Love Everlasting
Book 2 in the Isle of Hope Series
Published by Julie Lessman, LLC

ASIN: B01KE9PKUQ

Cover Design and Interior Format

Love Everlasting

BOOK 2 IN THE ISLE OF HOPE SERIES

JULIE LESSMAN

ACCLAIM FOR ISLE OF HOPE

"In Isle of Hope Lessman tells a poignant tale of first loves reunited and families reconciled. Both emotionally captivating and spiritually challenging, this sweet southern love story deals with issues of forgiveness and restoration. Fans of Lessman will be absolutely delighted with this riveting tale!"
—Denise Hunter, bestselling author of
FALLING LIKE SNOWFLAKES

"In Isle of Hope, award-winning author Julie Lessman weaves a story of how past choices collide with future consequences. Lessman's novel has it all: lush details, dynamic characters, and a storyline that keeps you turning the pages. The characters Lessman created in Isle of Hope confront their (in)ability to forgive – and as you fall in love with these characters, be prepared to question your beliefs about forgiveness."
—Beth K. Vogt, author of CRAZY LITTLE THING CALLED LOVE, and a 2015 RITA® Finalist and a 2015 and 2014 Carol Award finalist

"Fans of Julie Lessman's historical romances will love this modern day love story! Isle of Hope is a heartwarming and inspirational novel about forgiveness sought and restoration found. I'm enamored with the large and wonderful O'Bryen family and I thoroughly enjoyed the romances Julie skillfully crafted for both Jack O'Bryen and his mom Tess. A delight!"
—Becky Wade, award-winning author of MY STUBBORN HEART and THE PORTER FAMILY series including A LOVE LIKE OURS

ACCLAIM FOR JULIE LESSMAN

"Truly masterful plot twists ..."
—Romantic Times Book Reviews

"Readers who like heartwarming novels, such as those written by Debbie Macomber, are sure to enjoy this book."
—Booklist Online

"Julie is one of the best there is today at writing intensely passionate romance novels. Her ability to thread romance and longing, deception and forgiveness, and lots of humor are unparalleled by anyone else in the Christian market today."
—Rachel McRae of LifeWay Stores

"Julie Lessman's prose and character development is masterful."
—Church Libraries Magazine

AUTHOR ACCLAIM FOR JULIE LESSMAN

(authors listed alphabetically)

"With memorable characters and an effervescent plot that's as buoyant as it is entertaining, Dare to Love Again is Julie Lessman at her zestful best."
—Tamera Alexander, bestselling author of A LASTING IMPRESSION and TO WHISPER HER NAME

"In a powerful and skillfully written novel, Lessman exposes raw human emotions, proving once again that it's through our greatest pain that God can lead us to our true heart, revealed

and restored. Thoroughly enthralling!"
—Maggie Brendan, author of the HEART OF THE WEST and THE BLUE WILLOW BRIDES series

"Julie Lessman brings all her passion for romance rooted in her passion for God to A Heart Revealed. Emma Malloy is her finest heroine yet. These characters, with their own personal struggles and the ignited flame of an impossible love, fill the pages of this powerful, passionate, fast-paced romance."
—Mary Connealy, bestselling author of the LASSOED IN TEXAS, MONTANA MARRIAGES, TROUBLE IN TEXAS, and WILD AT HEART series

"What an interesting mix of characters. Rather than a single boy-meets-girl romance, Julie Lessman's latest novel takes readers on an emotional roller coaster with several couples—some married, some yearning to be married—as they seek to embrace love, honor the Lord, and uncover a dark truth that's been hidden for a decade. Readers who long for passion in their love stories will find it in abundance here!"
—Liz Curtis Higgs, bestselling author of THORN IN MY HEART

"Readers will not be able to part with these characters come 'The End'."
—Laura Frantz, award-winning author of LOVE'S RECKONING

"With an artist's brushstroke, Julie Lessman creates another masterpiece filled with family and love and passion. Love at Any Cost will not only soothe your soul, but it will make you laugh, stir your heart, and release a sigh of satisfaction when you turn the last page."
—MaryLu Tyndall, bestselling author of VEIL OF PEARLS

ISLE OF HOPE SERIES

Characters for Love Everlasting

The Hero:
Samuel (Ham) Cunningham: A pediatrician bachelor at Memorial Health and Jack's O'Bryen's coworker and friend.

The Heroine:
Shannon O'Bryen: A schoolteacher by day/ghostwriter by night, Cat's twin, Jack and Davey's sister, and Tess's daughter.

The O'Bryen Family:
Catherine (Cat) O'Bryen: Shannon's twin sister.
Tess O'Bryen: Shannon's mother.
Jack O'Bryen: Shannon's brother, married to Lacey, and coworker/friend with Sam Cunningham.
Lacey (Carmichael) O'Bryen: Shannon's and Cat's sister-in-law, Tess's daughter-in-law, married to Jack.
Davey O'Bryen: Shannon's, Cat's, and Jack's little brother, Tess's son.
Matt Ball: Shannon's, Cat's, Jack's, and Davey's cousin, married to Nicki, Lacey's cousin.
Nicki Ball: Matt's wife and Lacey's cousin.

Friends:
Dr. Ben Carmichael: Tess's love interest, Lacey's father, and Jack's father-in-law.
Chase Griffin: Associate Pastor of Hope Church, friend of the O'Bryen's.
Cameron Phillips: Tess O'Bryen's friend, Lacey's uncle, and

Ben's ex-brother-in-law.
Jasmine Augustine: Sam's and Jack's ex-girlfriend and a nurse at Memorial Health.
Mrs. Myra Penelope Lee: Owner/benefactor of Camp Hope for ill and handicapped orphans.
Mr. Will Hogan: Seasoned cowboy and all-around coach/handyman at Camp Hope.
Deborah (Debbie) Lynne Holbrook: Orphan at Camp Hope with health issues.
Karen Carmichael: Ben's deceased wife, Lacey's deceased mother, Tess's former friend and neighbor.
Mamaw Phillips: Lacey's and Nicki's grandmother.
Spencer Phillips: Lacey's cousin and Nicki's little brother.

DEDICATION

To Bonnie Roof—
One of the dearest friends I've ever known
and a true gift from God.
Our friendship—like God's love—will last forever.

I have loved you with an everlasting love;
I have drawn you with loving-kindness.
I will build you up again, and you will be rebuilt …
—Jeremiah 31:3-4

CHAPTER ONE

Isle of Hope, Georgia, Early Summer

"Okay, smile pretty—hot guys at three o'clock."

Shannon O'Bryen smiled, more because of her friend Margo's mumbled man alert than the need to charm any "hot guy." She shook her head when Margo tugged the neckline of her sequin halter dress a bit lower before casually skimming a pinky along the rim of her Diet Dr. Pepper. When her friend chatted nonchalantly about a book she'd just discussed with Shannon, Cat, Amy, and Becky not five minutes ago, Shannon grinned outright. But when Margo's finger slid from the rim into her soda, Shannon could do nothing but giggle. The sound set off a chain reaction of laughter around a table in the middle of a fancy fundraiser for Memorial Hospital at Mansion on Forsyth Park.

Peeking over her shoulder, Shannon expelled a sigh of relief, grateful the "hot guys" were only her brother Jack and his coworker, Sam Cunningham. Because although each of the girls around the table were looking for Mr. Right, Shannon was definitely not one of them—*despite* the slinky blue dress and four-inch heels her twin sister Cat had coerced her to wear. Nope, she preferred her Prince Charming confined between the covers of a book, thank you very much, where he couldn't stomp on her heart.

"Well, one viable 'hot guy,' anyway," Shannon's twin sister, Cat, said with a lazy smile. A breeze fluttered her long strawberry blonde hair, the salty scent of the marsh mingling with the hint of chlorine from the marble fountain in Savannah's historical Forsythe Park. Cat swayed to the music of a five-piece orchestra while Spanish moss swayed in the canopy of oaks overhead, the mischief in her eyes sparkling as much as the water dancing into the fountain. "My brother Jack is taken, but his pediatrician friend—*Dr.* Sam Cunningham—is still *very* available."

"And very, *very* attractive," Amy whispered, swallowing hard while Margo just stared with saucer eyes, sucking Dr. Pepper off her finger.

Margo gulped and quickly averted her gaze. "Uh … I think you dropped a 'very,'" she muttered, secretly tracking Jack and Sam as they wove their way through a glittering sea of people and tables in the candlelit promenade. "Far as I'm concerned, that guy just broke the hot scale, because he's *way* more than attractive."

Too attractive. Shannon watched as Sam flirted with every girl he could on the way to their table, Jack's warning that Sam was a "player" resonating deep in Shannon's soul. No matter the boyish twinkle in brown eyes that made every girl feel special or a crooked smile always tipped with tease, Shannon knew better. She had no doubt that beneath that magnetic façade was a man whose good looks and lust for women spelled doom for any girl sucked into his orbit—whirling them in a lovelorn spin that only made them dizzy.

And so sick that avoidance was the only cure.

"Heeeeeey, ladies, I'm in dire need of a dance partner, so who's willing to help me out?" Dr. Sam Cunningham ambled forward with hands in the pockets of his tux, his shirt and tie as disheveled as the dark curls that spilled over his forehead. *Which* was a total rarity for the man who was usually a walking photo shoot for a Gucci cologne ad, always dressed to the nines like a GQ model with a wardrobe to match.

"You're in dire need, all right," Jack said with a slant of a smile, his eyes far more sober than Sam appeared to be, "of a lift home." Looping an arm around Sam's shoulder, he zeroed in on

Shannon. "Shan, would you mind driving Sam home? I'm up soon on the podium for some announcements, so I can't take him right now, and he's pretty hammered. He's feeling no pain, but I'll tell you what—his bar tab will give him sticker shock on his next credit card statement."

Shannon blinked, stomach roiling over going anywhere with Sam Cunningham. "Uh … sure, Jack, but wouldn't a cab be better?"

"I don't wanna go home," Sam interrupted, a faint slur of his words a perfect complement to the glassy look in his eyes. "I wanna dance." Pausing as if he just realized he hadn't introduced himself, he dazzled the girls with his trademark smile, complete with a flash of dimples. "Please forgive me, ladies, but I'm Sam Cunningham, and I am hoping one of you might consider dancing with me." In true Cunningham style—at least according to Jack, who claimed Sam had a genuine soft spot for wallflowers and underdogs—he turned his famous bedroom eyes on the least likely girl at the table, who seldom garnered the attention of men.

Becky Dempsey was a brilliant mathematician who, unfortunately, looked like one too. Unable to wear contacts, sweet Becky was relegated to thick tortoise-shell eyeglasses that magnified her eyes so much, her pupils were as big as eyeballs. At six foot, she wore her brown hair in a short permed bob that matched her mother's and sported a host of allergies, not the least of which was to makeup and most food. As a result, she had a gangly frame, which did, fortunately, show off clothes to good advantage.

If they weren't from her mother's closet.

Sam awarded Becky a truly genuine smile. "How 'bout you, Miss …?"

"*Ohhhhhh*, no you don't, Ham," Jack said with a latch of Sam's arm, employing the nickname Sam had earned in residency because of his outrageous flirting and show-off tendencies. "Sweet Becky here doesn't need her feet mauled tonight, so let's get you home."

Sam jerked free of Jack's hold with amazing dexterity for someone swaying on his feet. "I told you, I don' wanna go home, O'Bryen. I wanna dance."

"Yeah, well you can dance your way to Shan's car, dude, because you're in no shape to do anything but crash."

"I'll drive him home," Cat offered with a look way too eager, jumping up so fast, she jolted the table and everyone's drinks along with it. She wriggled her brows at Sam while she reached for her purse. "I've been wanting to get to know you better anyway, Dr. Cunningham."

"Soun's like a plan to me," Sam said with a wayward grin. "Jack's been *waaaaay* too possessive of you girls, if you ask me." He gave Cat a slow wink. "Forbidden fruit, I suppose."

"In your dreams, Dr. Love." Jack flashed Cat a wry smile, resorting to his role of annoying big brother that Cat always accused him of. "Sorry, Catfish, but that would be the blind leading the blind, so I'll stick with the sober and sensible twin." He homed in on Shannon once again, the plea in his eyes weakening her defenses. "Shan, I really hate to ask, but I don't trust Sam in a cab because he'll just go to a club and drink some more."

"What are you, O'Bryen, my mother?" Sam scowled, and even that looked good on him.

Shannon chewed on her lip, not sure why Jack would put her in a situation like this with a Romeo he'd warned both Cat and her about.

"Come on, Cat, let's dance …" Sam extended his hand to her sister, practically tripping on the leg of a chair when he rounded the table.

Ignoring Sam's comment, Jack bent close to Shannon's ear, kneading her shoulder in a coaxing manner. "Normally I wouldn't let Sam within a mile of either you or Cat, sis, but he's hurtin' pretty badly because Jazz showed up with another guy." Jack glanced toward the dance floor to where Jasmine Augustine—a nurse at Memorial who was both his and Sam's ex-girlfriend—laughed and danced with some good-looking guy. "So I don't trust him to go straight home. *Nor* do I trust him with any female in this room but you, Shan." His smile was laced with apology, reminding Shannon of another conversation in Jack's office once, after she and Cat had met Sam for the first time.

"Sam and I are good friends, guys, but you two need to steer clear," Jack'd told them after Sam had left, his voice lowering to a mere whisper. He'd zeroed in on Cat, then, with that warning squint in his eyes. "Especially you, Catfish, because he's not like other players I know, only out for themselves. Deep down Sam's a pretty decent guy who actually cares about people, so I don't think he's really looking to hurt anybody." His mouth took a twist. "Unfortunately he does—a lot—because he's got this innate kindness and sensitivity that disarms most women, setting them up for the fall when he moves on." Jack had seared them both with a big-brother stare. "And trust me—he *always* does."

The fall. Shannon swallowed hard. *Yes, I remember it well ...*

Jack's heavy expulsion of air ruffled Shannon's hair, bringing her back to the present where Sam was flirting with Cat. He shook his head. "I swear, the clown is so lousy with bone-deep charisma, Shan, he can charm the spots off a kid with measles, which makes him all the more dangerous." He gave Shannon's shoulder a quick squeeze, fixing her with a look of regret. "So I need someone mature and levelheaded, sis, with an immunity to players, and the only one I know is you."

Shannon sighed. *Ah yes, my immunity to players. I've definitely been inoculated by the best.* "All right, Jack." She tossed her purse strap over her shoulder and rose with another heavy exhale of air. Pushing her chair in, she gave him a twist of a smile. "But you owe me, big brother."

"And then some," Jack said with a kiss to her head. He tucked a finger to her chin. "And don't let him bamboozle you. The man has a masters in roguery, so it might be good to lend him an ear, but nothing else." He tugged on her hair. "His address is 665 Parkway, Apt. B, and he keeps a key under one of the potted palms by his front door."

Her smile slid off-center. "The operative word being 'potted,'" she said with more sarcasm than normal.

He grinned. "I have his car keys, so Lacey and I will drive his Corvette home later, okay? Just get him inside and make sure he stays."

Shannon's mouth went flat. "You want me to tuck him in too?"

Jack chuckled. "Might be a nice touch, but not necessary." He leveled a finger at her with a mock glare. "I don't want you within twenty feet of his bedroom, young lady, you got that?" He winked. "I'm trusting you, Shan."

"Glad one of us does," she mumbled, shoulders slumping when she saw Sam dipping Cat in a dance move next to the table, almost dropping her.

"Okay, come on, Twinkletoes." Jack pulled Sam away from Cat to hook an arm over his shoulder, carefully guiding him down the wide, tree-lined walkway dotted with tables. He tossed Cat a warning glare over his shoulder. "And if I ever see you dancing with this joker again, Catfish, I'm going to toss you into the river, you got it? He's off-limits to you and Shan because he's dangerous to women's health."

"Yeah?" Sam mumbled, stumbling along beside Jack, "then how come it's *my* health that took the hit this time?"

"Have fun, you lucky duck," Margo called as Shannon led Jack and Sam to where she had parked her car. "Sure wish it were me."

"Me too," Shannon muttered, wondering if she could talk Jack into putting Sam in the trunk.

"Jack, I'm fine, I swear." Sam's argument sounded convincing enough except for a near miss with a chair, and Shannon couldn't help the ghost of a smile when her brother gave him a Gibbs smack to the back of the head. She could have kissed Jack after he dumped Sam into the back seat of the car instead of the front. *Especially* after a slight detour where Dr. Love puked on the parking lot, necessitating quick cleanup with wet wipes from the glove compartment.

Facedown on the upholstery, Sam ground out a low groan that coaxed another smile to Shannon's lips. "I think I'm gonna die …" he muttered. His voice was no more than a rasp as he lay prostrate across the back seat of her mother's 1999 Chevy Impala, his bristled jaw flat against her beige upholstery.

"No you won't, Ham," Jack said with a degree of sympathy. "You just need to get past this obsession with Jasmine and move on with your life, man. There are other fish in the sea."

A hiccup interrupted Sam's moan. "I don' want fish. I want her. She's one in a million."

"Yeah, and so's the headache you're gonna have come morning, bro, if you don't get some decent sleep." He shoved the rest of Sam's legs into the car and slammed the door, opening the passenger side to offer Shannon a penitent smile. "I can't thank you enough, Shan. Jazz dumped him for some new intern, and it's been a rough week for him, you know?"

"I'm sorry to hear that," she whispered, her heart aching for him despite his inebriated state. "Is there anything else I can do to help cheer him up?"

"Yeah, you can pray for him, and maybe even share some of that wisdom you're so famous for. Never seen Ham this down before, and it has me a little worried, you know?"

"Sure, Jack." She peeked into the back seat where snores could be heard while drool puddled on the upholstery. "I feel bad for the poor guy."

Jack grinned. "I knew you would because you have an oversized heart of gold, kiddo, but not too much, okay? Ham has been known to take advantage of the kindness of strangers."

A grin tugged at Shannon's lips as she glanced over her shoulder. "Doesn't look like he could take advantage of much of anything right now." She wrinkled her nose. "Except Mom's car seat."

"Yeah, well that's when he's at his most dangerous, I'm afraid, catching women off-guard with his little-boy charm. So unconscious or not, keep your distance, okay?"

She started the car with its customary sputter and growl, shifting into gear as she slid Jack a wry smile. "Distance would be a cab, Jack, but I'll keep that in mind."

"Good girl." With two firm taps of her roof, Jack closed the door, hands in his pockets as he watched her drive away.

A snort sounded from the back seat, and Shannon had no choice but to smile. A cab, definitely.

In another state.

CHAPTER TWO

Stupid fly. Sam Cunningham swatted at the insect, its stupid buzzing getting on his last nerve. It landed again, and he literally growled, flailing his arm to shoo it away. "Beat it, before I nail your butt to the wall."

"Now *that* I'd like to see."

Sam jolted up with a groan, drool smeared on the side of his mouth as he squinted into the eyes of an angel.

Okay, he couldn't be dead because his head was pounding too hard, and dead people didn't feel pain, right? Not unless … He shot straight up, head in a vise as he groaned in misery, kneading his temples. His stomach burned like the devil and his throat was so parched, it felt like it was on fire.

Uh-oh … *fire!*

Yep, he was dead.

And now, he was going to pay for his sins.

"You're not going to throw up again, are you?" A quiet voice asked, soft with sympathy.

He glanced up at the angel through slits in his eyes, his voice barely a croak. "I might. Where am I?" he rasped.

"The back seat of my mother's car, and I'm Jack's sister Shannon in case you don't remember." She gently tugged on his arm, obviously hoping to remove him from the vehicle. "Which would be a miracle, given the brain cells you destroyed tonight."

He grunted, gingerly attempting to unfold himself from the car while bowling balls ricocheted in his head. "I don' believe in miracles."

"You should—it's a miracle you're even alive after the alcohol you consumed."

"Wish I wasn't," he muttered, hand to his eyes as he teetered on the sidewalk, limbs as limp as the crumpled tie dangling around his neck. He sniffed. "What's that awful smell?"

"Vomit. You puked on your tie and shirt," she said, the empathy in her tone now laced with a hint of a smile.

He groaned. "*Noooo!* This is my best tie—a Ralph Lauren black." One eye opened a sliver. "Not in your car, I hope?"

"Nope, that's miracle number three—you puked in the parking lot, so Jack and I cleaned you up with the wet wipes we keep in the glove compartment."

"For sloppy drunks you cart home?" He managed to pry his eyes open all the way, noticing for the first time just how pretty she was.

"Nope, you're my first." She hooked an arm to his waist. "Ready?"

"Always," he said with a smile that was worth the pain, "when there's a pretty woman by my side."

She paused, face in a pinch as she stared up with mouth agape. "Seriously? You're going to hit on me when you can barely walk and smell like puke?"

He gave a faint shrug, smile sheepish. "Nothing ventured, nothing gained."

"I guarantee you, Dr. Cunningham," she said in a stern tone tempered with tease, "the only thing you're going to gain with comments like that is a whop alongside the head."

"Ouch." He grinned while she attempted to steer him toward his luxury villa with a strength and determination that belied her small size, her manner utterly patient when he stumbled several times. His hands shook as he fumbled to fish his keys from his pocket, striving for a smile that came out as a grimace. "I can take it from here," he said, then froze, his keys promptly plummeting onto his brick front porch. Panic set in when he broke out in a cold sweat, mouth salivating like he was going to throw up …

Nooooooooooo!

Body heaving, he spun around to a potted palm just in time,

retching into the planter for several agonizing seconds. He stood there, breathing hard while he remained bent over the poor plant, pretty sure he'd just puked up his intestines.

"Let's get you inside," a soft voice said, the gentle touch of a palm rubbing his back.

A groan scraped past his dry lips, and he white-knuckled the edge of the planter, not sure if the heat in his cheeks meant he was embarrassed or going to toss his cookies again. "Please go—I can take it from here."

The caress of a hand to his back continued despite his objection. "I'm sure you can, Sam, but it remains to be seen if you'll be sleeping out here next to a potted palm or inside in a clean, cozy bed. So, if it's all the same to you, Doc, I have strict orders to get you down for the night before I leave, so I'm here till I get the dirty deed done."

He rose slowly, wiping his mouth with his coat sleeve and feeling so much better after unloading his stomach, he actually managed a chuckle. "Ah yes, the 'sober and sensible twin.'"

"That's right, Dr. Love," she said, employing Jack's nickname while she turned the key in his door, "which means the party's over and you're done for the night."

"Wait …!" He spun around, heart in his throat. "Where's my car?"

"Jack will deliver it in the morning, Doc, so move it inside, please." She nudged him into his spacious marble foyer that never failed to elicit a feeling of pride, always reminding Sam that he'd finally arrived. A far cry from a flea-bitten room over a bar on the wrong side of the tracks, Sam's villa—along with his "preowned" pearl white Corvette—were his pride and joy. Absolute proof he was worth something, despite desertion by a two-bit mother and the rantings of a foster father who claimed he'd only amount to a pile of dung.

He fumbled to turn on the light, then reveled in the gasp that popped from Shannon's lips, her voice tinged with an awe he never tired of hearing. "Wow, this is some place, Doc," she whispered, peering up at the vaulted foyer with its sleek chrome and teak stairway that zigzagged against a wall of glass. Cream walls resplendent with equally pale modern works of art were beautifully complemented by a central circular mirror and white calla lilies in a tall pottery vase. Sam would have preened with pride if he wasn't covered in puke, because each and every piece was deliberately designed to evoke the clean and simple beauty he so craved in his own life.

"It's breathtaking," she whispered, leaving his side to wander the entryway with a look of awe as if she were Alice perusing Wonderland for the very first time. "Utterly clean and pure. Not at all what I expected of a notorious bachelor." She turned, the look of astonishment on her face making him grin and wince at the same time. "You didn't do this yourself, did you? I mean a designer put it together for you, right?"

"Nope, all mine," he said, chest swelling with pride even as his stomach rebelled with a twinge of nausea. He fought it off, suddenly aware he smelled like a pub on payday.

Her jaw actually dropped. "I don't believe it."

He forced a flirtatious smile, barely minding the throb in his head. "Every shade of paint, every stick of furniture, every piece of art," he said with a wobbly hand to his heart, "straight out of my depraved brain, I promise." He suddenly steadied himself with a hand to the wall, a flashback from his childhood making him dizzier than the booze in his body.

"I'll come back soon, I promise," his mother always said, night after night, the stench of alcohol on her breath making him nauseous. Only she never did, leaving a skin-and-bones five-year-old to fend for himself in a rat-infested room over a dive of a bar. And when her lush of a boyfriend gave her a choice between Sam and him? Sam's teeth ground hard as he swayed on his feet. No contest. Because his so-called mother was weak—seeking her self-worth in a loser who had absolutely no worth at all—while giving her son promises that were worth even less.

"*No,*" Sam stressed with a hint of a slur, focusing glassy eyes on a woman who for some strange reason, he wanted to know the truth. "I give you my *word,*" he emphasized with surprising clarity, "because you see, Miss O'Bryen, promises are nothing more than a puff of air. But my word is my unbreakable bond, as honest and pure as I can ever hope to be." The dizziness passed, and he stood up straight and tall, both his smile and the "player" in play once again. "Because despite my notoriously black reputation, I am inexplicably drawn to things that are simple and pure, honest and clean, and completely unblemished by my own sordid life."

Her gaze met his and held. "It's beautiful," she said softly, head tipped as if she couldn't quite figure him out.

"Thank you." He leaned on the knob of the open door, making every effort not to waver on his feet. "Unlike its owner at the moment, I'm afraid. It seems I'm in dire need of a shower."

She simply stared, her calm look of compassion so disarming that the smile slowly dissolved on his face. All at once, he felt his shoulders relax, the need to impress suddenly as absent as his sobriety. "Thank you, Shannon," he said quietly, somewhat baffled by the calming effect that she had, "for putting up with me tonight and getting me home." He took a stab at a smile that came out more as a flinch. "I'll have the inside of your car fumigated and detailed, so just send me the bill."

For some reason the kindness in her eyes put a hitch in his throat he could only blame on the booze. She slipped her purse off her shoulder, dangling it from one hand while she reverently glided the other across his polished teak half-moon table. "That won't be necessary," she said with a smile, "but I suspect a pot of coffee will be. Direct me to the kitchen?"

He studied her through blurry eyes, wondering if the aura of innocence he detected was real or just the effect of the alcohol on his brain. "You don't have to do that, Shannon. The vomit was already above and beyond the call of duty, so I'll give Jack a good report."

She huffed out a sigh bigger than her. "Sorry, Doc. Jack asked me to make sure you go to bed and don't go out again. Blame it on the curse of being the sensible and sober twin who follows orders, but if it's all the same to you, I'd like to follow through with coffee and even lend an ear if you like."

He stared for several dizzy seconds, then shut the door, figuring a cup of coffee was preferable to a vertigo spin in bed. "Sure. Kitchen's down the hall, and it won't take me three minutes to shower." He eyed the lofty staircase with a dull gaze. "Now the stairs? Might be more like twenty."

She paused halfway to the kitchen. "Need help?"

"Nope." He made his way to the staircase, trying hard not to weave. "The hangover will be wicked enough without Jack's fist if I get one of his sisters into my bedroom."

"O-Okay." She spun on her heel and all but sprinted down the hall.

But not before he saw the delicate rise of color in her face that lured a smile to his lips. He shook his head as he methodically scaled one step at a time, fisting the steel banister to hold himself up. He sure didn't blame Jack for banning him from his sisters, especially Shannon. There was something so sweet and wholesome about her that it almost made him want to protect her himself.

He paused at the top of the stairs to catch his breath, the thought of Jack's sister in his "lair" quirking his lips. Obviously Jack was concerned about Sam's welfare enough to put his sister in harm's way, which only deepened Sam's gratitude to the man who was quickly becoming a close friend. His mouth crooked. Even *if* he was annoyingly bent on saving Sam's soul.

Plodding into his massive bedroom, he peeled off his clothes, leaving a trail on his way to the master bath before turning the shower all the way to scalding. Feeling woozy, he braced his hands on the vanity, mind as foggy as the steam billowing behind him like thunderclouds portending a doozy of a storm. He peered into the mirror, muscled arms taut with his weight while red eyes and a sagging face shadowed with scruff confirmed the storm was already here.

And it was a stinkin' category five.

He dropped his head, the pain in his chest suddenly making the throb in his brain look like lollipops on immunization day.

Because he'd lost Jazz again. A second time.

And losing always left a bitter taste in his mouth.

You're nothing but a loser, kid, just like your old lady.

Kind of like spewing in a parking lot, only this time the nausea was in his heart. Peering up, he saw a ripped body honed at the gym and chiseled features Jazz once likened to a Greek god. Determination steeled his bones. Because inside he knew his feelings for Jasmine and hers for him went far deeper than a pretty face. "You'll be back, Jazz," he whispered, "because I'm the one you come to when you're hurting, and the one who makes you laugh when others make you cry."

Like Jack when he dumped you for Lacey.

An odd mix of resentment and regard churned in his gut along with the booze, reminding him that it had been Jack who had stolen Jazz away the first time, after Sam cheated on her. But then it was Jack who had sent her running right back after he'd upped and married Lacey. Jasmine had been devastated, but Sam had been ready, wooing her back with love and understanding and an iron-clad resolve to never stray again.

Until she dumped him for an intern.

Sam's eyes shuttered closed. Just like his so-called fiancée dumped him in college. Right after she had an affair with his professor, destroying Sam's confidence along with the man's marriage.

Mind and body wobbling, he quickly opened his eyes, desperate to purge the memory from his brain along with the alcohol from his system.

Stepping into the shower, he welcomed the hot water that battered him raw. Well, he'd lost Jazz twice, but he'd also won her twice, and if it took every trick in the book, he'd do it again. His jaw automatically hardened, resolve to win her back pummeling through his veins as hard as the steaming water pummeled his body. But right now he needed to numb the ache in his heart, so he'd start with a cup of coffee with a pretty woman who just might help fill the hole in his chest.

At least for a while.

He lathered with soap, aching with the need to feel worthy and clean. He suddenly thought of Shannon and instantly relaxed, the idea of coffee with her suddenly the only thing he wanted to do. He could use an honest sounding board after all the angst Jasmine had put him through. And he'd begin tonight by picking Shannon's brain as to how he might win her back. Because Shannon *did* mention lending an ear.

Stepping out of the shower, he expelled a burdensome sigh. And maybe, if she realized just how badly he was hurting, she'd lend him even more. Like a few innocent kisses—and only kisses—from a woman who could help ease some of his pain. Sagging over the sink, he ground his thumb against the throb in his temple, desperate to free himself of the awful loneliness that always haunted his brain. His eyelids weighted closed. Because he had to.

Jack's sister or no.

CHAPTER THREE

Shannon hummed while she finished grating cheddar cheese on a Denver omelet just as Sam padded into his stainless steel gourmet kitchen. The *same* amazing kitchen that had caused an immediate flare-up of Shannon's MSD. Her smile flatlined. Otherwise known as Martha Stewart Disease, an affliction that had been in remission for over six years now. Since she used to cook for …

Her eyelids drifted shut as she paused over the plate, the malaise that always accompanied thoughts of Eric still marginally potent, even if far less than before.

"Holy cow, what smells so good?" Sam sniffed the air, eyes flaring when she turned around with the plated omelet in her hands.

Offering a Mona Lisa smile, she placed it on a sunny yellow linen napkin she used as a placemat, with another napkin arranged in a special necktie fold. Her smile squirmed. In honor of the tie he'd soiled, of course, adorned by two ibuprofen.

His jaw dropped as he toppled into his seat with a low groan, ironically attired in Polo "player" pajama pants and a white T-shirt that showcased a toned and sculpted body. "This looks like breakfast at the Ritz," he said, his hygiene considerably improved with a clean-shaven jaw and curly damp hair that smelled like lemons.

Maybe too improved, Shannon thought as she poured him a cup of coffee, hints of musk, cedar, and vanilla causing an annoying flutter in her stomach. "What on earth is that scent?" she whispered, taking a quick step back.

His smile was more of a grimace that instantly revealed

dimples she hadn't paid much attention to before. "You like it? It's called Straight to Heaven by Kilian. Supposed to be one of the most expensive colognes in the world." A muscle flickered in his cheek as he reached for his coffee, nodding his thanks. "Jasmine gave it to me for Christmas."

"It smells really nice." Shannon hurried to pour herself a cup on the other side of the glass-and-stainless table, grateful for the comfortable distance it afforded.

"Man, this is incredible," he said with a sip of the steaming brew, pausing to sniff. "Wait—is that cinnamon?"

She shook out her own napkin, settling it over her lap with a smile. "I sprinkled it on the grounds because it's good for hangovers." She nudged a plate of toast forward, crispy-crunchy with lots of cinnamon and sugar. "Thus the cinnamon toast as well."

He gave her an open-mouthed stare, still spidered with red despite his squeaky clean appearance. "Are you for real? I mean, at first I thought you were an angel when I came to because your eyes were so …" He backpedaled a hand in the air, as if he couldn't make his brain work. "I don't know—gentle and kind. But now I'm not so sure you aren't." He managed a tired wink as he picked up his fork. "Because I gotta tell you, Angel Eyes …" A small moan melted on his lips when he tasted the food. "This omelet is pure heaven."

She smiled. "I assure you, Dr. Cunningham, I am not an angel, so let's just chalk it up to alcohol delusion, shall we?" Her lips canted. "After all, there was enough in your bloodstream to make a pub proud."

Closing his eyes, he rolled a bite of the omelet around on his tongue. "Wow! How on earth did you have time to do all this?"

She shrugged, enjoying his praise more than she should. "Well, despite the fact that your three minutes were more like an hour, I figured you could use some sustenance to soak up the poison." She took a stab at her own omelet, wishing she'd found some spinach and gruyere in his fridge. "And then, of course, I used to be somewhat of a cooking freak."

"*Used* to be?" His fork paused as he watched her, a gooey string of cheese dangling off.

She dusted her omelet with additional pepper while his question dusted her cheeks with heat. "A guy I was engaged to once liked to cook as a hobby, so we took cooking classes together." Avoiding his eyes, she pushed the omelet around on her plate, her appetite suddenly diminished. She shifted her tone to casual, unwilling to let anyone know how deeply Eric had scarred her life. Her food suddenly stuck in her throat. *And* how badly she'd failed herself and her family. Feigning a nonchalant shrug, she quickly swallowed the pain along with her omelet, coercing a glib smile. "So after we broke up, I guess I just lost interest."

Along with my interest in men.

"I see. So … it was a bad breakup, then?" His voice was nearly a whisper, gentle and low, as if he were afraid he'd inflict more pain by saying it too loudly.

She stared at her plate, no longer seeing the omelet for the awful memories that assaulted her mind. Swallowing hard, she slowly met his gaze, stunned that he'd picked up on what she'd worked so hard to hide, especially with a brain muddled by alcohol. Her rib cage constricted when she saw raw compassion in bleary eyes so tender, they sparked a sharp sting of tears at the back of her lids. "The worst," she whispered, quickly returning her focus to her food in the hope he would do the same, "which is why I gave up dating." Head bent, she silently nibbled at her omelet, grateful he let it go, as if sensing her need to distance herself from the subject. They ate in companionable silence, and she was surprised at how relaxed and natural it felt, as if he, too, were lost in the sins of his past.

When they finished, she rose to take her empty plate to the sink, anxious to steer the conversation away from her. Inhaling deeply, she reclaimed her seat and zeroed in on him with a jut of her chin. "*So*, Dr. Cunningham, since *I'm* not the one who drank herself into a stupor tonight, let's trade couches, shall we?" Her gaze softened as she folded her arms on the table, recalling

Jack's concerns over how miserable he felt Sam was despite his ever-jovial demeanor. A man who, in his endless pursuit of love and approval, Jack suspected, buried his pain in laughter and tease.

Just like I bury mine by being quiet and shy.

"Jack told me about Jasmine," she said gently, heart wincing at the flicker of pain that crossed his features. "And I ache for you, Sam, because I know how hard it can be when a relationship is over."

His Adam's apple ducked as he abandoned his fork for his cup, pushing away from the table to sag back in his chair. "It is, as we both obviously know, but it's far from over for me, I can tell you that," he said without a trace of a slur, the determination in his eyes apparently sharpening his focus and tongue. "From the moment I laid eyes on her, it's like the woman possessed my soul, convincing me she was the one." His mouth banked to the right. "Now I just have to convince her. *Again*."

He set his cup down and leaned in with arms on the table like her, a glint of steel glittering in those coffee-brown eyes. "Never been a quitter, Shannon, and I sure don't intend to start now. She'll have her fling with this new guy, and I'll have plenty of my own, but when she's ready" —he dipped his head in emphasis, penetrating her with a bloodshot stare— "and she will be sooner or later—she'll be back." He raised his coffee cup in a mock toast. "And I'll be ready because it's the dance that we do, until she finally figures out I'm the guy that she needs."

"Why?" She reached for a piece of cinnamon toast and nibbled the edge.

He frowned, dark brows digging low. "Why? Why what?"

She sat back to settle in, casually hugging one arm to her waist while she nipped at her toast, curious as to why Jasmine possessed him so. It was a mystery she'd had to solve herself with Eric in order to heal and discover who she really was. And although it was no mystery what Sam or any man saw in Jasmine—she was beautiful, smart, and the wealthy daughter of Sam's and Jack's boss—Shannon suspected Sam had never truly scratched the surface of "why." Never delved into the deep, dark recesses of his soul where the truth lay buried, just waiting to be revealed.

Like mine.

With a pensive crunch of her toast, she chewed slowly. "Why is she 'the one' for you and why are you the 'guy she needs'?" Wrinkling her nose, she took another bite, smile skewed as she studied him. "And why, in the name of love, would you even consider a 'fling' with anyone else if Jasmine 'possesses' your soul?"

Ruddy color crept into his cheeks as he offered a casual smile, leaning back with a muscled arm over the chair, as if just shooting the breeze. "Gosh, Shan, go for the jugular, why don't you?" He flaunted his dimples. "Not just sober and sensible, but point blank and precise too."

Tipping her head, she arched her brows in challenge, far more interested in facts than flirtation. "The jugular veins drain blood from the head to the heart, Dr. Cunningham, as you well know, so the answers to your heartache are most likely in the brain."

He squinted as if seeing her in a whole new light, lips parted in an open-mouthed smile tinged with annoyance despite a hint of respect. "Well, well, looks like somebody's been spending her Saturday nights curled up with Jack's anatomy book instead of the real thing."

She blinked, completely caught off-guard by his jab. Rising, she reached for his empty plate with a weary expulsion of air. She wasn't about to be target practice for some clueless player who'd rather coddle his pride than his heart. Nope, it was definitely time to go.

"Wait ..." Eyes naked with regret, he gripped her wrist, startling her so much, the plate dropped to the table with a thud. "Don't leave," he whispered, a sobriety in his manner she hadn't thought he possessed. "I'm a horse's behind, Shannon, and I'm sorry I sniped at you like that." He gently grazed her wrist with his thumb before letting go, gaze fused to hers as he picked up her plate. "Stay and talk. Please?"

He lumbered up to collect his, too, then dumped them both

in the sink. Returning to top off their coffee, he nodded at her empty seat while she stood stock-still. "Come on, sit—please? I'm interested in what you have to say," he said quietly, his hand shaking as he poured.

Arms barricaded to her chest, she silently studied him through wary eyes, miffed when her heart softened at the tug of his plea.

When she didn't move, he splayed a hand to his chest with a boyish smile, brown eyes so mesmerizing, they melted her resistance. "If I promise to behave?"

A trace of a smile tugged at her lips as she delivered a mock glare. "Behave? I'm not sure you can even define it, Doc, much less do it, but since patience is a byproduct of sober and sensible, you're in luck."

He grinned as he pulled out her chair. "Yes, I am, Miss O'Bryen, and Jack tells me you're a teacher, so I'm just glad there are no pointers or rulers around. Third grade, I believe?"

Tempering her smile, she slid into her chair with a fold of her hands on the table. "Yes, so as you can see, I'm completely qualified to deal with the likes of you."

"That appears more than obvious," he said, plopping back into his seat, the barest hint of mischief peeking through that same adorable hooligan guilt she saw in her eight-year-old male students. "Okay, then." Huffing out a heavy sigh, he folded his hands on the table like her, his humor slowly dissolving into a quiet vulnerability she suspected few people ever saw. "I can't exactly explain in concrete terms why Jasmine is the one because it's more of a rightness I feel when we're together—like we're a perfect fit."

Closing his eyes, he propped elbows to the table to massage his temples with the heels of his hands, face pinched as if striving to make sense of it all. "It sounds crazy, I know, but it's kind of like slipping on a perfectly tailored Armani suit, you know?" He peered up, face scrunched while he struggled to put his feelings into words. "It's so smooth and comfortable, you feel like a different person. Like when I slide into my Vette or walk into my townhouse after a long day, there's this sense of significance, value … order, even, that makes everything right in my world."

She released a quiet sigh, something cramping in her chest. "Don't be angry with me, Sam, but those things sound like trappings to me," she said quietly, "not love."

He glanced up, mouth tamped in a firm line. "Maybe, but it makes me feel whole, Shannon, worth something and better than I've ever felt before."

"Yes, but for how long?"

He blinked at her, then looked away. "Long enough."

"Until she's gone?" she whispered.

She had her answer when his jaw went rigid.

"That's how it was with me, too," she said softly, gaze trailing into a faraway stare. "The sun only seemed to shine when I was with him." A wispy sigh drifted out as she finally looked up, so very grateful to a God Who had opened her eyes. A faint smile lighted upon her lips as peace lighted upon her soul. "Until I learned it rose every single day with or without him. Sometimes blindingly bright, sometimes dark and dim, but always there, rain or shine." She took a sip of her coffee, flashing a smile to steer the conversation out of the gloom. "So tell me, Dr. Cunningham, just *why* are *you* the guy that Jasmine needs?"

He grinned and sat back, hands braced behind his neck in a relaxed pose that displayed an impressive bulge of biceps. "It's not obvious?"

Her smile swerved. "A wise man once said 'charm is deceitful and beauty fades,' so you gotta give me more to go on than that."

He flashed some teeth. "Charm and beauty, huh? Well, I'll take it, Miss O'Bryen, although I would have preferred tall and handsome."

"'Vanity of vanities; all is vanity,'" she quoted, remembering well how much that lesson had cost her. She dipped her head to peer up, lips pursed in a patient smile. "Hate to break it to you, Doc, but as superficial as we women seem when ogling hot guys, most of us crave way more than a pretty face. And if we don't, then we're likely more shallow than the relationship."

He squinted at her. "You don't pull any punches, do you?"

She shrugged. "No reason to. I'm a bottom-liner out of pure self-preservation. I was deeply wounded by charm and beauty, so surface things like that don't even make the cut anymore. I tend to bypass most of it to get right to the point." She absently scraped her lip with her teeth, a hint of apology in her eyes. "No matter how sharp that point may be."

"And here I thought you were the soft and vulnerable twin."

She grinned. "Used to be." Her smile faded as she veered off into a distant stare. "Till the truth shattered my world, almost taking my life with it."

He paused for several seconds, then cleared his throat, peering up beneath the darkest, thickest lashes she'd ever seen on a man. The tenderness in his gaze was so real and intense, it stuttered her pulse. "You know, I barely know you, Shannon, except for snippets here and there I've gleaned from Jack, but for some reason I wince inside hearing that. I don't know—it's just harder to see pain devastate someone soft and shy like you, who seems to have an innate gentleness about her."

Her mouth quirked. "Except during detox and discussions of depth?"

"Yeah." He scratched the back of his neck, smile sheepish. "Except then."

"Well, then, see?" Hopping up, she grabbed both of their empty cups and took them to the sink. "There's our first plus as to why Jasmine needs you—your empathy and compassion, Dr. Cunningham. But don't waste it on me, please. That same truth that shattered my world was also what finally set me free." Glancing at her watch, she was completely shocked that two hours had already passed since they'd arrived. She tossed a glance over her shoulder. "More coffee?"

"No, thanks. Your mission is to put me to sleep, remember? Not hype me up so I call a cab and go back out." He squinted at the ceiling as if trying to remember something. "'You shall … know the truth … and it shall set you free.'"

She chuckled while she rinsed the dirty dishes and put them in the dishwasher, returning with a dishrag to wipe off the table.

"Ah, a man who knows Scripture—now *there's* a plus in the 'Jasmine Needs' column. A show of faith—I'm impressed."

"Don't be," he said with a wry bent of his mouth. "I'm not big on God or prayer, and that's the *only* thing I remember from church. That and 'do unto others as you would have them do unto you.'"

"Ah, yes, which brings us to question number three." She sat back down, hands folded like before, her probing gaze pinning him to the chair. "Explain to me, Dr. Cunningham, just how you can have a fling with anyone else if Jasmine 'possesses your soul'?"

He grimaced. "Uh-oh, looks like I may have to scratch 'soft and shy.'"

She shimmied to the edge of her chair, suddenly extremely curious why men—even great guys like Jack before his faith was rekindled—had no qualms about toying with a woman's affections. "I mean, Jack says you're a pretty decent guy for a player," she said, ignoring his flinch, "and you've chosen a noble profession, so you obviously have a great love for children. You could have blown me away when Jack mentioned you've been part of the Family for Every Child mentor program for years now, which clearly indicates a heart for others." She leaned in on the table, arms crossed while she absently tugged on her lower lip with her teeth, softening her voice to cushion the blow. "So tell me, Sam, how can a nice guy like you who is supposed to be in love with one woman, tease and take from so many others without ever really giving back?"

"I give back," he said with a thread of hurt in his tone.

She hiked a brow. "Dinners, dates, and sleepovers? Sounds like more trappings to make *you* feel better. Call me picky, but that doesn't say love to me, especially for a woman who 'possesses your soul.'"

He sat straight up, frustration ridging his brow. "Hey, need I remind you it was Jasmine who broke up with me, Miss Bottom-Line? Not the other way around, so technically I'm a free man."

A weary sigh feathered her lips as she slumped back in her

chair, heart aching for this man who was so desperate for love, yet so clueless as to how to go about it. "But that's just it, Sam," she said quietly, "you're *not* free. You're trapped in a cycle of rejection. Jasmine rejects you, so you reject her back, then you turn right around and reject every woman you use to fill the hole in your heart."

"You're crazy—I don't reject anybody," he snapped. "Especially Jasmine. For crying out loud, I'm so crazy in love with her, I'm sitting here in my kitchen with the room spinning and a sledgehammer pounding my brain, talking psycho-babble with some girl I just met."

"Sorry, Sam," she said, brows sloped in a look of sympathy usually reserved for skinned knees and hurt feelings in the classroom. "But that's not love."

"Really." It was more of a statement than a question as he hiked a leg up on the rung of the next chair, one thick brow jutting high. "Then what's your definition, Einstein?"

Shannon drew in a cleansing breath, closing her eyes to focus on the only kind of love she would ever settle for again. "'Love is patient, love is kind and is not jealous; love does not brag and is not arrogant, does not act unbecomingly; it does not seek its own, is not provoked, does not take into account a wrong suffered, does not rejoice in unrighteousness, but rejoices with the truth.'" She opened her eyes, her heart flooding with the assurance that this was exactly what God wanted for her too.

And for Sam.

Her smile was pure peace. "'Love bears all things,' Sam, 'believes all things, hopes all things, endures all things.' And you know why?" She stood and pushed in her chair, that very same love she espoused now spilling from her gaze. "Because 'love never fails,' Dr. Cunningham, which is the best news I could possibly give you right now."

She lifted the strap of her purse off the back of the chair and slung it over her shoulder, heart bleeding for this man who had so much potential—and need—for love. "Because if you apply *that* kind of love in your relationship with Jasmine and every other woman, you won't fail either, Sam, in finding the kind of love that will truly make you happy." Her lips twitched with a near smile as she employed her sternest teacher tone. "Now I'm going home, Dr. Cunningham, and *you* are going straight to bed, understood?"

"*Yeeeesssss*, Miss O'Bryen," he said in a sing-song voice à la Eddie Haskell. He grinned with a wide stretch of arms before shuffling to his feet, fingers suddenly clutching the back of the chair when he started to sway. "*After* I walk you out to your car."

"No, sir." She marched around the table, waving him off on her way to the door. "You look like you can barely walk to your room, much less to my car, Doc, so I should be carrying *you* to bed."

"Mmm … not a bad idea," he said with a rakish waggle of brows that produced an immediate wince in his face. "Ow—that hurt."

"Aw …" She fluttered her lashes in sympathy before delivering a dry smile. "Good." He followed her to the foyer, hand to his head, and she couldn't help but laugh. "Pain, puke, and the promise of a hangover." Hand on the knob, she turned at the front door with an arch of her brow. "Tell me, Doc, does anything stem the player in you?"

He mauled the back of his neck with a cringe, his smile appearing to be in as much pain as him. "Well, the point-blank truth tends to suck a bit of the wind out of my sails."

She couldn't resist a chuckle as she opened the door, lobbing a grin over her shoulder before she slowly shut it again. "Good to know."

CHAPTER FOUR

A player, yes, but a sweet one. Shaking her head, Shannon yanked the door closed with a smile, squealing when it bounced back with a clunk and a groan.

"*Owwww!* First you bludgeon my heart, and now my arm." Sam moaned, rubbing his wrist while he sagged against the doorframe. "Okay, that settles it—you're not a third-grade teacher, you're a sadist."

Eyes wide, Shannon put a hand to her mouth, as much to stifle a giggle as from shock. "I am *so* sorry," she said, backing down his brick serpentine walkway when he started to follow, thinking that even sulking, he looked adorable. "But I did tell you to go to bed, did I not?"

"A bossy sadist at that," he muttered, padding behind her in his bare feet, hands in his pockets as he gingerly stepped over acorns and sticks.

"You haven't seen 'bossy,' mister, if you don't get your butt back inside right now." Keys in hand, she rounded her car and opened her door, pausing to sear him with a threatening look completely ruined by her flicker of a smile. "Goodnight, Sam—*again*." She slid into the driver's seat and turned the ignition, groaning when a familiar grinding occurred. The engine refused to turn over as she pumped the accelerator to no avail. "Nooooo," she moaned to herself, cheeks heating as she tried to remember what Jack had done to start the car when she'd flooded it at home, before the Memorial fundraiser. The smell of gasoline wrinkled her nose as she tried it again. "Come on, baby, I know you've endured drool, puke, and Sam Cunningham, but please don't take that out on me …"

Tap. Tap.

Smothering a groan, Shannon looked up when Sam opened the passenger door, brows in a bunch as he ducked his head in. "What's wrong?"

She resisted the urge to roll her eyes, figuring she'd given Doctor Love enough grief for one night. "It's been flooding lately, so now it won't turn on."

"Well, you're in luck, Teach." A slow grin slid across Sam's face as he shut the passenger door and ambled around to the driver's side, opening her door with a wink. "I happen to have a *lotttttt* of experience in turning things on, young lady." He bumped her shoulder. "Move over."

Succumbing to an eye roll, she scooted over on the cloth bench seat of her mother's Impala to let him in.

"Whoa! How short are you anyway?" he asked, fumbling for the lever to adjust the seat. "My knees are in my nostrils." He jerked it back hard and immediately groaned, plying his fingers to the sudden pain in his head. "Man, shouldn't have done that."

"You should be in bed," she said with a sigh.

"I know," he said, heating her cheeks with a wayward smile that caused her to inch further away. Pressing his bare foot on the accelerator, he kept it there while he turned the key, head cocked to listen to the starter. "Come on, baby," he whispered in a husky tone, alarming Shannon when the sound purled heat in her tummy, "I know you can do it." With a rhythmic grind that seemed to go on forever, the engine finally roared to life, drowning out her loud sigh of relief.

Sagging back in the seat, Sam slid her a sideways smile. "The trick is to keep your foot on the accelerator with no pumping, young lady, then keep grinding and pray like the devil."

Her mouth crooked. "The devil preys, but not that kind." She huffed out more air, lips pursed in a tight smile as she shooed him toward the door. "Okay, then, it's off to bed with you, Doc, but thank you, truly, for starting my car."

He didn't move, smile gentle as his gaze roamed her face, her hair, hitching her pulse when it drifted down her body and back.

"You're not the one who should be thanking me, Shan," he said quietly, "I should be thanking you."

She smiled, going for casual as she shuffled back a tad. "For adding to your headache with opinions you didn't want to hear?"

His face faded to serious. "Yeah, for that. Because I have to admit, though you ticked me off pretty good a couple of times" —those chocolate eyes held her captive, probing as if she were a mystery to solve— "for some strange reason, I feel a whole lot better than I did before, and I'm not exactly sure why."

Her smile was warm. "Because the truth is the cure for heartache?"

He stared, eyes in a squint. "Maybe. Or maybe you're just that good as a friend."

Her eyes softened, his words so sweet, she had to fight the urge to give him a hug. "I hope so."

"Me, too," he said, reaching to skim a finger down the curve of her jaw.

Before she could react, he leaned in and brushed a kiss to her cheek. It startled her so much, she jerked, which inadvertently aligned her mouth with his, barely inches apart. Heat coiled in her stomach as she froze, his shallow breathing mingling with her own. And then her oxygen ceased altogether when he slowly bent in, closing the distance as his eyes sheathed closed.

No! But her limbs and voice refused to work, the caress of his lips paralyzing all protest. Against her will, a low moan slipped from her throat, his kiss so achingly tender, her body felt drugged as it melted into his arms. *Oh, Lord, help me—it's been so long …*

"Shan," he whispered, his breath warm in her ear, easing her down on the seat so gently, she was barely aware. "Stay with me …" With a playful tug of her lip, his mouth took hers, disarming her with a dangerous warmth that swirled heat in her belly.

Stay with him.

Spend the night with him.

So he can take another piece of my soul.

Her mind seized, and then her heart. *"No!"* she screamed, shoving him away with such force, he bumped his head on the dash. "Out, get out, you … you … slimy letch!" She flogged him with her fists, not feeling a bit bad over the nasty knot he would have.

"Shannon, wait—" He raised his arms to protect himself, but she only whacked him all the harder, furious she'd been dumb enough to be played by a player. Especially after Jack's warning.

"He can charm the spots off a kid with measles, which makes him all the more dangerous. So I need someone mature and levelheaded, with an immunity to players …"

Yeah, right. Apparently an "immunity to players" doesn't inoculate one against "stupid."

"Shannon, let me explain, please—"

Chest heaving, she jerked one of her high heels off and bullied him with her size five-and-a-half stilettos. "The-only-ex-pla-nation-I-want-from-you-bucko," she hissed as she bludgeoned him but good, "is-how-to-get-you-out-of-my-car!"

"Hey, that hurts," he moaned. He clutched his stomach as he scrambled out, finally toppling into the street.

"Good!" She lunged to slam the door, too angry to gloat when he furiously scuttled back before she could take off his big toe. Shifting into gear, she spared him one last glance to make sure he was clear, satisfied to see the fear of God in his eyes. "I hope your stupid tie stinks forever," she shouted, moisture stinging as she gunned away from the curb.

Just like my judgment in men.

CHAPTER FIVE

"You've been a godsend, Cam." Carrying two tall, frosty glasses of her famous peach iced tea out to her patio, Tess O'Bryen placed one in front of Cameron Phillips—the uncle of her daughter-in-law, Lacey—who had just taken her out to lunch. "I can't thank you enough for all the help you've been."

"My pleasure, Tess." Cam hoisted his glass in a toast, his smile solid, steady, and warm, like the friend he'd been to her the last five months since her ex-husband Adam passed away. "I remember all too well the grief of losing Susan to cancer, which is one of the reasons I've spent so much time at sea on various naval commissions. Despite the fact it's my job, it was one of the few ways I found I could cope. So trust me—I count it a privilege to be here to help you shoulder your grief."

Offering a grateful smile, she sank into her white wrought-iron chair, welcoming the comfort of the heron-blue striped pillows that were beginning to show wear and tear. *Like me*, she thought, shamefully exhausted from their trek through the cemetery, where she and Cam had attended a Memorial Day service before lunch. They'd both put flowers on Adam's and Susan's gravesites. She laid her head back on the chair and closed her eyes, grateful that Cam understood her moments of silence and didn't press her to talk.

She'd only officially met Cam briefly last August at his daughter Nicki's wedding. And then again at her son Jack's and Lacey's wedding the next month after he'd finished his naval commission on the *USS George H. W. Bush*. So when he showed up at Adam's funeral, she'd been surprised. And *so* utterly grateful! Somehow, she hadn't expected her ex-husband's death to affect her so, especially since she hadn't seen him for two years prior to last summer, when he'd come back to make amends to his family.

Amends. Tears pricked her eyes. And then some. The pastor husband who had left her almost eight years ago after an adulterous affair with her friend and neighbor, Karen—Cam's sister—had somehow managed to burrow into his family's heart all over again. He'd been a changed man on a mission—to heal the wounds he'd inflicted before God called him home. And, oh, how he had! Becoming a best friend to her all over again and an unlikely hero to his children, making the last five months since his death oh, so hard.

And yet, oh, so wonderful! Knowing he was now in the presence of His Savior while his family no longer bore the burden of bitterness.

Only grief.

She took a sip of her iced tea, gaze trailing into her once-lush garden and yard, which now suffered neglect as much as she. But she hadn't expected Adam's death to bruise her so badly, imposing an awful malaise that was so unnatural for a woman Ben Carmichael once called "annoyingly perky."

Ben.

Loneliness struck with such force, a flash flood stung at the back of her eyes. With two daughters, two sons, a brand-new daughter-in-law she adored, and a crotchety blue heron who resided in her oak as an unofficial pet, she shouldn't be lonely. And yet, from the moment Ben—her crotchety neighbor, Lacey's father, and now love of her life—had kissed her goodbye in that empty hallway before Jack and Lacey's wedding last year, a hint of loneliness had crawled into her heart.

"So help me, Tess," he'd said, nudging her to the wall with an agony that had shocked both of them to the core. "I am so in love with you …"

Her answering moan had melted into his mouth before she gently pushed him away, the same torment in his face that she felt in her own. "Ben, I'm in love with you too—*desperately*—but this is not the time nor place."

And so he had left after the wedding, one of the country's top cardiac surgeons opting for a six-month medical missionary trip a friend had been badgering him about for years. To give her time with Adam and then time to grieve. Only six months had turned into eight, so when his once frequent letters and emails tapered off to only here and there, her loneliness had spread like the vile disease that had taken Adam's life. A sharp stab of pain wrung more moisture from her eyes. What if he had changed his mind about marrying her? What if he'd met someone else? What if he didn't need her anymore like she needed him?

Oh, Ben, where are you?

"Tess." Cam's voice was gentle as always.

Her eyes jerked open, so lost in her thoughts that she had to blink several times before Cam's face came into view. "Yes?"

She startled when he reached across the table to tenderly brush a tear from her cheek. "You know I don't mind the moments of silence between us because I understand." He slowly sat back down, kind eyes probing hers with a concern that had been a balm to her soul these last five months. "Because the silence is comfortable, like our friendship." He paused, a crease above a classic nose on a face most women considered attractive, she supposed, although she'd been too depressed to notice. One side of his full lips lifted into an off-center smile that popped a dimple, and she blinked, suddenly caught off-guard by military-short sandy hair and hazel eyes the exact shade of Ben's. "But when the friend I've come to care for starts shedding crocodile tears …" He cuffed the back of his neck with an adorable grimace that made her smile. "Well, I tend to revert to Navy mode, and the Rear Admiral in me takes over."

She caught her lower lip with her teeth, a glimmer of the former "Miss Perky"—Ben's nickname for her—twinkling in her eyes, no doubt. "Uh-oh … should I salute?"

He grinned and rose, downing most of his iced tea before pushing in his chair. "That might be best since we'll be at sea."

He rounded the table and hooked her arm, plucking her up.

"What? W-Where are we g-going?" she stammered, too aware of his commanding hold as she stumbled along while he led her down her driveway.

"To test-drive a boat."

She skidded to a dead stop, her one-inch pumps digging into her red paver driveway now crisscrossed with moss. "Are you crazy, Cam? I'm not dressed for a boat."

He scanned head to foot and back. His slow perusal of the *way*-too-short pencil skirt Cat talked her into and her sleeveless lavender silk blouse was so deliberate, it toasted her cheeks. "I'll wait. Go change."

She blinked, mind racing in a hundred different directions, none of them along the lines of grief counseling with a friend. He turned to buff her arms, thumbs slowly grazing the crook of her elbow. Her throat went dry as her neck craned *up, up, up* to a handsome face sporting a patient smile.

Good grief, when did he get so tall?

"It's Memorial Weekend, Tess, and you've been in a funk for five months now. The sun and sea air will do you good and who knows?" The hazel eyes twinkled like topaz. "You might even have a little fun."

"B-But … but …"

He glanced at his watch. "I have an appointment at 1500 hours—three o'clock your time—so we have to cut and run, Mrs. O'Bryen, because I'm never late."

"But you're not dressed either," she said, swallowing hard as she did a quick perusal of his crisp shirt and tie and neatly pressed Dockers.

He grinned as he tugged off the tie, then unbuttoned the top two buttons of his shirt with a wink. "I have shorts, Sperrys, and a Polo in the back seat, along with drinks and snacks in a cooler."

She crossed her arms with an open-mouthed smile. "Why does this sound premeditated, Admiral Phillips?"

"Because it is," he said with a swagger as cocky as his smile on the way to his Land Rover, "so get crackin'."

Shaking her head, Tess scurried inside, almost shocked at how giddy she felt. It had been years since she'd been on a boat other than Adam's dory, and she actually found herself humming as she changed into her white shorts and a nautical blue and white tank top. She hadn't even been on Ben's cabin cruiser, for heaven's sake. *Specifically* because their relationship was on the sly since Tess didn't want her family to know she and Dr. Doom—the name her children had coined for the grouch next door—were smitten. And as small as Isle of Hope was, there'd be too many tongues wagging if Ben had taken her out on his boat.

She gathered her shoulder-length blonde hair into a messy ponytail, then dug on her knees in the closet for casual shoes that weren't dirty or stained with paint. "Yes!" she shouted as she found the white deck shoes she'd bought late last summer, slipping them on before hooking her purse over her shoulder. Shooting a glance in the mirror, she wondered if she should put on some gloss, then paused. Her heart cramped when she remembered how much Ben loved her peach lip gloss.

Especially kissing it off.

"No! You are *not* going to ruin my mood, Ben Carmichael, not when you've been AWOL for almost two months!" With a thrust of her chin, she snatched her peach lip gloss from where she'd tossed it in the drawer after Ben left. It had been too painful a reminder of what they had lost, but now she slathered it across her pinched lips. "Take that, Dr. Doom," she muttered as she stashed both the gloss and sunscreen into her purse and marched out the door.

It was a perfect day. A cerulean blue sky and a sea-scented breeze billowing Cam's loose sea foam Polo as he test-drove a 50-foot Princess Motor Yacht that Marv, his salesman friend, let him take out on his own. They'd laughed all the way to the marina, then some more on the boat, where Cam—the consummate sailor—commandeered with feet straddled at the wheel while Tess lounged on the leather seat. When he finally dropped anchor, they bobbed on the water to the music of seagulls and waves, dining on cheese and fruit while Cam nursed a beer and she sipped a Seven-Up. The time flew faster than the seagulls winging overhead, and Tess couldn't remember a more relaxing day in a long, long while.

When the sun sank lower in the sky and brought a whisper of dusky pink to the horizon, Tess didn't want the day to end. "This is sheer heaven," she said as she tipped her face to the sun, arms hooked around knees tucked to her chest.

"I would have to agree." He shifted to the rear seat across from her, appearing very relaxed as his arm rested over the back. "Not just the boat and the water, mind you, but the company too."

Her heart stuttered as she shielded her eyes, more to deflect the interest in his than the glare of the sun. "So, what do you think?" She patted the seat with a smile, anxious to steer the conversation in a safer direction. "Are you interested in this beauty?"

He stared at her for several endless seconds before he answered, that maddeningly calm half smile skittering her pulse. "I think so," he said, eyes fused to hers while he upended the last of his beer. "And I'm not sure about the boat yet."

Gulp.

"Cam …" She sucked in a deep swell of sea air for courage, wondering how she could have been so stupid to not see this coming.

He held up a palm. "I'm not rushing you, Tess. I know what you've been through, but I thought it fair to let you know I enjoy your company and would like to spend more time with you, beyond our mutual grief."

Oh, boy.

Setting his beer down, he rose to sit next to her, fingers almost touching her shoulder as he draped an arm over the seat. "I'm seriously thinking of retiring from the Navy to spend more time with Spence, Mamaw, and any rug rats Nicki and Matt may have in the future," he said quietly, "especially if there were another reason to stay."

She all but leapt up from the seat, wringing the front of her tank till the stripes weren't straight anymore. "Cam, I enjoy your friendship, I do, b-but I think there's something you should know."

He peered up beneath shuttered eyes that had seemed so safe and soothing before, and she sat back down to face him head-on, scooting a hair away when his fingers casually brushed her shoulder. His patient smile never faltered. "Too soon?"

The lump in her throat bobbed like the boat in the water. "No … not too soon … a little more like too late."

He barely blinked, the look on his face far more serene than the waves churning all around.

"You s-see," she stumbled on, "I'm … pretty serious with someone else."

A breeze stirred one of his clipped tawny curls the wind had disheveled, and yet his demeanor remained unruffled. "I expected as much, although you never made mention. You're an amazing woman, Tess, and I've spent the last five months wondering why someone hasn't snatched you up." He paused, his manner casual. "Anyone I know?"

Heat broiled her face like a bad sunburn. It was awkward enough turning Cam down. If he found out it was Ben—the ex-brother-in-law he despised as much as Ben despised him—that unflappable calm of his would blow like a dozen foghorns. Besides, nobody was supposed to know, right? So, Tess was completely within her limits to withhold the truth for now. She thought of how Ben had barely contacted her in the last two months and not at all in the last two weeks, and her ribs constricted.

If it's even the truth anymore …

"It's someone with whom I was pretty serious before Adam returned," she said slowly, sidestepping the issue of identity, "so he left town for a while to give me time and space until …" Her voice trailed off, and she hated the stupid tears that blurred in her eyes.

But they only gushed all the more when Cam pulled her into a firm hug. The smell of Coppertone and a hint of his cologne—Guilty, by Versace, no less—only reminded her of what a good friend he had been when she'd needed one most. "It's okay, Tess," he whispered against her hair, the massage of his hand on her back providing a tranquility she'd come to expect from this rock-steady man. "I completely understand, and he's a very lucky guy." He pulled back to fish a Kleenex out of his pocket—a staple of his since he'd been spending time with Tess—and carefully dabbed at her tears. "But if it doesn't work out" —he paused, handing her a fresh tissue as he fixed her with that penetrating stare that always settled her down— "you know where I am."

She nodded and sniffed, swiping at her nose.

"But …" He lowered his head to fix her with a parental look laced with his trademark half-smile. "Just because I'm backing off doesn't mean we can't be friends. I'm going to need *lots* of advice on women now that I'm back home and looking to settle down, so I'd like to continue our occasional lunches if that's okay?"

Her rib cage expanded. "Sure, Cam."

"And maybe we can even double after you and this guy reconnect because I'd like to meet him."

No you don't, Cam, trust me. She gave a quick nod while she chewed the edge of her lip.

"Good." He rose and squinted at the horizon. "Well, I don't know about you, but I'm starving, so what do you say we head in for an early dinner before calling it a day?"

Relief expelled from her lungs in one undulating wave. "I'd like that a lot," she said, gratitude warm in her eyes. All tension blew away with the wind as she sat beside him on the fly bridge while he drove back to the marina. By the time they eased into the slip and tied up, they were laughing and sparring like siblings over who had the best barbecue—Sandfly or Wiley's.

"Mmm … sounds like a challenge to me." Opening the door to the marina office, he chuckled, steering her back to Marv's cubicle before hooking a loose arm over her shoulder. "So how 'bout Sandfly tonight, and we'll do Wiley's for lunch next time?"

"It's a date," Tess said, peering up with a tilt of her head as they arrived at Marv's cube. She slid Cam a sideways grin. "*And* a bet, Admiral, so prepare to lose because you're going down in flames."

"So, what do you think?" Marv glanced up with a smile when they walked into his office. "Ready to sign your life away?"

Tess's snappy response died on her lips when a black lab pounced on her chest, squealing and slathering her face with drool. Her grin immediately molded like plastic, all air sucked from her lungs as effectively as if they were vacuum-sealed.

Talk about going down in flames!

Neither she nor Cam answered the salesman's question because they couldn't—oxygen failed as they stared at Ben Carmichael, reining in his dog with a stony press of his lips. "Beau, sit!" he commanded, his gaze thin as it flicked from Tess to Cam and back, making Cam's arm over her shoulder feel like a two-ton weight.

Guilt flamed in her cheeks as she eased away from Cam's hold. *Ready to sign her life away?* Heart ramming her ribs, she tried to breathe, but there was no air to be found.

I think I just did …

CHAPTER SIX

"Wow, what the heck happened to you?"

Sam looked up as Jack strolled into his office without knocking, the toothy smiles on his framed Rugrat cartoon characters in direct contrast to the scowl on Sam's face. Stifling a groan, he wished he had locked the door after his final patient. The last person he wanted to see right now was Jack O'Bryen, not when Sam sported a truly impressive shiner and rainbow bruise on his cheek, compliments of Jack's sister. Which is why Sam had been avoiding Jack all day—easy enough to do since the three-day holiday backlogged them both.

Jack plopped into one of Sam's shocking orange Bola chairs and hiked his legs on the desk, head resting back as he eyed him with a shuttered grin. "Some girl finally wise up and knock you for a loop?"

Something like that. Sam sagged back into his chair with a groan, scouring his face with both hands so Jack wouldn't spot the fire heating his cheeks. "Hit my head on the dash," he said, rubbing his skin briskly to account for any flush that might remain. His hands dropped to hang limp over the arms of his chair like he'd been deboned as he faced Jack head-on with a dry bent of his mouth. "Don't ask."

Jack's brows cut low. "You weren't in an accident, were you?"

Close enough. Sam expelled a heavy sigh. *A freak accident where I was almost run over by your sister, who bludgeoned me with her shoe.* "Naw." He hesitated, stomach churning over the possibility that Shannon had told Jack he'd hit on her. He was pretty sure she hadn't, though, since he was still sitting here in one piece with only *one* black eye ... "Thanks for having Shannon drive me home, Jack," he said quietly, testing the waters with a tentative smile, keeping his words as neutral as possible. "She's a really nice person."

"Yeah, she is, Sam, which is why I'm so protective of her. A gentle spirit who wouldn't hurt a fly."

Sam fought the rise of a gulp. *Nope, not a fly …*

A twinkle lit Jack's gaze. "And a killer cook too."

"Yeah." Blood broiled Sam's face as he scratched the back of his neck, his collar collecting moisture. *You have no idea.*

"Heard she made you breakfast, then tried to talk some sense into you." Jack studied him with a curious air, as if trying to determine if Shannon had any effect on him. "Did any of it sink in, I hope?"

Sam jumped up to crank up the air, sweat breaking out on his sweat. "Sure."

One stiletto, several times in my chest.

"Good. Well, I owe her for taking such good care of you. Said she fed you and lectured you, then left you all comfy-cozy, flat on your back."

Sam blinked. *Well, on my back anyway …*

"So you owe her, too, dude, for taking such good care of you."

"I know." *Twice. Once for taking me home. And once for not telling her brother what happened after she did.* "I'll get her a gift card."

"That would be nice, Ham. So …" Jack said with a tap of his palms on the chair, "now it's your turn to do me a favor."

"Sure." Sam dropped back into his chair, mouth crooking as he took a drink of his bottled water. *Not press charges against your sister?*

"As you know, Lacey and I have a wedding to go to in San Diego on Saturday, so last night we got this wild hair—why not make a mini-vacation out of it? And Augustine is good with it, so it seems stupid not to take advantage, you know?"

Sam nodded, upending his water. "It'd be a shame not to, since you're spending the time and money to fly out there anyway."

"That's what we thought, too, so since you already volunteered to fill in for me at Camp Hope for next Saturday—"

"Volunteered?" Sam parked his hands behind his neck with a lazy grin, far more relaxed now that Shannon wasn't part of the conversation. Besides, he was actually excited to help out at the camp for orphans that Jack always talked about, where Jack and his family had volunteered for years. "You mean blackmailed, don't you?" Sam continued, "in exchange for not telling everyone in the office that your little sister had to babysit me after hauling me home?" His eyes narrowed in jest. "Not to mention siccing your last morning appointment on me today—Brian Campbell, no less—so you could take an extra-long lunch, probably to play kissy-face with your wife."

Jack drew air through a clenched smile. "Blackmail is such an ugly word, Sam. I prefer the concept of sharing the wealth with a good friend. After all, Brian Campbell's symptoms were quite rare, so it was a good case to be exposed to. Even Augustine said so."

"Yeah? Well he didn't puke on Augustine's tie; he puked on mine," Sam groused, still ticked that Augustine had laid down the law, demanding Sam wear a tie at the office like everyone else. Sam enjoyed giving horsy rides to his patients and picking the little ones up, which meant risking kid stains on some of his best ties, making Polo shirts his clothing of choice under his white jacket. His scowl went flat. But not anymore.

Jack's grin was diabolic. "Well, see? You and Brian obviously have a lot in common, Ham—you both puke on your ties."

"Cute, O'Bryen, but I'm not laughing." His pained smile was just shy of a frown. "Two of my favorite—*and* most expensive—ties, ruined."

"I'll tell you what." Jack snatched a sucker from the candy bowl on Sam's desk. "I'll buy you a new one if you fill in for me at Camp Hope on your day off as well as on Saturday." He crumpled the wrapper and stood, tossing it into the wastebasket behind Sam's desk. "Deal?"

Sam surveyed him through a squint. "Ralph Lauren?"

Shaking his head, Jack laughed, crunching the sucker to bits. He stood and nailed a two-pointer in the can. "You are such a snob, Cunningham, you know that?"

"You would be, too, O'Bryen, if your clothes came from Goodwill most of your life."

Jack's grin simmered into a smile laced with respect. "I know, Sam. You never cease to amaze me at all you've accomplished, given your background."

Sam's gaze lagged into a cold stare, suddenly aware why Jack was rapidly becoming one of his best friends. "Thanks, man," he whispered. "I never forget where I came from, even if most people don't have a clue." Releasing a heavy exhale, he shook off his melancholy and offered Jack a sincere smile. "And no tie necessary, Jack, seriously. There's nothing I'd rather do than help kids who haven't been given a fair shake, you know?"

"Yeah, I know." Jack made his way to the door, shooting a smile over his shoulder. "Appreciate it, Sam. I'll have notes for you on what's expected before I leave." He turned, smile wary as he slacked a leg. "Just promise me one thing."

"Sure." Sam grinned, pretty sure he knew what it would be.

Jack leveled him with a pointed stare, smile flat. "No messing with the female volunteers. They have enough on their minds without some hotshot charming them into a crush. Got it?"

Sam flashed some teeth. "Sure, Jack. Anything else?"

Jack turned at the door, a gleam in his eyes as he offered a salute. "Yeah. And whatever you do, Ham," he said with a twitch of a smile, "don't wear a tie."

CHAPTER SEVEN

"But I d-don't want to see the n-nurse; I want to r-ride a h-horsy." Little six-year-old Beth Erin Schwarzlose clung to Shannon's neck, voice quivering with disappointment as they entered the reception area of the Camp Hope plantation house.

"I know, sweetheart, but you can't ride a horsy if you're dizzy and throwing up." Shannon pressed a kiss to the child's cheek, worry lines creasing her brow at the heat of her skin. This was the downside of volunteering at Miss Myra's camp for ill and handicapped orphans—the heartbreak of seeing sickness steal what joy these precious children had. Shifting the little tyke in her arms, she wished she could give them far more than just volunteer time during the summers and on weekends. *Like a family that would love and nurture them*, she thought with a pinch in her chest.

Suppressing a melancholy sigh, Shannon poked her head in Miss Myra's office, worry lacing her tone. "I'm taking Beth to sick bay, Miss Myra, because she's not feeling well."

"I want to ride the horsy," Beth whimpered, red-rimmed eyes issuing a soggy plea to the camp's matriarch as Shannon gently rubbed the little girl's back.

Miss Myra glanced up, her perennial Southern air evident in a silk mauve dress perfectly complemented by a single strand of pearls. Most likely in her sixties, Miss Myra always appeared ageless to Shannon. Her classic ash blonde French twist and porcelain skin etched with fine lines was a perfect cover for a five-foot-one dynamo no one dared cross. Two tiny wedges appeared between Miss Myra's brows as she rose to circle her desk. Her high heels clicked on the wooden floor with the same sharpness and efficiency with which she transformed her family's plantation into a camp for orphans with illnesses, disabilities, and other challenges.

"There will be plenty of time to ride your horsy after you get well, darling." Depositing a kiss to Beth's brow, Miss Myra gently swept the little girl's hair from her eyes, gaze connecting with Shannon's. "Caryl Kane's the nurse on duty today, but she just left for lunch after the volunteer doc arrived, so just take her on back. Oh my, she's burning up," she whispered, the thread of concern in her tone matching the soft blink of brown eyes.

"I hope it's Dr. Nate," Shannon said, readjusting Beth in her arms before turning to head down the hall. "He's almost as good with the children as Jack."

"No, it's somebody new, according to Caryl, but I haven't had the chance to meet him yet, so you can be my scouting party." Miss Myra actually winked, a gesture so out of character that Shannon grinned. "But she says he's a real Southern gentleman, and I quote, 'quite a hunk' too."

Shannon chuckled. "Everybody's a hunk to Caryl," she called on her way to sick bay. Smiling, she shook her head over Caryl's comment. The young volunteer in her second year of nursing certainly seemed far more interested in the docs than a degree.

"I don't feel so good, Miss Shannon," Beth whispered, laying her head on Shannon's shoulder. "My tummy hurts."

Shannon paused on the threshold of sick bay—a former outdoor veranda converted into a sunny year-round mini hospital ward. "Do you feel like you're going to throw up again, sweetheart?"

"I don't know."

"Well you be sure to tell me or the doctor if you do, and we'll get you a pot, okay?" Shannon wiggled her nose in the crook of Beth's neck, making the little girl giggle as she carried her to a hospital bed. Along the far wall, a doc in a white coat emblazoned with a Superman logo squatted to give an insulin shot to a small child in a Little Tykes car. Giggles rose from a group of children that surrounded him while a young volunteer teacher looked on, the smile on her face practically aglow. "After all," Shannon said, "we don't want you puking on the doc or he might not come back."

Her breath caught in her throat when the doc glanced over his shoulder.

Or maybe we do.

Sam Cunningham—or "Sham Cunningham" as she'd nicknamed him in her mind—had the audacity to give her a grin and a wink, charring her cheeks. "This is my last injection, so I'll be right with you, Angel Eyes," he said with a twinkle, gaze flicking to Beth to render another wink. "And you, too, sweetheart." He turned back to his task before Shannon could deliver a scowl, his bedside manner obviously as deadly with sick kids as it was with unsuspecting women.

"Okay, what flavor shot do you want this to be, champ—vanilla, strawberry, or chocolate?" Sam reached for a clean syringe while gently rubbing an ice pack on the back of a little boy's arm. "Or if you want to go daring like me, you can go with something like Chunky Monkey or Peanut Butter Fudge or my personal favorites" —he tossed Shannon a grin over his shoulder— "Baskin Robbins' Wild and Reckless sherbet or Love Potion #31."

Shannon rolled her eyes.

"I'll just take vanilla, please," the little boy whispered, hands gripped knuckle-white on the steering wheel of the Little Tyke's car.

"You like to play it safe, eh?" Sam gently pinched some skin at the back of the boy's arm. "Well that's okay, buddy, because some of the nicest people I know like to play it safe. Now I'm going to hold this arm still, but let's make some noise with the other by beeping that horn, okay?"

The boy started banging the horn while Sam and all the others whooped and made car sounds, the needle in and out so fast, the little guy was vaccinated before he knew it. "Okay, partner, good job," Sam said, swabbing the boy's arm while he fished a Tootsie Roll Pop from his pocket. "You're all done." Opening the car door, Sam carefully lifted the boy out, taking great pains not to bump his vaccinated arm.

"Thanks so much, Dr. Sam," the volunteer teacher said before herding the children to the door, the adoration shining in her eyes enough to make Shannon sick. Trying to ignore the hugs and high-fives Sam doled out to each of the kids, Shannon sat next to Beth on the bed, hugging her close while the little girl's head lagged against Shannon's side.

Beth's little chest expanded and contracted with a sigh way bigger than she, and Shannon found herself doing the same as she watched Sam out of the corner of her eye. True, he may be a hero with women and kids, but she was grateful she'd been "vaccinated" against charming players like him. She closed her eyes, and the memory of his kiss instantly invaded, tugging another heavy sigh from her throat. Vaccinated indeed. Her lips took a twist as she hugged Beth close. *Including the booster shot last week in the car.*

CHAPTER EIGHT

"So … what's the problem with this little angel here?" Sam returned to squat before them.

Well, Doc, she's nauseous and has a fever, and I'm just plain nauseous.

"Miss Shannon won't let me ride my horsy," Beth said with a sad sniff, no hesitation at all in throwing Shannon under the bus for trying to do the right thing.

Shannon sighed. *Again.*

Sam smiled up at Shannon, and her stomach plunged at a mottled yellow and purple bruise around his eye. She put a hand to her mouth, feeling like a despicable human being. "Oh no, did I do that?" she whispered, nodding at his shiner.

His twitch of a smile was in perfect sync with the sparkle in his eyes. "Afraid so, Teach, but trust me—it's a lesson I learned well."

Shannon punished her lip with her teeth. "Sam, I am *so* sorry."

He peered up with that rare gravity she'd seen before despite the curve of his lips. "I'm not. I had it coming, Shannon, and besides" —he winked— "my patients think I look like a pirate, striking fear in the hearts of both maiden and man."

"Are you?" Beth asked, eyes wide.

Sam's gaze lingered on Shannon, the sober apology in his eyes at odds with the playful tone he just used with Beth. "Not anymore," he whispered before refocusing on his patient with his killer smile. "So … what's your name, pretty girl?"

"Beth," she said softly with a sweet smile, and Shannon could have sworn the little dickens fluttered her lashes.

"Wow, a beautiful name for a beautiful girl!" He rose and

placed a palm to her forehead. "You're definitely warm, so what hurts, sweetheart?"

"My tummy and my head." Beth gave him a sad-eyed gaze.

"And she threw up," Shannon said sweetly, satisfied when Sam took a step back.

"Okay, then." He turned around, dimples working overtime as he grinned at Beth over his shoulder. "How about I give you a horsy ride over to the table, Beth, so we can take a better look?" Butting up to the bed, he scooted low so Beth could climb onto his broad back, looping his arms to brace her legs. "Ready? Hold on tight, sweetheart, because here we go."

Shannon battled a smile when he galloped to the examination table yelling, "yee-haw!" and all sorts of cowboy jargon, unwilling to give him a chance to soften her heart. Yes, he was a kind and decent individual when it came to children, but when it came to women? She issued a silent grunt, her guard going up with a tight fold of arms as she followed behind. He was little more than a Casanova, and she wasn't about to give him a chance to con her again.

"Don't let him bamboozle you, Shan. The man has a masters in roguery, so it might be good to lend him an ear, but nothing else."

Another grunt made it to her lips, only this one slipped out, braising her cheeks when it drew the bamboozler's gaze with a curious smile.

"Okay, cowgirl," he said to Beth after he'd finished his examination, whipping a Tootsie Roll Pop out of his pocket like it was a gun. He aimed it at her with a Clint Eastwood squint. "I reckon you've got a touch of cowgirl virus, ma'am, so I'm gonna give you a swig of this here cowboy juice to help you feel better …" He paused to measure out some cherry-looking medicine that Beth gulped down, then handed her a Pedialyte juice box from the fridge. "I need you to drink as much of this here cherry juice as you can, little lady, then bunk down here for a while to get some shut-eye. Nurse Caryl and I need to keep an eye on you for a while, okay?"

The Tootsie Roll Pop bulged one of her cheeks as she nodded, garble coming out when she tried to talk. Sam calmly removed the pop for a moment while Beth blinked up at him. "But when am I going to get to ride my horsy?" she whispered, a glaze of tears starting to form.

Sam popped her sucker back in with a kiss to her head. "A day or two, sweetie-pie, I promise, but first you gotta get better, and a nice long nap will help that along." He picked her up and deposited her on one of the several beds tucked back in a dark corner of the room, placing her drink box on her nightstand and removing her shoes. "Finish up that lollipop, ma'am, and I'll be back to read you a story before you get some shut-eye, okay?" Fluffing the pillow behind her, he placed a kiss on her head and returned to where Shannon stood, thinking what a great guy he would be if he wasn't such a player.

"She's going to be out of commission for a couple of days, but I want to keep her in sick bay for a few hours to see how she handles the Tylenol and Pedialyte." He glanced toward the room where Beth was sucking on her Tootsie Roll Pop, the serious concern in her eyes in total contrast to the twinkle that always resided there. "And I want to watch her fever for a while because it's tipping close to 103. I don't like the look of her throat either, so if you can let her dorm mom know, Shannon, I'd appreciate it." Gaze connecting with hers, his caring and responsible air almost disarmed her.

Almost.

"Will do, Doc, thanks." She spun around and dashed for the door, anxious to put as much distance between her and Sam Cunningham as she possibly could.

"Shannon, wait—"

But she didn't. Miss Myra and her Southern etiquette would have had her head if she'd seen her bolting down the hall like one of the kids, as if she were fleeing for her life. But in a way, she was. Sam Cunningham had not only put the fear of God in her that night, he'd put something else far more sinister and dangerous.

Desire. Attraction. Longing.

A deep-seated longing for something she would never have with the likes of him.

Correction. She'd have the desire and attraction all right—that's what players like Sam did best—but the longing for something more, something real, something that would last forever? It wasn't in the DNA of a player who had no use for God, and Shannon had no desire for a relationship of any kind with a man like that. *Especially* one who had turned her world upside down with a single kiss. Something cold slithered her spine as she hurled the front door open. God help her, imagine the damage he could do if he stole her heart …

Ooomph! Shannon bounced off Caryl Kane on the other side of the door, almost spilling the two Cold Stone milkshakes the young girl carried in a cardboard caddy. "Caryl, I'm so sorry," she said as she steadied the student nurse who volunteered in sick bay, noting the freshly applied lipstick and potent scent of perfume.

"No problem," the young girl said with a bright smile, sidestepping Shannon to hurry down the hall.

No doubt to ply Dr. Love with a milkshake as cold as his heart.

A heavy sigh parted from Shannon's lips as she scurried down the steps, suddenly ashamed of her attitude toward Sam. Heaven knows that wasn't the type of person she wanted to be nor usually was, but Sam just brought out the worst in her it seemed—a sharp tongue and point-blank honesty aimed right at his heart. The corner of her mouth tipped. Because he was a man who tempted—not only with physical desire—but with the hope of bringing out the best in him. And that was a hope she couldn't afford.

Not with a player.

"Hey, Shannon, wait up."

She whirled, her stomach doing the exact same thing as she spied Sam on the porch of the plantation house, waving his milkshake to get her attention. Spinning back around, she picked up her pace to the stables, head down and jaw tight. *Lord, I don't want to be mean to him, so please, can you just make him go away?*

"Hey, wait up, please? I just want to clear the air with you ..."

"And I just want to clear my head *of you,*" she muttered, ducking into the stables to hide in the first stall. *Your face. Your smile. Your stupid kiss that won't let me alone.* She slid down the planked half wall hunched to her knees, closing her eyes while she held her breath and prayed he wouldn't come in.

She squealed and jumped when something touched her head. It jolted her so much, she toppled into the corner, legs sprawled and pride as flat as her butt against the wall.

Right next to a pile of poop.

Which pretty much described her sentiments as Sam Cunningham grinned from above, leaning on the stall while he sucked on a straw. "Hey."

Giving up the ghost, she went slack with a groan, eyes closed as her head clunked against the wood. "What do you want, Sam?" she whispered, realizing she'd have to give him his say before she gave him the boot.

"I'm not sure, Angel Eyes, but I think I may be a tad wounded that you'd rather hide in a smelly stable than talk to me."

"Sorry, Doc, but I just prefer this type of manure."

"Ouch." Setting his milkshake on the ledge, he rounded the wall with a husky chuckle, extending his hand to help her up. "Come on, Shannon, don't sugarcoat it—why don't you say what you really mean?"

"I'd like to," she muttered, ignoring his palm to pop up on her own. Huffing out a noisy sigh, she proceeded to brush bits of hay from her jeans.

He stilled her with a gentle hand to her shoulder. "Me too," he said softly, the humility in his tone drawing her gaze. "And if you don't mind, I'll go first." He'd ditched the Superman coat, so he slid his hands into the pockets of his Dockers while he took a step back, shoulders hunched as he stared at his feet. "I've … been wanting to apologize to you ever since that night. I was a jerk, Shannon, and I'm really sorry." He finally looked up, meeting her gaze with a solemn one of his own. "And I'd" —he cuffed the back of his neck while a knot jogged in his throat—

"I'd like to be friends if you'll let me because I really enjoyed talking to you."

She cocked her head, lips flat. "Sure you did."

"I did," he said with a crooked smile. He gave a slight shrug of his shoulders. "Well, most of it anyway, so I'd like to do it again. You know, shoot the breeze so I can pick your brain as a woman, maybe to glean some advice on how to get Jazz back? So, what do you say, O'Bryen? Friends?"

Her heart softened. And then her mind went into alert mode. Sam was the kind of guy who would be a great friend, she was certain, but he'd ruined that possibility when he'd made a pass in the front seat of her car. Not just because she didn't trust him, but because she didn't trust herself. That pass, that kiss had ignited something in her that made her want far more than a friendship, and for her, the temptation just wasn't worth the risk. "Apology accepted," she said quietly, "and we can certainly be friends, Sam, but …" Her heart squeezed at the look of vulnerability in his eyes, so foreign to the player she knew him to be. It took her back to the night he'd disarmed her in his kitchen with his sincerity and candor, making inroads into her heart that were never meant to be. "As far as shooting the breeze …" She paused, not wanting to hurt him, but not willing to give him the chance to hurt her either. "I don't think Jack would like that, and frankly, I'm not comfortable with it either."

He cocked a hip, hands perched on his thighs and a pinch in his brow. "You don't trust me," he said with a hint of hurt, his words a statement rather than a question.

Not even a little. "I … just don't think a friendly relationship would be wise." She tried to temper her words with a gentle smile, fighting the urge to just blurt out the truth like before.

Slashing a hand through his hair, he walked away, blasting out his frustration with a noisy breath before facing her once again. "Come on, Shan, I make one lousy move, and suddenly I'm a danger to your health?"

Yes.

He forged on, apparently stirred by her lack of response. "Look,

I'll admit I tend to get pushy when I drink too much, but it's not a common occurrence, Shannon, and I promise it won't happen again, at least not with you. So please don't let one stupid misstep on my part ruin the really great friendship we could have."

Arms clutched to her waist, she stared at the ground instead of his face, wishing there was some way she could just end this whole conservation with a smile instead of a scowl. All at once her gaze sharpened on his expensive brogues, polished to a gleam as he stood in a pile of manure. Chewing on the edge of a smile, she lifted her eyes to his, unable to thwart the shy grin that grew on her face. "Uh … not one stupid misstep, Sam," she said, gaze darting to his shoes and back. A giggle bullied its way past her lips. "Two."

CHAPTER NINE

How the devil did this happen?

The question blistered Ben Carmichael's brain as he sat in the shadows of his front porch at the inane hour of eleven-thirty on a Wednesday night, an O'Doul's in his hand and a scowl on his face. The *same* question that had badgered him for the last 48 hours.

When he saw Tess for the first time in eight months.

When he'd lost his violent temper for the first time in eight years.

And when he got into a fistfight for the first time ever.

Taking another belt of his non-beer, he winced, jaw still sore from the clip his ex-brother-in-law had landed at the marina.

Right *after* Ben had called him a questionable name and blackened his eye.

And right *before* Tess tore out of the marina office, madder than a hive of hornets.

Upending the can, he crushed it while the last dregs slid down his throat, groaning when he realized he'd just used the sore fist that had busted Cam's chops.

Even so, his lips curved in a satisfied smile.

Never liked him from the get-go.

Guilt instantly wormed its way past his gloat. *Real mature, Carmichael.* Now the woman you love thinks you're a street punk with a short fuse instead of her knight in shining armor, home to rescue her from her grief. Thoughts of Cam's arm around Tess's bare shoulders, of the sparkle in her eyes as their laughter filtered into Marv's office, suddenly flashed, and Ben's anger reignited all over again.

"I've never loved anyone like I love you, Tess," he'd told her the night she'd put their relationship on hold over eight months ago, *"and I will wait forever, if that's what it takes."*

He grunted, the sound harsh in a night filled with the heavy groan of a bull frog, obviously as unhappy as he. "Yeah, well looks like I was the only one …"

Dropping his head on the back of the chair, he closed his eyes, his newfound faith suddenly niggling at the back of his mind. *You didn't even give her a chance to explain. Just popped your cork like she wasn't the most important person in your world other than Lacey.* Self-condemnation sandpapered his conscience.

Let every person be quick to hear, slow to speak, slow to anger; for the anger of man does not produce the righteousness of God.

The mangled can dropped from his fingers as shame curdled in his gut along with the warm beer.

Nope, he just went off half-cocked, spewing jealousy and bitterness like a sewer gone awry.

Let all bitterness and wrath and anger … be put away from you, along with all malice.

"Okay, okay, I blew it," Ben snapped, "and I'll fix it, I promise. As soon as I can talk to Tess." He stared into the dark, his dock lights winking at him in the distance. "*If* I can talk to Tess," he muttered, painfully aware she'd been avoiding him since the incident. Not coming home till late that night with Bozo, then gone all day today and again tonight. She was obviously still ticked because she hadn't answered or returned his calls, texts, or emails, and with Jack and Lacey out of town, he couldn't bug them to help him out.

No, he'd have to wait her out till he could catch her alone to apologize and grovel if need be. After all, he'd made his bed and now he'd have to lie in it. His mouth compressed. *Problem is, I want Tess lying right next to me when I do,* the thought came, the feel of the engagement ring he'd bought last year a lumpy reminder in his pocket.

Lights swept onto the street to indicate the approach of a car. But when they disappeared at Tess's house, along with the sound of an engine that eased to a stop at her curb, Ben knew she was avoiding him still. Tess never parked in the street, always in the back of the house. Which meant she expected him to be lying in wait in his backyard for her to pull into her free-standing garage.

Wrong.

Lips flat, he strode to the corner of his eight-foot, Japanese privet hedge—the one he'd paid big bucks for eight years ago to shut the world out—painfully aware his temper had erected an even bigger barrier between him and Tess. Sucking in a deep draw of air, he attempted a casual stance as he leaned against the light post, hands in his pockets while he watched her retrieve her briefcase from the backseat. Slinging the strap over her shoulder, she carefully closed her car door with nary a noise, then turned toward her driveway.

And froze—body taut with surprise and stiffer than the wooden lamppost gouging his hip.

"A little late to be working, isn't it, Tess?" He pushed off from the post and ambled forward.

She visibly sagged. "Oh my goodness, Carmichael, you scared the living daylights out of me!" Hand splayed to her chest, her rib cage physically depleted like a blood pressure cuff releasing its air. "What on earth are you doing?"

Hands still plunged in his pockets, he approached with extreme caution, wishing more than anything he could just reel her into his arms and kiss her like he used to. "Waiting up for the woman I love since she hasn't returned any of my calls."

She buffed the sides of her arms as if she were cold, a noticeable duck in her throat. "I've been busy, Ben, but we'll talk soon, I promise."

He reached to take the briefcase from her shoulder, and his chest cramped hard when she jerked away. "Yeah, I know—busy avoiding me. But I learned from the best not to take no for an answer, Tess, *and* how to deal with my problems head-on, so I'm afraid 'soon' doesn't cut it."

"I'm not ready, Ben," she whispered, clutching the strap of her briefcase like a lifeline.

His smile was gentle. "I wasn't either, Tess, but I don't remember you cutting me any slack."

"Tomorrow." She took another step back. "We'll talk tomorrow, when we're both fresh, okay?"

"Nope, tonight," he said calmly, tugging the briefcase from her shoulder, "or I won't sleep and neither will you." He nodded toward his dock across the street. "My dock or yours—take your pick."

"And you call *me* 'pushy,'" she muttered, referencing all the many times he'd accused her of being a rammy neighbor. Heaving a cumbersome sigh, she nodded toward his dock and slid by to head in that direction.

He followed, lips twitching in a near smile at the way she marched with head high and shoulders square, reminding him just how much he'd missed her humor and stubborn resolve. When she reached his dock, she sat in one of the Adirondack chairs with hands folded on her lap, gaze fixed on the moon-striped river, which rippled and rolled as much as his stomach.

Setting her briefcase down, he claimed the chair next to hers, shifting it to face her directly. "Words can't express how sorry I am, Tess, for losing my temper," he said softly. "I was completely out of line, and I apologize." He paused, ducking his head to force her gaze to meet his. "Will you forgive me?"

She warded him off with a tight clutch of arms to her waist, the glaze of tears in her eyes twisting his gut. "Of course I forgive you, Ben, but I won't deny it worries me. I knew you had a temper because Lacey always alluded to it, but I honestly didn't believe it until I saw what you did to Cam."

He fought the need to grind his jaw, slowly easing back and resting his arms on the chair to keep his temper in check. "I haven't lost my cool since that night Lacey jumped off my boat over a year ago, Tess, and before that it's been years. But you have to understand that coming home after eight months of missing the woman I adore, only to see her in the arms of a man I can't abide, tripped an anger in me I didn't even know was there."

"Cam and I are friends, Ben, nothing more," she whispered,

her tone mellowing even if the intensity in her eyes did not. Her chin tipped up in challenge. "And frankly, after barely hearing from you weekly for almost two months and not at all the last two weeks, how on earth was I supposed to know you were even home since you never bothered to tell me?"

"I wanted to surprise you," he ground out, forcing a tranquility to his tone even though his gut was in knots. "I came straight to your house, but nobody was home, so I took Beau out on the boat to kill some time." His jaw notched up, even with hers. "The last few months of the trip were grueling, Tess, with 18-hour days and very little sleep, so I didn't always have the luxury of writing." His voice softened along with his heart. "The only luxury I did have, however, was thinking of you—which I did day and night."

Gaze tender, he leaned in to hunch on the edge of his chair, hands in a loose clasp over his knees while he zeroed in on the dark circles under her eyes. "How are you, Tess?" he whispered, suddenly worried that her overly perky letters hadn't revealed the depth of her mourning. After Adam had passed away in January, Ben had written her almost every day and called as much as he could, given the demands of his schedule and time zone. And although she'd seemed to struggle at first, the spunky and perky personality he'd fallen in love with had re-emerged quickly, both in her letters and phone conversations, much to his relief.

Until now. Now the woman before him not only appeared tired and worn, but so tightly coiled, she looked spring-loaded, ready to pop from the chair. He grazed her arm with a gentle touch. "You're still grieving, aren't you?" he said quietly, distraught that she hadn't let him know. "Why didn't you tell me, Tess? You know how much I wanted to be there for you."

She pounded the sides of her chair with her fists, jaw quivering as she seared him with a soggy glare. "Oh, don't you dare go all tender on me now, Ben Carmichael," she hissed, looking so much like a little girl throwing a tantrum, he couldn't refrain from a faint smile. "And you can just wipe that silly smirk off your face, too, because we have serious issues to discuss, mister."

"I know." He reached to glide the pad of his thumb along the curve of her face, grateful for the shiver his touch produced because heaven knows she was setting off Richter-scale tremors in him. "The most important of which is—I love you, Tess."

She slapped his hand away and jabbed a tight-fisted finger right under his nose. "Don't you dare try to sidetrack me, Dr. Doom, because I am serious here."

"I know that, too, babe." He gripped her wrist so fast, she caught her breath, smile soft as he slowly reeled her in. "Seriously beautiful, seriously perky, seriously perfect …"

"I'll-show-you-perky …" she bit out with a flurry of smacks that only made him chuckle as he scooped her onto his lap, grinning when she bucked like a catfish out of water.

"And I'm seriously crazy about you, too, Teresa O'Bryen," he said, burying his head in her neck to feather her skin with kisses before trailing up to suckle the lobe of her ear. "Marry me, Tess—please—and I'll even consider inviting your annoying friend to the wedding." He suddenly thought of Phillips touching her like this, and his jaw went to iron as he staked his claim with a possessive kiss.

Then again, maybe not.

CHAPTER TEN

Sweet Southern tea, what am I doing? Tess slammed two stiff palms to Ben's chest, hoping he hadn't heard the moan that almost slipped from her lips. "You're crazy all right, Carmichael," she said with a last-ditch flail of arms, desperate to keep him in line until she could drive her terms home. "And God help you if you think you can waltz in here—"

He cut her off with another kiss so urgent and deep, his groan tangled with hers as she melted against his chest. She dug her fingers into the hair at the back of his neck, trying to decide if she wanted to grab him or gouge him when his mouth slid along the curve of her jaw to nip at her ear. "God help me is right, Tess, because I want you more than I have ever wanted anything in my life."

"Ben, wait, please—"

He silenced her weak protest with another ravenous kiss, like a man starving for the only sustenance his soul could abide. "I can't, Tess—not any longer," he rasped, voice hoarse with a need he obviously could no longer deny. "I want to marry you now."

Oh, Ben … She went completely still in his arms, her fingers at the nape of his neck suddenly limp and flat. *Me, too, but …* She slumped back, facial muscles wilted with a sadness she'd only displayed one other time—the night he'd revealed a past that had almost cost him her love.

Her heart ached as he fumbled in his pocket for the diamond ring he'd so longed for her to wear, holding it out with shaky fingers. "Marry me, Tess—tomorrow, the next day, I don't care—but soon because I need you like I've never needed anyone before." Her resolve weakened when he cradled her face in his hands. “In my life,” he whispered, nuzzling her neck with a tenderness that immediately lured her eyelids closed. “In my house …” He mated his mouth with hers, exploring until he coaxed a soft mew from her throat. “And most definitely in my bed …” he said with an answering groan, voice husky as he devoured her body and soul.

Her breathing was as ragged as his when she finally pushed him away, soggy eyes revealing the depth of her love.

And her hesitation.

“Ben, I love you, I do,” she said quietly, the deep slash between his brows putting a stranglehold on her heart, “and I want to be your wife so badly, I can taste it—”

“Oh, me too,” he said, diving right back in to nibble her neck all over again.

“*But* …” She squirmed from his grasp with two rigid palms, arms locked to keep him at bay. “I have concerns.”

The air in his chest seemed to slowly seep out. “My temper?”

She shimmied off his lap to slip back in her own chair, the absence of his warmth chilling her as much as the vulnerable look on his face. “Yes, your temper, although it’s not my chief concern at the moment because losing it only twice in a number of years is not a deal breaker.”

His throat convulsed several times before he spoke. “Deal breaker?” he whispered, voice a near croak as he slipped the ring back into his pocket.

She studied him with caring eyes that longed to kiss away every worry line in his face. “Jealousy, Ben,” she said softly, bracing her arms to her waist again as if shutting him out. “I can’t abide jealousy because nothing will destroy a relationship faster than that.” Her gaze veered beyond him to absently trace the shore, a mist of moisture glazing her eyes. “I never fully realized it at the time, but jealousy was one of the root problems in my marriage to Adam. Our fights escalated the last few years because he wanted me to attend conferences with him, you see, but I never wanted to go. I used my job as an excuse, which infuriated him, of course, and it was certainly a factor in the rift between us."

She swallowed hard as she met his gaze once again. "But it wasn't the main reason." She looked away, skimming her arms as if she were cold, not knowing if it was the chill of a sudden sea breeze or her guilt, but either way, a shudder rippled her body. "It wasn't until Adam and Karen got involved that I realized just why I couldn't tolerate those stupid conferences where women flirted and fawned over Adam like I wasn't even there. I was jealous and couldn't handle it, so I chose to turn a blind eye to it all, trusting Adam far more than I should have." Expelling a shaky breath, she finally faced him again. "So when he ran away with Karen, the monster of jealousy finally took over my soul, blackening my heart until it snuffed out any love I may have had for my husband."

Ben reached to give her hand a squeeze. "That won't happen with us, Tess, I promise."

She stared at him for several seconds, regret etched into every pore of her face. "You can't promise that, Ben, because it's *my* Achilles' heel." A muscle jogged in her throat. "But I can promise *you* I will do everything in my power to make sure it doesn't happen to us."

He gave her a lazy smile while he slowly circled her palm with the pad of his thumb. "Put me under lock and key?"

She didn't crack a smile. "No, Ben, not you. Your temper."

He dropped her hand, eyes in a squint. "And what's that supposed to mean?"

Huffing out a sigh, she rose to pace the deck, her arms in a tight fold. "It means I have two conditions before I put that ring on my finger, Dr. Carmichael, and you can either comply or we can call it quits."

"You're joking." He stared, mouth dangling.

"Nope." Her chin jutted up as if to prove her point. "Dead serious, Dr. Doom, and no amount of kissy-face is going to change my mind."

He ground his jaw as he leaned back in his chair, elbows on the armrest and fingers laced. "And what exactly are these 'conditions,' Tess?" he said, giving her a death glare over the clasp of his hands.

She held up a finger. "One, I want you to deal with your bitterness toward Cam, because I refuse to marry a man where jealousy blackens his soul like it did mine."

His lips took a hard twist. "It won't, Tess, as long as he stays away from you."

Head cocked, she sucked air through teeth clenched in a tight smile. "Yeah, well, that's just it, Ben—Cam is my friend and as a widower whose wife died from cancer, he's helped me through my grief a lot, which means his friendship is here to stay—"

Ben shot to his feet. "Over my dead body," he snarled, "not if you become my wife."

She scrunched her nose. "Which is a pretty big 'if' right about now, Doc, so you might want to hear me out." She shrugged. "If not, I'll be happy to give your eulogy."

Leaning forward, he stared her down, hands perched low on his hips. "It would be downright irresponsible for you to even consider a friendship with another man, Tess, especially one I can't stand, and there isn't a marriage counselor alive who wouldn't agree with me."

"Maybe," she said with a slow nod, remembering that Adam had called her irresponsible once as well, and she supposed she had been. But this was different. Ben's ring wasn't on her finger yet, and unless he was willing to rid his heart of the bitterness he still harbored toward Cam, it didn't look likely. The barest semblance of a smile flickered at the edge of her mouth as she arched a brow, hoping a tease would soften the blow. "But then it's not the marriage counselors you want to take to bed, now is it, Dr. Doom?"

He turned away, slashing fingers through his hair. "This is nothing short of blackmail, and if you really loved me, you wouldn't do this."

"On the contrary, Ben, it's *because* I love you that I am doing this." His eyelids weighted closed after she rose to tenderly touch his arm, her voice gentle with the deep affection of a woman in love. "Why on earth would I stand by and allow the man I adore to be eaten up by bitterness when it's a cancer we can cure?"

His rib cage deflated in one, noisy bluster of air. "What else?" he bit out, tone as sharp as the hackles she'd apparently raised.

Silence reigned for several seconds before she whispered her second request. "I'd like for you and Cam to be friends."

He spun around so fast, it made her dizzy, his eyes wide sockets of shock. "Are you crazy?"

She moved in close to wrap her arms around his neck, tone husky to convey her intent. "Yes. Undeniably, unequivocally, and certifiably crazy in love with an unbelievably stubborn man with whom I hope to spend the rest of my life."

She stood on tiptoe to sway her lips against his, and he swallowed her up in a raspy groan. "God help me, I love you so much, it aches," he whispered, taking her mouth with a ferocity that mirrored the love that they bore.

She pulled away to cup his face with her hand, a sheen of tears in her eyes she hoped told him that she felt the same. "That's what I'm counting on, Dr. Doom," she whispered, nuzzling his mouth with a tenderness meant to drain all the anger from his soul. "But I promise you, Ben Carmichael, that once I say 'I do,' I'll do everything in my power to make the ache go away."

"You better," he said with a mock snarl, tugging her lip with his teeth, "if befriending Phillips doesn't kill me first." Emitting a growl, he wandered her throat before gently biting her earlobe, obviously to let her know he wasn't thrilled with her demands. "But you can't blame me if he spits in my eye."

"He won't," she said with an assurance she felt deep in her soul. "Cam's a reasonable man, Ben, so all you have to do is dig down for some of that hidden charm you've buried beneath the surface like gold. And I know it's there, Dr. Doom, or you wouldn't have stolen my heart like you did."

He grunted, tugging her back on his lap after sitting back down. "Yeah? Well you might have to do some pretty heavy convincing, Miss Perky, before I'm ready to share any charm." He burrowed his lips in the crook of her neck, making her squeal while his mouth wandered her throat.

"Well ..." She chuckled, twisting to do a little ear-tugging of her own. "Look at it this way. You won't just be doing it for your future wife, you'll be doing it for Karen," she said softly, reminding him of the struggle he'd overcome to forgive his ex-wife. "*And* yourself, Ben, since making amends to her brother will finally put all your demons to rest."

He pulled back to pierce her with his trademark Ben Carmichael glare, as if the significance of her statement had just hit him square in the chest. Inhaling deeply, he expelled it again in one long, arduous sigh of surrender. "I just hate to admit when you're right."

She feathered his ear with the softest of kisses before her mouth trailed to caress the bristle of his jaw. "I don't know why," she whispered, her chuckle lost in the sweet depths of their kiss. "I love you so much more when you do."

CHAPTER ELEVEN

"So, Caryl … how do you stay busy when there are no patients?" Sam tossed a syringe and empty vial of Glucagon into the disposal receptacle. He glanced at his watch, the six-year-old boy he treated for hypoglycemia long gone to the cafeteria with his teacher for needed sustenance. "Our patient won't be back for a few hours, so how does Jack kill time?"

Caryl paused as she wiped the examination table with disinfectant, eyes sparkling with interest. "Jack likes to stay busy, so he goes wherever he's needed—the fishing dock, stables, basketball court, or ball field, and then I call him when necessary. He's even been known to jump in the lake for a quick swim."

Sam stared at her as if she'd just told him Jack swam buck naked. "In the *lake?*" He didn't have to fake the shudder that rippled through him, the memory of almost drowning in a scummy algae lake at the age of ten shivering his skin. He wouldn't be here today if his foster mom hadn't finally dragged him out while her creep of a husband laughed and belched his beer. To this day, just the smell of a river or lake tainted Sam's tongue with the vile taste of dirty water, as polluted as the foster families to whom he was just a paycheck. "No, thanks—I prefer my water with chlorine, if you don't mind."

"Well, then …" She paused with a tilt of her head, a definite invitation in her tone. "I play a mean game of rummy if you care to take me on, Doc, or we also have every board game known to man."

Sam chuckled as he took off his Superman jacket, pretty sure Jack wouldn't want him playing games with a volunteer nursing student, rummy or otherwise. "Thanks, Caryl, but since this is my day off, I'd really like to get outside for a while, so how about a rain check?" Flashing a smile to assuage the disappointment he saw in her face, he strolled to the closet, gaze flicking out the windows to an azure sky tufted with clouds. His adrenalin immediately started flowing at the thought of helping out on a challenging and vigorous activity that would get his heart pumping.

Baseball.

Basketball.

Shannon O'Bryen.

His smile eased into a grin because that was definitely one woman who gave him a real workout in even attempting to be her friend. But Sam had never shied away from hard work or a challenge a day in his life, and he wasn't about to start now. Even *though* Shannon made it perfectly clear she wanted nothing to do with him, a fact that only intrigued him all the more. Because she was one of the few single women he actually felt comfortable with and whose company he enjoyed without the thought of anything more.

The memory of their kiss in the car flashed in his mind, and heat scorched through his body with a fury that both shocked and annoyed. He'd been drunk, that's all, a vice that always enhanced attraction for him, so it was no big deal. His brows dug in, creasing the bridge of his nose as he slipped his coat onto a hanger. Sheer gratitude for Shannon's help and input on Jazz and nothing more.

The thought of Jazz suddenly dimmed his good mood, and closing the door harder than intended, he vowed to find a way to win her back. His gaze snagged on a volunteer schedule tacked to the wall, and a slow smile curved on his lips as he scanned the list.

Outdoor Basketball—2:00-3:00 PM—Shannon O'Bryen and Lauren Miller.

Basketball? Being petite, gentle, and shy, Shannon hadn't struck Sam as the killer athletic type, which somehow made friendship with her all the more appealing. Of course, his chest still had dents in it from her stilettos, so he'd obviously misjudged her, no matter how angelic she'd appeared. But a basketball court was the perfect place to forge a friendship with a woman whose brain he could pick regarding Jazz without messy complications. A woman he could trust. A woman who was honest. *And* a woman who wasn't attracted to him, a situation that didn't sting quite so much once he realized how valuable it could be.

"I'll be back." He offered a smile and a salute to Caryl, then strode down the hall and out the front doors of what he fondly referred to as "the big house." Relishing the sunshine that soaked into his navy Polo, he followed the distant sound of a basketball. Making a left at the stables, he found her, she and another girl surrounded by a group of pre-teen kids while she demonstrated a perfect lay-up. Fascinated, he watched from a distance, her body poetry in motion as she dribbled several times before bounding off one foot to sweep the ball into the air. It swished into the net as neatly as she'd swished him out of her life with the jab of her heels.

No one noticed when he came closer. Hip cocked to the chain-link fence, he studied Shannon while she demonstrated the shot a few more times. Her instructions to the kids impressed him as much as her skill with omelets—*not to mention* hot pink basketball shorts that revealed beautifully toned legs, making his mouth go dry.

"Okay, guys, if you can shoot a free-throw, you can easily learn a lay-up," she told them, "and it's important to know how because they're hard to defend, as Lauren and I will demonstrate." Taking her position, she backed up and took a few dribbles while Lauren—all of four-foot-eleven, maybe—tried to counter, but she was no match for Shannon, whose ball glided in as if the net were calling it home. "See? A good lay-up is really hard to stop."

"True, but there *are* ways." Sam strolled onto the court, fingers twitchy to get his hands on the ball.

Shannon spun around along with the others, her messy ponytail as off-kilter as the look on her face.

"Doctor Sam!" one of the boys shouted, a prior patient who gashed his lip on a slide to home plate on Sam's last visit. "I'll bet you can stop her."

"Well, I'd sure like to try if Miss Miller doesn't mind?"

A volunteer who looked to be in her thirties, Lauren Miller gracefully stepped aside with a wide smile. "Have at it, Doc, because I need all the help I can get with Slam-Dunk here."

"Slam-Dunk, huh?" Sam's gaze met Shannon's, grinning when her lips pursed in a polite smile. "That's what they used to call me in college." He winked just to get on her nerves. "And some nurses at Memorial still do."

"All right, everyone," she said, turning her back on him to address the group. "Not only will I demonstrate how easily you can get by the defense with a lay-up, but I'll show you how to put another 'player' in his place." She got into position, dribbling the ball while she seared him with a look. "And I use the term literally."

He chuckled as he took his stance between Shannon and the net, body loose while he addressed the group with hands held high in defensive mode to block her shot. "Okay, guys, the trick is to prevent the guy with the ball from getting under or even close to the basket like th—" His words died on his lips when she gave a slight fake to the left and slid by him so fast, the ball whooshed over his fingertips into the net before he could even jump.

"Nice trick, Doc," she said with a smirk, bobbling the ball back and forth while she resumed her position. "Got any others?"

"Just one." Returning to his position, he pinned her with a narrow gaze, ready to close off the side she favored for her turn, which had been on the right all three times. Before she could get the shot off, he blocked her right side, forcing her to the left. He grinned when the ball bounced off the rim with a beautiful clunk. Snatching it mid-air, he turned back to the kids. "Whenever possible, you want to block whichever side the player favors to make him or her go in another direction." He bounced the ball several times before tossing it back to Shannon with a wink. "Because you *always* make them adjust to you," he said with a cocky grin, pinning her with a penetrating look.

"Can you play a game with us, Doctor Sam?" his former patient asked, and Shannon cut him off at the pass with a glance at her watch.

"Sorry, guys, but our time's almost up, and Miss Myra will have my head if you're not cleaned up in time for chapel, so we'll play a game next Saturday, okay?"

Groans filled the air as the kids—a motley mix of pre-teen boys and girls—trudged from the court while Shannon gave Lauren a hug. "Thanks for filling in for Cat, Lauren—you were a huge help, and I think the kids had a lot of fun with a game between the guys and the girls."

Lauren tugged the basketball from Shannon's hands before shooting Sam a smile. "My pleasure, Shan, but I think the fun started when the real competition arrived. I'll put the ball back in the gym closet for you so you can head out early for that special dinner you mentioned." She tossed a wink over her shoulder. "Have fun."

"Thanks, Lauren." Without a word to Sam, Shannon marched to the fence where a backpack hung over the post. Looping it over her shoulder, she took off for the parking lot, forcing Sam to catch up.

"Special dinner, huh?" he said with an easy grin, falling in step beside her. "Sounds like a hot date. Hope you're not wearing stilettos ..."

She whirled around with a tight-lipped smile, which he realized was her version of a scowl. "Are you following me?"

"Bite your tongue," he said with an innocent lift of brows, hand to his chest. "I'm a player, not a stalker, remember?"

"Same difference," she muttered, turning on her heel to practically sprint to her car. "Both put the fear of God in me."

"Well, lucky for you we're friends, right?" He reached to take her backpack, grinning when she screeched to a halt to play tug-of-war in the middle of the lawn. "Come on, Teach, let me carry your books for you, will you?"

She sighed and let go, mouth clamped as she picked up her pace. "Thank you."

"Hey, where'd you learn to play hoops like that?" he asked. "You're good."

The tiniest crack of a smile appeared as she tramped over the lawn, eyes straight ahead. "When you're the quiet twin with an overly competitive jock for a sister and an older brother who hates to lose, one becomes adept at holding her own." She gave him a cursory glance. "Survival of the fittest."

He grinned and rubbed his chest. "Yeah, I know, and I have the holes in my chest to prove it."

She peeked at him out of the corner of her eye, her pace slowing as she gnawed at her lip. "Did I really hurt you?"

"Only my pride," he said with a smile, grateful she was actually talking to him at all. His mouth took a right. "Oh, and my backside, but I won't show you *that* bruise 'cause it ain't pretty." He made a great show of rubbing the back of his head. "Not to mention the lump on my skull that, amazingly enough, lingered long after the bruises on my face." He adjusted her backpack on his shoulder. "Which kind of gives a whole new meaning to the phrase 'head over heels,' you know?"

A smile squirmed on her lips despite the haze of color that dusted her cheeks as she picked up speed, eyes trained on the parking lot like a heat-seeking missile.

"Hey, I have a proposition for you," he said, loping after her while her backpack bounced on his back.

She never missed a beat as she hit the pavement of the parking lot, homing in on her car. "You want me to teach self-defense to the women you date?"

"Cute, but no." He waited while she fished her keys out of the backpack and opened her car, leaning in to start it so she could roll down the windows. "I'd like to pick your brain as a woman about how to get Jasmine back because I'm obviously doing something wrong."

She slacked a hip, arms in a fold as her smile tipped off-center. "You think?"

"Yes, Miss Smarty Pants, I think. Wednesday's my day off, and I know you get through here about three, so how about a quick coffee consult after—say, four at Cutter's Point? Because I need a coach, and you're perfect."

"Because I'm immune to your charm and see all your faults?"

"Yeah, I guess," he said, her casual assessment stinging more than it should. He rubbed at his chest as if those stupid heels had spiked him all over again. "But I'd wish you'd sugar-coat it a little more, kiddo, because I'm starting to get a complex. So … are you free next Wednesday afternoon at four?"

"I don't sugar-coat, Sam." She reached for her backpack, attempting to tug it off his shoulder. "Or coach anything but basketball and softball."

He tightened his hold on the backpack, giving her the half-lidded smile that usually worked wonders on the nurses at Memorial. "Come on, Shannon, one hour of your time over a cup of coffee is all I'm asking—is that so difficult?"

"With you, yes," she said with a pull of her backpack, which didn't budge beneath Sam's iron grip. "Sorry, Doc, but I'm allergic to players, so I can't because I'll break out." She gave the backpack another yank.

He held the backpack out of her reach, reduced to begging. "Shannon, *please?* I need you bad, and I'll pay whatever price you say."

One perfectly shaped brow jagged high. "A little privacy, maybe?" Heels digging in, she tried to wring the pack from his grasp. "Sorry, Sam, I'm not your girl, so I'll thank you to give-me-my-backpack …"

"Nope, not till you say yes," he quipped, digging in some heels of his own.

"Over-my-dead—" She gave one final wrench that sent her and the backpack flying backwards, her butt hitting the pavement hard.

"Backpack?" he finished for her, pouncing on a number of papers that went flying before the wind could carry them away. He added them back to a packet of sheets he picked up, all fanned out on the ground, then extended a hand to help her up. "Sorry, but this is just another reason you should say yes, because now we'll have matching bruises."

Ignoring his hand, she popped up a lot quicker than he had the night she'd kicked him out of her car, a hint of her Irish temper flaring for the very first time. "No-no-no-*no!*" she said in a near hiss, emphasizing each word with a hasty pluck of papers, one batch at a time. "Don't force me to get a restraining order, Cunningham, because I will."

She took a stab at grabbing the final bunch in his hand, but he snatched it away, his mouth dropping open when he realized what it was.

LOVE EVERLASTING
A novel

"Oh my gosh," he said with a chuckle, speed-reading the first page, "you're writing a *romance* novel?"

"Give-me-that-*now*!" she said, her words clipped while she jump-shot in the air, trying to snatch the papers he held over her head.

"'*True Love. An oxymoron if ever there was,*'" he read in a sappy voice, continuing on with a chuckle while she clobbered his chest. "'Olivia Brighton issued a rare grunt as she stormed up the stairs to her apartment, desperate to get inside before anymore tears leaked from her eyes.'"

Shannon whacked him hard, leaving an impression of her fist to match the holes from her heels. "Give-me-those-papers-right-now-or-so-help-me-I will-knee-you …"

He backed away a healthy distance, laughing as he waved the papers. "I'll tell you what, Angel Eyes, for the sweet and shy twin, you sure are feisty." He rifled through a few more pages, his grin growing with every line. "Whoa … and sexy, too, you little vamp! Who knew?"

That did it. Hurling her backseat door open, she yanked out a bat and chased him around the car till his sides ached from laughter. "Your knee caps are in trouble, mister, if you don't give that back right now."

"Okay, okay," he said with a grin, taking great precaution in handing the manuscript over. "But I sure never figured you for writing a …" He paused, face in a scrunch as he tried to remember what Jazz called the racy books she read with bare-chested men on the covers. He snapped his fingers. "A bodice ripper, that's it."

"It is *not* a bodice ripper," she muttered, stuffing the papers back into her backpack. "It's a sweet romance where people are fully clothed. And it's not mine."

He squinted at her, hands low on his hips. "You didn't write it?"

Her mouth compressed.

"*Ah-ha!* You *did* write it, but you don't want anybody to know, do you?"

She expelled way too big of a sigh for such a little girl. "I'm a ghost writer, okay? But I signed a secrecy clause and nobody knows, so you can't breathe a word."

A grin inched across his face. "Nobody?"

She tossed the backpack into her back seat and closed her back door, peering up with a plea in her baby blues. "My family knows I freelance as an editor for a publisher friend of mine. But they *don't* know I'm actually *writing* a romance novel for one of my publisher's most important authors who has run into some health issues. So you have to promise not to say a word."

He gave a lazy shrug, butting a hip to her car. "No prob, Shan. After all—what are friends for?"

Her pretty pink biker tank rose and fell in relief before she slid into her car, the tension in her face easing into a weary smile. "Thanks, Sam, I really appreciate it."

"Sure thing, kiddo, mum's the word." He closed her door and leaned in, arms folded on the open window. "Glad we sealed the deal."

Her hand froze on the gear shift. "What deal? We don't have a deal."

He traced a finger down her arm to rile a little fire in her. "Sure we do, Angel Eyes—my silence for your coaching."

She slapped his hand away as her eyes narrowed. "Blackmailer on top of a stalker and player? Gee, Doc, you get better by the moment."

"I know." He tapped on her door with a waggle of brows. "Just imagine how good I'll be after you're done?"

She groaned and dropped her head on the wheel.

"Cutter's Point, Wednesday at four." He pushed away from the car and gave her a dazzling smile. "I need you, Shan," he said, hands over his chest in true drama, befitting his nickname. "My heart's sick over Jazz, so I'm in a really bad way."

"I know, me too." She jerked the car into gear, and he jumped back for safety while she glanced in the rearview mirror. Broiling him with a look, she gunned the accelerator and tore out of the lot, her final words making him grin. "Only mine's indigestion."

CHAPTER TWELVE

"Uh-oh, Jack's gonna toss somebody in the drink …" Sprawled across Shannon's bed with a bowl of nuts, Cat popped a peanut in her mouth as she laid on her side, elbow cocked and head in her hand. "But it's definitely worth the swim, Shan. I'm jealous."

"It's *not* a date," Shannon emphasized, her clenched response sounding far more like Cat than herself. "It's coffee at Cutter's, for pity's sake, just to talk."

Cat wiggled her brows. "You mean he actually uses those luscious lips for other things?" she teased, her comment warming the blood in Shannon's cheeks.

Lacey snatched a handful of peanuts from Cat's bowl and scooted against the headboard, knees to her chest. "I don't care, Shan," she said while Shannon pinned her hair in a haphazard messy bun designed to discourage male attention, "Jack's gonna blow when he finds out. If he's told me once, he's told me a dozen times he doesn't want Sam anywhere near you or Cat."

"Which kind of ticks me off," Cat groused, "because I'm twenty-six, and the last thing I need is two mothers."

"Jack won't find out if you don't tell him, Lace." Shannon glanced at her sister-in-law in the mirror, grateful she could trust Lacey to keep her secret. "Believe me, Jack has *nothing* to worry about because the last thing I need—*or want*—right now is to spend time with Sam Cunningham. I'm up to my eyeballs in edits on several books my publisher's been waiting for, so all I really want to do is cozy up with my manuscript, not some pushy player looking for advice."

Lacey zipped her mouth. "My lips are sealed, Shan—you have

my word."

Cat's husky chuckle drifted from the bed. "But I'll bet Sam's won't be …"

"And trust me," Shannon continued, not even validating Cat's remark with a response, "I don't want Dr. Love anywhere near me either, but it's just one time so he can pick my brain on how to win his girlfriend back."

"Your brain?" Lacey pursed her lips in a sweet smile. "You mean you actually have one? After all, you did say 'yes' to Sam Cunningham."

"For heaven's sake, it's a cappuccino in a public place for maybe an hour," Shannon stressed with a stronger tone than usual, more to convince herself than her sister and sister-in-law. "Then I never have to talk to the man again."

Cat sighed. "That's okay—that's one guy where talking is overrated. I'd just want to look at him." A dangerous grin slid across her face. "Well, maybe not just look."

"I'll take a picture for you," Shannon muttered, slipping a tank top over her head.

A peanut halfway to her mouth, Cat paused with a serious look as if she couldn't believe her luck. "Gosh, Shan—would you?"

"*Please* tell me you're wearing a blouse over that," Lacey said, nodding at Shannon's form-fitting tank—the loosest one she owned with the least amount of cleavage.

Shannon shimmied on an old pair of jean shorts. "Oh, for crying out loud, Lace, it's almost 90 degrees, and I'm wearing my grungiest shorts, beat-up athletic shoes, and not a stitch of makeup, so doesn't that convince you I have no interest at all?"

"No, because you're one of the few girls who can pull it off, Shan—a natural beauty."

"Why, thank you," Cat said, preening with a pose in the mirror.

Rolling her eyes, Lacey refocused on Shannon, mouth swerving sideways as she popped a peanut. "And trust me, Shan, when it comes to Sam Cunningham and women, *nothing* is for 'heaven's sake.'"

"Oh, I don't know," Cat said with a sigh, rolling over on her back to stare at the ceiling with a dreamy smile. "Sounds like heaven to me …"

"Oh my gosh, when on earth did you get so guy crazy, Catfish?" Lacey launched a peanut, bouncing it off Cat's head. "Are we going to have to lock you up after dark?"

Cat picked the nut out of her hair and aimed it right back. She heaved a heavy sigh, lips in a pout. "Don't have to, 'Mother.' Between Mom's eagle eye and Jack's Rapunzel mindset in keeping me away from his friends, I'm trussed up tighter than Fort Knox."

"That's because to Jack, you and Shan are pure gold and always have been. He loves you and wants to keep the wrong guys away, so sue him."

Cat halted to squint at Lacey, peanut in hand. "You think I can?"

Lacey grinned and fired another peanut.

Blasting out a heavy sigh, Cat stared at the ceiling, melancholy tingeing her tone. "Shan and I will probably die lonely old maids because there sure aren't many guys around here."

"Not lonely," Shan affirmed, rifling through her wallet to make sure she had money. The last thing she wanted was for Player-Boy to buy her anything. "Happily accomplished and content—at least me." She slipped her purse over her shoulder and sat down on the edge of the bed next to Cat, grabbing a few nuts. "You? You could be settled with babies and a white picket fence in the next three years if you'd just give the guys at Hope Church a chance."

"Yeah," Lacey piped up, "both Luke Calloway and Jordan Murphy have asked you out, but you just blow 'em off, Cat. So why is that?"

Cat scrunched her nose. "Don't be ticked, Lace, but I'm looking for a little more excitement in my life right now, and somehow, I don't see it at Hope Church." She tossed a peanut in the air, snapping it with her mouth. "I guess I have this thing for bad boys, you know?"

"Yeah, I know," Lacey said with a wry twist of lips. "That's what worries me."

Cat rolled on her side like before, head propped. "Yeah? Well, welcome to the club, Carmichael, because you sure put us through the wringer before you got religion."

"What about Chase?" Shannon asked as she slipped a sock on her foot, thinking the good-looking associate pastor at Hope Church was just what her sister needed. "He's the best of both worlds, Cat—a bad boy who found religion, just like Jack."

"Yeah, he's hot, no doubt about that." Her face screwed in a frown as if she were contemplating the option. "But pastor types like Chase have such strict policies, not to mention preaching at you all the time, and I want to have some fun for a while. Call me crazy, but right now I'd trust a bad boy way before a preacher because at least he's looking for fun, too."

"Call you crazy?" Lacey grunted. "You *are* crazy, O'Bryen. I should have Jack fix you up with a psych major."

Cat glanced up, a sparkle of excitement in her eyes. "Ooooo … you think he would?"

Shannon chuckled to deflect her worry over a sister whose interest in spiritual things was on the wane. "Then you'd be locked up for good, sis, once he finds out how crazy you are."

"Yeah, crazy fun," Cat said with a gleam of trouble in her eyes.

Shannon pinched her sister's waist, Cat's slow spiritual decline at the top of her prayer list these days. "Uh, you do remember the pact we made with Jack way back when, right? Where we promised to wait until marriage for certain kinds of 'fun'?"

A heavy sigh blustered from Cat's lips. "Yeah, yeah, just another example of Jack's lock and key, Shan, but don't worry. I'll do my best to honor it, but only because I love you."

"And God?" Lacey asked, a sobriety in her eyes despite the smile on her face.

"Yes, Mother, I love God, so you can tuck your sermon back in your pocket." Cat sat up, as if she were ready to flee any conversation that included spirituality. "I just don't have to *like* Him a lot right now, that's all."

Shannon's heart constricted. A 'dislike' that had clearly been deepening over the last few months.

Since Daddy died.

"So don't go all gloomy on me, guys," Cat said quickly, all humor suddenly depleted in both her tone and her voice. "God and I are just taking a break from each other for a while till I can hash out a few things in my mind, that's all."

"He's real good at hashing things out, Cat," Lacey said quietly, "but not if you don't talk to Him."

"Yeah, well, I'm still a little ticked over Daddy, Lace, so maybe it's better I wait." She hooked an arm around Shannon's shoulders. "Besides, you have bigger problems right now since the sweet and spiritual twin has a date with the dangerous Dr. Love."

"I keep telling you—it's *not* a date!" Shannon insisted, unlatching Cat's arm when she bent to put on her shoe. "You guys already know I have a strict no-dating policy, so I guarantee it won't be this twin giving anyone any problems."

Lacey nudged Shannon's hip with her foot, her tease laced with warning in spite of the grin on her face. "It better not be, Shan, now or ever, because Jack and I have enough trouble on our hands keeping your evil twin in line."

"Ha!" Cat said, rising from the bed with a lazy stretch. "I'd say Shan's the one with trouble on her hands because according to half the nurses at Memorial, Sam Cunningham is an addiction without any cure." She bent to press a kiss to her sister's head before tweaking her neck. "So stay on your guard, sis, because I'd sure hate to see the good twin go through a nasty withdrawal."

Shannon huffed out a sigh, bending to tie her other shoe.

Join the club.

CHAPTER THIRTEEN

One leg jiggling over his knee, Sam drummed his fingers on the patio café table at Cutter's, glancing at his watch for the umpteenth time. "Where the heck is she?" he muttered, well aware it was two minutes to four, so Shannon wasn't technically late. But it felt like he'd been waiting for days, the Pepcid AC he took a while ago doing nothing for the churning in his stomach. He could blame it on the four cappuccinos he'd had since he'd arrived an hour ago, he supposed. Or the ten-mile jog this morning before he went home and changed, which had been more of a run for his life than a jog. Or even the stupid bees that buzzed around the pot of petunias hanging next to his table. He swatted at one who zipped too close. Bees made him downright nervous because he absolutely despised getting stung.

Much like Jasmine was about to do.

He upended his cup, then scowled when sludge trickled down his throat. Nope, it didn't take a medical degree to diagnose the awful pains in his stomach because he knew exactly why they were there. Jazz was coming over tomorrow to pick up the rest of her things.

Including her favorite swimsuit.

For a trip to the Bahamas.

With the intern.

"Where are you, Shannon, I need you," he said under his breath, switching legs to twitch the other over his knee while the leather tie on his tan Topsiders flopped in the air, as goosey as him. He looked at his watch again before scanning the parking lot, the sight of her car pulling in both expanding his rib cage in relief and racing his pulse more than the stupid coffee. She got out of her car and he exhaled slowly, thinking she had to be one of the purest, most natural women he'd ever seen, sun glinting off strawberry blonde hair thrown into an adorable messy bun as unpretentious as she.

A slow smile slid across his face as he watched her, always amazed how unspoiled she looked with her clean peaches-and-cream complexion and smattering of near-invisible freckles. Like a Georgia peach, just beginning to turn lush and ripe. Even from across the parking lot, he could see a spark of fire in those blue eyes, and his smile blossomed into a grin at the tight press of her lips. Generous lips usually full in repose, the color of pale raspberries and just as sweet.

Not that he was ever going to taste them again. His mouth quirked as he snatched his cell off the table and slipped it into the pocket of his creased Brooks Brothers shorts. Because Shannon couldn't abide him as a man, which made her the perfect choice as a female friend. As much as Shannon's sweet and pure appearance inspired nibbling, he'd discovered since that night in his kitchen that he liked having a woman as a good friend, so he wasn't about to botch it up again. This friendship was too important.

Because Jazz is too important.

"Hey, you didn't have to bother dressing up on my account," he teased as he rose, her bare-bones getup only reinforcing her wholesome appearance. His grin ramped up to double dimples when those porcelain cheeks ripened with a blush, wondering why on earth he got a kick out of tweaking such a sweet and shy kid. Maybe because that sweet mouth pinched in restraint and those searing blue eyes challenged him to trip that glorious temper no one else ever saw, unleashing words no one else ever had the guts to say.

The truth.

"So … what's your pleasure, Angel Eyes?" he said, pushing in his chair.

The edge of her mouth ticked up. "A tall, frosty glass of peach iced tea." She batted his hand away from the small of her back when he tried to usher her inside. "At home."

"Your wish is my command," he said, looping her waist to whirl her back toward the parking lot. "Just lead the way, kiddo."

"Not a chance, Doc." Slapping his arm away, she ricocheted back to the entrance like a paddleball on a string, ducking inside before he could even open the door. "Jack would blow a gasket if he saw me out with you, which come to think of it, might be a good thing." She lobbed a one-sided smile over her shoulder. "*Way* cheaper than a restraining order."

She marched right up to the counter and ordered a peach iced tea, then tussled with him about paying for her own, losing the battle when the young woman deferred to him with a dazzling smile.

"You know, it's downright criminal how you get your way with women." Shaking her head, Shannon made a beeline for the outside patio.

"Not all of them," Sam said with a wry smile, racing to open the door for her, "which is why you're here, remember?"

"Really?" Shannon seated herself at the table, offering a flutter of lashes that tickled him because it seemed so out of character. "I thought it was because of extortion."

He grinned and slid in his chair, questioning his sanity in purchasing a fifth cappuccino. "Come on, Shannon, 'extortion' sounds so crass. Let's just think of it as two friends helping each other out."

Cracking a skewed smile, she perched on the edge of her chair with hands neatly folded on the table. "Like I said—extortion. But since we're both here and I'm not wearing heels, why don't we get down to business?"

"See? That's what I like about you," he said with a chuckle, "you don't mince words; you get right to the point." He took a healthy swig of his coffee, eyeing her over the rim with a teasing look. "With or without stilettos." Setting his cup down, he sucked in a deep breath and propped his arms on the table, all of his good humor bleeding out along with a long, bumpy sigh.

"She's going to the Bahamas with him," he said quietly, just saying the words out loud a reality crash that sent his stomach into a free fall. Head bowed, he gouged his eye socket with the pad of his thumb. The happy-go-lucky persona he worked so hard to maintain with an upbeat manner and maniacal regimen suddenly stripped away to reveal the wounded man inside. For some reason he couldn't ascertain, Shannon's presence allowed him the luxury of brutal honesty, exposing deeply buried feelings no one ever saw—sometimes not even him.

"Oh, Sam …" Shannon's whisper carried all the tender compassion he'd known it would, the barest touch of her fingers to his a balm he'd seldom experienced before. Certainly not from a mother who'd deserted him at the age of five nor from a long line of foster parents more interested in the subsidy than in him. And one sure didn't unload true feelings and failures with other guys, not even good friends like Jack, and never *ever* with women. Especially a woman like Jazz. No, he'd learned long ago that image was all he really had to ward off the pain, all he could really count on to keep him afloat when others deserted him. And they always did.

Eventually.

His dad. His mom. His foster parents. His fiancée in college.

Even Jazz.

Shannon gave his arm a gentle squeeze. "I can't tell you how sorry I am."

"Yeah, me too," he muttered, voice barely audible as his gaze lagged into a vacant stare, memories of past relationships tainting his mind. Far as Sam could tell, love was little more than a commodity, as fleeting as the people who stole in and out of his life, a revolving door of rejection that always hit him hard. Which is why image was everything. A message to the world that he had it all, no matter how many people screwed around with his heart.

Unfortunately, Jazz was not only an important part of that image, she was the one woman who'd managed to make him care despite his "player" charade—that careful façade that had both bolstered his confidence and kept rejection at bay.

Until Jazz.

The one challenge he had yet to conquer.

His mouth tamped in a tight line. And he'd never walked away from a challenge yet. Without thinking, he downed his cappuccino in a series of scalding glugs, as if it were the whiskey with which he'd numbed the pain at the Memorial fundraiser. Slamming the cup on the table, he shoved it away, his voice taking on an edge. "But, it is what it is," he said, huffing out a noisy sigh. He peered up. "Now I just need to figure out how to get it back to what it 'was.'"

Serious blue eyes stared back, soft and serene, reminding him just why he'd nicknamed her Angel Eyes. "How about … to what it *could be* instead?" she said quietly, and his pulse hitched hard for several precarious seconds, the impact of her words as loud as if she'd blasted them through a megaphone.

He sat straight up, adrenaline pumping through his veins along with the caffeine. "Yeah … yeah, that's exactly what I want." Shaking his head over the brilliance of her statement, he fanned fingers through his hair with an open-mouthed smile, wondering how on earth he'd managed without a female friend like Shannon all of this time. "I mean, that wasn't what I was after in the beginning, I'll admit. I just wanted what we had before—a nice, cozy relationship with lots of fun. But since I've lost her twice now, it's been like a kick in the head, you know? Making me realize just how much I care about her and want her in my life."

He grinned outright, the revelation escalating his mood as much as the cappuccino. "I never even thought about it being any better." Tunneling his hand through the curls at the back of his head, it latched there as he stared at her in awe. "I swear, Shannon, you're amazing. One sentence. One mind-blowing sentence, and you change everything for me, parsing it down to something so startlingly simple."

Those blue eyes softened with sympathy. "Not so simple, Sam, because it means *you* have to change in order for the relationship to change."

"I can do that," he said with the utmost confidence, jaw firm. "If I can put myself through med school and college, score a spot in Augustine's practice—the chief pediatrician at Memorial—and compete in an Iron Man Triathlon, I can do this." He glanced at his watch. "And I'll start tonight when Jasmine comes over to pick up a swimsuit she left and the rest of her things. All I need is your input as to what you think I should say and do."

A twinkle lit in her eyes. "Uh, we're talking a major overhaul, Dr. Love," she said with a patient smile, "and one hour over coffee and tea isn't going to cut it."

"My thoughts, exactly." He rose and pushed in his chair. "But two or three will at least get me started and hopefully prevent me from making a fool of myself tonight." He cleared the trash from the table and pitched it in the receptacle before hooking her arm to pull her up. "So … how are you at miniature golf?"

Shannon blinked, snatching up her tea before he pushed in her chair. "Pardon me?"

He gave her a lopsided smile as he tugged her toward his car. "I've had five cappuccinos, and I'm ready to jump out of my skin, kiddo, so I need to do something active while you give me advice on how to handle tonight." He paused, eyes in a squint. "You are good, aren't you?"

"At advice?" Eyes wide, the heels of her Nikes seemed to drag across the asphalt.

"No, I already know that. At miniature golf." Opening the passenger side of his car, he winked, leg slacked while he waited for her to get in. "I learn best when crushing competition."

Mouth unhinged, she perched a hand on her hip, challenge luring a smile to her lips. "Good, because I advise best when crushing pride."

He grinned, palm extended to invite her to get in. "Then crush on, Teach, because I've got an awful lot to learn."

"Yeah, me too," Shannon said, her smile taking a slant when he closed her door. "Like how to say 'no.'"

Sam chuckled as he strode around his car to get in on the other side. "Now, you know you don't mean that, because this will be fun. Besides," he said, glancing over his shoulder before easing out of his spot. He gave her a wink. "Something tells me this could be the beginning of a beautiful friendship."

CHAPTER FOURTEEN

A *beautiful friendship?* Shannon stifled a grunt as she watched Sam bag a hole-in-one on the third hole.

"Score!" He swooped his ball out of the cup with a little-boy grin that scored more than his stupid hole-in-one.

Yeah, a real beautiful friendship. For Dr. Love, maybe, but for me? Shannon recorded his score on the tally sheet with a quiet sigh. *Not so much.* Not when the man she swore to avoid forever had railroaded her into having fun with him, laughing with him, seeing him in a light that didn't bode well for her heart.

In a mere thirty minutes at Putt 'N Stuff golf, she'd seen a side of the "player" that not only surprised her, but alarmed her as well. Whether opening car doors for her or guiding her with a protective hand to the small of her back, to shamelessly flirting with the elderly cashier or paying for Carol Green's mini-golf with her two grandsons Trevor and Tyler—Shannon soon understood Sam was a person who thrived on serving others. Jack had told her as much, but she'd let the player reputation sour her opinion of a man who mentored foster kids and coached basketball for inner city youth. It didn't take long to see he had a way of making everyone feel special, and in a clutch of her heart, Shannon finally understood one reason why. Because the little boy inside—the abandoned orphan lost in the foster-care shuffle—wanted to feel special too.

"Hey, awesome shot, Sam!" one of Carol's grandsons said whose mini-golf game he'd paid for. His brother and Grandma Carol quickly echoed their approval, and Sam grinned like he'd just won the U.S. Open.

"So, Teach," he said as he ambled back, club over his shoulder, "how should I handle tonight? You know, when Jazz comes over?"

"How do you want to handle it?" she asked, strolling to the next tee.

He grunted. "By ignoring her, but she has a key, so it's too late to change the locks."

Shannon assessed the obstacles on the green before taking her stance, feet a shoulder width apart as she eyed the hole. "Interaction is important, Sam, and you don't have many other opportunities to talk to her, do you?"

"Just on rounds twice a week since she's a Peds nurse at Memorial, then sometimes weekends when I'm on call. But not often unless she comes into the office to see her dad or I run into her at Memorial hangouts."

With a putt fine-tuned in high school golf class and backyard sessions with Jack, Shannon sailed the ball smoothly over a hump to bank off the back edge, missing the hole by six inches or more. She wrinkled her nose. "Then you have to take advantage of this opportunity," she called over her shoulder as she finished the hole with a birdie. "How have you reacted to her in the past when you've run into her after she's broken it off?"

"Hey, nice one, kiddo." Club over his shoulder, he cocked a hip, one hand buried in his pocket while his smile faded into a scowl. "I usually give her the cold shoulder till she needs one to cry on, and then I cave because I can't stand to see her unhappy."

Shannon retrieved her ball, wondering how a guy with such a soft heart could so casually toy with the hearts of so many women. She halted halfway on the mini-green, a sudden thought taking her so by surprise, she actually grinned outright. "Well, then …" she said as she approached with a reflective grate of her lip, suddenly realizing just how valuable Sam could be in the novel she was ghostwriting. *Love Everlasting* was book three in a trilogy by one of her publisher's top-selling authors, but the poor woman had had a breakdown and couldn't write a word. So now Shannon was on the hot seat with a skeletal synopsis about a playboy and a princess. Adrenalin coursed as she suddenly saw

Sam in a whole new light, wondering if God was trying to kill two birds with one stone: saving Sam along with Shannon's sketchy manuscript. She paused in front of him, almost giddy over the research that he could provide. "Then let's introduce her to the new Sam, shall we?"

He squinted while he recorded her score. "I don't know, Shan—I'm kind of fond of the old one."

Her smile canted as she strolled back to check out the tally. "Yeah, well, whose fondness you looking for, Doc—yours or Jasmine's?"

"Okay, I'll give you that one." He handed her the scorecard before teeing up, besting her birdie with another hole in one and a cocky smile. "But the mini-golf win is all mine."

She logged in his score with a scrunch of her nose. "Gosh, Doc, between your inflated ego and bloodthirsty competitive streak, we may never find the other Sam."

"We have to, Shannon—my life depends on it."

She glanced up, the sobriety of his tone stilling her hand on the scorecard. The serious Sam was back—his faint smile at odds with the solemnity in his eyes.

Her heart softened. "It does, Sam, more than you know. Women want men with depth and values, not fast cars and fancy moves. They want a man they can respect. That's the main way a woman falls in love. Prove to Jazz you've changed and are worth her love and respect."

"And how do I do that?" he asked quietly, probing her with a look that said golf was suddenly the last thing on his mind.

She sighed, well aware there was only one way she knew for a person to really change, and she wasn't sure Sam was ready to hear it. But he needed to—badly—and for the first time ever, she actually understood why God might want her to become his friend. An honest-to-goodness friend who put aside her own desires to impact someone else with the truth. In the slow blink of Sam's eyes, she felt her perspective shift, suddenly seeing beyond the expensive clothes, good looks, and effortless charm to a man whose life truly did depend on what Shannon could give.

Faith.

And what Sam could give as well, the counter thought came.

Heartbreak.

Shaking the fear off, she jotted his score and handed the card back, her mind made up to be the person God had called her to be. Not a woman attracted to or repelled by a player she'd hoped to avoid, or even a ghostwriter desperate for research. Nope. But someone who had a chance to impact that player for good and change not only his life, but his eternity as well. A mission to mend the badly bruised heart of a rejected little boy, who drew his confidence and love from perishable things.

Warn the rich people of this world not to be proud or to trust in wealth that is easily lost. Tell them to have faith in God ...

Shannon studied him now, this self-assured man whose very confidence was as much a façade as the image he strove to project and knew God had graced her with his trust. The trust of a man who didn't trust—or open up—to many people. A golden opportunity to lay down her own fears and insecurities for the sake of another, opting to trust the very God she espoused with her own vulnerable heart.

Greater love has no one than this: to lay down one's life for one's friends.

"How do you do it?" she repeated, awed by the peace that suddenly flooded her soul. "You do it by learning to respect and love yourself, Sam, seeing yourself through God's eyes rather than through your own shallow trappings."

His gaze was wary. "Religion? You're really going to play that card with me?"

"It's not a card, Sam," she said softly, "it's a lifestyle that can not only help you win the game, but the very desires of your heart."

His low chuckle vibrated the air as he shook his head. "I'm not looking to warm a pew, Teach; I'm just looking for how I should handle Jazz tonight."

She tilted her head to assess him in that point-blank manner that always seemed to penetrate his charm and pretense. "*Which,* you would learn in that pew if you decided to warm it. But the basics? Forgive her, treat her with kindness, be there for her as a friend *without* strings attached." She patted his face with a parental air, his sandpaper jaw reminding her he wasn't that little boy she often saw beneath the surface. "Unconditional love, Doc, the kind that God gave to us."

"And that really works?" He squinted at her, disbelief crinkling his brows.

Her smile indulged. "Worked for me, big boy, and the Good Book says 'love never fails.'"

He cut loose with a grunt. "Yeah, well you can't prove it by me."

"That's because your love is self-absorbed and self-serving," she said in a matter-of-fact tone.

His jaw fell open. "Gosh, Shan, why don't you tell me what you really think?"

"I'm trying," she said with a squirm of a smile. Teeing her ball, she glanced up to see the wounded look he always teased her with that was more real than anyone knew. Her smile broke through, honest and tender and sweet for a friend she suspected she would come to care for a lot. "Because one of my most annoying qualities is telling my friends the truth, Sam, so I always will." The affection in his eyes suddenly fluttered her stomach, and cheeks growing warm, she quickly looked away to focus her gaze on the ball, palms suddenly sticky on the club.

At least, most of the time ...

CHAPTER FIFTEEN

"Soooo, Daddy ... I've been dying to ask. How did it go with Tess?"

Ben looked up, smiling despite the question that annoyed. Lacey looked like his little girl again, legs tucked to her chest as she leaned against Jack on the back seat of Ben's Formula while they bobbed in the ocean. Arms circling her knees, she worried her lip, obviously dying to ask since she'd returned from their vacation on Sunday. *Especially* since he'd told them about his marina debacle with Tess right before they left.

Jack chuckled and tweaked the back of her neck. "Uh, maybe your dad's not ready to talk about it, Lace. Ever think about that?"

Ben cut loose with a weighty sigh as he sat on the other side, one arm draped over the leather back while he sipped an O'Doul's with the other. As always, his black lab, Beau, snored at his feet. "No, I actually *do* want to talk about it, Jack, because I think I may need some counsel." He cuffed the back of his neck to deflect his embarrassment over a cardiac surgeon in his forties seeking advice on his love life from two kids. Particularly when those kids were his own daughter and the son-in-law whose mother he loved. He expelled another awkward breath as he gave Lacey a sheepish look, feeling a lot like he was back in high school. "Well, I guess you could say it went better than the marina, but not by much."

"What do you mean?" Lacey asked, a pucker of concern ridging her brow.

His smile thinned, Tess's limitation of their time together since their negotiations a week ago putting a crimp in his mood. "I mean Tess has certain" —against his will, heat crawled up the back of his neck— "'*conditions*' before she'll allow us to pick up from where we left off."

"Conditions?" Jack frowned, the male in him obviously balking like Ben had.

"Yeah." Ben set his beer aside, hands clasped between parted knees. "She wants me to clear the air with Cam."

Lacey winced, shoulders in a scrunch as she gritted her teeth in a commiserative smile. "Gosh, Daddy, that won't be easy. Uncle Cam thinks your middle name is Lucifer."

It was Ben's turn to wince, well aware there was plenty of bad blood between Cam and him over the miserable husband he'd been to Cam's sister, ruining her life. His jaw hardened. *And* given the way Phillips was hanging all over Tess when they'd entered Marv's office, he could probably times that by two. His mouth shifted sideways. "Thanks, Lace—good to know, although it's not much of a surprise."

"You said 'conditions.'" Jack absently raked his nails up and down Lacey's arm, brows knit over eyes dark with concern. "More than one?"

Ben upended his O'Doul's, almost wishing it were a real brew rather than the non-beer Tess had badgered him into. "Yep, only two, but the second one is a real doozy." His smile tasted as flat as the beer. "She wants us to be friends."

Lacey's brows shot straight up. "You and Uncle Cam?"

"Yep, ol' Lucifer and the Admiral," Ben said with a hoist of his bottle, "as thick as the noose Tess put around my neck."

"Oh, Daddy …" Lacey tugged her lower lip with her teeth, hazel eyes so like his own warm with sympathy. "I'm sure Tess will be fine with you just forgiving him and clearing the air, don't you think?"

"Ha!" Jack's jibe said it all. "Not the Tess I know." He shook his head with a grimace. "Mom's like a steel trap when it comes to 'conditions.' Just try and slip out, and you're likely to lose a leg."

"Or your heart," Ben muttered, his gaze drifting out over the water in a dead stare.

"Yeah, knowing Mom, she's probably playing hardball." Jack's sigh carried on the breeze. "No compliance? No dinner, fishing, friends, or whatever else we wanted. Growing up, it was Mom's way or the highway, so I don't envy you, sir."

Ben managed a faint smile at Jack still calling him "sir" after almost nine months of marriage to Lacey. But then Ben hadn't been around since the wedding when Jack and Lacey moved into his house to dog-sit Beau. "Me either, Jack." His smile took a twist. "She's sticking to her guns on no dating or official get-togethers till her conditions are met, which relegates me to phone calls, texts, or stolen moments if I'm lucky enough to catch her out on the patio. Which is why I need your help—both of you."

"Anything," Jack said, their relationship considerably warmer now than years ago when Ben considered Jack no more than a punk who dated his rebellious daughter. "Just name it."

Head bowed, Ben peered up beneath a half-lidded gaze. "I know you two probably see Mamaw and Cam on a regular basis, so I was hoping Lacey could enlist Mamaw's help in both praying I can clear the air with Cam and putting a bug in Cam's ear that he needs to do the same."

"Sure, Daddy, Mamaw will be glad to do that, I'm sure." Lacey's smile was tender, reminding Ben of the miracle God had performed in healing his relationship with his estranged daughter. "And, of course, Jack and I will be praying about it too."

The edge of Ben's mouth lifted the slightest bit. "I'm counting on it, sweetheart."

"What else?" Jack wanted to know, his eagerness to help easing Ben's smile into a near grin.

Ben reached to scratch Beau's head while the black lab slept at his feet. "I have no earthly idea how I should go about this. Tess gave me Cam's cell number and I've left several messages, but he refuses to call me back." Sucking in a deep draw of air, he expelled it again as he sagged back in his seat. "And it'd be too awkward for me to just show up on his front door, so I figured

I'd wait to run into him this week at the marina. Marv says he has an appointment on Saturday to test-run another boat."

"That's a good plan," Lacey said with a nod of her head.

Ben's smile zagged sideways. "If it works. I'm worried he's going to take a swing at me or just plain tick me off with his bullheaded stubbornness before I can even get him to talk."

"Oh, you'll manage, Daddy." The assurance in Lacey's tone was tempered by a squirm of a smile. "After all, you're both mule-headed Irishmen, so you have a lot in common."

Jack pinched Lacey's waist. "Including a certain mule-headed Irish daughter and niece."

Ben grunted. "Who pales in comparison to a certain mule-headed Irishwoman holding a gun to my head."

Lacey giggled, the sound winging in the air along with the seagulls above. "Try to look at it as a loving incentive, Daddy, instead of a gun, for a man Tess knows *all* too well."

Ben shot her a narrow gaze. "Hey, whose side you on, kiddo?"

A tender look of love welled in her eyes, along with a sheen of tears. "Yours, Daddy, the father I love with my whole heart and soul," she whispered, "and one of God's greatest blessings in my life."

Emotion clogged in Ben's throat as he battled the sting of moisture beneath his own lids. "Right back at you, sweetheart." He deflected his gaze to the glimmering waves, which rolled as much as his stomach. "Well, I guess if you and Tess got through to a hardhead like me, I suppose there's hope for me and Cam. But it sure won't be easy."

Lacey scrambled out of Jack's arms to sit next to her father, looping a gentle arm to his waist. "No, it won't. But we're Carmichaels, Daddy—we're big on grit and God, so all you have to do is talk to him." Her eyes sparkled with tease. "And maybe grovel a tiny bit." She ducked to smile into his eyes. "You know, like I had to do with you?"

Ben groaned, kneading the bridge of his nose. "Don't remind me."

"Okay, but I *will* remind you how far you've come, Dr. Doom, from being the Terrible Hermit Ogre of Bluff Drive to a man with whom Tess O'Bryen wants to spend the rest of her life." She kissed him on the head. "And that ain't no small feat, Daddy, for either you *or* for God."

"I suppose." He hooked her close with an arm around her shoulders, returning her kiss with one of his own. "But I'll be hanged if I know how I'm gonna do it."

"But you will," Lacey said with a squeeze of his waist, "and if you don't?" She rose and straightened the collar of his Polo with a saucy smile before giving him a wink. "Run the other way if you see Tess with a rope."

CHAPTER SIXTEEN

"You're a genius, you know that?"

Shannon whirled around with a basketball in her hands, annoyed that the sound of Sam's voice sent butterflies flitting through her stomach like they were OD-ing on Starbuck's.

Tucking the ball under her arm, she swiped her face with the sleeve of her "Cutter's Point" T-shirt Sam insisted on buying for her after he trounced her in mini-golf. "That's debatable," she said, pretty sure a genius wouldn't get involved with a hunk of heartache like him. "But why?"

She posed the question with a slack of her hip, feeling a bit on the scroungy side after a basketball game with her kids. Especially when Dr. Love looked like he stepped out of a Polo ad in a crisp, fitted shirt open at the collar and designer jeans, sleeves rolled to show off tan forearms scattered with dark hair.

He ambled onto the court, hands in his pockets and a grin on his handsome face, swiping the ball from her so smoothly, she never knew what hit her.

Kind of like their friendship.

"Your advice about how to handle Jasmine, Miss Brilliant."

Shannon suppressed a smile. Ah, yes—chapter fifteen of *Love Everlasting.*

He dribbled the ball around her several times like he was Tom Hanks in the movie *Big*, a grown man with the heart of a kid, and she could do nothing but grin, shaking her head. His expensive shoes lifted off the pavement as he let the ball fly, allowing it to spin into the net with a satisfying swoosh before he retrieved it. His teeth gleamed white against bronze skin as he dribbled back to her side.

"Show-off." She snatched the ball to hurtle a three-pointer into the net, effectively dropping his jaw. "I want details, hotshot, not fancy footwork."

"I was hoping you'd say that." He latched his thumbs into the front pockets of his jeans and strolled alongside as she headed toward the gym. "I'm high on success and cappuccino, so I thought I'd tell you all about it while we jog on Tybee Beach. I've got a change of clothes in the car."

She peered at him out of the corner of her eye. "Did it ever occur to you I might be busy?"

He paused as if giving it serious thought before he shrugged with a sheepish grin. "Not really. Ran into Cat at the big house, and she said you had nothing going after you got off at three, so here I am."

She sighed. *Yes, you certainly are, in all your annoying glory.* "Guess I need to chat with my social director about screening my schedule," she said with a side smile, irked that her pulse was already sprinting on Tybee while her body dragged from a full day at camp.

"So, what do you say?" He nabbed the ball to carry it for her. "I'll even buy you dinner after, to pay for lesson number two."

She skidded to a stop, gravel crunching beneath her Nikes. "Lesson number two?"

"Come on, Shannon, I'm on a roll here," he said, bobbling the ball back and forth, "and I need a professional who can tell me what to do."

She plunked a hand on her hip. "And there aren't any shrinks in that big hospital building you work in?"

He pulled out the stops with his perilous smile and a little-boy plea in those coffee-colored eyes. "Sure there are, but I need a romance professional, Angel Eyes." He slung an arm over her shoulder, and the scent of his Straight to Heaven cologne made her wish she could go straight home. "Besides, most of them are my guy friends, and I need a female who will shoot me straight."

Her smile took a right turn. "How about a female who will

just shoot you?"

"Nope." He had the nerve to wink. "Already got plenty of those."

Her sigh floated into the air. "Well, I'll pass on the run and the dinner because I'm whipped and already look like I finished last in a marathon. But Cat has a softball game if you want to sit with me in the bleachers."

An inverted V wedged above his classic nose as he held the gym door open for her. "I was actually hoping for a bit more privacy. You know, somewhere quiet where we could talk?"

She sailed past, attempting to mollify him with a bright smile over her shoulder. "We'll sit on the top row, and I promise we'll be completely alone." Her smile twitched as she stored the ball in the equipment closet and closed the door.

Just us and thirty loyal supporters …

"But what if Jack's there?" He looked so pathetic, she almost felt sorry for him, inclined to give in like she always did with Cat.

"Jack never comes to Cat's games anymore. She's in two leagues, so nobody can keep up except me."

"But … what about dinner?"

Shannon almost laughed out loud at the deprived look on his face.

Ah … so this *is what it's like having a little boy!* She swept past him at the door, making a beeline for the parking lot. "Hot dogs and Diet DP works for me, big boy, how 'bout you?"

His grunt pretty much confirmed he didn't agree, but he didn't have a choice. She may be coerced into a friendship with a notorious heartbreaker, but it didn't mean it had to be on his terms.

"Do they at least have corndogs?" he asked, a hint of a sulk in his tone.

"You bet, and cheese dogs, chili dogs, and even a Coney dog, although I won't vouch for the state of your stomach an hour later."

"Can't be much worse than it is now," he muttered, "worrying over Jazz." He hooked her arm as they neared the parking lot, steering her to his Corvette. "I'll drive."

She glanced up after he opened the door, sliding into the leather bucket seat as if she belonged there. "Hey, what happened to being 'high on success and cappuccino'?"

He grunted again before closing her door and circling, his smile off-center as he got in on the other side. "Corn dog indigestion, setting in early."

Shannon slowly stretched back in the seat to the mellow sounds of Keith Urban's "Making Memories of Us," keenly aware they were making memories of their own, she and Sam. *As friends.* The idea wrapped around her like the rich, honey sound of Keith Urban's melody, easing the tension from her bones. "You like country music?" she asked with a lift of brows, expecting the Memorial heartthrob to crank up clubbing music like Usher or Rihanna.

He slipped her a sideways smile. "We'll let that be our little secret, okay? I do have a reputation to protect after all." Easing the Vette out of the parking lot, he seemed to loosen up, one hand relaxed on the shift lever while he drove with the other. "Country music just seems … homier to me, you know? More Mom and apple pie." His mouth swagged to the right. "Which considering I never had a real mom, seems to fill the bill."

Against her will, her heart cramped, reminding her once again that Sam's upbringing was anything but normal, explaining a little bit more each time they were together just why he was the way that he was.

A player desperate for love.

A person desperate for approval.

And a man desperate for peace.

Instead of talking about himself and Jasmine, he surprised her by peppering her with questions about her upbringing on the short ride to the ball fields. She readily complied, suspecting he was hungry to hear about what a real family was like, a close-knit family where faith was front and center. According to Jack, Sam had no family, much less any real exposure to faith, which was one of the reasons Jack had reached out to him during their residency despite their keen competition over women.

"The poor guy's a virtual orphan," Jack had told them once, "with no living relatives except some drunk of a dad who never married his mom." Shannon remembered being heartbroken for Sam at the time, even before she'd ever met him.

When they were seated at the top of the bleachers with hot dogs, corn dogs, French fries, and drinks, Sam went silent while they ate their dinner, his gaze fixed on the softball game in a dead stare. It wasn't until he wadded up his trash that he finally broached what was on his mind.

"She wants to be friends," he said quietly, even though there was no way people three rows below could hear given the whooping and shouting over a close play at the plate. He stared straight ahead, munching on his third corn dog while he watched a game he probably wasn't seeing.

Shannon studied his somber profile, drawn as always to the serious side of Sam Cunningham, the real man behind the pretense. "But that's a good thing, right?"

He turned halfway, lips curving in a sad smile. "Yeah, it is, even though it's light years from where I want to be."

She tipped her head. "Ah, yes, but light years from where you were, yes?"

"Yes, indeed." He slid her a sideways grin as he tweaked her neck, both his touch and the affection in his eyes sputtering her pulse. "And all because of you. She actually said she missed talking to me and she's glad we can be friends."

"Well, I'd say that's definite progress, Dr. Love." Shannon popped the rest of her hot dog in her mouth and balled up the wrapper and napkin.

"I'll say. We were on such good terms when she left that she even promised to bring me back these special cigars she knows I like from her trip to the Bahamas." Sam took the trash from her hands and tucked it in the cardboard drink carrier along with his own before setting it aside. "So, Coach, I'm definitely going to see her again, and I need the game plan before I do."

Shannon leaned back, arms braced to the bleacher seat as she peered at him out of the corner of her eye. "Are you sure you're up to the challenge, Ham? Because we have some big work to do."

"I beg your pardon." Sam squeezed her leg muscle right above the knee, making her squeal. "There isn't a challenge you can issue, Angel Eyes, that I can't handle with ease."

"All right, hotshot, we'll just see about that." She leaned back again, eyes on the game. "You're going to have to convince Jazz that she's the only woman for you. *And* that you're willing to wait."

"Piece of cake," Sam said, the self-assurance in his tone causing a smile to tickle her lips.

"With*out* dating anybody else."

Silence.

She gave him a sideways peek, and her smile bloomed into a full-fledged grin at the gape of his mouth.

"You can't be serious," he said, his voice a near croak. Facial muscles slack, he stared at her as if she'd just suggested he become a Tibetan monk.

"Completely, Dr. Love, but the real question is—are you?"

His mouth snapped shut as those brown eyes darkened, his bristled jaw hardening with the same resolution that obviously took him from a street-poor orphan to a top pediatric practice. He turned his attention to the game, mouth compressed. "For how long?"

"As long as it takes to convince her you're the man she needs, Sam. The loyal, serious, committed man who will love and protect her all the days of her life. Not the player waiting in the wings while he's making a play for every other woman, sowing doubts about if you'll ever be faithful as a husband." She paused. "So, basically forever, Dr. Love, because she's the woman you want, remember?"

A muscle quivered in his cheek, the hard set of his jaw telling her he was wrestling with his doubts. He finally expelled a lengthy sigh that seemed to deplete all the caffeine from his body, leaving him with a calm that drained all the tension from his face. "Bring it on, Coach," he said softly, the faintest of smiles lining his lips.

"Okay." Shannon shifted to face him. "I can't promise you this will work, Sam, but I *can* promise you that the only way this *will* work is if she's convinced you've changed for the better. And I guarantee you nothing will accomplish that quicker than if word gets around that you've given up other women."

"Done." He squinted at her. "What else?"

"Then you get real serious about being her friend. Which means spending time with her in a nonthreatening way."

"Nonthreatening?" A slow smile eased across his lips. "Oh, you mean like I have with you?"

Shannon swallowed a gulp. "Yeah, like you have with me," she said with a quick drink of her DP, upending it to deflect the blush she felt rising up her neck.

"So, you mean things like meeting her for cappuccinos to catch up or innocent games of mini-golf where she can vent over what a jerk the intern can be?" His playful grin coaxed a smile to her face.

"Yes," Shannon said, "as well as things like taking her favorite smoothie to the hospital where everyone sees that she's special to you, or taking her to lunch, even if it *is* just to talk about the other guy. Woo her," Shannon emphasized, ducking her head to pin him with a pointed gaze, "without her ever even knowing." She felt a twinge in her heart.

Kind of like you're doing with me.

"Okay." He focused on her as if she were one of his professors in med school, as serious as she'd ever seen.

"And whatever you do, my friend," she said, warning thick in her words, "do *not* make a move on her. *She* has to be the one to do that, because then you'll know she wants *you* to make a move. But—and this is going to be the hard part, Sam …" She drew in a deep breath heavy with the scent of popcorn and hot dogs, "if she *does* make a move, you have to say no."

He blinked, jaw swagging low. "Are you crazy? The woman

turns my blood to lava, Shan, white hot and ravenous. How am I supposed to say no?"

One side of Shannon's mouth crooked up. "The same way you got through seven years of med school and residency, Dr. Love—sheer fortitude." She fluttered her lashes. "Unless, of course, you're not strong enough to say no …?"

His eyes narrowed. "Self-control is my middle name, Teach. I didn't get through med school on my looks, you know."

A smile squirmed on her lips. "No, just residency …"

He wagged a stern finger in her face, a smile twitching at the edge of his lips. "You know what? People think you're the sweet and shy twin, Shannon O'Bryen, but you have a wicked tongue. And for your information, you little brat, I am a brick wall when it comes to will power, a virtual man of steel, just like Superman."

"Yeah?" She arched a brow. "Prove it."

His mouth took a swerve. "Don't have to. Straight A's in high school, college, and med school should be proof enough, kiddo, especially for a foster-care orphan who worked three jobs at a time." His chin jutted up. "Besides, even professors in med school gave us reasons why, Angel Eyes, so suppose you tell me just why I should do something as stupid as that?"

The smile faded on her face as she pierced him with a solemn gaze. "Two reasons, Sam. One, she's looking for a man she can trust, remember? And that's not somebody who takes advantage of another guy's girl, which she apparently is if she's going to the Bahamas with him, right?" She cocked her head. "What's his name, anyway?"

His mouth went flat. "Derek. Or as I prefer to call him—'Derelict.'"

She shook her head, a smile itching to break through, but she fought it off. This was too serious of a point to temper with a smile. "So, if she makes a move and you give in? You risk your credibility as a friend and a man she can trust. Understand?"

He grunted his response, obviously not happy with her assessment. "Yeah, well, we'll cross that bridge when we come to it."

She jerked his chin to face her, forefinger and thumb pinching hard while her brows arched in command. "No, we will cross that bridge right *now*, Dr. Love, or we can nix these 'lessons.'"

The edge of his mouth flickered with a near smile despite his narrow gaze. "You're a bigger bully than old Mrs. Cranston in the third grade, O'Bryen, you know that? And she was the meanest teacher I ever had."

"Yeah?" Shannon grabbed the lobe of his ear. "Well, ol' Mrs. C.'s gonna look like a field trip when I'm done with you, Dr. Love, so buck up or back out." She gave his ear a hard tweak. "I want you to promise me right now, buster, that you will keep your mitts off of Jasmine whether she comes on to you or not."

"Ouch!" He slapped her hand away, broiling her with a mock glare. "I think I prefer the stilettos."

"It can be arranged, bucko, if you even think about crossing me, so I want your word now—hands off the ex, got it?"

"Hands?" He splayed a palm to his heart, a devious smile sprouting on his lips. "Consider it done."

She nabbed his chin again, holding it tight. "Hands, lips, nose, body, and every other trick you have in the little black book of yours, Doc, capiche? No moves whatsoever." She let him go, shoulders squaring with a firm fold of arms. "Unless, of course," she said with a measured smile, "that's too difficult for you?"

He swallowed the dare like a carp on dog food. "Bring-it," he bit out.

"Good." She swiveled forward to watch the game, the progress they'd made making her hungry. "Then you can thank me with another hot dog and DP. And don't skimp on the relish this time."

He rose with a chuckle, swiping up the trash on his way. "Sure thing, Mrs. O.," he said, staring down with a slack of his hip. "Anything else?"

"Yeah." She peered up with a tilt of her head, shading her eyes with her hand. "One final tip. If you ever play mini-golf with Jazz ..." She battled a grin that just itched to break free, already plotting chapter sixteen in her mind. “For the love of all that’s humble and sweet, Doc,” she said with a wry twist of her lips, “for once in your do-or-die life—let the poor woman win.”

CHAPTER SEVENTEEN

Crash!

Sam jolted at his desk when his closed door banged hard against the wall in an office where he'd thought everyone had gone home.

"So help me, Cunningham, I will take you out right now if you're hitting on my sister." Jack stormed in with fire in his eyes, slamming the door behind him with another bang that jangled Sam's nerves. He strode forward and yanked one of the chairs in front of Sam's desk out of the way with a clatter while Sam shot to his feet, hand raised to quell Jack's temper.

"Calm down, Jack, Shannon and I are only friends, I swear."

"Don't give me that garbage," Jack hissed, palms flat on the front of Sam's desk as he leaned in, the tic in his temple keeping time with the rapid thud of Sam's heart. "That's classic 'Cunningham 101: Friends with Benefits,' you slime ball, and I ought to tear you limb from limb for even glancing at my sister."

"Hey, man, it's your fault in the first place," Sam said, standing his ground with his own searing glare. "You're the one who had her drive me home from the fundraiser, O'Bryen, so can I help it if Shannon's an amazing listener? One who parses a problem down to size with some of the most honest, real advice anyone has ever given me?"

The tic slowed as Jack's eyes narrowed to slits. "Like take a flying leap off a tall building?"

Uh, yeah. Or from the front seat of a car ... Sam's eyes softened as he absently rubbed the center of his chest, the memory of Shannon's stilettos tugging a sheepish smile to his lips. "As a matter of fact, Jack, yes—among a few other choice barbs, so trust me, I got the point.

Permanently tattooed on my chest.

Jack rose to his full height, a twitter in his cheek confirming that his anger still simmered dangerously close to the surface. "I want the truth, Ham—did you hit on Shannon?"

The fire in Jack's eyes was apparently catching because Sam felt it whoosh up the back of his neck. *Nope, more like the other way around …*

Smile fading, Sam sucked in a deep draw of air, figuring he owed Jack the truth. He cuffed the back of his neck, slowly taking his seat. "I won't lie to you, Jack—I did kiss Shannon out of appreciation for taking me home, making me breakfast, and talking some sense into me, but I swear, it was nothing more than an innocent kiss." The heat from his neck crawled up into his face at how close he'd come to way more if Shannon had been willing.

Jack slanted in again, hands knuckle-white on Sam's desk. "Then *why* does your face look like the backside of a baboon?" he said in a slow, deadly voice, rife with warning.

Avoiding Jack's burning gaze, Sam swallowed a knot of nerves, his Adam's apple chugging so many times, he thought it was broke. "Because it was a" —*gulp*—"really nice kiss," Sam said with a croak, "that made me want more, but I assure you Shannon nipped that in the bud right away when she pummeled my chest with her stilettos and kicked me out of her car." He swallowed hard. "Literally. Right on my baboon butt."

Jack blinked, a smile twitching at the corners of his mouth as he quietly straightened. "No kidding?"

Sam grunted, a sheepish grin sliding across his face. "Yeah, man, with divots that would make a nine iron proud. So trust me, Jack—I ain't going down that road ever again."

"Trust you?" Jack said with a flash of teeth, apparently satisfied enough to drop into Sam's chair with hands braced to the back of his neck. "Not in a million years, Ham, but I will admit it's awfully good to hear that Shan can take care of herself."

"And then some, I assure you." Sam reached into his mini-fridge under his desk to grab two Red Bulls and sat down, closing his computer before tossing one at Jack, who caught it handily. "So, when I say Shannon and I are only friends, man, I mean it. And to be honest?" He popped the tab. "Shannon's too important of a friend now to risk screwing that up, especially since she's a genius when it comes to coaching me on how to get Jazz back." Smiling, he raised a toast. "You wouldn't believe the strides I'm making with Jazz, and all because of your brilliant sister."

Jack toasted him back and took a healthy swig, throat glugging as he watched Sam over the rim of the can. "Man, that hits the spot—thanks." He rested his arms on the chair, bracing the can while he relaxed his head on the back. "So I don't need to break your legs?"

Sam chuckled. "Please don't—I need them if I'm going to win Jazz back."

"To crawl on your knees?" Jack said with a lazy grin.

"Surprisingly, no." Sam took a drink of his Red Bull, a feeling of peace settling despite the caffeine he was pumping into his body. He smiled. "Your sister is teaching me a whole new tact," he said with a leisurely scratch of curls at the nape of his neck, his smile easing into a grin, "and unlike my methods before, begging is not part of the routine."

"Good to hear, Ham. Women like a man in control, especially a woman like Jazz."

Sam issued a grunt. "Yeah, well I've always been the one in control in relationships until Jazz dumped me."

"*And* the two-timing co-ed," Jack reminded him gently, almost making Sam sorry he'd opened up about the woman he'd fallen hard for in college, the one he'd hoped to marry. His smile disappeared into a thin line as he recalled how over the moon he'd been when he put his ring on Amber's finger, pledging his love forever. Only forever turned out to be till every Friday night rolled around when she went clubbing with her friends, screwing Sam over with a revolving door of other men.

Including a married professor.

A heavy blast of air blustered from Sam's lips. "Don't remind me."

"So, what's Shannon's plan?" Jack studied him with frank interest, his faith in his sister obvious by the affection in his tone.

Sam sank back into his chair, resting his head on the back like Jack while giving him a faint smile. "I swear your sister should be a counselor, Jack. Not only has she taught me how to be a friend to Jasmine" —he paused to give Jack a knowing look with a crook of a smile— "and *only* a friend, but she's helping me to build my self-respect in ways I never dreamed I could. She's pretty much whittled away the player in me to not only reveal a guy women can trust, but a guy I can trust too." His smile bottomed out. "Of course being your sister, she also gets her licks in with not-too-subtle references to God that annoy me to no end."

Jack's chuckle bounced off the office walls. "That's my girl. I'll tell you what, Sam, she's definitely something special."

"Yes, she is," Sam said quietly, thinking how much fuller, deeper, and more peaceful his life was since he met Shannon. He glanced up to lock gazes with Jack, the sobriety in his tone a promise he intended to keep. "She's rapidly becoming my best friend, Jack, and you have my word—I will never hurt her."

"I believe you, Sam." Jack's chest inflated with a deep swell of air before he expelled it in one long, arduous sigh. "At least not intentionally, but I gotta tell you, bro, I'm more than a little concerned about that killer charm of yours. I've seen too many women fall under your spell, Dr. Love, and I just want to make sure Shan doesn't become another victim."

Victim. Sam winced, pretty sure he deserved that. He tossed out a grin, hoping to counter Jack's underlying message with humor. "Are you kidding? When it comes to Shannon, I'm the victim here, and don't make me take my shirt off to prove it. Besides," he said with a hoist of his Red Bull, "it took weeks before she'd even give me the time of day, and she still won't go anywhere without a lot of people around. Trust me—I literally had to bribe her in the first place, to even break through her defenses."

"Yeah, 'break through her defenses.' That's what I'm worried about, Ham, because I learned first-hand in residency that nobody breaches a girl's defenses quite like you." Jack rose, stretching his arms back with the Red Bull in his hand and a wry smile on his lips. "So I hope you don't mind, old buddy, but I plan to put the third degree to my little sister just to make sure she's not falling for your charm."

"She's not," Sam said too quickly, suddenly remembering the passion in Shannon's kiss when she melted in his arms. A kiss that had enough return heat to convince Sam she wanted more as much as he did. "But it doesn't matter, Jack—I would never risk hurting Shannon or my friendship with her."

"I'm afraid it *does* matter, Sam, because if I sense she has even the slightest bit of attraction to you, I'm going to ask you to back off and leave her alone. Which shouldn't be too much of a problem for you if you get back with Jazz. Because take it from personal experience—that woman isn't going to want Shannon around, friend or no." Jack paused. "Agreed?"

Sam's throat constricted, the thought of Shannon out of his life not settling all that well. "Agreed," he said quietly, hoping it didn't come to that.

"Good. Then thanks for the Red Bull, man. I was dragging before I came in here, but this fired me right back up."

"I doubt it was the Red Bull," Sam said with a jag of a smile. "You were seeing red way before that."

Jack grinned. "Yeah, I was, but I feel a whole lot better now." He took a drink and sat on the edge of Sam's desk, assessing Sam with compassion in his eyes. "So … you and Jazz—things are looking up?"

"Yep, and all because of your amazing sister, coaching me every step of the way."

"Cool." Jack nodded, a tender smile shadowing his lips for a woman Sam supposed was as great a sister as she was a friend. He stood. "Well, I gotta go before Shan's 'amazing' sister-in-law disowns me."

Sam laughed, slanting back with a casual fold of arms. "Yeah, right. The woman's so out of orbit for you, she's over the moon."

Jack ambled to the door, lobbing a grin over his shoulder. "Yeah, I know. Just like Jazz will be once you lock her down."

"Thanks, man." Sam opened his computer, Jack's reassurance leaving a warm feeling in his chest. "Appreciate it."

"See you tomorrow," Jack called, turning halfway with a sudden notch between his brows. "Oh … almost forgot." He strolled around to Sam's side of the desk with his Red Bull to apparently throw it away. But before Sam could take it, Jack dribbled the dregs over Sam's head.

"Are you crazy?" Sam vaulted to his feet with a growl, snatching the can from Jack's hand while he grilled him with a glare. "What the devil was that for?" he shouted, amber liquid dribbling off his nose onto one of his favorite ties.

Hands in his pockets, Jack strolled to the door with a satisfied chuckle, glancing back while he fisted the knob. "*That*, old buddy," he said with a smile a whole lot dryer than Sam's tie, "is for kissing my sister."

CHAPTER EIGHTEEN

Oh, goody. The shoe's on the other foot. Tess glared at the privet hedge that separated Ben's yard from hers, flipping a page in her magazine so hard, it tore in half. Her lips took a twist. *And it's pinching my feet along with my mood.*

Which is exactly why she was barefoot at the moment, sitting on her patio in the dark with only a pale shaft of light from her open kitchen door.

For. The. Last. Stinkin'. Hour!

She lifted her feet to study the freshly painted Peach Passion on her toenails, nicely complemented by skimpy white short-shorts she'd borrowed from Cat and a snug crop top the exact shade of her toes. The *same* crop top she'd worn the night Ben had told her he wanted to be way more than neighbors last summer, when he couldn't keep his eyes—or hands—off of her. Normally she avoided snug or skimpy anything, especially where Ben was concerned, but after two weeks of barely seeing him at all, she figured this was war. She'd even ditched the usual messy ponytail for the loose shoulder-length style he seemed to love because she obviously needed to remind him of just what he was missing by not coming around.

Glancing at her watch, she noted the late hour of eleven o'clock and huffed out a noisy sigh, her patience as thin as the flimsy page of her *Better Homes & Garden*. "Where the heck are you, Carmichael?" she muttered, more than a little peeved she hadn't seen him all week and only once the week before for pizza on her patio the night the kids were gone. Even *though* the concept of "some distance" had been all her idea.

"What? I can't see you till I meet your conditions?" he'd

rasped after he'd walked her home following her ultimatum on the dock, the question laced with shock.

"Of course you can, Ben." She attempted to soothe him with a gentle skim of his bristled jaw, her tone soft. "Once or twice a week for an occasional chat on your patio or dinner on mine when the kids are gone, but no official dating until you clear the air with Cam and *no* sneaking around like before." She pretended to shudder. "I don't like sneaking around—makes me feel like we're doing something wrong. Besides, I think we need some distance." She'd stood on tiptoe then to brush a tender kiss to his lips, feeling strong and confident and oh, so very in control.

Her mouth jabbed into a scowl. *Unlike now.*

Slapping the magazine on the table, she jumped up and started to pace, clearly more frustrated with her mandate at the moment than Dr. Doom, apparently. Just what did he think he was doing anyway? Yes, it had been her idea for limited time together, but for pity's sake, she hadn't expected him to comply, and certainly not so completely! She paused mid-pace with an awful thought, her heart slowing to a painful thud that nearly drowned out the rising hum and click of cicadas. What if he'd decided her demands were too high? What if he realized the occasional chat or dinner was more than enough? What if he came to the conclusion that she was too demanding to marry? Tess swallowed the lump of panic in her throat.

What if he decided to see someone else?

Pulse sprinting, she gnawed on her lip till most of her Peach Kiss lipstick was gone, the scent of her new lemon swirl body lotion—Ben's favorite—as potent as her fear. Men didn't like ultimatums, she knew, and especially a man like Ben, a virtual hermit set in his ways for the last eight years. Until *she'd* invaded his space. She grated her lower lip with her teeth, wondering when she'd turned into such an insecure, jealous stalker.

Uh, when he invaded my heart?

"Ben, where the heck *are* you?" she hissed, slapping a palm on her patio table, grateful her nine-year-old son Davey was spending the night at his best friend's house while the twins worked a campout at Camp Hope with Jack and Lacey. Tears blurred in her eyes before she could stop them, and dropping back in her chair, she stared at the hedge with an ache in her heart. *I miss you ...*

Screeeeeeeech.

Tess froze, the sound of Ben's slider sending her pulse into overdrive as his backyard light flooded the sky over the hedge like the dawn of a new day. Beau squealed and darted into Ben's backyard before the slider squeaked closed again, and Tess tugged her top in place, ready to pay the elusive Dr. Doom a late-night visit. Palms damp and mouth dry, she snatched up the plate of monster cookies she'd made, promising herself she wouldn't lose her temper. Nope, all she wanted to do was give him a smile as sweet as his favorite cookies and jog his memory as to what was on the other side of that stupid hedge. Head high, she marched right around that idiotic Wall of Jericho he'd put in eight years ago and entered his side gate. Her mouth took a swerve. The same gate that had once sported a padlock worthy of Fort Knox before Jack finally took it off after he and Lacey moved in.

Beau came running at the clink of the latch after she closed it, and unwrapping the Saran from two pieces of bacon, she tossed the treat into the air, Beau's Underdog leap coaxing a smile despite her testy mood. "Enjoy, big boy, because one of us needs to."

With a square of her shoulders, she strode right up to Ben's slider, sucking in a deep breath before she practiced a bright smile. "Easy does it, Teresa," she muttered, giving the glass the perky and friendly tap she'd employed so many times in the past. "The man's done nothing wrong." *Except comply with my stupid rules.* Smile in place, she waited.

And waited.

And waited, tempted to make more noise than Beau as he squealed. The lab nosed the door with a stream of pathetic whimpers that coincided with those in her head.

"Come on, Ben," she mumbled, "you've got an antsy dog out here." She rapped the glass with her knuckles, her frustration rising along with poor Beau's. "Not to mention an antsy fiancée."

Uh ... almost fiancée, she reminded herself through a clenched smile, suddenly ticked that Ben had not only stayed away, but now he wasn't even answering his stupid door. One hand cupped to the glass, she peered into his dark family room, spying lights in both the kitchen and down the hall. "Come on, Carmichael, I know you're in there ..."

Oh, how she hated what this was doing to her! Before Ben, she'd been content, happy-go-lucky, even-keel. She paused, the truth niggling over what Ben referred to as her "too perky" personality. Well, even-keel for the most part. But since Ben had left for his medical mission trip, she'd been calm, supportive, the height of maturity in getting her and her family past the heartbreak of Adam's death. And yet the moment Ben returned, she'd lost it all, morphing into a hot-tempered, stubborn bully, and she didn't like it one little bit. And now the thought of Ben pulling away, possibly pursuing a woman who was less of a shrew scared her silly, heaping jealousy and fear on top of an already volatile mindset.

Before she knew it, she was banging on the glass for all she was worth, eyes squeezed closed as she pounded on the door, determined to give Dr. Doom a piece of her mind along with her cookies. *So help me, Ben Carmichael, if you don't open up right now ...*

Screeeeeeeech.

Her eyes popped open when the door whooshed sideways on the track, interrupting her mid-air assault. "Tess! What a nice surprise." Ben butted a hip to the doorjamb, arms in a relaxed fold that only accentuated well-toned biceps in a turquoise Polo. His deep tan and windblown sable hair salted at the temples suggested a day on his boat, ratcheting up her temper another notch while hazel eyes studied her with a twinkle. A lazy smile inched across lips that hadn't kissed hers since her "nuzzle ban" a few nights after the dock discussion, when Ben wanted to pick up where they'd left off. Only she figured a man as hard-headed as Dr. Doom needed a little extra incentive, so she'd topped it off with no kisses, no lap snuggles, and no inside visits until he and Cam were as tight as ticks.

Yeah, that worked well.

The sparkle of humor in those mesmerizing eyes gleamed as bright as the flash of white teeth when his smile slid into a grin. "I'd invite you in, Ms. O'Bryen, but Tess's rules," he said with a slight shrug, his husky drawl laced with tease, "and I'm nothing if not compliant."

She gritted her teeth, her smile as plastic as the Saran over the cookies. *I'll give you compliant …*

"Are these for me?" He reached for the plate of cookies, and she jerked them away so fast, two of them flew off the plate despite the Saran, happily snarfed up by Beau.

"No!" she bit out before she realized what she'd done, her frustration festering out of control. She hiked her chin up, fire burning in her eyes. "They're for Jack and Lacey," she said, justifying the fib based on the fact that they *did* live in Ben's house and she *did* bake them cookies on occasion.

Just never delivered them late at night.

"Something wrong, Tess?" Ben's manner turned serious as he slipped his hands in his pockets, but the twitch of a smile and eyes warm with affection gave him dead away.

"No, Dr. Doom, there isn't, so you can wipe that smirk right off your face." She rammed the cookie plate hard into his chest, doubly annoyed when it felt like a brick wall. "Here," she snapped, "this is the third batch I've baked in two weeks, but you wouldn't know since you never seem to be home."

He grabbed the plate, skimming her hand with his thumb before her arm jerked away. His smile was tender. "I thought you baked these for Jack and Lacey," he whispered, his husky tone getting on her nerves when it rippled her stomach.

"I did," she hissed, too far gone to save face. "Because you're obviously too busy to even come by."

"I've been spending most of my spare time on the boat these last few weeks, Tess." Sobriety stole the humor from his eyes as he set the plate of cookies on his sofa table, his gaze never leaving hers. Stepping outside, he closed the door behind him. "You know—to think. Pray. Talk."

Talk? Her imagination went wild, detonating the bomb ticking inside.

She bludgeoned a finger to his broad chest. "Are you seeing someone else, Ben Carmichael?" she shouted, not giving a whit if anybody could hear her ranting in the middle of the night.

"Yes," he whispered, tugging her close with a shuttered look that immediately snatched all protest from her throat. Before she could object, he burrowed his lips into the crook of her neck, mouth skimming up to suckle the lobe of her ear. "I am."

Any other time, Ben's lips would have melted her on the spot, but this time she didn't feel a thing but the awful stab of his response, and immediately she started pummeling his chest with a sting of tears in her eyes.

"My ex-brother-in-law," he said quickly, reeling her back in with a soft chuckle as he brushed a kiss to her lips. Cupping her jaw with one hand, he held up the other with two fingers crossed, a bit of the devil sparkling in those amazing hazel eyes. "We're like this, you know."

She blinked, mouth falling open before he sealed it with an intimate kiss. Stifling a moan, she pushed him back, palms flat to his chest while she fought off more tears. "You and C-Cam?" she stuttered. "You made amends?"

"Not just amends, Tess." He traced a finger down the side of her face, the look of love in his eyes all but swelling her throat. "He's my new fishing buddy, although I will admit, the boy has a lot to learn."

"B-But how?" she whispered, caressing his shadowed jaw with a feeling of awe, hardly able to believe Ben had done this for her.

He shrugged and leaned back against the house with a faint smile, arms circling her waist to draw her in close. "God railroaded me, I'm afraid, prompted by your prayers, no doubt. Ever since you laid down the law, I was dragging my feet on confronting Cam face-to-face." His smile kinked. "Until I ran into him in Marv's office a few weeks ago after I took Jack and

Lacey out on the boat."

His chest rose and fell in a heavy sigh. "You were right, Tess," he said quietly, his smile fading into a sobriety that bordered on reverence. "Cam was the last holdout in that hedge of bitterness I built over the years, and God knew it needed to come down. So we talked, we yelled, then we talked some more, and I asked his forgiveness for ruining his sister's life." His jaw stiffened as he looked away, as if embarrassed by a sheen of tears. "Because I'm done harboring hurt, Tess." His gaze reconnected with hers as he stroked her hair with the same tenderness she saw in his eyes. "And I don't want anything to ever ruin this precious love that we have."

Her chin began to quiver.

"So it would appear," he continued with a tap of her nose, "that your objections to marriage have been effectively laid to rest." He leaned in to tease her mouth with his own, his words feathering her skin with a delicious heat. "Bitterness toward Cam corrected. Check." He strayed to gently tug on the soft flesh of her lobe. "Jealousy toward Cam corrected. Check." His laughter rumbled hot against her ear with a teasing flick of his tongue, coaxing a faint moan from her throat. "Friendship with Cam established. Check, Check." He finished her off with a kiss that made her go limp in his arms before he dug into his pocket for the ring he tried to give her before. "So Phase One accomplished, Ms. O'Bryen," he whispered, "and now we move on to Phase Two, yes?"

Overcome with both gratitude and desire, she lunged to hug him with all of her might, tears staining his shirt as she pressed her cheek to his chest. "Yes, yes, yes, and oh, Ben, I love you so very much!"

His husky chuckle tumbled her stomach as he placed the ring on her finger, a dangerous smile matching the heated look in his eyes. "Enough to break a few rules with a little temptation? Like snuggling on the couch to watch a movie?" He slowly traced the shape of her lips with the pad of his thumb, his intentions abundantly clear. "And I have Häagen-Dazs …"

Tess gulped. *Häagen-Dazs and Ben—Lord have mercy!*

Swallowing hard, she put as much distance between them as she possibly could, given the tight circle of Ben's arms to her waist. "Häagen-Dazs is one temptation I'll succumb to anytime, Dr. Carmichael, but out here on the patio, if you will." Tugging free from his hold, she stood on tiptoe to slowly graze his lips with her own before holding out her hand to admire her ring. "Because the way I feel about you right now, Doc?" A warm shiver pebbled her skin as she hurried to claim one of his Adirondack chairs, tucking her legs to settle in with a shaky wink. "I sure don't trust myself inside."

CHAPTER NINETEEN

"I'm telling you, woman, you missed your calling." Sam wiped the sweat from his face with the bottom of his "Pediatrician … I see little people" T-shirt, revealing a tan six-pack that depleted all moisture from Shannon's throat. "I swear you're one of the smartest people I've ever met," he said, repeating a compliment he often doled out during their counseling sessions. "And I've met some pretty brainy chicks in med school, Shan, but you're a bloomin' genius, you know that?"

In plotting a relationship between the player and the princess in her novel, yes. Shannon humored him with a patient smile as they headed toward the Camp Hope gym after a basketball game with the kids. *But in pursuing a friendship between a player and a ghostwriter?* Shannon's smile went south. She couldn't be too darn smart if she was starting to look forward to these "sessions" more than she should. After several times of hanging out following camp and almost daily texts, her friendship with Sam had grown to the point where she'd rather spend time with him than write or hang out with her friends—two things that had always satisfied her loneliness before.

The only bright spot was that her romance novel was coming along swimmingly, the need to channel all her pent-up feelings for Sam fueling her cause. And although the growing closeness between them alarmed her at times, she truly believed the spiritual groundwork she was laying far outweighed the risk to her heart. A risk she completely gave to God since she now believed her friendship with Sam was in His plan all along. "Define genius," she said as he bobbled the basketball back and forth.

He focused on the ball while he spun it on his finger, providing ample opportunity to study him unaware. *A dangerous thing to do.* The more she saw of the "real" Sam with his wellspring of vitality, the more she was drawn into the vortex of a man who at the core, possessed an almost childlike humility and hope. A little-boy innocence of sorts that was so at odds with the self-confident charmer about town. There were times like now when the player was nowhere in sight, giving way to a crazy and carefree man whose energy for life was so strong, it sent her heart spinning more than the ball on his finger. "You know, a woman so in touch with her feelings—both spiritually and emotionally—that she's a beacon of truth to all those she knows and loves."

Shannon deflected the heat in her cheeks with a wry smile. "Gosh, Doc, you make me sound like the Statue of Liberty."

He paused the ball mid-spin, his faint smile belied by the intensity in his eyes. "That's because you are, Shannon, to me anyway. You've liberated me, kiddo, in more ways than you know."

"I'm glad," she whispered, uttering a silent prayer she could one day usher him into the true freedom of faith. "So, Dr. Love … why am I a 'genius' today?"

Mischief curled on his lips as he palmed the ball with one hand, his sideways glance offering a teasing dance of brows. "Apparently Jazz and Mr. Wrong are having issues, and she's coming to me for advice."

"Really?" Shannon's heart sped up, a mix of pride and joy colliding with a hint of malaise. "What happened?"

He tossed the ball back and forth as they approached the gym, his smile suddenly ebbing along with the prior victory in his tone. "She showed up at my place last night crying," he said quietly, "so we talked for a long while, deeper than we ever have before." He opened the gym door for Shannon and followed her in, unleashing a heavy sigh as he put the ball away. "And I'll tell you what, Shan—tore me up so much, I just wanted to swallow her up in my arms and make the hurt go away." He fell in step beside her on the way to the parking lot. "So I asked her to stay for popcorn and a movie."

Shannon skidded to a stop, several pebbles flying when she spun to face him. "You didn't try and …" She fought the rise of a gulp, not really wanting to hear his answer.

His mouth tipped. "No, Teach. I did just what you told me, as difficult as it was. Comfort, coffee, and nothing else." He opened her door and she slid in, waiting for him to get in on the other side. "And let me tell you," he continued after he started the ignition, "the woman was all over me before the credits could even roll, almost pouting when I wouldn't put out." He gave her a wink before easing the Vette out of the lot. "Kinda felt like you, Shan."

Shannon gaped at his profile in awe, hardly able to believe the playboy in Sam had turned away the woman he loved. "You mean you didn't even kiss her?"

Strains of Keith Urban's "But for the Grace of God" filtered through the car as a slow smile wended its way across his lips. "Sushi okay?" he asked, ignoring her question.

"No, sushi is *not* okay," she said with a slap of his arm. "You *know* I don't do slimy."

He flashed a grin with a wiggle of dark brows. "Yeah, I do, remember?"

She whacked him again, face burning over his reference to the one and only pass he'd ever made. "I need real protein, Doc, not designer fish food, and you didn't answer my question. Did you kiss her or not?"

"Nope." With a smug smile, he got on the Harry S. Truman Parkway, and she knew he was taking her to Sandfly BBQ, one of her favorite obsessions.

After him, of course. Her smile bottomed out over a thought she had no business thinking. *Buck up, O'Bryen—this is friendship, remember?*

"I didn't kiss her, Teach, but she sure kissed me." He shot her a grin before accelerating to his usual breakneck speed on the highway.

Shannon's jaw dropped, pretty sure her eyes were as round as his headlights. "Oh my goodness, Sam, what did you do?"

His broad shoulders lifted in a casual shrug, smile soft as the Vette ate up the miles. "I just pushed her gently away and told her I respected our friendship and her relationship with the boyfriend too much to mess either of them up. So she left."

Shannon hadn't realized she was holding her breath until it seeped through her lips. "Before the movie?"

"Yep." He glanced her way, a definite gleam in his eyes. "But not before laying one on me at the door that almost made me cry before I pushed her away. I sent her home more than a little frustrated, I guarantee you, but she wasn't alone. But it was all worth it, though, because I can sense a shift in her, you know? Like the winds are starting to blow my way." He winked. "Shouldn't be long now before she dumps the chump and we're back together for good."

Shannon drew in a deep breath, slowly releasing it again. "You so sure about that, Doc?" she said quietly, pretty certain it wasn't going to be as easy as that.

He squinted at her as he exited the highway, a deep cleft at the bridge of his nose. "What's that supposed to mean?"

"Think about it, Sam," she said, voice soft to cushion the blow of what she was about to say. "She's left you twice before, so what makes you think she's gonna stay this time?"

"Hey, I've changed, haven't I?" There was a thread of hurt in his tone.

Her smile was gentle. "Marginally, yes, but I suspect it's only a temporary change to win her back, not deep-down change to convince her you're the man for her."

He pulled into the parking lot of Sandfly BBQ and jerked the hand brake up a little too forcefully, clearly frustrated. "Come on, Shan, have a little faith in me, will you?"

"I'd really like to, Sam," she whispered, heart racing at the subject she was about to broach, one Sam didn't cotton to, based on their many conversations. But deep down she knew it was time, and her friendship with him was worth nothing if she couldn't supply him with the truth. She ducked her head to peek up with the deep affection God had so abundantly deposited into her heart. "In fact I'd like to have a whole lot of faith in you where it counts, Sam—deep down in your soul. Life-changing faith, like the kind we can only get from God."

He hurled his car door open with a groan that made her smile, practically stomping around the vehicle to open her door as he always insisted on doing. "You're going to ruin our BBQ if you keep this up—"

She held up a hand before she rose from the car, brows elevated in teacher mode. "No, wait—hear me out, please." He extended his hand to assist as always, and she popped up, stepping aside to let him close the door. "Einstein said, 'Insanity is doing the same thing over and over again and expecting different results.' Which is what you'll be doing, Sam—settling back in to the same old routine that didn't satisfy her before."

His jaw condensed as he steered her up the steps into the small but wide Streamliner railcar building, palm firm at the small of her back. "Okay, okay, so how do I change that?"

"You don't, Sam—God does." She slid into a booth and faced him with hands folded on the table, offering a grateful smile when the waitress delivered menus and took their drink order.

He shook his head as the waitress left, snatching up the menu to study it. "Oh no, Angel Eyes, we're not going there."

She waited till he laid it down again, then leaned in, her smile warm with affection. "Tell me, Sam—do you trust me?" she asked, tenderness lacing her tone.

He stared at her for several tics of his jaw before his scowl surrendered into a sigh. "Yeah, I trust you," he muttered, "way more than God, I can tell you that." He managed a forced smile of thanks to the waitress when she delivered their drinks. "But you already know how I feel about that, Shannon. God wasn't there for me when I was shuffled from foster home to foster home, so I don't see any reason to be there for Him now."

She paused. "But you *do* believe in Him, right?"

He pushed the menu away, face pinched in a frown. "Yeah,

I believe in Him. But only because of this crazy cop who took me under his wing after I got into trouble on the streets. And *only* because *he* pounded it into my brain that God cared about me, saying that was the reason he reached out to me in the first place—because God told him to."

Sam's gaze lapsed into a dead stare, a sudden sheen of moisture glazing his eyes, which immediately pricked tears at the back of Shannon's own. "He was a crazy old coot, but I'll tell you what. Whether God told him to or not, Gus Garavelli was the only one who ever really took the time to know me, care about me. The only one who even bothered to steer me straight." He swiped at his eyes, the strain in his face softening as one edge of his mouth tipped. "Used to bribe me to go to church with him—in exchange for shooting baskets or taking me out to eat, and other cool stuff he knew I'd wanted—so I did." His eyes connected with Shannon's. "I still wasn't too keen on God, mind you, but I couldn't deny there was a strength in Gus that drew me, a faith in him that gave me hope." He reached across the table to take Shannon's fingers in his, his touch tender. "Just like I see in you, Shan."

The waitress returned, and Sam released Shannon's hand to order for them both. When she left again, Shannon paused, absently twining the wrapper from her straw around her finger as she broached a question weighing on her mind. "This Gus Garavelli," she said quietly, "is he still in your life?"

Sam grunted, ripping the paper from his own straw. He crumpled and hurled it at the smiling-pig mold on top of the BBQ sauce caddy. "Nope. Died of a heart attack during my first year of college, which pretty much crushed me, leaving me alone all over again." He lifted his DP in a mock toast, his smile as plastic as the pig's. "So, yes, in honor of a stellar human being named Gus, I do retain a faith in God, Angel Eyes, but our relationship is rocky at best."

"Yes, but that's the beauty of faith," she said as she set her drink aside. "God's precepts work even when our relationship with Him doesn't."

His gaze narrowed as he studied her with another scowl, grabbing the menu to peruse it again like a barrier against the conversation. "And what's *that* supposed to mean?"

"It means if you get back with Jazz and honor God by staying celibate till marriage, He will bless you."

The menu dropped to the table, Sam's eyes as wide as the paper coasters beneath their drinks. "Are you on drugs? You want me to commit to Jazz, put a ring on her finger, and *not* make love to her till we say 'I do'?" Thrusting the menu aside, he issued a grunt. "Impossible."

"For you on your own, maybe, but not with God's help."

His smile went flat as he slanted back with a tight fold of arms, assessing her through sullen eyes. "No. I value your advice, Shannon, you know that, but that is just flat-out crazy and wouldn't work at all, so you may as well forget it."

Watching him over the rim of her glass, she took a leisurely sip. "Okay," she said with a nonchalant air, her smile as sweet as the drink in her hand, "but it sure worked for Jack."

Sam blinked, lips parting as awareness eased the hard line of his jaw. "It did, didn't it?" he whispered, mouth curving in a slow smile as the truth dawned in his eyes. "I remember now because Jazz and I remained friends after we broke up, so I was her sounding board when she started dating your brother." A grin inched across his handsome face. "Man, how he ticked her off with his strict moral code, driving her up the bloomin' wall. But there was a part of her that liked it too, she said. Kind of like it gave Jack this strength of character that ramped up her respect and attraction. Jack was a challenge, and she was determined to take him down, only he took her down first when she fell head over heels." He shook his head. "Now I wonder if his playing hard to get just made her want him all the more …"

"No wondering about it, Sam, because it sure didn't hurt," Shannon said with a gentle smile. "And he wasn't 'playing hard to get.' He was committed to a moral tenet established by God, even though he was angry at Him. A moral tenet, I might add, that not only kept him from marrying the wrong woman, but gave him the desire of his heart in Lacey, the girl he'd been in love with since high school."

He sent her a shuttered look, skepticism tingeing his tone. "And you really believe that all happened because he followed some tenets?"

Her chin rose in a rare show of pluck. "Not '*some* tenets,'" she said with a firm set of her jaw, "God's tenets. And, yes, I absolutely believe that, especially after Jack's faith was restored. Because, Dr. Love, faith and obedience in applying God's precepts—are the epoxy glue that strengthens relationships. A two-step bonding, if you will."

"Okay, let me get this straight." He leaned in, forearms on the table and that resolute look in his eyes. "You're saying if I apply this so-called 'tenet' with Jazz, it will not only strengthen our relationship, but it will help me win her back once and for all?"

She angled in, too, nose-to-nose with a man she knew thrived on a challenge. "Yes, it will definitely strengthen your relationship and very possibly win her back."

"Possibly?" He slugged back a tall swig of his drink, brows bunched over the rim.

"If Jazz is the woman God has for you, then yes, I believe this could very well win her back. But if she's not?" She lifted her shoulders in a definitive shrug. "Then this will probably chase her away, preventing you from marrying the wrong woman in the first place, like it did for my brother."

Sam's lips gummed into a thin line. "Don't worry, Teach, she's the one," he said with another healthy swig of his DP. "The woman's been under my skin since the first moment I saw her, and me under hers, so I'll do whatever it takes to close the deal."

"Whatever it takes, huh?" Shannon grinned, hoping to close a 'deal' of her own. She lifted her glass in a toast. "Even faith?"

He stared for several seconds, his jaw shifting almost imperceptibly before he clinked his glass to hers. "Even faith," he said in a near growl, glass tipped straight up as he downed the rest of his drink.

"Good. Because I have a feeling that's what it's going to take,

Dr. Love. And the fringe benefits? Not only do you completely solidify Jazz's opinion of you as a man of strength and character, but you convince her it's *her* you want and not just her body. Effectively reaffirming the change she's seen in you as a man she could marry. And all because of a 'so-called' tenet where you honor God's precepts."

Gouging fingers through his hair, Sam sagged back in the booth, his gaze veering off into a cold stare as if he just realized what he was about to give up. "Gosh, Shan, I don't know if I have the strength to do that—*or* the faith."

"Nope, but you're in luck, big boy, because I know just the place you can get it."

Sam paused, lids narrowing to slits. "Why do I think I'm not going to like this?" he bit out, those beautiful coffee-colored eyes deepening all the way to dark roast.

She gave him a secret smile, chapter twenty-two of *Love Everlasting* already sketched out in her mind. The waitress delivered two platters of ribs with all the trimmings, one for her and one for Sam, and her stomach rumbled on cue. "Thank you," she said with an appreciative smile, suddenly ravenous—both for ribs and for Sam to scratch the surface of a faith that could set him free. "Oh, and ma'am …" Shannon offered the waitress a shy smile. "Would it be possible to get a few more wet naps?" she asked meekly, chewing at the edge of her lip with a penitent look. "I have a sneaking feeling I'm about to make a real big mess."

"Yeah, I know the feeling." Sam delivered a mock scowl, drilling Shannon with a gaze that only made her grin. He unfolded his napkin, his smile veering toward dry. "And something tells me it ain't gonna be pretty."

CHAPTER TWENTY

"You sure it's not too short?" Sam peered into his visor mirror after he'd parked the Vette near the Mansion on Forsyth Park, brows scrunching over the scalping he'd gotten at the barber. His mouth went flat. On the very day he planned to set the hook with Jazz at the Memorial Awards Banquet. He ruffled the close-cropped curls on top of his head, attempting to rumple them to the disheveled look he preferred. "Closest thing to a military buzz I've ever seen," he said with a heavy exhale, flipping the mirror back down. He offered Shannon an off-kilter smile. "Maybe I should tell Jazz I enlisted, so she'll beg me to stay."

Shannon calmed him with a smile, taking the edge off his nerves better than the occasional Xanax and after-hours beers he'd opted for after Jazz dumped him. She reached to tousle his hair, her touch melting his stress. "I like it," she said with an approving eye. "More professional physician, less shaggy playboy." She sat back in her seat, an angel in pale chiffon. "Very mature, especially in that Armani suit." Her mouth squirmed with a smile. "And far less dangerous."

He grinned. "I kind of miss 'dangerous,' but 'mature' is a definite plus since juvenile behavior is my hallmark, right?"

"Only on the surface," she said with a look of affection that warmed him from the inside out. She tapped a finger to her heart. "In here, you're a changed man, Dr. Cunningham."

His grin faded to soft. "Only because of you, Angel Eyes." Emotion thickened the walls of his throat, reminding him how lucky he was to have Shannon as a friend. Soft, kind, supportive, beautiful, and brilliant. He took in the wispy strays of strawberry gold from an elegant and graceful twisty bun, noted the tenderness in eyes soft with affection, and was certain he'd never met a more angelic being. Her creamy complexion glowed in the dim lighting of the streetlamp, and he could no more stop his gaze from trailing down the modest bodice of her dusky pink dress than he could stop the slow thud of his heart. To him, she was purity personified, creating an unsettling tug-of-war between cherishing her as a friend and wanting her as a woman. "Have I told you yet how mind-blowingly beautiful you look tonight, Teach?"

A soft blush settled in those petal-soft cheeks. "At least five times," she said with an adorable grimace, "but you haven't convinced me yet, so I'd save those compliments for when they count—with Jasmine."

"Well, if I can't convince you, there'll be plenty of guys gawking inside who will, kiddo, so get ready." He got out of the car and strode around to open Shannon's door, surprised as always at how petite she was, even in heels. Placing a protective palm to the small of her back, he guided her toward the elevator. "You should have let me drop you off at the door," he groused, wishing he wasn't so paranoid about valet parking. "You look too classy to be hoofing it to the hotel."

Her soft chuckle sounded like music. "I don't mind, truly. Especially since I'm wearing sensible heels instead of stilettos."

His laughter filled the tiny elevator. "Thank you, God," he said with a devious wink.

By the time he ushered her into the lavish Viennese Ballroom of the luxurious Mansion on Forsythe Park Hotel, he was keyed to the max again. The thought of how close he was to making Jazz his pumped equal mixtures of adrenalin and hope through his veins. Because he was close—he could feel it. And he could see it in Jazz's eyes every time he met her for coffee or the occasional friendly dinner to discuss her romantic woes with the intern. It had been months in the making, but they had forged a bond Sam had never achieved in all the time he and Jazz had dated. A bond firmly anchored by his initial declaration that *she* was the woman he loved per Shannon's suggestion, and the one he was willing to wait for, completely forsaking all others. A solid-gold suggestion to be sure, allowing Jazz the comfort of a close friendship with Sam minus the usual stirring of jealousy over other women he'd dated.

Until tonight.

A slow grin eased across his lips as he escorted Shannon through the sea of linen-clad tables, each resplendent with calla lily centerpieces and candlelight flickering over crystal and china. No, tonight was the night he hoped his friendship with Shannon might spark a little bit of the green-eyed monster in his green-eyed beauty. Oh, Jazz knew Shannon was his friend all right, but she had no idea how close they were, which is why he'd asked Shannon to go with him to the banquet tonight.

"You mean like a *date*?" Shannon had said, her voice little more than a squeak.

"*Not* a date," he'd emphasized, "as friends. So you can lend me moral support when Jazz shows up with Bozo."

"Oh, I see. And possibly making her jealous when you show up with another woman?" Those "angel eyes" had narrowed as she folded her arms, brows arched in a schoolmarm scold.

But he'd just given her that little-boy grin that always seemed to breach her defenses, and she'd caved as usual. "Admit it, Shan, it's perfect. Jazz knows I'm committed to her because I've given up dating other women. But it can't hurt to tweak a little jealousy when she sees me dancing and laughing with my new best friend, right?" He winked. "Especially my very beautiful, very sexy, very bright best friend."

His words had gorged her cheeks with blood, and he hadn't been able to resist a hug, tugging her close to deposit a kiss to her head. "You are so adorable, you know that? Hands-down the sweetest, most innocent woman I have ever met."

Which is why she was absolutely perfect as his date tonight. With an easy smile, he guided her to her family's table at the back of the room, where Cat was wildly waving a napkin. Jazz had already lost one man to a "prude" of a friend when Jack broke it off to marry Lacey, so it only stood to reason that Shannon—Lacey's equally spiritual sister-in-law—would threaten her too.

If Jazz cares at all.

And that was what Sam planned to find out tonight, hopefully hooking her back into a relationship with him once and for all.

"What took you so long, Ham?" Jack said when Sam seated Shannon at a table with Jack and Lacey, Jack's mom and Lacey's father, Cat and her date, and Jack's cousin Matt and his wife, Nicki. "You almost missed the first course."

Extending greetings to the ladies and handshakes to the men, Sam took the last seat between Shannon and Jack. Smile faltering, he bent close to Jack to explain his delay, voice low while Shannon chatted with her mother and Dr. Carmichael. "Sorry to run late, man, but I got a call on Sandi Borgens," he said quietly, quickly taking a sip of his water.

Jack's brows dipped. "I thought Sims was on call this weekend, not you." His voice dropped an octave, the thread of concern in his tone matching Sam's. "Everything okay?"

"Yeah, for now. But the little sweetheart had a relapse, so I wanted to check it out and talk to her parents."

Jack cuffed Sam's shoulder while Lacey chatted with Cat and her date, Chase Griffin. "You're a good doc, Ham."

Heat crawled up the back of Sam's neck as waiters delivered their salads, and issuing his thanks to the staff, he deflected Jack's praise with a cocky flash of teeth. "Yeah, well let's hope it's enough to kick your butt tonight, O'Bryen," he quipped, referencing the "Rookie Pediatrician of the Year" award they were both up for.

Which wasn't the obsession it had been before, Sam suddenly realized as he harpooned a cherry tomato, pretty much blowing him away. At one time winning meant everything, but since his countless sessions with Shannon, it now paled in comparison to winning at love. The deep-down, bottom-line kind of love that lasted a lifetime. "Love everlasting," Shannon had called it, but she always tacked God onto it, which Sam wasn't inclined to do.

At least, not yet.

"If Wilson doesn't kick our butts first," Jack responded with a stab at an olive, his casual attitude about winning as surprising as Sam's. He and Jack had been killer competitors throughout residency, Sam's drive to win meeting its match in the nose-to-the-grindstone resident who was now one of his best friends. Even *after* Jack stole Sam's crown as Memorial's heartthrob their final year.

Along with my girl.

But Sam wasn't one to hold a grudge, especially against Jack, a good friend he flat-out liked and respected more than most men he knew. And like Shannon so wisely pointed out, it was Jack's involvement with Jasmine after Sam blew it that forced Sam to finally see the error of his ways—never a bad thing.

Love seeketh not its own.

It does not behave itself unseemly.

Jack's mom, Tess, leaned forward with a bright smile. "So, Sam, good luck tonight."

"Gee, thanks, Mom," Jack said in a mock wounded tone. "Appreciate the support."

Affection glowed in Tess O'Bryen's face. "Aw, sweetheart, you'll always be a winner to me."

A low chuckle rolled from the lips of Jack's cousin, Matt Ball. "Yeah, the Mommy's Boy Award."

Jack grinned, finger-shooting a crumb at Matt from his half-eaten roll. "Better than being a loser, Ball."

"You're a winner to me, too, Jack," Cat piped up, a bit of the devil gleaming in blue eyes so like Shannon's and yet so different. "Except at shrimping and crabbing, of course, where I will always be queen."

"'Queen of Crabbing?'" Cat's date said with a lift of sandy brows, a laid-back guy who turned out to be Jack's pastor and best friend as well as a friend of the family. He chewed his salad in a leisurely manner, broad shoulders and hard-chiseled features more reminiscent of a bodyguard than a minister. He tweaked the back of Cat's neck with a lazy smile. "Now there's a crown that fits with all the crabbing you do at volleyball whenever you lose."

Jack grinned, finger-shooting another crumb at Cat. "Or when I decimate her in fishing tournaments."

"Or when it's her week for dishes," Shannon volunteered with a flutter of lashes, her love for her sister evident from the sparkle of tease in her eyes.

Cat's jaw sagged in an open-mouthed smile, the spark of trouble in her gaze leaving no doubt as to which twin was the handful. "Even you, Shan?" she said with a true flair for drama, hand splayed to the bodice of a red dress that hinted at far more cleavage than Shannon ever displayed. "I'm wounded—you're supposed to defend me to the bitter end."

"I do, Catfish," Shannon said with a sweet look of sincerity as only she could. "When Jack says you're a big, fat pain, I tell him straight out that you are *not* fat."

Sam laughed along with the others, soaking up the playful banter of family like a parched wasteland thirsting for rain. Jack was one of the luckiest guys around, in Sam's opinion, with the incredible family and friends that he had. But at least Sam was gaining ground with Shannon as his friend.

And soon, God willing, Jasmine as his wife.

His mind stilled despite the chatter and clink of silverware. *God willing?* The random thought caught him by surprise, making him uneasy over the notion that Shannon might be making more headway than he thought. Shaking the feeling off, he zeroed in on Lacey's dad, the notorious Dr. Snark of Memorial, of whom he and every other intern had steered clear. "Congratulations, Dr. Carmichael," he said across the table, "for your nomination as Physician Philanthropist of the Year. That's quite an honor, sir."

Memorial's chief cardiac surgeon and Shannon's neighbor glanced up with a polite smile, his manner far more amenable than his cranky reputation warranted. But according to Jack, Ben Carmichael was a new man with a newfound faith, something that totally intrigued Sam in light of his own recent overhaul at Shannon's hand.

Taking a drink of his water, Dr. Carmichael assessed Sam through hazel eyes that held a humility he hadn't expected. "It is, Sam, and please, call me Ben. But I have to admit, for a man who seldom gave of himself philanthropically until the last year, the idea of an award makes me more than a little uncomfortable."

"Oh, poo," Tess O'Bryen said, giving her neighbor's arm a quick squeeze. "Ben's given of his time and services to the less fortunate for years now, Sam, culminating in an eight-month medical mission leave this last year." She launched into a thorough rundown of Dr. Carmichael's achievements that quickly caught the ear of Chase Griffin, whose questions prompted a conversation on the other side of the table.

Shannon leaned close to Sam. "Mom claims they're just neighbors and friends," she whispered, "but Cat and I think there's more to it than that, thus the staunch defense."

"Interesting." Sam observed the body language between Tess and Ben, the idea of Jack's mother involved with Lacey's father intriguing, to say the least.

By the time dessert had been served and awards had been won—including Rookie Pediatrician to Wilson and Physician Philanthropist to Ben—Sam was like one of the family. Seldom had he felt so included and at peace as he did sitting next to Shannon, thriving on being part of the camaraderie they all shared. So much so, he'd almost forgotten about Jazz after the dancing began, enjoying a private moment with Shannon while everyone at their table was out on the dance floor.

"Uh-oh, target approaching at nine o'clock." Shannon's soft alert congealed the last of Sam's English trifle in his throat, forcing it down along with a sudden knot of nerves.

Pretending not to notice Jasmine heading their way, Sam hooked a casual arm over Shannon's shoulder, bending close to whisper in her ear. "Do you have any idea just how much I appreciate you, Angel Eyes?"

When her cheeks bloomed bright red, he laughed out loud, massaging her shoulder before pressing a soft kiss to her head.

"Hey, Sam."

He and Shannon glanced up, his arm around Shannon's shoulder the stabilizer he needed. *Especially* with the luscious Jasmine Augustine mere inches away in a clingy dress that sapped all moisture from his mouth. "Hey, Jazz." Sam rose, working hard at nonchalance as he fought the urge to tell her she was a knockout, which were always the first words off his tongue whenever he saw her dressed up. He gave Shannon's shoulder a squeeze. "You know Jack's sister Shannon, right?"

"Sure. Hey, Shannon—great dress."

"Thanks, Jasmine," she whispered softly, "I like yours too."

Turning back to Sam, Jasmine paused as if waiting for his approval, and Sam practically had to bite his tongue. One thing that had surfaced when he and Shannon talked was about the control she thought Jasmine held over him because he wanted her more than she wanted him. "A woman doesn't want a man she can control," Shannon said. "She wants a gentle man strong enough to stand up to her because that means he's strong enough to protect her, love her. Which means for the time being, Sam …" He remembered how she'd gently gripped his chin like he was some hyperactive kid whose attention she needed to corral. "You're going to have to refrain from giving Jazz her way—with your time, your attention, your attraction to her, and your compliments that she's so used to hearing."

"Watch me," he'd told her with the utmost confidence. But that had been before Jazz had come on to him in his apartment, *and* before the recent hint of longing in her eyes.

"I'm sorry you didn't win," she finally said, grazing his arm with perfectly manicured nails.

He shrugged. "Not a big deal." He smiled, features softening when his heart began a slow thud, acutely aware of what *was* a big deal—winning the heart of the woman he loved. "There are more important things in my life now," he said quietly, pulse picking up when he saw hope flare in her eyes.

Their song began to play, and memories hit Sam hard, taking him back to the best year of his life when Jazz was all his in the second year of residency. *Before* he blew it in the call room one night, when another nurse came on to him and Jazz found out.

"I hope you don't mind, but I thought it'd be fun to dance to our song again, so I requested it." Her gaze flitted to Shannon and back. "That is, if Shannon doesn't min—"

"Where's Derek?" Sam interrupted, suddenly feeling like a heel at the thought of leaving Shannon alone.

"He's not coming till ten, so I—"

"Absolutely no problem whatsoever." Shannon bolted to her feet so quickly, Sam had to steady her when she wobbled. "I need to visit the little girls' room anyway, so he's all yours, Jasmine."

"Perfect." Peeking up through sooty lashes, Jasmine twined her fingers through Sam's as Shannon turned toward the door.

"Hey, wait." Sam halted Shannon with his free hand, a crease of concern wedged between his brows. "You sure you don't mind?"

Reaching up, Shannon gave his cheek a gentle pat, her sweet smile at odds with the somber look in her eyes. "Come on, Doc," she whispered in his ear, this is what you've been waiting for, remember? I'll see you in a bit."

He watched her walk away and wondered why he suddenly felt so alone.

"Sam?" Jazz squeezed his fingers. "Ready?"

Shaking the feeling off, he turned to the woman of his dreams, struck all over again at just how beautiful she was. "Sure," he said with his trademark smile, leading her out on the floor.

I hope.

CHAPTER TWENTY-ONE

"You do realize it's killing me not to nibble your neck." Holding Tess at a respectable distance on the dance floor, Ben whispered through gritted teeth. His polite smile was more than a little forced in front of a sea of family, friends, and coworkers who thought he and Tess were only friends and neighbors.

With a gentle smile, Tess discreetly squeezed his hand, the pink glow in her face a perfect match for the wispy pale pink dress she wore. "Yes, just like it's killing me not to snuggle in and lay my head on your chest, Dr. Carmichael, but there's no sense in setting rumors afire before we're able to tell both of our families we're dating."

Smile askew, he issued a low grunt. "It's not rumors I want to set afire," he muttered, scorching her with a heated look that deepened the blush in her cheeks. He grinned when she actually distanced herself several inches despite his arm clamped to her waist.

Lips pursed in a tight smile, she narrowed her eyes to that adorable look of warning that always made Ben smile. "I know patience is a virtue you're not fond of, Dr. Doom, but we agreed to break our families in *slowly* to the idea of our engagement, did we not? First announcing we're dating at an official family get-together, then another in a few months to disclose the engagement? And since the soonest everyone could get together for a BBQ was next week, you may as well put your matches away, Doc, because there will be no fires until we say 'I do.'"

"What about smoke?" he said in a husky tone, his lidded gaze drifting to her lips and back, hoping some of that fire in her cheeks was coursing through her veins just like his.

Her lips tipped off-center. "No problem. I'll just have a nice, tall glass of ice water ready in case things get too hot." The smug smile on those beautiful lips confirmed she'd have no problem doing that, just like she'd done in the beginning of their friendship when she found him stinkin' drunk one night in his recliner.

"Might be worth it," he said, giving her a quick spin that coaxed a tiny squeal from her lips. He heard the catch of her breath when he dipped her back at the end of the song, lingering long enough for his gaze to burn into hers. "But I'll behave, Ms. O'Bryen, because you're definitely worth the wait." He swooshed her back up, and she thumped against his chest breathless, allowing several intimate seconds for his gaze to caress hers. "I love you, Teresa O'Bryen," he whispered, and it took everything in him to refrain from showing her just how much.

"Ditto, Ben Carmichael." And the proof was in her eyes.

Smiling, he guided her to the table with a hand to the small of her back, managing a quick caress of his thumb to her waist before seating her again.

"Goodness, I didn't think pastors could maneuver a dance floor so well, Rev." Cat smiled up at Chase as he pulled out her chair, her blue eyes sparkling while her strawberry blonde hair spilled over bare shoulders. "Left over from your days as a Navy Seal, no doubt, when danger required being quick on your feet."

"Still does," he said with a languid smile, draping his suit coat over the back before taking his seat. He reached for his iced tea. "Now more than ever."

Ben smiled, pretty sure that was true if Pastor Chase Griffin was interested in Tess's more spirited twin, the daring daughter who seemed to be straying from her spiritual roots, according to Tess. Ben's gaze ventured to where Jack was ushering Lacey back to the table, and his heart skipped a beat, still amazed at all God had done to heal his relationship with his daughter.

Lacey plopped into her chair, smiling up at Jack with the same adoration she'd shown when she was a teenager. "Have to give it to you, O'Bryen—you haven't stepped on my toes once since we've been married," she said, reminding Ben how Jack had trampled Lacey's feet at her junior prom. "And you've even picked up some pretty fancy moves."

Ben leaned close to Tess. "Taught him everything he knows," he said under his breath, grinning when she jolted after he tweaked her knee under the table.

"Yep, that's Jack—light on his feet." Jack's cousin Matt flicked Jack's head on the way to seating his wife, Nicki. "*And* in his head."

Jack lounged back in his chair with a lazy grin, arm looped over Lacey. "Yeah, Ball, that's why I have a medical degree and you spend your days teaching little boys how to sweat in a smelly gym."

"What can I say?" Reaching for his drink, Matt smiled as he offered a slight shrug. "When God handed out grace and athletics, you obviously had your nose in a book."

"Hey, Shan, where's your date?" Cat licked her spoon after finishing off the rest of her dessert.

"He's *not* my date," Shannon emphasized with a tinge of pink in her cheeks, "he's my friend." She glanced over her shoulder to where Sam was dancing with Randy Augustine's pretty daughter, and Ben thought Shannon's shoulders slumped the slightest bit. He tossed back the rest of his water, hoping Tess's softer twin wasn't falling for the likes of Cunningham, whose Romeo reputation at Memorial was well-known.

One song ended and another began, and Chase jumped up and rounded the table, tugging an open-mouthed Shannon to her feet. "Love this song, Shan. Let's dance."

Shannon balked, heels digging in while she clutched the back of her chair. "Chase, really, you don't have to do this."

"Of course I do—it's one of my faves." Not taking "no" for an answer, he steered Shannon onto the dance floor and into his arms, not far from where Sam Cunningham was on his third dance with Memorial's most popular nurse.

Lacey sighed as her gaze trailed after Shannon and Chase. "He is such a great guy."

Jack arched a brow, smile flat. "You do realize, Lace, that I'm still here, right? Listening to you brag on the guy you dated before me?"

Lacey reached up to graze Jack's mouth with a tender kiss. "You mean the one I *dumped* for you? Oh, you bet, big boy—I always know when you're around."

"Hey, where's Shan?" Sam returned to the table alone, sliding into his chair before upending his water.

"Dancing with Chase," Lacey said, glancing to where Chase and Shannon were laughing while he dipped her, "and I'm sure hoping it's the first of many because those two would be great together."

"Chase?" Sam squinted at the dance floor with a hint of a frown before zeroing in on Cat. "But I thought you and Chase—"

"Oh, bite your tongue, Doc," Cat said with a mock shudder. "I mean Chase is a great guy and great to look at, sure, but I'm afraid my taste doesn't run that pure."

"Unfortunately." Lacey delivered a wry smile.

"I'll second that." Jack raised his drink in a toast before taking a swig.

Cat jumped up when the band began another song. "Oh, man, I love this one! Come on, Doc." She tapped on Sam's shoulder while dancing in place. "This one's too good to waste."

"I'll second that." Matt pulled Nicki back up and followed Sam and Cat to the floor with Lacey and Jack right behind.

Face and posture nonchalant, Ben slowly reached under the tablecloth to clasp Tess's hand, taking advantage of the fact they were alone. "Have I told you lately just how over-the-top crazy I am about you, Ms. O'Bryen?" he said, leaning back while his free arm rested over the next chair.

She peeked up out of the corner of her eye, the dewy blush on her cheeks making her look like a woman far too young for him to date. "Uh … out on the dance floor?" Her smile shimmered with the peach gloss he just ached to taste.

"No, ma'am. That was a simple 'I love you.'" His thumb teased the inside of her palm. "This is certifiably, undeniably, put-me-in-a-padded-cell crazy over the only woman alive who can transform me into a total fool for love."

She squeezed his hand under the table, her response husky with affection. "Then no, Dr. Carmichael, you haven't told me lately," she said, blue eyes glowing misty with love, "but you certainly have shown it."

"Why, Ben Carmichael—I thought you weren't bringing a date."

Ben's body went to stone at the sound of the statement, all blood leaching from his face when he glanced over his shoulder. "Cynthia …" He sprang up from his seat, voice cracking like some pimple-faced kid fresh into puberty. *You're supposed to be in Libya …*

Tess swiveled to stare up at the woman Ben had dated prior to her—the one Tess referred to as "Dr. Barbie"—and heat roared into his face while his Adam's apple ducked in his throat. The *same* woman with whom he'd spent his last month in Libya, who'd wanted to pick up right where they'd left off before Tess.

She slid a perfectly manicured hand down the arm of his suit coat, the scent of her Poison perfume reminding him of the temptation she'd posed on the final stint of his medical mission trip. "I checked with your secretary, and she said you were flying solo, Ben, so I was disappointed to see you came with a date."

Flustered for one of the few times in his life, he actually stuttered, the sight of his colleague in a snug sequined dress with ample cleavage making his hands sweat. "This is not a d-date," he said quickly, waving a hand between him and Tess, pretty sure his stupid promise to keep their engagement a secret would trip him up. "Tess is Jack O'Bryen's mother and my neighbor."

Cynthia's face perked up. "Wonderful, then you owe me a dance."

Ben bit back a groan. "Sorry, Cynthia, but I'd rather not leave Tess alone." He turned to Tess, stomach lurching at the tight press of her smile. "Tess, you remember my colleague, Dr. Cynthia Andreyuk, don't you? You two met last summer."

Tess's smile was so bright, it made the candles on the table look dim. "Of course, nice to see you again."

Cynthia lasered Tess with a cool look, her lithe five-foot-nine in stiletto heels making Tess look like a little girl. "Ah, yes, you're the sweet neighbor who bakes brownies for Ben."

Bobbing her head, Tess patted Ben on the back like a bosom buddy. "Among other things or else the man would starve, wouldn't you, Ben?"

Ben absently loosened his collar with a finger, his grin as stiff as Tess's. *Yep, and something tells me I will again …*

Cynthia sidled close to ruffle her fingers through the hair at the back of his neck. "Oh, I don't know—we had some pretty long days in Libya as I recall, but we always managed to eat." Slipping him a seductive wink, she bumped his hip with her own. "Among other things."

Ben's heart stopped the moment Tess's body went stiff, her eyes dilating in apparent interest. "Libya?" she said with a rapt tip of her head. "You were in Libya?"

Cynthia hooked her arm to Ben's, and he froze. All words fused to his tongue while she smiled up at him as if they shared a secret.

A deadly secret.

One about to explode in his face.

"Oh, only for a month," Cynthia gushed, obviously caught up in the wonder of her very first medical mission trip. "But it was one of the most fulfilling experiences of my life."

"I'll bet." Tess's smile stretched so wide, Ben thought it might crack.

"So …" Cynthia pivoted to adjust the lapels of Ben's suit coat. "Come on, Ben," she said in a pouty tone, "how 'bout that dance?" She peered at Tess over a bronzed shoulder, her smile patronizing at best. "Your neighbor won't mind, will you, Tess?"

Ben gripped Cynthia's hands to remove them from his chest. "Cynthia, no—"

"Don't give it another thought, Ben, please." Tess snatched the chain strap of her evening bag from the back of her chair and slung it over her shoulder, jaw tight enough to snap. "I certainly don't intend to."

His stomach lurched as he reached for her hand. "Tess, wait—"

She jerked free, shoving her chair in so hard, the glasses teetered on the table. "He's all yours," she said with a quivering jut of her chin, constricting his gut when he saw a sheen of tears in her eyes. "For the rest of his miserable life."

CHAPTER TWENTY-TWO

"Hey, you're awfully quiet, Teach, or have I been talking your ear off?"

Shannon managed a smile as she glanced over at Sam while they waited at a red light. *Although* it wasn't hard to do given the way he'd been bubbling over since they'd gotten in the car—like a boy at Christmas who'd just scored the latest Sony PlayStation with five of his dream-list games. Her smile tipped as she patted one of her ears. "Nope, ears still here, so I must just be tired, although happily so after hearing such good news."

For Sam.

Not me.

The flash of his grin filled both the car and her heart as he veered onto the highway, from zero to sixty in under five seconds—both Sam *and* the car. A smile tickled at the edge of her lips.

"I've said it before, Shan, and I'll say it again—you missed your calling as a shrink or counselor, my friend, because every single thing you've told me to do has worked like a charm."

She expelled a quiet sigh. She should be happy—Sam's burgeoning romance with Jasmine was going as well as Princess Olivia's with the playboy, well on track for their "*Love Everlasting.*" Chest expanding with the need for more air, Shannon leaned back in the leather seat with a wry smile. "Charms imply magic, Doc. I prefer to think of it as prayers and a healthy dose of self respect."

His low chuckle vibrated like the chassis beneath them. "Well, whatever you want to call it, kiddo, it sure worked."

For one of us, at least. Resting her hand on the open window, Shannon closed her eyes. How she wished the balmy breeze that fluttered stray wisps of her hair could blow the malaise from her mind as well.

His fingers skimmed her arm, and warm chills followed in their wake, having little to do with the crisp air or rush of speed in a Vette on a highway. "And it's all due to you, Shan, the true 'Doctor Love.'" Flipping his blinker to exit the expressway, he shot another grin. "Hey, you could go in business as the Date Doctor! You know, like in the movie, *Hitch*?"

Her lips curved as she shook her head, eyes still closed while she rested against the seat. "No credentials, Doc. One really bad relationship doesn't exactly qualify on a resume. Besides," she said, opening her eyes to pin him with a look, "after you, I'm going back into hiding."

For good.

"Well, that's a crying shame, Teach, because you've got a real knack."

I know—falling for the wrong guys.

"I mean, if you'd told me two months ago that Jazz would hint at breaking up with Mr. Wonderful to come back to *me*" —he melted her with a crooked grin— "which is a first, by the way, since I'm the one who asked her to come back the last two times—I would have said you're nuts. And yet, here I am, the 'good friend' she says she can trust and rely on, getting positive vibes from the woman I love." He unleashed a soft exhale of air, the sound pure contentment. "She told me tonight she thinks she made a mistake dating the intern and wanted to know what I thought she should do."

Shannon's breath hitched in her throat. "What'd you tell her?" she whispered, half hoping he hadn't taken her advice to play it straight with integrity rather than swooping in for the kill.

Both his smile and tone were steady and calm. "Told her what you told me, Teach—that choosing a person to love for life is huge and one of the most important decisions she'll ever make. Said she needed to think about it long and hard, weighing his love for her against his love for himself. *And* that she needed to make darn sure it was a love that could weather life's storms and fickle feelings." He looked her way, a deep and serious respect glowing in his eyes. "Unconditional love, Shannon, like you taught me, where we sacrifice our needs for the sake of the person we care about, establishing a rock-solid love we can count on no matter what."

"A love everlasting," she whispered, the kind of love her soul had ached for with Eric. And the kind of love that was only rooted in faith.

"Yep." A twinkle lit in his eyes as he slapped on the blinker again when they approached her exit. "And then I quoted one of the smartest people I've ever met." He glanced her way to deliver a wink. "I said 'a love worth having is a love worth praying for,' so she needed to do that too."

Tears stung at the back of Shannon's lids.

"So, you see, Teach, *you* taught me about the kind of forever love I never even knew existed or had even seen before, and I'm pretty sure Jazz hasn't either." His chest rose and fell in a satisfied sigh. "Till now." Voice husky, he grazed her arm again. "I owe you my life, Shannon, in more ways than one, and I wish there was something I could do to express how grateful I am."

She angled toward him, displacing his fingers. "Just be happy, Sam," she whispered, unable to thwart the sheen of tears in her eyes, "that's all the thanks I need."

"Hey …" He reached to caress the side of her face with his thumb, dark brows pinched with concern. "What's wrong? This doesn't change anything between us, I promise. We'll always be friends, kiddo, so why the saltwater?"

Because … *we'll always be friends.*

She quickly swiped at her eyes, relieved when he pulled into her driveway where the darkness could hide the heat in her cheeks. "I guess I'm just worried about my mom," she said quietly, grateful it was the truth even if it wasn't all of it. She took the tissue he pulled out of his console. "Cat said Mom left early because she didn't feel well, asking Chase to give her a lift home since Jack drove his two-seater. But she's not answering her cell, so I suspect she forgot to recharge the battery again." Shannon dabbed at her eyes, a semblance of a smile resurfacing. "She calls herself a space cadet, which certainly fits when it comes to her phone." Drawing in a deep breath, Shannon released it again in a wavering sigh. "But Ben left right after that, promising to check on her, so hopefully she's okay."

"Yeah." Sam turned the car off and shifted to face her, reaching across to twine his fingers through hers. "Probably just a headache from the band—it was pretty loud tonight. Which is fine for us wild clubber types, but not for normal people." He squeezed her hand, his voice suddenly as serious as his eyes. "I treasure your friendship, Shannon," he said quietly, grazing her knuckles with his thumb, "and oddly enough, your prayers." He sagged back into his seat, breaking the clasp of their hands. "Because God knows I'm going to need a boatload to say no to Jazz if we get back together." He cut loose with a grunt. "Especially if I propose, *which* given this new morality kink you've introduced into my life, should be rather soon."

"It'll be worth it, Sam, I promise."

He assessed her beneath dark lashes. "Well, you've never lied to me yet, Angel Eyes, so I'm putting my money on you." He jagged a brow. "Unless, of course, gambling is off-limits in your world too?"

"No comment." A smile twitched on her lips as she gathered her purse and shawl.

He stilled her with a hand to her arm, the tenderness in his eyes warming her from the inside out. "As God is my witness, Shan, I've never met anyone as wholesome as you, not to mention a woman with such a pure heart."

She shook her head, blood broiling her cheeks. "Nobody has a 'pure heart,' Sam, least of all me."

"I don't buy it. Believe me, I've dated my fair share of liberated women, and after just months knowing you, I'm pretty sure you rank right at the top of the purity scale. And I'll even bet that moron you dated gave you plenty of grief for your commitment to stay pure, didn't he?"

"He did," she said quietly, too ashamed to admit that she'd failed in that commitment, at least not to this man she was hoping to nudge toward morality.

"See? That's what I mean—you're an anomaly in today's society—untainted and pure."

Her pulse stuttered along with her words. "Oh, Sam, no—"

"Strangely enough," he continued, cutting her off with a wink, "despite my proclivity for wild women, I've always been a sucker for 'pure,' so who knows?" One edge of his mouth crooked as he opened his door. "I just might like celibacy till marriage more than I think."

Shannon's heart pounded as he circled the car to open her door. *Tell him.*

He grinned. "And then again, maybe not, because it sure isn't going to be easy. But the way I figure it, Teach, is if you can do it, I can too." He helped her out and gave her a quick hug before walking her to the door. "And if all this works out the way I hope and Jazz and I *do* tie the knot someday, Jack may be my 'best man,' Shan, but when it comes to counselor and best friend? You'll always be my 'best woman.'"

She blinked.

He pressed a kiss to her forehead. Thanks for being my date tonight. It sure didn't hurt for Jazz to see me dancing with a hot babe and having fun, good friend or no."

He gave a wave on the way to his car, and she returned a half-hearted one of her own. She watched until his brake lights disappeared down the street before she slipped into the house, a cramp in her heart.

Yeah, best woman. She swiped at the tears springing to her eyes. *Wrong girl.*

CHAPTER TWENTY-THREE

Never thought I'd say this, but thank you, God, for that stupid hedge.

Dabbing a tissue to her swollen eyes, Tess rose from the chair she'd tucked in the shadows behind her patio, her hiding place for the last hour while she'd waited for Ben to go to bed. He'd banged on all her doors and phoned and texted nonstop, but she'd ignored it all. Including the last call and text over forty minutes ago, right before his backyard light went out, turning the stupid hedge into an insurmountable black wall.

Like my heart.

She'd been so upset, she'd driven home and gone straight to bed, feigning sleep when both Shannon and Cat had peeked in, never more grateful Davey had spent the night with Spence. She didn't want to talk to anybody right now, least of all the man who had just shattered her heart into a million pieces.

"We had some pretty long days in Libya as I recall, but we always managed to eat." Tess's eyelids weighted closed as she swayed on her feet. *"Among other things."*

Other things.

The stupid leak in her eyes started up again and she blew her nose hard, the earlier click of his slider lock indicating Ben was safely in bed and long gone.

"Just like me tomorrow morning," she muttered, her bags packed and stowed in her car while a note to the twins lay on the kitchen table.

Cat and Shan, I left early to spend a few days with Lynne Feuerstein at her Hilton Head beach house, probably till Tuesday. Spoke with her last night, and she needs a good friend right now—lots of heartache going on.

Tess fought the rise of more tears as she fisted the envelope that contained Ben's ring. *And it's all mine.*

I already called Davey to let him know, so if you could just pick him up from his overnight at Spence's and keep an eye on him for a few days, I'd really appreciate it. You can reach me on my cell. I promise it's charged. Love, Mom.

Releasing a shuddering sigh, she swiped at her eyes and marched down the driveway with purpose. She needed to get away to think and pray, and as a recent widow, Lynne had been begging her to come, so the timing was perfect.

Unlike Tess's love life.

With a quick glance at her watch, she peeked around the hedge, satisfied to see that Ben's Range Rover was obviously in the garage and all lights were out. *One o'clock.* She'd never gone over to his house this late because Ben was usually in bed early, even before he and Tess had gotten together. An image of the leggy Dr. Andreyuk standing in Ben's kitchen a year ago in a barely-there bikini suddenly surfaced, taunting her with a whole new take on being "in bed," and the waterworks started all over again.

"No!" She strode toward the wooden gate with shoulders back and head high. "I will not allow Ben Carmichael to do this to me," she hissed, resolve coursing through her veins as she unlatched the gate that was, thankfully, on the other side of the house from where Dr. Doom and everyone slept.

Dr. Doom. Tess unloaded another grunt. Now *there* was a nickname that certainly nailed it to the wall. "Just like I plan to do to you once I get my hands on you … you …middle-aged Romeo," she muttered, relieved that anger was finally chasing the tears away. But nails and walls would have to wait because she was in no frame of mind to confront Dr. Doom right now, not unless she was fond of manslaughter.

Which was a distinct possibility at the moment.

Tiptoeing to the corner of the house, she paused, surveying Ben's darkened backyard. Satisfied all was quiet, Tess inched her way to the slider door where Ben had installed an oversized mailbox last year. *Right* after Lacey left a bag of homemade cookies tied to the handle when Ben wasn't home. Poor, sweet Beau had snarfed the entire bag of cookies down before Ben could even stop him, puking them all over Ben's bed. Tess opened the mailbox with painstaking care, an evil smile sprouting on her lips at the memory.

Poor Ben.

Her mouth took a slant. She was tempted to go home and bake cookies just to do it all over again. The slant curved into a deliciously slow smile.

Laced with MiraLAX and ipecac.

"I thought you didn't like sneaking around?"

With a throat-cramping squeal, Tess vaulted at least three inches in the air while the envelope flew even higher, pretty darn sure she was going into cardiac arrest. "Are you deranged?" she shrieked, gaping at Ben as he nonchalantly rose from a lawn chair hidden in the bushes at the back of his yard. She slammed a palm to her chest, rib cage heaving so hard, she thought she might puke. Which could come in handy if he came close enough ... "Oh my gosh, what kind of crazy lunatic sits in the bushes in the middle of the night?"

"The same kind that stalks into a neighbor's yard at one in the morning, I guess," he said in a casual tone, strolling forward with hands in the pockets of his Gap pajama bottoms. If she wasn't so ticked, she would have rolled her eyes at the T-shirt Lacey gave him for Christmas that said, "When Hearts Break, I Fix 'Em."

Yeah? Well not this time, Doc.

He nodded to the envelope at her feet, a faint smile on his lips as he slowly approached. "What'd you bring me? Restraining order, lawsuit, or cyanide?"

She jutted her chin, shoulders squared for battle. "I guess you'll just have to find out after I leave." Spinning on her heel, she tossed a squinty-eyed glare over her shoulder as she strode toward the gate. "I'd say 'good night, Doc,' but I wouldn't mean it. And unlike some people I know, I don't lie."

Oh!

In one violent whoosh, the breath left her lungs when he pinned her to the wall of his house, biceps taut as he held her in place with a grim smile, not even breaking a sweat. Never would she imagine a middle-aged man could move that fast, but then Ben kept himself in great shape. She squirmed to break free. *For Dr. Barbie, no doubt.*

"You didn't really think I'd let you walk away, did you, Tess?" he said in a calm tone that held the slightest bit of an edge. "After camping out in the weeds to catch you on one of your infamous midnight treks?" His lips curved in a tight smile, eyes far more sober than the tease in his tone. "You are *so* predictable, Ms. O'Bryen."

Her brows slashed high. "Yeah? I'll-show-you-'predictable,' you … you … womanizing, two-timing, lower-than-dirt brute!" Thrashing beneath his iron grip, she reared up a knee, which he promptly disarmed with a knee of his own, butted tightly against hers to lock her in place.

"So, is this how it's going to be, then?" he said, finally showing some exertion with heavier breathing. "Being married to you? Running away instead of discussing things like a rational human being?"

"No!" she screamed, temper so fried, she didn't give a flying leap who heard. "Because newsflash, bucko—you're not *gonna* be married to me!"

"Wanna bet?" Ben jerked her from the wall and swept her up in his arms, carrying her bucking and hissing into his house. "We're going to talk, Tess, and Jack and Lacey stayed at the hotel, so you can scream, kick, hit, or soak me, but you're going to listen to my side of the story."

His arms were like a vise, blocking all resistance, and it took everything in her not to bite him on the shoulder. "You mean the story you failed to mention?"

Chest heaving, he dumped her on his white leather sectional without ceremony, riling her further when it bounced her like a trampoline. "Yes, and for this exact reason." He stood over her, hands on his hips and feet straddled, obviously ready to pounce if she even thought of bolting. "I was planning to tell you the night on the dock, but then you told me about your problem with jealousy, and I thought it was best to let sleeping dogs lie."

She singed him with a glare, arms slanted back on the seat of the sofa. "Sleeping dogs or sleeping wolves, Doc? Because I'm a little confused."

Squatting before her, he reached out, and she lurched back a full foot, arms rigid on the seat to spring up if he even tried to lay another finger on her. "Tess," he whispered, genuine hurt in his eyes, "look at you. I've only seen you like this one other time—when I took a swipe at Cam, and both times it was because of jealousy—your Achilles' heel, remember?"

The flow of blood in her veins collided with a dam of bitterness as hard as the truth that hit her right between the eyes.

Jealousy. That insidious little sin that took her down every single time. The blight on her soul that crippled her marriage to Adam, and now was trying to do the same with Ben. Her eyelids sank closed as her head lowered in shame.

"Tess," he said quietly, the touch of his hand causing water to swell beneath her lids, "that isn't the same woman who barged in my life and made me face the truth that set me free." His fingers entwined with hers, and against her will, tears slipped from her eyes. "The same woman who stole my heart without me ever having a say." He gave her hand a squeeze. "And the only woman who could ever—*ever*—possess me heart and soul."

Her face crumpled like a soggy Kleenex, and before the sob could quiver from her lips, he swallowed her up, holding her close while she wept in his arms. "I love you, Teresa Catherine O'Bryen, and as God is my witness, you are the only woman my lips have touched since I kissed you goodbye in the hall at Lacey's wedding." He pulled back, lifting her chin with his finger as he gave her a tender smile. "Other than my daughter."

She started blubbering all the more, sniveling through each of the five Kleenex Ben nudged in her hands. When the heaves tapered off, she sagged against his soggy chest, a mountain full of sodden tissues piled in her lap. "Anybody ever tell you that you have a real knack for inflicting guilt, Ben Carmichael?"

His low chuckle feathered her ear as he brushed a kiss to her cheek. "No, but I'd say that's the ultimate compliment, Ms. O'Bryen," he said with a gentle knead of her back, "because I definitely learned from the best."

CHAPTER TWENTY-FOUR

"Hey, Doc, we've missed you at Club 51."

Sam glanced up from his book and half-eaten dinner at Memorial's cafeteria to flash his trademark smile at Patty Rude and Annie Sturtevant, two of his favorite nurses on Peds. Appetite gone, he pushed his tray to the middle of the table while Patty sidled close to check out his plate of roast beef and mashed potatoes. She wrinkled her freckled nose. "And comfort food in the hospital café instead of happy hour at Rocks on the Roof?" Her palm immediately pressed to his forehead. "Are you feeling okay?"

Comfort food. For some reason Shannon's sweet face flashed in his mind, and closing his book, he shot a crooked grin, stretching both arms overhead to reveal a loosened tie and shirt beneath his white coat. "Actually, never better."

"And reading a book on a Friday night instead of clubbing?" Annie butted a hip to the table and picked up his book, scrutinizing it with a kink at the bridge of her nose. "*Wild at Heart.*" A sultry smile crossed her lips as she wiggled her brows. "Tell us something we don't know."

Patty snatched the book from Annie's hand. "Yeah, like where did 'Wild at Body' go the last few months, Dr. Cunningham?" She squinted at the cover. "Discovering the Secret of a Man's Soul,' eh?" She turned the book over. "Huh. Maybe I need to borrow this after you."

Annie chuckled as she ruffled the curls at the back of Sam's neck. "We already know the secret of Dr. Love's soul, don't we, Ham?" She leaned close to whisper in his ear. "Blonde hair, bedroom eyes, and a body that won't quit?"

Sam blinked, the sudden image of Shannon's sweet face taking him by complete surprise.

Patty slid into the opposite chair, sympathy soft in her gaze. "You got it bad for her, don't you, Sam?" she whispered.

He looked up with a half smile. "Is it that obvious?"

"Your *absence* is obvious," Annie stressed, taking the chair next to him. "When the number-one eligible guy at Memorial disappears from the social scene, it sets rumors abuzz." She laid a hand on Sam's arm. "And the rumor *is* you're biding your time, waiting for Jazz."

He leaned back with a mysterious smile. "Maybe."

"Well, if it is ..." Patty drawled, "a little birdie told us there's trouble in paradise, so you might want to give her a call soon, because I think she'll be needing a shoulder to cry on."

Annie pinched his arm. "Among other things," she said with a wink.

Sam grinned. "Thanks, ladies, I appreciate your support."

Expelling an exaggerated sigh, Patty rose while Annie followed suit. "If you weren't so hung up on Jazz, Dr. Love, I'd give you *way* more than support."

Sam forced a smile that felt plastic while Shannon's words circled in his brain.

"If you really love Jasmine, Sam, then love her honest and true and selfless, because that's the greatest love of all. And *commit to her alone, body and soul."*

His eyes had practically bulged. *"But I'll die!"* he'd argued, jaw distended over what Shannon wanted him to do.

"Feel this," she'd said, pressing his fingers to her wrist, *"do I feel dead to you?"*

"Gotta go, Sam." Annie broke into his thoughts. She leaned to give him a side hug. "But we'll be looking for new rumors soon, you hear?"

"Yeah," Sam said with a weary sigh after the two girls had left. He picked up his book and sighed. *But they won't be the kind you're wanting to hear.*

"Hey, I've been looking everywhere for you." Jack eased into

Patty's vacated chair with a grin. "Your light was on and your briefcase still there, so I knew you had to be around, but I sure didn't expect it to be here." He scanned the sterile "cough-a-teria" as Sam called it, nodding at a few colleagues who waved. "You hate this place, man, and on a Friday night too? Shouldn't you be out clubbing or breaking hearts somewhere?" Squinting, he reached across the table for Sam's book, eyes going wide. "Wow, dude, you sick or lose a bet with Shan or something?" He turned the book over to study the back. "This is a spiritual book."

Sam snatched it back, his smile wry. "I lost a lot of things when I started hanging out with your sister, bro, some of which were part and parcel for my Friday nights."

Jack slanted back in the chair with a grin that was way too broad. "Yeah, the kid has that effect on people, but I gotta give it to her—I never thought you'd be one of them."

Sam's mouth zagged off-center. "Me neither."

So …" Jack leaned in, elbows on the table. "I have a favor to ask."

"Sure you do." Sam tilted back in his chair with a knowing smile. "No other reason you'd be tracking me down on a Friday night with a wife like Lacey waiting at home."

Jack's grin was downright cocky. "Yeah, I know, but it's actually because of Lace that I need the favor."

"Shoot." Crossing his arms, Sam studied one of the few men he respected in life when it came to faith and family.

Jack absently scrubbed the back of his head. "Lace is pretty stressed right now because she's got this cock-eyed notion she won't be able to have kids."

A frown creased above Sam's nose. "Why would she think that? You just got married."

"I know." A tinge of color bled up Jack's neck as he averted his gaze. "But we've been trying since the honeymoon, and the longer it takes, the more" —he cleared his throat— "well, 'focused' she becomes, if you get my drift, almost like she's got a one-track mind."

Sam grunted, lips swerving into a wry smile. "Doesn't sound like a problem to me, dude, especially since your sister has clipped my wings."

"Trust me, man, that's not the problem," Jack said with a lovesick grin that almost made Sam jealous.

What would it be like to love a woman that much?

Jack's smile dimmed somewhat, and Sam homed in, noting the deep concern in his friend's tone. "I'm worried about her, Sam, because I don't want to see her hurt, you know? But the more we try and fail, the more stressed she becomes, which just eats me up alive. So I was thinking that maybe we need to get away for a while, a second honeymoon of sorts where we can relax and—"

"Make babies?" Sam supplied, wondering why on earth something like that could set off a stupid twinge of envy in his gut.

Jack's sigh ruffled the crumpled napkin on Sam's tray. "Yeah, God willing, hopefully priming the pump for even more babies. At least, that's our prayer."

God willing. A smile automatically tilted Sam's lips over an expression Shannon used all the time. "So, how can I help, Jack? Since you're doing all the heavy lifting?"

Relief skimmed across his friend's face along with a grateful grin. "Can you fill in for me at Camp Hope this week? I know it's short notice, but Amy Tyner in X-ray booked a suite at a couples' resort in the Bahamas for her and her boyfriend, and the jerk dumped her. So she loses a hefty deposit if she doesn't use it. She asked me if I knew anybody who could take it off her hands, and since Augustine okayed switching my vacation in late August to this Wednesday through Monday of next week, I jumped on it. So all I need is for you to cover Camp Hope."

"Consider it done, my friend," Sam said with a smile, "and may I say I find it highly suspect that the married couple won out on this one."

Jack rose to his feet, a cheesy grin in play. "Yep, the wealth of the wicked is reserved for the righteous, my friend, so you listen real good when my sister speaks, you hear?"

"Don't have to worry about that," Sam said with a mock scowl. "As far as I'm concerned, your sister is E.F. Hutton, so trust me—when that woman speaks, I listen."

"Good to hear." Jack shoved in his chair. "Can't tell you how much I appreciate this, man, really, and I'll return the favor, I promise."

Sam's mouth hooked. "Naw—just name a kid after me, O'Bryen, because Samuel means 'heard by God,' according to your sister, so it looks like He's answered your prayer. The one about me filling in for you at the camp, that is." He winked as he picked his book back up. "You're on your own for the other."

"Thanks, Sam." Jack paused, resting his hands on the back of the chair. "I know I ask you this every week and every week you say no, but if you're ever interested in going to church with Lace and me early on Saturday nights, just say the word, okay?" He grinned. "And I'll even sweeten the pot if you do, buying you a Cold Stone smoothie every afternoon for a week." He tapped the chair with both palms. "See you, Sam, and thanks again."

Jack turned to go, and Sam huffed out a sigh. "Hey—you still play volleyball at your church on Saturday nights?"

Pivoting slowly, Jack cocked his head. "Yeah, once or twice a month, and this Saturday night, in fact. Why? You looking for exercise?"

"Maybe. I told Shannon I might try it one of these days. What time?"

"Seven, after the service, with pizza after the game." Jack went completely still, as if holding his breath.

Sam nodded. "Thanks, man. No guarantees, but I'll keep it in mind."

"Sure thing, Ham." Jack raised a palm in a wave and headed for the exit.

"Oh, and, Jack?"

Jack spun around, the look of hope in his eyes enough to make Sam laugh out loud. "Yeah?"

"*If* I do?" He grinned as he picked up his book with a shake of his head, wondering what on earth he was getting himself into. "Make it a strawberry mango on Monday."

CHAPTER TWENTY-FIVE

"Give me a break, Lace. You've been married for all of—what? Ten months?" Cat popped the cork on her fishing rod over and over, emitting a loan groan when she missed a bite. "I mean I want to be an aunt as much as you want to be a mom, but these things take time." She tossed a peanut in the air and caught it with her mouth.

"Not always," Lacey said with a glum look, slouched deep in her Adirondack chair next to Cat and Shan as the three of them fished on the O'Bryen's dock. She breathed in the earthy scent of the marsh and the salty smell of the Skidaway River and sighed. "Your mom said she got pregnant with Jack on the honeymoon."

"Yeah, well that's Jack," Cat said, tone dry as she recast her line in the water. "A chronic overachiever. He probably negotiated with God on his due date."

Lacey popped her cork once to every three of Cat's, her interest in fishing as flat as her fertility at the moment. "Can't argue with you there. When I started dating your brother at sixteen, his idea of a fun date was studying at the library."

A soft chuckle drifted from Shannon's lips as she settled back in her chair, rod loose and expression calm, no nervous popping of the cork for her. She got a bite and quietly stood to her feet, hauling in a keeper like it was no big deal. Hooking the fish on her stringer, she dropped it back in the water and then took her time baiting her hook, her heavy haul of fish proof that patience paid off in fishing.

Lacey expelled a silent sigh. *And in having babies, too, no doubt.*

"How long have you been trying?" Shannon asked, casting

her line in a perfect arc over the water, her quiet skill in sports often overshadowed by Cat's hyper-competitive delivery.

Lacey's mouth compressed. "Since the honeymoon, and I've read that after a year of trying, you should see a fertility specialist, so we're almost there." She huffed out another sigh, the mournful sound of a loon in harmony with her own melancholy mood. "And I had high hopes for the Bahamas, but nothing happened."

"Nothing?" Cat whipped her rod up and recast her line with a soft whoosh, slipping Lacey an impish smile. "Well, *that's* your problem then, goof. Something has to 'happen' for *it* to 'happen.'" Her brows did a Groucho Marx. "Or didn't Jack learn that in med school?"

Lacey rolled her eyes and popped a peanut off Cat's head. "You are such a goober, you know that?" A secret smile skimmed across her lips as she popped her line. "Trust me, there was so much happening on that trip, we barely got any sleep."

"*Ewwwwww*, stop!" Cat put a hand over her ears. "I don't want to hear what you do with my brother."

Lacey grinned. "Hey, you brought it up, not me."

"You know, Lace," Shannon said, manner reflective, "you still have two more months in your first year, so don't count yourself out yet. And then fertility is different for every woman too. We know a teacher at school who said she always wanted five kids, but wasn't able to have even one till she was married for five years. Would you believe she now has her five kids—*each* five years apart?"

"Yikes," Cat said, working her lip while she reeled in her line. She shot Lacey a wink before she recast. "That poor woman will be a room mother for life."

Shan's smile was soft as she leaned to give Lacey's shoulder a squeeze. "Give it another few months, Lace, and we'll hit it hard in prayer, too, because we all know how important that is in the mix, okay?"

"Thanks, Shan." Lacey slipped Shannon a sideways smile, a sparkle in her tone that helped chase her gloomy mood away. "And speaking of prayer, you've obviously been making great headway with Sam because Jack says he's actually thinking about coming to a volleyball game one of these Saturday nights."

Shannon blinked. "Really? He didn't mention it, but knowing Sam's aversion to church, I'll believe it when I see it."

Cat actually stopped popping her line. "*Our* Dr. Love? In a church building? Wow, Shan, if he's even *thinking* about it, then you *have* made some progress."

"Yeah, we have," Shannon said quietly.

Lacey glanced her way. *Too quietly.* She zeroed in on the sudden slump of Shannon's shoulders and the way her rod remained still, not popping once while her gaze trailed into a sad stare over the water. Stomach lurching, Lacey laid a hand on her friend's arm, her voice as gentle as this woman she loved. "Shan?"

Shannon didn't answer, and Lacey leaned forward to peer into her face. That's all it took for a sheen of tears to glaze Shannon's eyes. Dropping her rod on the dock, Lacey shot up from her chair to give Shannon a tight hug. "Oh, honey, what's wrong?"

Cat froze, rod suspended as she glanced over her shoulder. "Shan?"

"I … I …" Voice quivering, Shannon calmly placed her rod on the dock and then crumpled into Lacey's arms, body heaving as her words choked from her throat.

Words Lacey had never wanted to hear.

"I … think I'm in love with him …" Shannon said, fluid and grief congesting her tone.

"Oh, Lord, no, *please*—" Cat's rod clattered onto the wood as she rushed to squat beside Lacey, hands trembling while she stroked Shannon's hair.

"Oh, honey, are you sure?" Lacey whispered, hoping against hope that it was just a crush and not something that would "crush" Shannon's spirit.

Shannon nodded as she pulled away, swiping her arm across her face to mop up the tears.

Furiously fumbling into the pocket of her jean shorts, Lacey handed Shannon a slightly used tissue, the one weepy benefit of possible infertility—she always had tissues on hand.

"Come on, Shan," Cat said with a plea in her eyes, "you've only been friends with the guy for a little over two months. How on earth can you be so sure you're in love?"

Shannon blew her nose hard, then rewadded and dabbed at her eyes, voice nasal. "Because s-suddenly the only time I'm h-happy anymore is when I'm with him, Cat, and when I'm not?" She hiccupped and sagged back in the chair, gaze wandering into another dead stare. "He's all I think about. I have no interest in food, my friends, my writing—"

A low groan scraped from Cat's throat as she slumped onto the dock, head in her hands. "Nooo, not your writing too! That's what happened with El Jerko."

Shannon grunted. "Yeah, I know, that's why I'm so sure I'm either in love with the idiot or well on my way."

Cat jumped up. "Oh, no—not if I have anything to say about it, sweet cheeks." Hands on her hips, she glared down at her sister. "You're either going to ditch this friendship first thing or cave on that stupid no-dating policy of yours, because you are not going to go through another heartbreaker like this—I can't take it!"

"*You* can't take it?" Lacey said a lift of her brows. "It was Shannon who lost a year of her life, Catfish, as I recall."

"Yeah, Carbuncle, and I suffered right along with her—*major.* After all, we share the same blood, the same DNA, the same brains—"

"The same sweet personality?" Lacey hiked a brow.

Cat's blue eyes thinned considerably, lips twitching in sparring mode. "Somebody's gotta bring up the rear in this family, Carmichael, between Doc Brilliant and Mother Teresa here, so I'm just doing my job."

"And an excellent one at that, Catherine Marie, I assure you, but must I remind you—*again*—that I am now an O'Bryen, not Carmichael *or* Carbuncle."

Cat squinted while she aimed a peanut at her best friend. "Sorry, Lace. You'll always be a crusty carbuncle to me, sister-in-law or no."

"*Mother Teresa??*" Shannon said in a hoarse voice, a hint of a smile in her tone as she lasered Cat with a look worthy of her twin. "I should be so lucky, then I'd be long gone from this mess I'm in, totally content in the arms of God."

"But you're in the arms of God *now*, Shan," Lacey said softly, hope pumping through her veins over the only thing that would get Shannon through. She ducked her head to peer up into her sister-in-law's red-rimmed eyes, peace suddenly flooding her soul. "I don't know if you're in love with Sam Cunningham or not, Shan, but I do know that God will get you through if you are. And you'll come out on the other side stronger, happier, and more blessed than you've ever been before, and we'll be right there beside you, cheering you on."

A smile trembled to Shannon's lips as she squeezed Lacey's hand. "Thanks, Lace. I do know that, and I can promise you it's the only thing that's keeping me afloat."

"Good," Cat said with a thrust of her chin, "because I'm getting ready to throw you a floatie, sis, and so help me, you're gonna take it or I'll make your life miserable."

"You mean more than now?" Shannon asked in an innocent tone, her serious expression causing Cat to go stock-still. "Gotcha," Shannon said with that sweet smile that Lacey loved, slipping off her chair into a squat next to her sister. "You are my other self, Catherine Marie," she whispered, her soggy look a mirror reflection of her sister's as she brushed a stray hair from Cat's face, "the best half of the whole."

Cat was a stoic, so seldom had Lacey ever seen tears in her eyes, but she saw them now, bright and shiny as she clung to her sister in a ferocious hug. "I love you, Shan, with everything in me," she whispered, "and so help me, God, I will gut any guy like a catfish who ever hurts you again, you got that?"

Shannon's gentle laughter drifted on the breeze like a breath of hope as she plopped down next to her sister. "And I may just let you, sweetie, although this one doesn't really deserve it." The smile faded from her face. "Friend or otherwise, the man's a keeper."

"So, keep him." Lacey joined them to sit on the dock, leaning back with palms braced to the wood and legs crossed at the ankles.

That certainly stirred Cat's pot, lighting sparks in her eyes. "No way, Lace. She needs to distance herself from Sam Cunningham as much as she can."

"Agreed," Lacey said quickly, "on the distance, not on how much."

"What do you mean?" Shannon said, head in a tilt.

"I mean, keep the friendship, Shan, but at arm's length." Lacey shifted to get more comfortable. "Which frankly, shouldn't be too hard once Sam's back with Jazz because trust me, the woman does *not* like other women in her man's life, friends or otherwise."

Cat pelted a peanut at Lacey's head. "Oh, great idea, Carbuncle—let's just keep her in the lion's den where the beast can eat her heart out."

Lacey stared Cat down. "*Not* if she has another lion to protect her," she emphasized with a smug look in Cat's direction before facing Shannon once again. "Which means, Shannon O'Bryen, that as much as I hate to admit it, I agree with Cat—you need to start dating again."

"You do?" Cat blinked several times, obviously not used to Lacey agreeing so readily. A slow grin lit up her features. "Well, of course she does!" She grabbed Shannon's hand with a giggle. "And I know just the guy to fix you up with too!"

"Oh, noooooo you don't," Shannon said. "You are *not* going to pawn Mrs. Brewer's son off on me, Catfish. *You're* the one she wants as a daughter-in-law, not me."

"Mrs. Brewer?" Lacey's gaze bounced from Cat to Shan.

"A cafeteria monitor at the school where we teach," Shan explained, attempting to scoot away from her sister.

Cat clamped on to Shannon's arm to prevent her escape. "Okay, okay, we'll send Horatio sailing."

Lacey's jaw dropped. "Horatio? A woman actually named her son *Horatio?*"

"After Horatio Hornblower," Cat said, smile shifting sideways, "one of her favorite heroes. *Which* actually fits pretty well because both Horatio and his mother are from a long line of horn-blowers." Cat tugged Shan back. "Then how 'bout that sweet guy at church? You know, the one who turns sixty shades of red whenever you and I come around?"

Shannon's smile was patient as she inched even closer to Lacey. "Yes, Russell Sternberg *is* sweet, but in case you haven't noticed, Catfish, the poor guy is shyer than I am, so I doubt there'd be much talking going on."

"Not necessarily a bad thing," Cat teased.

Lacey pelted Cat with a hailstorm of peanuts. "I swear, O'Bryen, somebody needs to put you in shackles till you grow up."

"Don't think Mom hasn't threatened," Shannon said, pushing several stray peanuts through the cracks in the dock before Cat could pop them in her mouth.

Lacey shook her head, wishing Cat could find a decent guy she actually liked who would help get her back on track. Expelling a wispy sigh, she refocused on Shannon. "Well, what about Chase?" she said, waiting for Shannon's reaction. "I think you two would be a good match."

"No way," Cat volunteered, finishing off the rest of the scattered peanuts. "He's too serious, too mature, and way too spiritual." She paused, nose in a scrunch. "Which come to think of it sounds pretty perfect for Shan. But unfortunately, ol' Pastor Chase hasn't shown much interest in anyone since you threw him over for Jack, Lace."

"That's not true," Lacey said with a niggle of guilt. "He dated Mary Preston, Katy Hendricks, and Wendi Kitsteiner after me."

Cat delivered a deadpan smile. "One date each does not qualify. Face it, Lace—you ruined the man for other women."

"I did not." Lacey's chin rose several degrees, along with her defenses. "I'll have you know that Chase specifically asked me about Shannon after Jack and I got engaged, wanting to know if she was seeing anyone."

Cat could have been a statue, her look of stun etched in stone. "You're kidding," she said, a definite hint of hurt in her tone.

"He must have meant Cat, not me." The shock in Shannon's voice was equal to Cat's.

"Nope." Lacey shook her head, actually encouraged that Cat seemed disappointed over Chase's interest in her sister. A good sign, indeed, when a godly man like Chase didn't completely turn the wild twin off. "He meant *you*, sweetie-pie, but when I told him that you were 'unequivocally against dating at this phase of your life,' which is what you drilled into my head, yes?"

Shannon nodded.

"I can unequivocally say he was not only concerned, he was downright disappointed."

"He was?" the twins said in stereo, a matched set with gaping mouths.

"Yes, he *was*." Lacey squeezed Shannon's hand. "He likes you, Shan. Didn't you see that when he asked you to dance at the awards banquet? He kept you laughing and talking through three songs, for crying out loud, till Dr. Love cut in."

"I thought he was just being nice." Cat ground a peanut into the wood with her thumb.

"So did I," Shannon whispered, face reflective. "I mean he's always taken time to talk and tease with me at volleyball, but then he does that with *all* of the girls."

"Not with me." Cat's quiet tone sounded more like Shannon than herself. Brushing peanut crumbs from her shorts, she hopped up and retrieved her fishing rod. "Lacey's right, Shan. Chase and you would be good together." She whipped her line into the water with a hard snap of her rod. "I mean, he's not my type, of course," she said as she popped her cork too quickly, "but that type is just perfect for you."

Lacey's heart cramped. *You, too, Catfish, if you would just open your eyes.*

"So, it's settled, then, right?" Cat glanced over her shoulder, homing in on Lacey. "Sister-in-law Dearest will handle setting you and the pastor up, right, Lace?"

"Right." Lacey ducked to assess Shannon's expression. "If it's okay with Shan."

A weary sigh drifted from Shannon's lips as she stood to her feet. "Sure, Lace, why not? There aren't many men around who could get me to go out, but Chase is definitely one, so if he's game, I guess I am too."

"Great!" Lacey jumped up to give Shannon a hug. "You won't be sorry, Shan, I promise," she whispered as Cat slashed her line hard through the air, sinking Lacey's stomach along with her hook.

But something tells me Cat might be …

CHAPTER TWENTY-SIX

"Oh, goody, just what we need—another hot dog on the boy's team!" Cat unleashed a mock groan, bobbling a volleyball as Sam strolled into the gym of Hope Church, the smell of fresh varnish and old sneakers taking him back. She grinned, the lust of competition shining in her eyes when she pelted him with the ball. "Jack says you went to nationals in college, hotshot."

Sam caught the ball in split-second time, returning Cat's grin with a cocky one of his own while Jack, Lacey, Shan, and Chase broke from a group of people to join her, their welcoming smiles making him feel right at home. "Yeah, but you'll be happy to know we blew it in the semi-finals, so you can lower that pedestal a few feet."

"Or dig a hole deep enough for both *it* and you," Cat said with an evil smile, giving Sam's cheek a pinch, "when the girls bury y'all."

"In your dreams, Catfish." Jack looped an arm over Sam's shoulder, relieving him of the volleyball. "In fact, in a show of mercy, I think we should go with mixed teams tonight rather than guys against the girls, don't you, Rev?"

Chase ambled forward with a smile and hand extended in greeting. "No comment," he said with an easy grin, his grip firm as he shook Sam's hand. "Welcome, Sam. It's good to see you again. I'm the associate pastor here at Hope Church, and at the moment" —he tweaked Cat's neck, causing her to scrunch her shoulders in a giggle— "the buffer between Jack and his volatile sister."

Cat slapped him away. "I am *not* volatile," she said with a pert thrust of her chin, amazing Sam as always that two women who looked so much alike could be so very different. "I'm what most people would call spirited."

Jack chuckled as he fired the ball at his "spirited" sister. "And you don't want to know what I call her." He left Sam to hook Cat's waist, giving her an affectionate squeeze. "Trust me, Catfish. Dr. Jock here was on a variety of scholarships in college, not the least of which was volleyball."

"Good grief, Doc," Shannon said, giving Sam a side hug. The pretend scowl on her face came off more adorable than threatening. "Are there any sports you *don't* do well?"

He flashed a grin. "Come on, Shan, I'm a 'player,' remember?" Draping his arm over her shoulder, he bumped her hip with his own. "It's what I do."

Two wins and one loss later, Sam was genuinely surprised how much he was enjoying himself. After sparring with Cat some more, Jack had introduced Sam to the rest of the players, which Chase insisted on dividing into mixed teams of guys and girls.

"To eliminate murder and mayhem in a church gymnasium," Chase said, eliciting groans from the more athletic female contingent like Cat and several others, who wanted to take the guys head-on. Sam's gaze had softened when it landed on Shannon, who simply smiled and chatted with two girls while calmly awaiting her team assignment.

All in all, it was a fun evening of tough competition from the girls, confirming Sam's suspicion that there weren't many sports Shannon and Cat didn't do well in either. The two of them were a finely tuned spiking machine, which added yet another layer of respect to Sam's already high opinion of Jack's sisters.

The pizza after the game was great, and Sam never even missed the beer he always had with it. He was having too much fun talking trash and sports with Jack and Chase or flirting with the girls to notice that this wasn't the usual sports-bar gathering he was used to. So when the pizza was gone and several impromptu games of basketball were over, Sam realized he didn't want the evening to end. And there was nobody he'd rather continue it with than his new best friend. Seeking Shannon out, he watched as she wiped down the patio picnic tables with another girl, reaching across with a wide stretch. And then like a spiked ball out of the blue, she caught him off-guard with a flash of attraction so strong, his gaze roamed from her snug-fitting shorts down her beautiful legs before he was even aware.

"So, you coming back, I hope?" Chase asked, and Sam's gaze jerked back, heat ringing the collar of his Memorial T-shirt.

"Are you kidding? Athletic dominance and free pizza?" He offered a handshake, suddenly aware Chase Griffin was one of the few pastors he actually liked. "How can I resist?"

Chase slapped him on the back. "Was hoping you'd say that, Sam, although I suspect that killer spike of yours will up my humility a tad."

"Join the club, Rev." Sam scratched the back of his neck, smile sheepish. "Jack says you've got a pretty mean spike as well, spiritually speaking, that is."

"Maybe." The smile in Chase's eyes tempered somewhat, replaced by a scrutiny that made Sam squirm inside like he'd just missed a free ball. "If you're looking for deeper meaning in your life."

Sam laughed. "Uh, more like a deeper relationship, Rev, because Shannon's convinced me I'm going to need all the help I can get to land the girl that I love."

Chase nodded slowly, hands parked on his hips. "Jasmine, right? Jack mentioned you've been interested in her for years now."

Sam issued a good-natured grunt. "Yeah, especially after Jack stole her away from me." He nodded toward Lacey and Jack heading their way along with Shannon and Cat. "But the gods smiled on me when Lacey came along, knocking Jack out of the picture for good, so thanks to Shan's sound advice, I'm almost home free."

"God," Chase said with a faint smile.

Sam paused. "Excuse me?"

"God smiled on you, singular, not plural," Chase said with

a friendly cuff of Sam's shoulder. "And I'll be happy to help anyway I can, Sam, so if you ever need to talk, just give me a call."

"Thanks." *I think.* Sam quickly turned his attention to Jack. "It was a great evening, Jack, so thanks for inviting me."

"Which time?" Jack said with a grin, arm slung loosely over Lacey's shoulder. "Seriously, I'm glad you came, Ham—it's nice to compete against you again."

"Uh, he was on your team, Jack, remember?" Lacey pinched Jack's waist.

"Don't kid yourself, Lace. Ham is a die-hard competitor in everything he does, whether striving to be the best on a team or owning the best candy jar in the office."

Sam shrugged, offering a humble flash of teeth. "Can I help it if everybody likes Reese's miniatures better than Tootsie Roll Pops?"

"*Yes*," Jack said, flicking the back of Sam's head as he passed by. "Knowing you, you probably researched it to death. Come on, Lace. After the week I had, I'm about ready to drop, and I prefer it be in a bed rather than on a gym floor." He flopped a hand in the air on their way out the door. "So long, everyone."

Goodnights rang out across the gym as people slowly filtered out, leaving Sam and Chase to pull up the rear with Cat and Shannon. "Hey, Shan," Sam said while Chase locked up, "you and Cat feel like some ice cream?"

Cat exchanged glances with Shannon before she executed a perfect yawn. "Sorry, Sam, but I'm bushed, too, and I'm on early shift at camp tomorrow, so I need to head home. Rain check?"

"Sure thing," Sam said with an understanding smile, feeling a little guilty to be so relieved over having her sister to himself. He looped an arm to Shannon's waist and gave her a squeeze. "Looks like it's just you and me, Angel Eyes. Unless, of course, the Rev wants to tag along?" He glanced at Chase, who had just approached, praying he would say no.

"Where to?" Chase asked, giving Sam a strange feeling when the Rev exchanged looks with Shannon.

"I'm taking Shannon to get ice cream, if you're interested."

"Actually, Sam …" Shannon's voice lowered to a whisper as she turned away from Chase to address Sam with a pretty blush in her cheeks. "Chase and I were planning to go to Lulu's Chocolate Bar …"

"But you're welcome to join us if you want," Chase said quickly, the glance between him and Shannon like a blow to Sam's chest. *Not* to mention his ego.

Lulu's Chocolate Bar? The premiere date-night dessert venue in Savannah? The one he'd taken umpteen women to before he'd taken them "home"—his, not theirs?

"Absolutely," Shannon said in a rush, the gentle hand she laid on his arm burning right through along with the acid in his gut. "They have great ice cream, or so I've heard."

"Yeah, they do," he whispered, too stunned to even render a smile. *Shannon? On a date?* Sam grappled with what to say, how to act, the freeze in his brain as powerful as anything Lulu's could offer. *But … she gave up dating—isn't that what she'd told him once?*

As if reading his mind, she inched closer to Chase, the concern in her eyes making him feel like a heel. "I don't usually date, as you know, Sam, but when Chase tempted me with Lulu's …" She gave the Rev that sweet awkward smile that Sam absolutely loved, probably trying to lighten an embarrassing situation, then turned back to Sam with an uneasy shrug of her shoulders. "I figured I better take the opportunity because I've always wanted to go."

I would have taken you … Sam cleared his throat, taking a step back with a palm in the air. "Hey, no worries, Shan. I need to head home anyway, but you're going to love it, I promise."

"Are you sure you don't want to join us, Sam?" Grating her lip, Shannon offered a worried smile, her kind and nurturing nature obviously kicking in full force.

"Naw." He took a few more steps back, anxious to distance himself. "You two go and have a great time, and I'll call you tomorrow, okay?" Offering a wave, he made a beeline for his car.

"Sam?" Shannon's voice practically bled regret.

"Yeah?" He spun around with a strained smile, hands buried in his pockets.

"How about I treat you to Lulu's next week, to celebrate the progress you've made with Jazz?"

Jazz. The woman he loved and hoped to marry. He sucked in a sharp breath, then slowly expelled it again, wondering why the thought suddenly left him as cold as the ice cream at Lulu's.

"Sounds good," he said with another wave, his smile sad over the tenderness so innate in Shannon O'Bryen. A rare woman who worked diligently to spare people's feelings and tried so hard to make everyone happy. He slammed his car door, gunning the engine as if to vent, barely aware when the Vette squealed out of the lot.

A gentle soul, who would never, ever think of rocking the boat.

Sam downshifted with force, engine grinding in protest as he unleashed a harsh grunt.

Yeah? Then why in the name of friendship … was he suddenly so seasick?

CHAPTER TWENTY-SEVEN

Shannon winced when Sam squealed out of the parking lot, wishing she had told him about her date with Chase. He was her best friend, after all, and they told each other almost everything. But Chase had just called to ask her out this morning, and Shannon had never really expected Sam to show up at a church in the first place. Expelling a silent sigh, she faced Chase with a chew of her lip. "I'm really sorry, Chase. Sam is usually one of the most happy-go-lucky people you'll ever meet, so I don't know what got into him tonight."

"I do." Chase ushered her to his Ford Explorer with a gentle hand to her back.

She peeked at him out of the corner of her eye, not exactly sure what he meant. "You do?"

"Come on, Shannon—you're a very bright woman, which is one of the reasons I wanted to get to know you better." He glanced at her, eyes warm and his smile calm and caring, which immediately helped to settle the jitters in her stomach. "So I just expected you to see it. But my guess is you're too close to the situation to even suspect it." He opened the passenger side of his SUV and waited for her to get in before closing the door.

"Suspect what?" she said when he got in on the other side, the nerves in her middle rebelling again.

He started the car and looked over, his gentle eyes probing hers. "That Sam's attracted to you."

All blood whooshed from her face before it returned with a vengeance, broiling her cheeks. "Oh, Chase, you c-couldn't be m-more wrong," she whispered, her complexion flaming all the hotter over her stutter. She buffed her arms as if she were chilly, the butterflies in her tummy doing somersaults on a trampoline. "Sam and I are nothing but friends, and I assure you there is absolutely no attraction on his part." Teeth tugging the edge of her lip, she quickly looked out the window, barely seeing the blur of buildings passing by.

Please, Lord, don't let him ask about my attraction to Sam …

"You really don't see it, do you?" he said, tapping a CD into the player. The lively pulse of Matthew West's "Hello, My Name is Regret" filled the vehicle, mirroring her thoughts exactly.

Regret Sam had been a player.

Regret she'd been wounded by one.

Regret she was in love with a man she could never have.

"See what?" she whispered, not really sure she wanted to hear what he had to say.

He flipped on the blinker and glanced in the rear-view mirror before turning onto the highway, silent for several seconds until they were safely cruising in the far-right lane. "The way he looks at you, like a guy who's checking you out."

A nervous laugh tripped from her lips as she gave him a shaky smile. "Sam checks *every* female out, Chase—it's the player in him no matter how hard he tries to stifle it."

"Yeah, he does, I'll give you that, but you're his good friend, Shannon, and I've only seen one other guy check a friend out that way." He slid her a sideways look. "And that was Jack with Lacey."

She stared, her pulse slowing to a hard thud. *Impossible!* "No," she said with a firm shake of her head, "you couldn't be more wrong. The man spends hours and hours talking about Jasmine, desperate to win her back."

He gave a slow nod, eyes on the road. "I believe that, and I believe *Sam* believes that, but the look I saw in his eyes tonight when he found out you and I were dating?" He glanced her way, smile wary. "Call me gun-shy, but he looked and acted just like Jack did when I started dating Lacey—jealous."

Shannon peered out the window as she thought about what Chase was saying, pretty sure he was way off base. Drawing in a deep swell of air, she huffed it out again and faced him dead-on. "Well, if he was, Chase, it was only because Sam's very possessive and protective. He told me it was one of the problems he and Jasmine had in the past, his jealousy whenever another guy even looked her way. *Especially* if she looked back."

Yes, of course, that was it. Sam's possessive nature. Even with friends.

Expelling a cleansing sigh, Shannon relaxed against the headrest, her smile—and her stomach—finally tranquil. She was absolutely certain she wasn't sexy, striking, or sophisticated enough to *ever* be Sam Cunningham's type. "As close as Sam and I have gotten over the last three months, it's understandable he might be a little jealous of another guy spending time with his best friend." She shot Chase a lopsided smile. "*Particularly* when that best friend didn't tell him she'd nixed her no-dating policy to go out with her pastor."

Slapping his blinker on, Chase concentrated on exiting the highway, finally slowing for a red light before he returned her smile. "That would be a bit of a shock, I suppose." He gave her a little-boy grin that seemed so out-of-character for the solid and steady associate pastor. "I know it was for me." He reached to squeeze her hand. "Thanks for ditching your no-dating policy, Shannon. I've been wanting to go out with you for a long time."

"Since Lacey got back with Jack?" she said softly, her heart aching for the hurt he'd experienced in that situation, tough ex-Navy Seal or no. As Jack's best friend, he'd finally confided to Jack that losing Lacey had been difficult, but that he was certain God had a Lacey for him somewhere.

"Yeah." His profile sobered as he steered a corner, finally easing up to the curb on a fairly crowded street. He parked and turned off the car before shifting to face her. "I knew I wanted someone who took their faith seriously, with a moral code way above the norm, and trust me, Shannon, that's not easy to find." The streetlight shadowed his handsome face as he reached for her hand again, clasping it loosely on the console. "I had a pretty bad experience with a girlfriend when I was in the service. She was wild and free like so many of the women today, so now I steer clear of that type of girl, which is why someone like you is so appealing."

"And safe?" She tipped her head, delivering a teasing smile.

He squeezed her hand and let go, resting his on the console. "I hope so," he said quietly, his eyes suddenly sober. "If you don't mind, I'd like to ask a personal question about your relationship with Sam. Not because I'm nosey, mind you, but because I need to know upfront what I'm dealing with in a relationship with you."

"Ooo-kay …" she said slowly, her comfort level taking another dive.

"I'd like to know what your feelings for Sam are, if you don't mind."

"I told you, Chase, we're just friends."

"I know," he said with a quiet smile, "but I need to know how deep your feelings are for him, Shannon. Lacey told me the same thing in the beginning, but she was still in love with Jack, and I didn't know it." Sucking air through a tight smile, he threaded his fingers through short sandy hair. "If it's all the same with you, I'd rather not be blindsided this time, if you know what I mean."

"I do," she said softly, wishing she could say the same. Her unexpected attachment to Sam had blindsided her as well, pulling the rug out from under her heart.

He twined his fingers through hers, meeting her gaze with a sober one of his own. "So, tell me, Shannon—are your feelings for Sam deeper than friendship?"

She averted her gaze, swallowing a lump in her throat. "I think so."

Giving her palm a squeeze, he pulled his hand away and slowly exhaled. "I thought so," he said quietly, "so thank you for your honesty."

Heart lurching, she turned to face him, desperate to make him understand. She placed a hand on his arm. "I never meant for this to happen, Chase, I swear, and to be honest, I wish there was something I could do to change it."

"There is," he said with a patient smile. He gave her hand a gentle pat and got out of the car, peering in with gentle resolve etched in his face. "And we'll start with one of Lulu's decadent desserts and take it from there."

She gave him a wobbly smile when he opened her door. "You mean you still want to take me out? Even knowing how I feel about Sam?"

"Sure," he said with a slow grin, helping her out. "As long as I know where I stand going in, I'll just do what Sam did and become your good friend." He closed the door and slipped his fingers through hers once again, leading her to the quaint coffee-house storefront of Lulu's with a lazy smile. "Because friendship with you is something I definitely want, Shannon, and who knows? Maybe I can help you get over Sam too." He opened the door to Lulu's, and mouthwatering smells wrapped her in a delicious hug, rich and warm, like the relaxed feel of Chase's hand in her own. "But win or lose," he said with a smile that was rampant with tease, "it should be a whole lot of fun just watching Sam squirm."

CHAPTER TWENTY-EIGHT

Sam wasn't sure how long he'd been staring at Tara Hart's chart, hands poised over the keyboard, but so far he hadn't typed a thing. Granted, congenital heart disease wasn't something he wanted to dwell on, especially when it belonged to a sweet six-year-old girl, but even so, he had no business letting his mind wander.

For the zillionth time this week.

He closed the computer and sagged back in his chair, eyes closed while he rested his head. The scene with Shannon and Chase last Saturday night replayed in his brain like a bad video he couldn't get out of his mind.

"I don't usually date, as you know, Sam, but when Chase tempted me with Lulu's …"

Dating.

Temptation.

Weren't those things she should have mentioned to a best friend? He certainly would have and did, in fact, every single time they got together, so why didn't she?

Why do you care so much?

His pulse slowed to a crawl at the random thought. Why *do* I care so much, he wondered? Eyelids lifting, he dissected his reasons. Because he cared what happened to her, of course. Shannon was the best friend he'd ever had, man or woman, and he was very protective. He didn't want to see her get hurt. She was an innocent, a true rarity in today's world, sweet and trusting, especially with him since they'd gotten so close. And frankly, no one had ever trusted him like that before. He unleashed a grunt as he gouged fingers to the bridge of his nose.

Who was he kidding? *He'd* never trusted himself like that before. Not until Shannon. And not until the rock-solid faith she was slowly sowing into his life.

I need to apologize, he suddenly realized, staring at the Superman growth chart on his closed office door. *For acting like such a jerk.* There'd been no reason for his juvenile behavior. He cared deeply about Shannon and she deserved to be loved like he wanted to love Jazz, and Chase was actually perfect for her.

Clean cut.

No nonsense.

A pillar of faith, just like her.

Sam scowled, barely aware he was even doing it.

Okay, he was worried about her, so sue him. He pushed forward in his chair and flipped open his computer, grateful Chase was a stand-up guy who hopefully wouldn't take advantage of her. Sam's mouth crooked. Not that she'd let him. The woman was a wall of iron embedded with heels, untainted by the world.

His fingers hovered over the keyboard once again while his gaze wandered into another faraway stare. Which was one of the things he loved most about her, come to think of it. Her simplicity, her innocence, her morality—unspoiled and pure.

Unlike Jazz.

The thought was so out of left field, he actually blinked, downright ticked off for even thinking that way. Jazz was a modern woman, for pity's sake, just like he'd been a modern man, part of a society where anything goes. Pleasure-seekers all, yes, but searching for love in all the wrong places. And utterly blind to something Shannon had taught him well.

Love does not act improperly, is not selfish …

He sighed as his gaze veered off into another dead stare ...

Tap. Tap. Tap.

Sam looked up when Jack stuck his head in the door with a suspicious grin on his face. "Hey, buddy, your last appointment is here."

Sam's gaze darted to the clock on his wall and back, brows in a scrunch. "I don't have anymore appointments today."

Grinning, Jack pushed the door open, and Jasmine walked in. The scent of her Bombshell perfume was true to its name, all prior thoughts of anything else in his brain completely blown to bits.

"Oh, but you do, Dr. Cunningham," she said with a seductive smile, "and I'm afraid it's an emergency."

"Jazz …" Her name faded on his tongue as he rose to his feet, gaze traveling her body in natural reflex. Skin-tight jeans and a well-fitting white crop top made his mouth go dry, offering inviting peeks at a tanned and toned stomach. Attraction buzzed through his body like electricity, making it hard to concentrate. "This is a nice surprise …"

"I'm heading out, Ham." Jack gave him a knowing wink. "But I'm sure you can take it from here. Good night, Jazz."

She glanced over her shoulder, silky blonde hair trailing bronzed shoulders. "G'night, Jack, and thanks for the encouragement."

Jack waved and closed the door, and Jazz faced Sam again, a hint of timidity in her manner that he'd never seen before. "Hi," she said softly, teeth nibbling on those luscious lips that had once been his drug of choice.

"What encouragement?" He rounded his desk and perched on the front edge with a smile, arms crossed in a loose fold. "And I thought today was your day off—what are you doing here?"

She moved in close enough to make his pulse sprint when her body almost grazed his knees. "I came to see you, silly, since I haven't seen or heard from you in over a week …"

He blinked. *Had it really been that long?* He scratched the curls at the back of his head, heat creeping up his neck. "Sorry, Jazz, it's been pretty crazy at work …"

"Weekends too?" she whispered, the barest trace of hurt in her tone.

The heat converged in his face. "Yeah, I'm pretty slammed on weekends, too, unfortunately. I'm still mentoring and coaching inner-city basketball like before, but now I'm occasionally volunteering at Camp Hope—"

"That never stopped you before," she said softly, halting his pulse altogether when she idly smoothed the curls he'd rumpled at the nape of his neck. Her eyes were pools of concern, like the time she'd been insecure about her relationship with Jack. "At least not on Saturday nights as I recall …"

His shoulders lifted in an awkward shrug, smile sheepish. "You're going to laugh when I tell you this, I know, but Jack's been pestering me for months to go to his church, so I finally caved."

Her eyes grew. "*You* went to church?"

He grinned. "Well, not church *exactly*, but I played volleyball with the singles and young marrieds' group in the church gym, so you know Jack—it's only a matter of time till he gets me in the pews."

Jazz traced a gentle finger down his arm, her eyes following the motion rather than looking at him. "Was she there? Your new best friend?"

"Jack's sister?" Heart stammering, Sam sensed the first shred of jealousy he'd ever seen in Jasmine before—at least with him.

"Yeah." Her lashes flipped up as she stared at him with a tinge of apprehension. "Shannon, is it?"

He expelled a long wavering breath, hardly able to believe the shoe was finally on the other foot with the woman he loved. "Yeah, Shan was there. Why?"

She gave a little shrug, as if feigning indifference. "No reason. It's just that I thought you and I were friends, too, Sam, but I don't see you nearly as much as Shannon does."

There was a time when he would have teased her about being jealous, gloating that he could elicit a response out of her like she always did with him. But not anymore. Now his heart ached that he'd hurt her. Unleashing a heavy sigh, he drew her into a tight hug. "Jazz, you know I love you, both as a friend and as the only woman I've ever really wanted. But you belong to Derek right now, and I doubt he'd appreciate my spending so much time with you."

"I don't belong to Derek," she whispered.

The air swirled still in his lungs. Pulse pounding, he held her at arm's length. "What do you mean 'you don't belong to Derek'?"

"I mean I broke it off," she said with a shy chew of her lip, the sheen of hope in those green eyes shimmering with possibilities. "I finally figured out I'm in love with my old boyfriend." Caressing his jaw with her fingers, her eyes drifted closed as she grazed her lips against his.

The familiar taste of her triggered a rush of want so strong, he all but devoured her with a husky groan. "So help me, babe, I've waited forever to hear that," he whispered, blood pumping through his body at a ridiculous rate. He pulled away to cradle her face in his hands, hardly able to believe she was finally his. "Are you sure? Because there's no going back. You're the one I want, Jasmine, and this time I mean forever."

Tears brimmed in her eyes as she lunged, the depth of her kiss sending red-hot lava through his veins. "I'm sure, Sam, but if I wasn't, Jack's encouragement would have put me over the top."

"Yeah?" he said with a curious smile, tenderly brushing the hair from her face. "And what was that?"

"That the kind of love I was looking for was right under my nose, and if I didn't grab you, it would be the biggest loss of my life." Her lips curved in a tease. "After him, of course."

Sam grinned outright. "He said that?"

She nodded, skimming the side of his face with her fingers as her smile softened into awe. "He also said your love for me is so deep, it actually pushed you toward a faith that's transformed you into one of the finest men he knows and one he's proud to call a good friend."

A prick of moisture stung at the back of Sam's lids, catching him off-guard as he drew her close, burying his head in the crook of her neck. "He's right, you know, about my love for you, Jazz," he whispered, "but the true credit belongs to the power of faith." Shannon's image suddenly came to mind, and with it, a surge of gratitude swelled in his chest.

And a woman with a whole lot more of it than me.

CHAPTER TWENTY-NINE

"So, you forgive me for acting like a moron?" Sam glanced up as he retied his Nikes on the bench at the Tybee Island Pier and Pavilion, sweat glistening on a sculpted torso that put a lump in Shannon's throat.

"Of course I forgive you," she said, quickly diverting her gaze to the rolling azure waves as they lapped at Tybee's white-sugar shore. She took a drink of her water bottle and closed her eyes to breathe in the clean scent of the ocean. The sea breeze fluttered her ponytail and cooled the moisture on her skin, her sports tank damp from their six-mile run on the beach. "I planned to tell you all along, Sam, the next time I saw you, but uh … you kind of caught me off-guard." A smile squirmed at the edges of her mouth as she took another drink. "Didn't expect it to be at church."

"Yeah, I figured that was a factor." He grinned that lovable crooked grin as he upended his water, face shifted to the side so he could watch her while his Adam's apple glugged. Wiping his mouth with the side of his arm, he grinned and poured the remainder over his head, drowning his dark curls like a kid under a hose. "I think I caught God off-guard, too, since there weren't any bolts of lightning for me to dodge."

She grinned, wondering if she'd ever get past this melted, gushy feeling inside whenever she spied hints of the little boy in Sam. The one who had been so wounded and hurt, yet hid behind the fun-loving façade, never letting anybody know. The same one she always wanted to nurture and love.

And kiss?

"*Stay with me …*"

Heat swallowed her whole at the memory of that night in the car, how one kiss had so disarmed her in a span of a few seconds. Sam emanated a raw magnetism that even Eric hadn't possessed, shocking her that one man could have such a powerful effect. Battling a shiver, she took another drink, eyes closed as she drained the bottle straight up.

"Ready?"

Not really. "Yeah," she said with a toss of her empty bottle into the trash receptacle, falling in beside him as they strolled the long span of pier back to the beach.

"So …" He slowed his pace as always when he noticed her huffing to keep up. "Guess who paid me a visit at the office?"

Shannon's shoes slid on the sand when she ground to a stop on the pier. "*Jasmine?*"

He grinned and tugged on the bottom of her tank to keep her moving. "Yep."

"What did she want?" Shannon's voice was breathless, an odd mix of euphoria and fear.

His teeth flashed white against a perfect tan. "We're back together, Shan, for good."

She skidded to a dead halt, heart plummeting deeper than the ocean on either side of the pier. "That's … that's … incredible," she whispered, forcing the brightest smile she could manage considering the painful cramp in her heart. "You did it!"

"No, *you* did it." His eyes were tender as he gently buffed her arms with his palms.

"No, *God* did it, Sam," she whispered, unable to thwart the tears in her eyes.

His chiseled features melted into affection. "Through your amazing faith, Shan, and a boatload of prayer."

She tipped her head to stare up at him, so very proud of the man he'd become. "And your faith, too, my friend, not to mention your adherence to God's precepts."

The smile dissolved on his face as he cuffed the back of his neck. "Yeah, well about that." He continued walking, and she fell in step, her stomach suddenly as restless as the waves battering the sandy shore. "It's not going to be as easy as I thought," he said quietly, hands plunged in the pockets of his running shorts. He kept his gaze pinned to the weathered dock as if he were avoiding her eyes, his mood suddenly somber. "We've only been together two nights, Shan, but it's been a battle when I take her home. She wants to stay at my place or me at hers, but I told her we weren't going there this time, and naturally she threw a fit." He stared up at a blue sky scudded with clouds. "Which I really can't blame her, I guess, because we practically lived together before."

Shannon swallowed hard, a knot of jealousy wedging in her throat.

He huffed out a noisy sigh. "Not to mention she's the sexiest woman on the planet, and I've been without now for four months, practically a first since puberty."

Shannon wasn't prepared for the awful stab of pain that seared through her chest. *The sexiest woman on the planet …*

"But …" His mouth compressed, jaw sculpted in iron. "I told you once I'm not a quitter, Shannon, and that when it comes to self-control, I'm a wall of steel, so I'm not about to quit on the faith you've introduced me to no matter how tough Jazz makes it. And trust me, she's a master." He shook his head, a wry bent to his mouth. "Which means I need your prayers more than ever until I can get that woman to the altar."

That woman. The one he loved and planned to marry.

"You have them, Sam, you know that." She paused. "But I believe I can go it one better."

He peered at her out of the corner of his eye. "Yeah? How?"

She stopped to face him, holding out her hand. "Give me your word," she whispered.

His jaw tightened almost imperceptibly as he stared first at her hand, then up into her eyes. "That won't be necessary, Shan. I can do this."

"I know you can, Sam," she whispered, gaze fused to his. "I just want to help."

Hands on his hips, he glanced out over the water, as if trying to decide if it was worth it or not. He'd told her once that his mother had broken promises to him over and over before she'd deserted him forever. Which is why he always gave his word rather than a promise when it was something that truly mattered. Something forged in iron that he fully intended to keep, like he'd told her one evening at the onset of their friendship. "I've spent a lifetime restoring integrity to a name bonded in shame," he'd whispered, eyes lagging into a far-off stare, "so my word is at the core of who I am, Shan, and I will never, ever betray it like my mother betrayed me."

"Well now, see?" she had responded with a peaceful smile, "you and God have something in common then, Sam, because the Bible says, 'when God wanted to guarantee His promises, He gave His word, a rock-solid guarantee' because 'God cannot break His word.'"

"It says that?"

"It does," she'd answered with a grin and a playful pinch to his cheek. "So, like Father, like son, I guess."

He had grunted his doubt at the time, but Shannon could see his disbelief was on the wane. And now, here he stood before her on the pier, wrestling with a choice between lust and love. A man with one foot in the world and one in faith, not yet fully committed to the God who could provide the strength he would need. But Shannon could. Her heart thudded as slow and sure as the seconds dragging by. Through prayer and the bond of Sam's word.

But whoever keeps his word, in him truly is the love of God perfected.

He finally unleashed a noisy sigh and placed his hand in hers, giving it a firm shake. "You have my word," he said quietly, the sobriety in his eyes confirming it was a promise etched in stone from a man she could trust.

Her smile beamed brighter than the sun. "You won't regret this, Doc. I promise."

"Yeah?" He looped a loose arm over her shoulder, giving her a light squeeze. "I already do, kiddo. But if there's one thing I've learned about you in the short time we've been friends, Shannon

O'Bryen, is that *your* promises are true."

"Just like your word," she said with a grin, "which could very well be the first thing we've ever had in common."

"Naw, we both like basketball and miniature golf, right?" He pressed a random kiss to her head. "Which is only one of the gazillion reasons I love you, Angel Eyes."

Cheeks warm, she opted to change the subject. "So when do you plan to propose?" she asked, slipping from his hold to jog backwards in front of him.

He shrugged, hands back in his pockets. "As soon as I can, but we'll have to give her dad a little time to adjust before I put a ring on his daughter's hand."

"Does he like you, I hope?" She shaded her eyes as she squinted up, aligning her stride to his once again.

He grinned. "Come on, Shan, what's not to like?" He tweaked the back of her neck, scrunching her shoulders. "You're the only one who couldn't stand me."

A grunt tripped from her lips. "I find that hard to believe, with all the hearts you've trampled, Dr. Love."

"Ah … ah … ah, young lady, I did not trample. I carefully and gently transitioned from lover to friend with devoted diligence, which is why I remain friends with the women I've dated." He wrinkled his nose. "Well, most of them, anyway. So to answer your question, yes, Randy Augustine does like me. I mean, he hired me into his practice after all, so that speaks for itself, I guess. But I also think he feels a kinship because we were both in the foster system and had to work our way up."

"Well, that's certainly a plus. Do they go to church?"

Sam laughed. "I doubt it. Jazz is not exactly the religious type, and Augustine's on the links every Sunday morning."

"So bring Jasmine to church with us on Saturday night and stay for volleyball after," Shannon suggested. "You'll need a church to get married in, and Hope Church is one of the prettiest on the island."

"With you?" One thick, dark brow angled high. He shook his head. "Unfortunately, she's a little sensitive about you, Shan.

Frankly, if it were up to her, I wouldn't hang out with you at all."

Shannon's rib cage shrank, the thought of not seeing Sam on a regular basis suddenly bleeding the air from her lungs. "Maybe that's for the best," she whispered.

For both Jasmine and for me.

He halted so fast, she was already several steps ahead when he caught up at the entrance of the pier to brace his hands to her shoulders. "No way, Shan, we're buds, and Jazz is just going to have to accept that."

"Not after you get married," she said softly, knowing full well her friendship with Sam would have to come to an end. "Your wife's needs and desires come first, Sam, remember? If you were my husband, there's no way I'd want you hanging out with an old female friend."

He stared at her for several seconds, then expelled a heavy sigh and dropped his arms, continuing onto Tybrisa Street. "Well, then, we'll just have to become couple friends." He slid her a wary look while he placed a hand to her lower back, guiding her out of the path of a bike. "Speaking of which—how was your date with Chase?"

Her body automatically relaxed at mention of Chase, the man who'd offered to help her keep it together while Sam was pursuing Jazz. "Good." She slid into Sam's car when he opened the door, smiling at the memory of both Lulu's on Saturday night and biking with Chase on Sunday. As one of Jack's best friends, Chase fit right in with her family, especially since Jack and Lacey still lived next door till they found a house of their own. It surprised Shannon how quickly she and Chase slipped into a comfortable and easy friendship, affection lighting her eyes for a man she knew would become a close friend. "He's a great guy, and I like him a lot, although we've only gotten together about three times."

Sam's gaze felt like a laser as he started his car. "Three times since *Saturday*?" he asked, a ridge above his nose. "Sounds like things are moving pretty fast."

She glanced out her window to deflect the blush she felt in her cheeks. "No, we're just hanging out, that's all, having some fun."

The car didn't move. "Just fun … or more?" he asked, and she turned back at the edge in his tone, her eyes softening when she remembered Chase's words.

"Call me gun-shy, Shan, but he looked and acted just like Jack did when I started dating Lacey—jealous."

"Well, I'm not having the same problem you are with Jazz, if that's what you mean," she said with a tender smile, "so you can rest easy, Dad."

"Good to know." The car started with a growl that matched the look on Sam's face as he backed out of the parking spot with great care, face relaxing into a smile when he waved to a young couple with a toddler in a stroller, waiting until they crossed the street. "I just love kids," he whispered, his whole demeanor changing as he watched the couple with a sense of longing in his eyes. "I hope and pray I have a houseful someday, although I doubt I can talk Jazz into more than two." He shifted and eased the Vette down the street, shooting a grin Shannon's way. "But I sure love their honesty and innocence, you know? Which" — he reached over to give her knee a quick squeeze— "is one of the things I love most about you too. Seeing that kind of purity in kids is one thing, but in an adult?" He shook his head as he signaled to change lanes. "You're a rare find, Shannon O'Bryen, in such a jaded world."

The lining of her stomach turned to lead, weighing her down with the need to tell him the truth. "Sam … there's something you need to know…"

The theme to *Jaws* began to play on his phone, and he snatched it up, silently mouthing an apology. "Hey, Jazz, what's up?"

Shannon slowly released the breath she was holding as Sam calmly talked Jasmine through some computer emergency, his tender and caring tone making her heart ache. By the time Jasmine finally let him go, they had pulled into Shannon's drive, where Jack and Matt were playing basketball.

"Hey, you two, you're just in time for some two-on-two—interested?" Jack strolled down the paver driveway with the ball under his arm. "I need some real competition because goofball here's about to put me to sleep."

"That's what happens when you lose, dip-stick," Matt called with a hand to his mouth, reaching for the hose to get a drink. "Boredom sets in."

Jack leaned on Shannon's side of the car. "Come on, guys, I need some exercise, and the only workout Ball gives me is with his yapper."

"Trust me, Jack," Sam said with regret in his tone, "there's nothing I'd rather do than trounce you in basketball, but Jazz called with a hard-drive issue, and I'm her IT guy."

Jack opened Shannon's door with a grunt. "Trust you? The day you'd rather trounce me in basketball over spending time with Jazz, dude, is the day I'll begin to worry."

Shannon got out and quietly closed the door. "Thanks for the run, Sam. I do believe I'm warmed up enough to feed these two guys some humble pie."

"Ha!" Jack tossed the basketball in the air and caught it before looping an arm over his sister's shoulder. "You've been hanging with Ham way too much, Shan. You're starting to sound as cocky as him."

"Nope, she's just better at basketball—like me," Sam said with a grin as he put the car in gear. He stopped to squint at Shannon. "Hey—you were in the middle of telling me something when Jazz's call interrupted, so what were you going to say?"

"Nothing that can't wait for a more opportune time," she said with a smile, giving him a wave when he finally backed out of her drive. She stole the ball out of Jack's hands and sprinted toward their homemade basketball court, dribbling all the way.

A more opportune time.

Eye on the net, she gave careful aim, soles launching into the air for a 3-pointer that sank as fast as her mood.

Like when she needed to end a friendship.

CHAPTER THIRTY

Sam was having a blast. He glanced over at the bleachers in front of the baseball field where the Camp Hope Farewell Field Day was taking place, and his stomach took a dive.

But Jazz sure wasn't.

Sitting on the top row by herself away from the crowd, she filed her nails, a bored look on her beautiful face. His heart cramped. He hated to see her unhappy, but Camp Hope was an important part of his life now, and he'd hoped she would enjoy this final event for the orphans whose term at Camp Hope was over. Just like Sam had made an effort to enjoy the stuffy fundraiser dinners she dragged him to for museums and the arts. Not that he had anything against music or culture, but people were far more important in his opinion. *Especially* little people, something he was beginning to realize Jasmine had an aversion to.

His gaze flicked to the grubby-faced little guy who'd just sat down next to Jazz, causing her to inch several feet away. Sam handed Cat the stopwatch for the upcoming relay. "Take over for a few seconds, will you, Cat? I've got to run interference between Rupert and my girl. The kid may only be eight years old, but he's got an eye for the ladies like I've never seen."

"And you should know," Cat quipped, giving him a wink.

"Hey, I've cleaned my act up thanks to your sister, Catfish, so go easy, will you?" He gave her a noogie on her head before striding toward the bleachers, taking them two at a time to plop down between Jazz and Rupert. He hooked a protective arm over her shoulder and drew her close. "Hey, man, this is my woman, so you need to go find your own."

"Aw, shoot," Rupert said with a good-natured scowl, ebony face gleaming in the sun, "ain't none half as pretty as your woman, Doctor Sam, so I don't know why you cain't share." Giving Jazz a wink, he shuffled away with a sheepish grin.

"Hey, you okay?" Still smiling about Rupert trying to horn in on his girl, Sam leaned close to nibble on Jazz's ear.

"I am now," she whispered, turning to lay one on him that made him forget where he was. "When can we leave?" she whispered, skimming a hand down his thigh that shot fire through his veins, reminding him of the struggle he had with Jazz every time they were alone. "I suddenly have an irresistible urge for some couch time."

Couch time.

As opposed to *bed time*, the compromise Sam agreed to for watching movies and snuggling. Only it was rapidly becoming a wrestling match every time Jazz lay in his arms, taking every ounce of control he had to keep their relationship aboveboard.

"After the sack races, which are up next," he said, twining his fingers with hers to steer her hand from his leg. That's the last game I'm involved in before the BBQ, which I bet you would enjoy—"

"Oh, no you don't, Dr. Cunningham. I've had my fill of grimy faces and sticky hands today, thank you." She swayed her lips against his, going in for the kill with a kiss that nearly made him groan. "The only sticky hands I want mauling me at this point, mister, are yours."

"Hey—Doctor Love!"

Sam pulled away to glance down at Cat at the base of the bleachers, hands on her hips. "We're up in the sack races, so get a move on."

"I couldn't agree more," Jazz whispered in his ear, the flick of her tongue kindling a slow burn in his gut. "I've been waiting for you to get a move on for a while now, Doc, so let's get this show on the road and we'll have some sack races of our own."

"Hey, great idea!" He gripped her at arm's length, pulse sprinting overtime. "Why don't you be my partner in the race, babe?" His smile veered wayward. "It's the perfect opportunity to get me in the sack …"

"Cute." Her Angelia Jolie lips took a slant. "But I'm holding out for the real thing, Doctor Love."

"And it's on its way, babe, I promise." He kissed her nose. "Soon."

"Not soon enough to suit me," she said with a pout.

"Me, either, Jazz, trust me." He gave her a quick kiss before making his way down the bleachers, wishing this were the water balloon toss so he could cool off.

"Sure you can focus after that?" Cat watched his approach with a knowing smile, gunny sack slung over her shoulder while the participants lined up for the race.

"Give me a break, Catfish," he said with a lazy grin. "Winning is what I do best."

She shot a glance up to where Jazz was on the phone, and gave him a wink. "Not according to Jazz, I'll bet."

"Get your mind out of the gutter and into the bag, O'Bryen, will you?" He snatched the sack from her shoulder and held it while she slipped her left leg in, then did the same with his right, gripping her around the waist. "I need you as focused as me because I hate to lose."

"Not as much as me," she muttered, gaze darting down the line to where Chase and Shannon were teaming up for the race.

Sam followed her line of sight, and his jaw compressed. "Wanna bet?"

CHAPTER THIRTY-ONE

Shannon was laughing so hard, she could barely breathe, both she and Chase in a tangle of arms and legs at the finish line after they came in second place.

Right behind Sam and Cat, of course. *The Jugular Twins.*

"Going for the finish line in a dive, eh? Nice move, Rev," Sam said with a grin. "Too bad it didn't work."

Breathless, Shannon looked up at Sam and Cat, who stood over Chase and her with smug smiles.

"No, but it sure was a whole lot more fun," Chase said, helping Shannon to her feet. He shook Sam's hand, then Cat's, delivering the easy smile that was a key indicator winning at sack races wasn't his top priority.

Now souls? Shannon brushed off her shorts, hooking an arm to Cat's waist to give her a congratulatory squeeze before shaking Sam's hand. In the brief time she and Chase had been hanging out, she'd learned that the state of a person's soul was his win of choice, given the countless discussions they'd had about both Cat and Sam.

"I need meat," Chase said as the aroma of BBQ wafted their way. He draped an arm over Shannon's shoulder. "Hungry?"

"Ravenous." Tightening her ponytail, she flashed a smile at Sam. "Lacey and Jack said they'd save us a table, so you better go get Jasmine."

Sam glanced toward the bleachers, smile flat. "Wish I could stay, but I promised Jazz Sandfly BBQ."

"Oh, a BBQ snob—I see how it is." Cat ruffled Sam's hair.

He slapped her hand away with a mock scowl. "Yeah, well, hot dogs and burgers don't rank too high on her BBQ scale, Catfish, so I owe her after she sat through an afternoon of sweaty games and grubby kids."

"Not to mention Rupert," Cat said with a chuckle.

"Well, we'll miss you." Shannon gave Sam a hug.

"Speak for yourself," Chase said, draping an arm around both Cat's and Shannon's shoulders to usher them toward the picnic tables down by the lake. He tossed Sam a grin. "See you around, Doc."

Cat glanced back at the bleachers as she, Chase, and Shannon made their way to the table. "Is it just me, or do Sam and Jasmine seem like a mismatch?"

"I don't know. Being in love is a tricky business," Chase said. "You don't always get to pick who you're going to fall for."

"Humph." Cat snatched up a pebble and hurled it. "I plan to. I know exactly what I want in a man, and I refuse to settle for less."

"Less being …?" Chase eyed Cat with a faint smile, his arm still hooked over Shannon's shoulder.

"Boring. Unadventurous." Cat sailed another rock. "You know, hamstrung by a mindset that doesn't allow him to experience life or love to the fullest."

"You mean like me?" Chase said, the humor in his eyes undaunted by Cat's opinion.

"Well, now that you mention it, Rev, yes."

"Cat!" Shannon couldn't thwart the shock in her tone.

"I mean, come on, Shan—here he is, one of the most totally hot guys we've ever seen, and he's so mired in morality, he can hardly have any fun."

"Stop it, Cat," Shannon whispered loudly. Her gaze darted to the table where Lacey was waving them down while Jack played Power Rangers with their brother Davey and his best friend, Spence. "Mom would have a cow if she heard you talking like that, especially to the associate pastor of our church."

"So you think I'm totally hot, huh?" Chase said with a lazy smile.

Cat shrugged. "Sure, but what good is it if you can't have any fun?"

"You'd be surprised how much fun I have, Catherine Marie," he said in a husky tone, giving her neck a tweak before he sat down next to Shannon.

Shannon battled the squirm of a smile when Cat's face whooshed bright red.

"Can we eat now, Lace—please? We're starving to death, aren't we, Spence?" Shannon's brother Davey hopped up and down like he had to use the little boy's room, a Power Ranger action figure fisted in both hands.

"Uh-huh," Davey's best friend agreed in a quiet tone that made Shannon smile, along with the sweet owl glasses he wore.

"And look—Debbie's so hungry, she's crying!" Davey pointed at the precious orphan that Lacey and Jack befriended last year before Ben Carmichael saved her life with heart surgery. She sat slumped over the table with tears in her eyes, chin silently quivering on top of folded arms.

"Debbie?" Lacey leaned forward to peer into Debbie's sorrowful face, then immediately gathered her up in her arms. "Sweetheart, what's wrong?" she whispered, rocking the little girl while Debbie sobbed against Lacey's neck.

"Deb?" Jack abandoned his Power Ranger to sit beside Lacey, stroking the little girl's hair. "Why are you crying, Peanut? Come here …" He tugged Debbie from Lacey's arms and set her on his lap, gently brushing the tears from her eyes.

Small for nine years old, Debbie's little body shuddered with sobs while Lacey wiped her nose with a tissue. Blonde ringlets that had grown back after cancer treatment were now coiled in disarray, bobbing with every heave of her chest. "B-Because I h-have t-to leave and I w-won't ever s-see you a-again …" she whispered, barely discernable for the congestion in her voice.

"Oh, baby." Jack clutched her tightly, the sheen of moisture in his eyes identical to Lacey's. "Miss Myra promised us you'd be placed with a foster family close by, which means Lace and I will come see you as much as you like."

"You p-promise?" she said with a hiccup, swiping at the tears in her eyes.

"You bet, sweetheart—pinky swear." Lacey held her little finger out to the sniffling girl.

Heaves slowly dissipating, Debbie curved her tiny finger around Lacey's and then with a quiver of her lip, she launched into Lacey's arms, clutching her tightly. "I l-love you, L-Lacey," she whispered before she turned to lunge back to Jack. "You, too, Jack, more than anybody in the whole, wide world."

Jack and Lacey's watery gazes locked, and Shannon was pretty sure she was going to cry too.

"Hey, I'm hungry—who wants BBQ?" Chase jumped up from the table.

"Me-me-me!" Davey shouted, echoed by Spence's more modest assent.

"You hungry, Deb?" Chase asked. "Because yours is the first plate I'm gonna get if you are."

Debbie nodded against Jack's chest, an impish grin lighting on her lips. "Can I have two hot dogs? And lots of dessert?"

Chase gave her a wink. "Whatever your little heart desires, munchkin, as long as Miss Shannon helps me to carry it all."

Cat hopped up with a roll of her eyes. "I better go, too, or you're liable to end up with more veggies than dessert with these two."

"For your information, Catfish," Chase said with a shuttered drawl, "I have a near-decadent weakness for anything sweet."

Faking a yawn, Cat broke from the ranks to sashay in front of Shannon and Chase, smile dry as she delivered a smirk over her shoulder. "Seriously, Rev?" She zeroed in on Shannon with a pointed gaze before baiting Chase with an arch of her brow. "Tell me something I don't already know."

CHAPTER THIRTY-TWO

Skimming his jaw with one last swipe of the razor, Jack rinsed the shaving cream and dried his face, mouth slanting at the notion that he was shaving at ten o'clock at night, something he'd never done before. At least not until the honeymoon when Lacey woke up the first morning with awful razor burn. His mouth tipped in a gentle smile.

God bless her. She'd been so mortified by the heavy rash that broke out on her face that she'd talked him into hiding out in their honeymoon bungalow all day and all night. His smile eased into a grin.

Not that she had much persuading to do.

He patted his clean-shaven face with her favorite cologne—Obsession—which fit perfectly because if ever a man was obsessed with a woman, it was him. Lacey Carmichael O'Bryen was the love of his life, and he would do anything for her. His lips inched up as he dragged a comb through his dark, unruly hair, still damp from his shower.

Including shaving every night since.

But he sure wasn't complaining. Applying deodorant, he assessed the tan he'd managed to maintain from their Bahamas getaway, bicep bulging with the motion. Nope, because attached to his late-night shaving ritual was Lacey's own personal obsession of getting pregnant, which meant Dr. Jack was on call every night of the week. He slathered toothpaste on his toothbrush with a decadent grin.

With his very sexy and very determined wife.

Swishing water in his mouth, he spit it out and wiped his face with the towel. "Ready or not, Mrs. O'Bryen, here I come," he said under his breath, pretty sure Lacey was more than ready, a baby foremost on her mind. And frankly, he was too. Not that making love to his wife every night was a hardship by any means, but seeing her disappointed month after month certainly was, and he wanted his bubbly and lively Lacey back. He jerked his pajama bottoms up a fraction of an inch as he shot a smug smile into the mirror. And hopefully soon, God willing, he could share news with her that would do just that.

Turning off the bathroom light, Jack entered the darkened master bedroom Lacey's dad insisted they keep after Ben returned from his mission trip. Making his way to the bed, he was surprised his very thorough wife didn't have her lavender-scented candle lit. He grinned as he eased under the sheet. The one she'd read promoted both relaxation and romantic mood.

Wrapping his arms around her from behind, he nibbled her neck while he spooned her close. "No ambiance tonight?" He skimmed his palm down the length of her body, caught off-guard by the feel of pajama bottoms instead of skin. Ignoring a niggle of worry, he burrowed into the crook of her shoulder, gently feathering the lobe of her ear with his mouth. "No worries, babe, candlelight or pitch dark, you're all I need to set the mood …"

"Jack?" Her voice sounded off.

"Yeah, Lace?"

"Would you mind terribly if we just cuddled tonight?" She reached to brace his arm to her waist, wrapping her own arms around his. "I don't feel so great."

"What's wrong, babe?" he asked, brows crinkling as he slowly turned her to face him, stomach plunging at the moisture he felt when he gently kissed her cheek. "Lace—why are you crying—are you in pain?"

Eyes squeezed shut, she started to shake her head, but the moment her face crumpled with tears, he swallowed her up, holding her tightly as they lay side by side. "Aw, babe, we'll have lots of babies, I promise, whether biological or adopted, you have my word."

"I … know," she whispered, "b-but that's not the only reason I'm sad."

"What, then?" He pressed a kiss to her hair.

"It's D-Debbie."

Jack's pulse stalled.

"It's just not fair, Jack." Lacey sat up to wipe the tears from her face, and he reached for a tissue from the nightstand, nudging it into her hand. "That sweet little girl has had so much rejection and pain in her life and now she has to start all over again with heaven knows how many other foster families." She blew her nose, words nasal from weeping. "All of whom will probably never really want her because of her risky health issues ..."

Her voice trailed off into another sob, and Jack held her close, rubbing her back in a soothing up-and-down motion. "Babe, God has a plan for Debbie's life, I promise, and it will be good."

"I believe that, Jack, I do, but how long will it take?" Lacey pushed away, her eyes wide and wet while frustration threaded her tone. "The poor kid's been waiting her whole life just to get well and be loved, and now she's gotta wait some more? Without any guarantee she'll find a family who will love her or want her?"

Her lower lip began to quiver, and Jack held her face in his hands, fusing his gaze to hers. "Lace, there *is* no greater guarantee than God's love, and although His timing is not always in sync with ours, He *will* provide a loving family for her soon, I promise."

"But that's just it, Jack, you *can't* promise that," she whispered, jaw trembling as she swiped at more tears on her face. "Nobody can."

He stared at the woman he loved more than life itself and knew he should wait. Knew he should just love her and comfort her and keep the promise he'd made. But the pain in her eyes stabbed straight into his soul, and suddenly nothing mattered more than making it go away.

Even if it meant breaking a promise.

Drawing in a deep swell of air, he slowly traced the line of her jaw with the pad of his thumb, hoping to still its awful tremor of grief. "No, nobody can promise absolutely, Lace, but I believe I can come pretty darn close." He leaned in to caress her lips with his own, gently cupping her face like the precious treasure she was. "Maybe not on the timing," he said softly, his breath warm against the dampness of her skin, "but definitely on a loving family for Deb."

She jerked away, breathing erratic as she stared at him with saucer eyes, fingers digging into his arms. "What do you know, Jack?" she rasped, the hope in her face completely doing him in. "You have to tell me or I will never be able to sleep."

His smile was tender. "You won't either way, babe, but that's okay, because I know one or two ways we can pass the time."

Hopping up on her knees, she grabbed his shoulders and rattled him hard, the fire in her eyes making him grin. "So help me, Jack O'Bryen, if you don't tell me what you know right now …"

He chuckled and flopped back on the bed, hauling her along with him while he nestled his mouth into the curve of her neck. "Well, I had an opportunity to talk to Miss Myra a few weeks ago, and she confided it's a fairly young couple with no kids who actually met Debbie already and promptly fell in love." He paused to fondle her earlobe with kisses. "So … they're actually talking adoption rather than foster care."

Lacey popped up from his chest, her smile half-hearted at best. "Are they a decent couple? Can they afford her healthcare? And both Miss Myra and Will have approved of them?"

Grinning, he tugged her back down. "Yes, a very decent, church-going, solid-income couple with a close-knit extended family who will be over the moon to welcome Debbie."

"They're not too old, are they?" The worry in her tone made him grin.

"Well, he's a bit long in the tooth, I'm afraid, but she's much younger and a teacher, I understand."

Her sigh feathered the bare skin of his chest. "Well that's good because Debbie is going to need all the extra tutoring she can get." She jolted up again, panic lacing her tone. "They do live in

Savannah, right, or at least not too far away?"

He brushed a wisp of hair from her face, fingers straying from her ear to her jaw. "No, babe, they don't live in Savannah, but close."

"How close?" she rasped, clutching so tightly, he was certain he'd have handprints embedded in his chest.

A tiny squeal squeaked from her lips when he whooshed her onto her back, hovering over her with a wayward gleam in his eye. "This close," he whispered, bending to tenderly skim her mouth with his own.

Her body seized right before she dug her fingernails into his arms like meat hooks, tears pooling in her eyes as she shoved him back. "Don't toy with me, O'Bryen, or I will *so* make you pay."

Rolling onto his side, he brought her along, flashing some teeth while he cocked an elbow to rest his head in his hand. "Actually, I'm pretty fond of toying with you, Mrs. O'Byren," he said with a tender smile, voice fading to a whisper, "but I'm also fond of making you happy. *Which* is why I talked to Miss Myra months ago about possibly adopting Debbie."

Lacey blinked, the whites of her eyes growing in the dark before she launched into his arms with another squeal so loud, Jack was grateful Ben was still out. And then, in the span of a heartbeat, she jerked back again, fingers still clutched to his arms. "B-But … b-but you refused to even consider the possibility of adoption when I mentioned it months ago. You said maybe years down the road if we couldn't have children of our own, but not this early in our marriage."

A grin curled his lips. "Had to do something to throw you off the track." He slowly grazed the curve of her jaw. "And it *was* 'early' in our marriage, if you recall." He arched a brow. "Uh … like on our honeymoon?" His smile softened into serious. "We were always on the same wavelength with Debbie, babe, but I didn't want you to get your hopes up till I could make sure it was a definite possibility with no roadblocks." He brushed his lips gently against hers. "I can't stand to see you disappointed,

Lace, especially with all the frustration you've gone through trying to get pregnant." He gave a slight shrug. "So I figured derailing your thoughts about Debbie in the meantime was the best course of action till I made sure it could actually happen."

Eyes misty, she flung herself into his arms once again. "Oh, Jack, I didn't think I could love you anymore than I do, but I adore you!"

His chuckle fluttered her hair as he returned a hug of his own. "That's good, babe, because I plan to be around for a long, long time, taking good care of you and Debbie and all of her brothers and sisters." His tone sobered as he held her at arm's length, hoping the sobriety in his eyes would temper her joy with caution. "But … you need to know, Lace, by telling you this now, it means I had to break a promise I made to Miss Myra not to say anything until she has a few more details tied down, just in case."

The smile dissolved on Lacey's face, which tore at his gut.

But not as much as it would if things didn't work out with Debbie …

A lump wallowed in her throat. "I understand, Jack, and I won't say a word, but how … long will it take?"

He coaxed her head back to his chest. "Miss Myra tells me the process is broken down into three basic parts: certification, placement and transition, and then severance to adoption. Which means there'll be mandatory trainings to attend, paperwork to file on our finances and health, a background check, and a home study. She says it can take anywhere from a few weeks to a few months barring any problems. Then, depending on how busy the courts are, an adoption date can be set within a couple months or longer once all appropriate documents are submitted and processed. Which, by the way" —he pressed a kiss to her nose— "are all ready to go, just awaiting your signature."

"Problems," she whispered, the dread in her voice heavy against his chest. "What kind of problems?"

He kissed her head, wishing he didn't have to tell her, but he knew the damage would be far greater to be blindsided if the adoption fell through. "With parental termination," he said quietly, "although the likelihood is remote given Debbie's mom's history and lack of interest."

Her sigh breezed across his skin. "Well, we're just going to have to pray about it then, every step of the way."

"I'd say that's a given, babe."

He winced when her nails dug into his sides once again as she cut loose with a joyous shriek. "Oh. My. Goodness!" She smothered his chest with a flurry of kisses, working her way up to capture his mouth with such passion, his moan was lost in her kiss. She broke loose with another high-pitched squeal as her feet danced against his. "I am so over-the-moon excited, Jack O'Bryen," she said with a giggle, burrowing her head into the slope of his neck, "that I'm pretty sure I won't sleep even a wink."

"Yep …" His low chuckle rumbled against her hair as he rolled her back over, swooping in to capture her mouth with his own. "My plan exactly."

CHAPTER THIRTY-THREE

"You *do* realize I'll have to get up very early to run extra miles after this meal, don't you?" Sam groaned as he pushed away from the glass patio table on Jazz's river-view condo veranda, pretty sure additional sit-ups were in his future too.

Arms crossed, Jazz leaned in to give him the benefit of her low-cut tank top that tempted as much as the seductive smile she wore. "Not if I give you a workout here," she said with a mischievous wink, rising to collect the dirty dishes from the table.

Opting to steer clear of Jazz's idea of a workout, Sam stood to help, relieving her of the dishes in her hands. "Nope, you cooked, I clean. House rules."

"But this is *my* house, mister," she teased, sliding her arms around his waist from behind, "so why are *you* the one making the rules?" Her fingers fiddled with a button on his dress shirt, which had long been stripped of his tie and opened at the collar, with sleeves rolled to his elbows.

He craned his neck to press a kiss to her hair before piling more dishes on his stack. "Because I'm bigger than you, Miss Augustine, *and* because at this venture in our relationship, I'm the one with enough self-control to keep us in line."

"Humph." She removed her hands, but not before allowing a rebellious glide down the sides of his thighs, reminding him once again that Jasmine did not agree with his new moral code. "I liked you better before you got religion," she said with a pout.

Sam could do nothing but grin on his way to the kitchen. "No you didn't, babe, so you may as well admit it." He placed the dirty dishes on the counter while she followed him in, rinsing spaghetti sauce off each one before stacking them in the dishwasher. "Deep down you like my commitment to faith just like you liked it in Jack because you, Jasmine Joy Augustine," he said with a stern arch of his brow while he loaded the dishwasher, "are just like me—a sucker for a challenge."

Rinsing a tomato-sauced dishrag under the tap, she sighed as she squeezed it, orange water streaming into the sink. "And you, Dr. Cunningham, have become most proficient at offering them, it seems, especially in areas near and dear to my heart."

He hooked her waist before she could leave to wipe off the table, brushing a tender kiss to her lips. "But just think how fun it'll be on our honeymoon," he whispered.

Those gorgeous blue eyes narrowed while her mouth took a twist. "It was fun *before*, Sam," she muttered, smile as flat as her tone. "I just hope you remember how."

He dove for her neck, making her squeal when he nibbled the soft flesh of her ear. "Don't you worry about my memory, Nurse Augustine, because it's only exceeded by my skill in making love."

"Yeah, that's the problem, Doc," she said with a pout, wet dishrag in hand as she looped her arms around his neck to give him a lingering kiss. "I remember *all* too well, and it's killing me." She apparently gave the dishrag a squeeze because a stream of cold water dribbled down the collar of his Armani slim-fit shirt.

"Hey!" Sam gripped her arms and pushed her away before swatting at the dribble of water at the back of his neck. "Okay, Augustine, orange water on my best dress shirt? This is war …" Snatching the wet rag, he locked her to his chest with one hand while he rinsed the rag under the tap with the other, Jazz's giggles bouncing off the walls as she thrashed in his arms.

"Sam, I'm sorry," she said with a heave, laughter rippling her words. "I'll never do it again, I promise—"

"I know, babe, but just to make sure …" Butting her to the counter, he cut her off with a possessive kiss that took the fight out of her as she melted into his arms … right before he squeezed and dribbled the sopping rag down her back.

She squealed and darted away, scrambling to the other side of her island table, hands braced to a chair. "Okay, Sam, we're even now," she said, voice breathless and eyes lit with a mischief he didn't trust for one solitary moment.

He slowly walked toward the island, grin decadent as he sloshed the rag back and forth in his hands. "That's just it, babe—I'm not looking for 'even,'" he said with a shuttered look, "I'm looking for world domination."

She bolted for the sink, snatching up the sprayer so fast, Sam didn't know what hit him until a blast of water pelted him in the face, drowning him, his shirt, and his favorite Cole Haan shoes. "Domination sounds nice, Sam, but if you think you're going to win this battle, you're all wet."

Ignoring the geyser of water splatting off his face, he confiscated the sprayer with ease, both of them laughing as he immobilized her with a steel hold, drenching her until she was soaked. "Give up?" he breathed in her ear, giving the spray a rest.

"Always." Her body relaxed in his arms as she surrendered with a languorous kiss that turned up the heat so high, his clothes should have been dry. One hand cupped to the back of his neck, her other slid down the front of his shirt to slowly undo the buttons. "We need to get out of these wet clothes," she whispered.

Alarm curled in his belly along with desire, and he quickly held her back, grip gentle but firm. "We both know that's not a good idea," he said quietly, his body aching with need. He deposited a soft kiss on her nose before grabbing a wad of paper towels. Squatting to mop up the floor, he glanced up, mind grappling for something they could do while they dried off outside. "Hey, you ever play basketball?"

"What?" She stared at him like his brain was soggy, too, her nose in a cute, little scrunch.

"Basketball," he said as he finished cleaning up his mess. "I have a ball in my trunk, and there's a park down the street that has a court." He rose to his feet, sailing the sodden paper towels across the room into the trash with a grin. "Yes! Two points."

"Sam …" Shoulders slumping, she tipped her head in a patient look that said there was no way she was playing basketball. "I would rather not run around on some public court in this heat, if it's all the same to you." She reached out to undo another button of his shirt. "Let me just throw your shirt in the dryer, okay? And I'll change clothes so we can snuggle on the sofa and watch a movie."

Just the mention of lying on a couch with Jasmine at the moment spiked his body temperature several degrees. He cuffed the back of his neck.

Uh, yeah, horizontal's not working for me right now, babe …

"Come on, Sam," she said in that pouty tone that always weakened his defenses. She slid her hands into the open V of his shirt, thumbs massaging his chest. "I've been wanting to watch *Fifty Shades of Gray* anyway."

He stifled a groan. *More like Fifty Shades of Temptation. No, thanks.* He carefully removed her hands from his chest, distancing himself as he twined his fingers through hers. "Miniature golf then. Come on, Jazz, I really need to work off that meal."

She moved in close again with that sultry look in her eyes, and he tightened his grip to hold her at bay. "Out in the fresh air," he emphasized with a jag of his brow.

"So, I'll open a window," she purred.

Plopping his hands on her shoulders, he turned her around and prodded her toward the door, expelling a silent sigh when she actually went. "Go change, and I'll take you to play miniature golf," he said as he rebuttoned his shirt. "You're gonna love it. I promise."

"I'd rather love *you*," she said with a mock scowl over her shoulder.

"You are, babe. Trust me."

She turned at the door, eyes troubled as she clutched at the jamb, as if girding herself for what she was about to say. "You *are* still attracted to me, Sam, aren't you?"

Heat scorched his collar as he slacked a hip, hands on his thighs. "Are you serious?" Dropping his head, he laughed, never in a million years wanting her to know that his desire for her was considerably tamer than before, except when she kissed him or came on to him like she always did. But that was part of the commitment he'd given to Shannon, wasn't it? Knowing he couldn't give in because he'd given his word? Not to mention the seeds of faith both Shannon and Jack had planted, no matter how small. He shook his head, peering up with a tender smile. "You are the sexiest woman alive, Jasmine Augustine, and trust me—I will devour you on our honeymoon."

Eyes somber, she gave him the barest of smiles before it faded as quickly as it had come. "Did you ever …" She chewed on her lip as if unwilling to utter a question that would produce an answer she didn't want to hear. A lump bobbed in her beautiful throat. "Ever make love to her?"

His blood turned to ice. *Her?* Heat blasted his cheeks, knowing full well who she was talking about. She'd hinted more than once that she blamed Shannon for his "lack of interest" in what he'd so readily taken from Jazz before. A powerful mix of fury and shame surged through his body—anger at Jazz for sullying Shannon that way and shame that at one time he would have done the same if given the chance. Then. Not now. "Lust isn't love," Shannon had told him once, "serving self instead of others," and for the first time, Sam understood that concept like never before. Because Shannon's "no" to him and to herself that night had said "yes" to a friendship that was saving his soul. He swallowed hard. A soul as empty as his life had been before she had driven him home the night of the fundraiser.

"You did, didn't you?" The tears swelling in her eyes twisted his gut.

"No, I didn't," he said quietly, slowly approaching to tenderly gather her in his arms.

She crumpled against his chest with a sob, and he bent his head to hers, eyes squeezed shut as he held her close, stunned at how truly sacred lovemaking actually was. Not moments of lust and selfish pleasure as he'd always seen it before, but a merging of souls as well as bodies, a holy covenant sanctioned by God. Just like Shannon had said.

And the two shall become one flesh.

Moisture stinging beneath his lids, he pressed a gentle kiss to her hair. "Which is why I want to wait, Jazz, because I want to love my wife the way that love was actually meant to be."

Sniffing, she nodded against his shirt. "Okay, Sam." She pulled away and swiped at her eyes, her smile tremulous at best. "But do you mind if we go get ice cream instead?" She lifted on tiptoe to brush a soft kiss to his lips. "I think I need to cool off."

"Me too," he said with a smile, buffing her arms. "So go on and change, and we'll go to Cold Stone, okay?"

"Oh, yum!" She gave him a quick hug before heading to her room, tossing a grin over her shoulder. "Nothing cools a body down like a water fight and Cold Stone."

"Yep." Sam ambled back to the sink to wipe it down, a sense of calm and peace flooding his soul.

That and the prayers of a very good friend.

CHAPTER THIRTY-FOUR

"Come on, baby, come home to Mama ..." Deck shoes braced on the dock and knees slightly bent, Shannon set the hook with a sharp jerk, reeling in the biggest fish of the night to put the girls ahead of the guys.

"Whoo-hoo, Shan!" Lacey high-fived Cat and Nicki when Shannon hefted the good-sized bass in the air. "Woman power!" she said, hurrying over to help Shannon weigh in her catch.

Jack offered his wife a patient smile as he recast his line. "Settle down, babe. We still have fifteen minutes in the tournament to put you ladies in your place, so I'd save your celebration if I were you."

"Yeah, Lace," Nicki said with a lift of her Dr. Pepper, content to cheer her team on from the sidelines since she was odd woman out and not overly fond of fishing, "we'll have lots of time to celebrate when the guys have to wait on us, hand, foot, and finger."

"Hey, woman," her husband Matt said with a jag of a thick blonde brow, "we're still newlyweds, so you're supposed to be supporting and kissing up to *me,* not the females."

Cat made a perfect cast. "Uh, I doubt there'll be much 'kissing up' tonight, Cuz, not with you smelling like stink bait, right, Nick?"

"The woman has a point," Nicki said with a nod of her head, "at least not without a long, *long* shower."

"Hey, Chase ..." Jack shot a wicked grin over his shoulder. "Make sure you double-check their measurements, will you? Lacey's been known to fudge."

Lacey gave Jack the stink-eye as she and Shannon measured

her fish, tone indignant. "I beg your pardon—Shannon would never do anything fishy, O'Bryen, unlike *my husband* whose chances of 'kissing up' tonight are looking slim to nil, with or without a shower."

"Uh-oh, somebody's in trouble." Chase ambled over to where Lacey and Shannon were recording the weight and length of the fish. He peered over their shoulders with a crooked smile. "Not sure I can continue to be friends with a girl who outfishes me, Shan," he said with a shake of his head. "Even pastors have their pride, you know."

Cat tossed an evil grin his way. "Not when they fish like you, Rev," she teased. "The only thing I've seen you reel in is humility."

"That's because I focus more on fishing for souls, Catfish," he said with a lazy smile, "a fisher of men and cocky women rather than sea life."

Nicki chuckled. "Well, then this one must keep you *prettttty* darn busy," she said with a sassy nod in Cat's direction, her prior enmity with Cat years ago long since dissipated, thank God. "The poor kid reminds me of myself before I mended my wild ways, Rev, so keep trolling, buddy, and you'll reel her in yet."

"In his dreams." Smile flat, Cat popped her shrimp cork several more times, squinting at a river shimmering with the fiery fuchsia of dusk.

"And in my prayers," Shannon whispered, earning an understanding hug from Lacey before her sister-in-law sauntered back to her rod.

"Don't worry. We'll hook her yet, Shan," Chase said quietly.

Shannon expelled a weary sigh as she put her fish on the stringer in the water, grateful that the banter and laughter of the others drowned out Chase's comment. "I hope so. Believe it or not, her faith in God was as strong as mine at one time." She reached for a shrimp from the bait bucket and rebaited her line, her tone melancholy. "But Dad's affair with Lacey's mother all those years ago pretty much damaged it, just like it did to Jack."

"Yeah, but God won after all the smoke cleared," Chase

reminded, "and He'll win with Cat, too. You'll see. That stubborn sister of yours doesn't stand a chance with all the family and friends praying for her." He followed Shannon to the far edge of the dock away from the others, slipping Cat a troubled look out of the corner of his eye. "I just hope it's before she gets into too much trouble."

"Me too." Shannon launched her line across the inky waters in a perfect arc. "But I'll tell you what, Chase, when He *does* get His hands on Cat again, I'll be rejoicing louder than all those angels in heaven."

"Just like with Sam?" he said quietly, his perceptive gaze warming her cheeks.

"Yes." Her voice was the softest of whispers, hope swelling in her chest as she offered Chase a gentle smile, reminded once again just how much she missed Sam. She hadn't seen him in almost two weeks due to a vacation he took with Jasmine's family the first week, then playing catch-up with his job and volunteer work the second. *Not* to mention Jasmine's demands on his time, which Shannon suspected were partially to limit Sam's time with her. Her rib cage expanded and contracted with a wistful sigh. But the truth was, Shannon didn't blame Jasmine one bit. If Sam belonged to her, she wouldn't want him hanging out with any other females either. Shaking off her melancholy, she forced herself to focus on how much Sam had grown in his faith since the night of the Memorial fundraiser, and joy immediately flooded both her heart and her smile. "But he's close, Chase, I can feel it, and I'm so proud of how much he's changed over these last few months."

"Because of you." There was respect in his tone, along with a strong affection that Shannon sensed was growing between them both.

She popped her cork more quickly than usual, uncomfortable as always with praise. "No, because of *God*," she emphasized, quite certain it was God Who'd given her the grace to be Sam's friend in the first place. And even more grace now to be *only* a friend.

"When is he planning on proposing to Jasmine?" Chase's question was casual, but Shannon perceived an underlying concern. True to his word, Chase had become her good friend over the last month, coming over or taking her out at least three times a week, making it clear he was waiting till Shannon was ready for more.

She glanced up at him, wishing Sam wasn't so embedded in her heart because Chase was everything she'd always wanted. A godly man devoted to his faith.

Not a player devoted to himself.

"Tonight, as a matter of fact," she said, thinking about the text he'd sent her earlier in the week, asking her to pray that the evening went well. Forcing a smile she hoped didn't reflect how she truly felt inside, she glanced at her watch, then out at the water where her cork popped too many times to be effective. "By now Jazz should be sporting a hefty-sized diamond."

The gentle touch of Chase's hand on her shoulder drew her eyes to his. "I know you're still in love with him, Shannon, but I promise you—everything will work out."

She offered a tremulous smile. "I believe that, Chase, I do, with all of my heart. *And* I truly believe God will get me past these unfortunate feelings" —her throat convulsed against her will— "and hopefully soon. But right now, what I want more than anything is for Sam to be happy."

"Hey, Shan," Cat said, squinting toward Bluff Drive in the distance, "what's Doctor Love doing here?"

Shannon's heart stopped at the sound of Cat's question, stomach flipping as always whenever Sam was near. She spun around so fast, Chase had to steady her, her pulse stuttering along with her words. "S-Sam ..." she whispered, spotting him getting out of his car parked under a streetlight. Hands in his pockets, he started walking across the lawn to their dock until his somber gaze collided with hers at the front of the ramp, effectively halting him halfway. He offered a half-hearted wave, the solemnity of his pose begging her to come.

"Something's wrong," Jack said, shifting his focus from Sam to

Shannon, Sam's unwillingness to approach the group speaking volumes to both her brother and her. He took the fishing pole from her hand. "Go talk to him, sis."

She peeked up at Chase, and he nodded, his knowing look eliminating all hesitation as he gave her back a gentle rub. "Go. I need to head home soon anyway, so I'll call you tomorrow."

Nodding, she squeezed his hand before hurrying from the dock, heart sprinting along with her body as she ran to where Sam stood like a statue. "W-What on earth are you d-doing here?" she rasped, stomach constricting at the look of grief in his eyes. "And why aren't you with Jazz?"

"I needed to talk," he whispered, his deadly serious expression joining forces with the gravity of his tone to wreak havoc with her pulse. His gaze flicked to where Chase had turned back to the river to fish alongside Jack, and a knot ducked in his throat. He took several steps back, as if to leave. "Look, I'm sorry—I didn't mean to interrupt. It can wait till tomorrow—"

She stopped him with a hand to his arm. "No, it's fine, Sam, really. Chase said he's leaving shortly anyway."

Chest rising and falling with a heavy sigh, he slipped his fingers through hers and led her toward his car, his silence unnerving her.

"Sam, you're scaring me," she said as he opened the passenger door. "*Please*—tell me what's wrong."

Without answering, he closed her door and circled to his side, head bowed as if he had the weight of the world on his shoulders. He got in and closed his door, finally meeting her gaze. "I broke it off with Jazz tonight," he whispered, the brown of his eyes black with intensity.

Shannon couldn't breathe. His words snatched all air from her throat while her brain grappled with what he was saying.

Jazz is out of his life?

Jaw tight, he started the car and put it in gear, his glance fraught with regret. "Do you mind if we go somewhere quiet to talk?"

"No, of course not," she whispered, reaching out to gently massage his arm, his pain becoming her own.

His hand immediately covered hers, and her pulse skipped when his thumb caressed the back of her wrist. Giving her hand a light squeeze, he returned his grip to the steering wheel while he peered straight ahead. Obviously lost in his thoughts, he silently drove to Tybee, their favorite running beach over the last few months. He seemed somewhere far away, so Shannon didn't push, knowing Sam would talk when he was ready.

He parked the car on Tybrisa Street and got out to open her door, helping her out as always before leading her to the Tybee Island Pier and Pavilion. Awash in the watercolor pinks and purples of dusk, the pier was quiet tonight, with just a smattering of couples sitting on benches overlooking the water. Usually Sam ushered her with a guiding hand to her back, but tonight his fingers laced firmly with hers, gaze pinned on the covered pavilion at the end of the pier. He steered her to an isolated bench on the far side, giving her palm a slight press before he sat down, tugging her along. "I hope you don't mind, Shan, but I needed someplace quiet and calm to talk through this," he said, his face chiseled in gravity. "And somewhere we could be alone."

Her heart stumbled at his words, its beat erratic as he continued to hold her hand, thumb grazing her palm. Near breathless, she broke the connection to shift and face him, his touch muddling her mind far too much for coherent discussion. "No, I don't mind," she whispered, arm straddling the back of the bench while she discreetly inched away to give herself the distance she needed. She girded herself with a deep draw of sea-scented air, the gentle whoosh of the ocean on the shore providing a tranquility she desperately needed. "Sam, what on earth happened?"

Offering a faint shrug, he expelled a tired sigh before sagging against the bench, head bowed while he pinched the bridge of his nose. "You're too good of a teacher, Shan," he muttered, "so it's all your fault."

She blinked, a tad nervous to hear why she was to blame. "I … don't understand."

He rested his head on the back of the bench, profile somber

as he stared at a sky heavy with stars. "All this time I thought I was in love with Jazz, that she was the one I wanted to spend the rest of my life with." The faintest of smiles shadowed his lips as he peered at her out of the corner of his eye. "But you taught me what real love is, Teach, and being with Jazz these last few months made me realize that's not what we had." He shook his head slowly, the motion melancholy as his gaze returned to the sequined sky. "What we had wasn't love. It was a mutual lust fueled by jealousy and control, each of us too mired in pride to even consider the other's feelings." His voice gentled as he quoted the Scripture she'd worked so hard to drill into his head. "Love does not envy, it does not boast, it is not proud, does not demand its own way, is not easily angered, keeps no record of wrongs ..."

Shannon's breath shallowed considerably, her brain battling an emotional tug-of-war between remorse and relief. Remorse won out as she strove for words to restore his hope. "But love is also patient, Sam, and kind. It always protects, always trusts, always hopes, always perseveres."

"True, but not in this case. Not if it's not the right person," he said quietly, slowly pivoting on the bench to face her head-on. He rested his arm across the back until their fingers almost touched. "I discovered that making love wasn't love at all, and when it was removed from Jazz's and my relationship, there was very little left. You taught me that physical intimacy outside of God's precepts muddies the waters, making it difficult to see things clearly, things that truly matter in a life-long relationship." He paused, absently cuffing the back of his neck, the gesture almost awkward. "You were right. Without sex, Jazz and I suddenly couldn't communicate, couldn't agree, couldn't connect like two people in love should." The tips of his fingers gently grazed hers, robbing her of speech as well as air. "Not like you and I can, Shan," he said softly, the look of tenderness in his eyes swirling warmth in her middle. "So it's all your fault, Angel Eyes, because it looks like you've ruined me for other women."

CHAPTER THIRTY-FIVE

Shannon jumped up, body trembling as she clutched her arms to her waist. "Sam, I'm so sorry—I never meant to cause problems between you and Jasmine, I promise."

She took a step back when he slowly rose, towering over her. "Not consciously, I suppose," he said with a faint smile that tightened her stomach. She stopped breathing altogether when he stepped close enough to buff warm palms on her bare arms. "But subconsciously?" She couldn't move, limbs paralyzed when his fingers slowly traced up her skin to glide over her shoulders, leaving fire in their wake as they skimmed up to cradle her face in his hands. His brown eyes softened with such affection, she thought she might faint. "I'm hoping and praying it was your plan all along," he whispered, voice husky as he bent in, his shallow breathing merging with hers. "Because the truth is I'm falling in love with you, Shannon, and my only regret is that it took me so long to figure it out."

She had no control over the tears that swelled in her eyes, and when he bundled her to his chest with a low chuckle, she literally sobbed. His strong arms banded her close until she could feel the wild beat of his heart, as chaotic as her own. He pressed a gentle kiss to her head. "Uh … I'm hoping that means you're falling for me, too, and not that you feel sorry for me?"

A laugh broke from her lips that ended up quivering into a sodden heave, causing Sam to pull away with a grin. His smile was tender as he brushed the hair from her eyes. "You know, Shan, all this crying and laughing isn't doing a whole lot for my ego. So if you don't mind, can you tell me if you feel the same because if you don't, I'm going to need some heavy-duty therapy from my best friend."

Her lips trembled into a soggy smile as she nodded, hardly able to believe that Sam Cunningham felt about her the same way she did about him.

"Say it, then," he whispered. A glimmer of the vulnerability he seldom revealed infused his words with an urgency that matched the intensity in eyes, naked with need.

Against her better judgment, her heart slowly unfurled like a rosebud ready to embrace the sun. With a rush of love, she cupped a shaky hand to his jaw while his handsome face blurred through her tears. "I'm afraid I'm falling for you, too, Sam Cunningham, whether I want to or not."

A heart-melting grin eased across his face as he swooped her up in his arms, spinning her 'round and 'round until she was as dizzy as her heart. Setting her back down, he threaded gentle fingers into her hair and drew her close. "I've never met a woman like you, Shan," he whispered, his eyes caressing her face as if it were the first time he was really seeing her. "So gentle, so kind …" His gaze settled on her lips, and her heart slammed against her ribs when he slowly bent in, mouth hovering over hers as if awaiting her consent. "So incredibly beautiful and pure …" His words faded into her mouth as he nuzzled her lips with such excruciating tenderness, a moan ached in her throat. "You even smell pure," he whispered, his breath warm against her skin, "fresh and clean, like the scent of vanilla."

Her mouth curved beneath his. "I should smell like fish."

"Angel fish," he said, mouth wandering to fondle the lobe of her ear, "which are remarkably beautiful, by the way, just like you. Leading me to believe you're not only the perfect friend, Angel Eyes, you're the perfect woman as well."

"Sam …" She shook her head, a sudden twinge in her chest. "There is no perfect woman," she whispered, eyes sober as she pulled away with a melancholy smile.

His chin nudged up as he swept her hair over her shoulders. "Maybe not, but you're as close as I've come, Shan, and I want to get to know you as a woman. Which means …" He melted her resistance with a crooked smile, brown eyes twinkling with tease. "High GPA and med degree notwithstanding, I'm not as smart as I think if it took me this long to figure that out."

Her smile took a rare slant. "Unfortunately, I figured it out a while back, which hasn't always made this friendship very easy."

"Unfortunately?" He cocked a brow. "Hey, I don't know about you, Teach, but I'm pretty happy about this unexpected turn of events." A crease appeared at the bridge of his nose. "Aren't you?"

She paused, her true emotions tangling into a ball of knots, right along with her stomach. *Happy that Sam wanted more than friendship?* She swallowed the fear that instantly clogged in her throat. Her eyes flickered closed when she realized what that meant. Not only had she fallen in love with another player against her will, but he wanted to return that love, to know her as a woman.

Vulnerable.

Weak.

And fragile enough to break.

Again.

A shiver skated her spine as she took a step back, not sure she wanted to risk it. Yes, Sam was changing, but so far it wasn't the soul-deep change that she needed. Nor was she sure he could even change enough to commit to a love that would last a lifetime. A love everlasting, like God had given to her. A feat difficult enough for most human beings, much less a player with a propensity for women.

"Shan?"

Her eyes snapped open at the gentle slide of his palms up her arms.

"I won't hurt you, I give you my word," he whispered, the affection in his eyes easing her fears for the moment. He ducked to give her a gentle smile. "How about we start out nice and slow, with an official first date on Saturday?"

Hesitating, she peeked up with a chew of her lip, fighting the pull of his charm.

"Come on, Shan, I promise to behave. Scout's honor." He snapped to attention, two fingers to his brow in a salute.

Her smile slid sideways. "You weren't a Boy Scout, Ham."

"No, but I wanted to be," he said, the pucker above his nose all for show. "Can I help it if I was a poor, abandoned orphan shuffled through foster care and never given the opportunity?"

Shifting her stance, she folded her arms with a slack of her hip. "So you're playing the orphan card, are you? Low blow, Dr. Love."

He scooped her close with his wrists locked behind her, and her pulse went haywire at the dangerous proximity of his body against hers. "Whatever it takes to get you to say yes," he whispered, eyes darkening with the same look she'd seen that first night in her car. "Even this …"

Before she could utter a single syllable, his mouth took hers with a gentle dominance that literally stole her breath away. Firmly cupping the back of her head, he kissed her exquisitely slow and deep and utterly possessive. Never had a man disarmed her so, the taste and touch of him drowning all restraint in a sea of want while heat purled through every inch of her trembling body. Eyes closed, she was still in a stupor when he pulled away, his fingers all but singeing her skin as they softly feathered the curve of her face. "Give me a chance, Shannon," he said quietly, "please."

Breathless, she could do nothing but nod, her mind too dazed to say no while her heart screamed yes with every treasonous beat of her pulse.

He leaned in to nestle his mouth close to her ear, his words hot against her cheek. "Saturday, seven o'clock, I'll pick you up, all right?"

She blinked, still too hazy to form a coherent sentence.

Tucking a finger to her chin, he skimmed her jaw with his thumb while he seared her with that determined glint in his eyes. "If you don't answer, Teach, I may have to kiss you again …"

"I … need to t-think a-about it, Sam." Her words rushed out

in a hoarse stutter as she jerked away, arms clutched to her waist like a barrier. "Then I'll let you know, okay?"

"When?" The steeled look on his handsome face told her he wouldn't give up easily, if at all.

"Soon," she said with another step back, the blood still pounding in her brain. "After you take me home." Heaven help her, she needed space if she was going to make a rational decision.

Lots and lots of space.

He huffed out a sigh tinged with frustration. "All right, kiddo." Hooking her elbow, he practically dragged her down the pier, the clamp of his sculpted jaw telling her he wasn't happy, but he'd do it her way.

For now.

But she knew Sam Cunningham almost better than he knew himself, which is why she paused when he opened the passenger door of his car. "I want your word, Sam, that you won't kiss or touch me again until I make my decision."

Those very lips that had stolen her will only seconds before now compressed into a thin smile that was anything but. "You have my word," he said in a clipped tone, circling the car after he slammed her door with more force than usual. She knew he was angry because he didn't speak on the way home, profile etched in stone as he focused straight ahead. He was a man who wasn't used to a woman telling him no, especially when he'd just laid his heart on the line. But this was too important a decision to allow Sam to have his way without prayer and the counsel of people she trusted. This was her life and her heart at stake here, and possibly her very soul, so she had no desire to make the same mistakes all over again.

Veering into her driveway, he turned off the engine and got out of the car, completely silent as he ushered her to the front porch. Hands deep in his pockets, he patiently waited while she retrieved a key from beneath a potted planter and opened the door. Hand on the knob, she turned, a twinge in her heart over the hurt in his eyes. "I care about you deeply, Sam," she whispered, "both as a friend and as someone with whom I could have so much more. But my heart was wounded once, almost beyond repair, and I will never go there lightly again."

His eyes softened, appearing to chase his prior anger away, and the faint smile he gave her was achingly tender, revealing the soft side of Sam that had stolen her heart. "The kind of love I think we could have together, Shan, is so much more than I ever dreamed. So I'm more than willing to wait."

Emotion thickened the walls of her throat. "I truly appreciate that, Sam, because the only type of love I'm willing to risk my heart on is one that will last forever, so it's definitely worth the wait."

He reached to gently prod the door open, nodding for her to go in. "Good night, Shannon. I'm praying you'll say yes, but either way, I will love you forever."

Tears welled like a flash flood, and reaching out, she caressed his bristled jaw, her hand quivering as much as her heart. "Good night, Sam," she whispered, slipping inside while the look of love in his eyes forever branded her brain. *And if my gut tells me no* ... Her eyes lumbered closed.

Maybe goodbye ...

CHAPTER THIRTY-SIX

Here goes nothing.

Sam slipped out of his Vette and quietly closed the door, wishing he didn't have his good shoes on as he picked his way down a gravel drive to the rustic cabin Chase Griffin rented on a small lake. From what he could see in the dark, it was a good-sized A-frame of sorts that faced a moon-striped body of water too big to be a pond. Tucked away in the trees, Chase's house was one of a smattering of lakeside summer cottages, each far enough apart to ensure privacy.

He's going to think I'm crazy. Loosening the tie he'd worn on what had become his last date with Jazz, Sam sucked in a deep draw of loamy air and slowly mounted the steps to the front door, pretty sure Jack's pastor friend already thought that, but then so what? It was true—he *was* crazy.

Over my best friend.

Shaking his head, Sam raised a fist to knock on a knotty pine door, questioning both his brains and his sanity in not realizing he'd been falling in love with Shannon all along. Unfortunately, it took being with Jazz several months to come to his senses, but once he had, the reality struck like a mega-watt bolt of lightning, leaving him more than a little stunned. But no more stunned than Shannon, he supposed, when he'd told her he was falling in love with her tonight. His mouth compressed. Or himself, for that matter, when she'd told *him* she needed time to think and pray about dating him at all.

He expelled a weary sigh. A girl like Shannon had never been his type. Sweet. Shy. Serious. And *way* too pure to give him the kind of love he'd wanted. Which is why it had never even crossed his mind that she was *exactly* the kind of girl who could give him the kind of love he *needed*. Not the physical kind he'd been searching for since high school, but a kind that could satisfy his heart and soul as well as his body.

Body? A veritable hot flash zipped through him at the memory of the kiss he'd given her on the pier earlier, and his blood simmered with a passion he'd never experienced before. A melding of mind, body, and spirit that blew lust right out of the water, confirming to him once and for all that Shannon was everything he wanted in a wife and a lover—an unpolluted woman.

Innocent. Intelligent. Inspiring. And downright irresistible.

The perfect antidote to all the women who had betrayed him in his life.

His knock immediately prompted a dog within to bark, the ferocious sound confirming he was outmatched should a fight ensue if Chase refused Sam's request to back off from Shannon. Sam's mouth went flat as he knocked again. "Yeah, real smart, Cunningham—let's tick off the ex-Navy Seal and his pit bull."

The sound of footsteps on the other side of the door shook him from his thoughts, and he immediately stiffened, reminding him this was no social call. As much as he wanted to handle this calmly and maturely, he couldn't shake this tension he felt inside, this edgy drive to eliminate the competition. Shannon was too important, and Chase was too much of a threat.

The door opened halfway, and Sam was face-to-face with the guy he didn't want anywhere near Shannon, whether Shannon agreed to date Sam right now or not. His mouth morphed into a scowl. *Which* immediately softened at the sweet whine of a German shepherd the rev was holding back by the collar.

Before Sam could stop himself, he squatted to scratch behind the dog's ears, the shepherd's tail wagging so much, it stirred up a stiff breeze. "Hey there, buddy."

Man, how he'd always wanted a dog growing up! But many of his foster families barely fed *him*, much less a mutt. And as a single man seldom home, he refused to coop an animal up all day and all night.

"Sam!" Chase opened the door wide, his broad smile obviously unaffected by Sam's mild glare. "This is a nice surprise."

Surprise? Definitely. Nice? No way.

Allowing himself a final scrub of the dog's snout, Sam rose, his good mood dimming along with his smile. He plunged his hands in his pockets, fighting the sudden itch to let fly with a punch to that rugged pretty-boy face.

Knock it off, Cunningham, he silently berated himself, *Chase is a reasonable guy.* "Can we talk?" Sam said, his tone suddenly as sharp as the jealousy lancing his gut.

"Sure, come on in." Chase motioned for him to enter, and you would have thought Sam had T-bones in his pockets the way the shepherd went wild, tail whirlybirding while he tried to slather Sam nonstop.

"Sam, *sit!*"

The dog instantly did, and Sam's mouth fell open. "Seriously? Your dog's name is Sam?" He bent to ruffle the shepherd's fur, peering up with a zag of his mouth. "Or was that command for me?"

A grin eased across Chase's face as he closed the door, indicating for Sam to follow. "Him," Chase said with a chuckle, ambling into a woodsy room as rustic on the inside as the cabin was on the outside. "Short for Samson. Although since you appear to be his new hero, maybe I should change it to Samuel."

"Naw, Samson suits him—shaggy and strong like his namesake." Sam strolled behind Chase into a tidy, but old-fashioned, knotty-pine kitchen with a generous window overlooking the lake. He slid onto a matching bar stool at a Formica counter.

Chase laughed as he opened an ancient refrigerator. "Somehow I never pegged you as a Bible guy, Doc." He glanced up from the fridge. "Red Bull, OJ, or coffee?" His mouth tipped. "Or nearly expired milk since I may have one or two monster cookies left over from some that Shannon gave to me."

At the mention of Shannon's name, Sam's mood went south, as sour as that milk was likely to be in another week. "Thanks, but I won't be here that long," he said in a clipped tone, jaw suddenly tight.

Eyes in a squint, Chase stood to his full height with a hand propped to the open fridge door. "Something eating at you, Sam?"

"Yeah, as a matter of fact there is." Sam tried to temper his scowl, but it was no use. The rev was an okay guy, he supposed, but right now he was too big an obstacle in Sam's quest for Shannon, fraying his nerves. Steeling his backbone, Sam jutted his chin. "I broke it off with Jasmine tonight because I've discovered that I have deep feelings for Shannon," he said, eyes unflinching, "so I'm hoping you'll respect that, Chase, and be willing to back off."

Chase closed the door with a cool look before he butted against the counter, muscled arms in a tight fold. "Not an easy thing to do, Doc, since I have feelings for her, too, you know."

Sam's chest constricted. "Are you in love with her?"

Head cocked, Chase studied Sam with an unreadable expression. "I'm on my way," he said quietly, "and I'm not about to back off if she's just another conquest to you, Sam."

In a rare show of temper, Sam slammed a fist to the bar. "I'm in love with her, all right?" His voice came out harsh, shocking even him. He swallowed hard. "And she's in love with me." His voice tapered off to a near whisper. "So I'm asking you nicely, Rev, to do me this favor—please."

"And who told you she's in love with you?" Chase asked with a shuttered look, as if questioning Sam's integrity.

Sam felt a tic in his temple. "She did. Tonight. After I told her I thought I was falling in love with her."

"I see." Without another word, Chase moved to a Keurig coffeemaker—the only new thing in the house—and punched in a K-cup and a mug below, his back to Sam while he waited for it to brew. Muscles that rivaled Sam's own rippled through Chase's thin T-shirt as he reached for a dog biscuit from a cookie jar, and Sam's mouth clamped in a tight line. Whether Shannon agreed to a serious relationship with Sam right now or not, he was determined to oust all competition. His jawbone compressed with resolve. Because one way or the other, she *would* agree eventually if he had his way, and Sam didn't want some muscle-bound minister messing that up.

Mug and dog treat in hand, the rev avoided eye contact on his way to the great room while his pup followed close behind. Tossing the treat in the air, Sam Jr. snatched it as Chase hunched on the edge of a brown leather sectional overlooking the lake, the setting real cozy while he sipped on his coffee.

Only Sam wasn't here for cozy. "So, what's your answer, Rev?" he said, rising to stroll into the main room.

"I'd get some coffee if I were you, Sam," the rev said in an unequivocal monotone as he stared out the window, the tic in his jaw matching the one in Sam's temple.

Frustration suddenly swarmed Sam's collar, lighting his fuse. "I don't want coffee, Griffin; I want your word you'll back off from Shannon."

Chase finally looked up, his steely gaze piercing Sam straight through. "Sure, Cunningham, I'll back off." He took a slow sip of his coffee, drilling Sam with a flinty look that had, no doubt, served him well as a Navy Seal. "On three conditions."

Sam bristled. "And those are?"

Chase took his time with another sip, setting the cup down before slanting back with an arm straddling the top of the sofa, his smile hard. "One, you treat her honorably, respecting her moral boundaries. Which means, Dr. Love," he said with a threat in his tone, "if you're really serious about her like you say, then you toss your little black book in the trash and commit to her and only her. And no fast moves like you pull with other girls either. Shannon is a class act, Sam, and she deserves your respect and protection. So if I feel even a quiver of concern that you're pressuring her in anyway" —he paused with a dip of his granite jaw, his intent more than perfectly clear— "I will mess you and your pretty face up real good, Doc, pastor or no, you got that?"

Sam met his stony look with a stubborn one of his own. "Yeah, I got that. But for your information, *Rev*, Shannon's innocence and purity are two of the things I love about her most, so I have no intention of messing with that *or* her."

"Can I have your word on that?" Chase pinned him with a challenge that scalded the back of Sam's neck.

"I don't have to give you anything," Sam snapped, his tone sharp enough to embarrass him if he wasn't so hot under the collar. He paused to massage the sudden throb between his eyes, desperate to curb an anger he suspected was completely fueled by fear. Expelling a shaky breath, he forced civility into his tone. "But I'll give Shannon my word that my intentions are purely honorable."

Without so much as a blink, Chase stared him down. "Then can I have your word on that?"

Sam let fly with a rare curse, the sound exploding into the air along with his temper. "Yeah, you have my word on that, Preacher Boy, so you happy?"

"Not yet." He rose and strolled into the kitchen, pulling another cup from a cabinet. "I still have two more conditions, Doc." He tossed the used K-cup in the trash and deposited another into the Keurig. "I want you to start coming to church on a regular basis," he said with a hard glance over his shoulder. "Not any of these occasional visits when the mood strikes either, Sam, because Shannon deserves a man of faith, not some player just going through the motions."

Sam worked hard to bridle his impatience. Not because he didn't want to attend church regularly because he did, especially with Shannon. It was the rev's mandate that ticked him off. "Not a problem because I know how important it is to Shannon."

"*And* to you," Chase emphasized, strolling back into the great room with another cup of coffee. He set it down in front of a log chair and ottoman woven in a Navaho pattern of rusts, browns, and blues. "Take a load off, Sam. You probably need to be sitting when I tell you condition number three."

"Already told you, I'm not staying that long." Ignoring the inviting call of the coffee, Sam cocked a hip, hands in his pockets.

"Sure you are," Chase said with an overly confident air that got on Sam's last nerve. "It goes along with condition number three."

"Which is?" Sam singed him with a glare.

Picking up his mug, Chase settled back into his comfy leather sofa with a soft whoosh, eyeing Sam with a knowing smile. "Why, your own personal Bible study group, Dr. Cunningham, every week with you, me and Jack. Beginning tonight."

Sam's mouth dropped open. "You're out of your mind."

"So are you, Dr. Love, if you think I'm going to just step away and let some hotshot player with little or no faith beat my time with a woman I care about."

"Yeah? Well, maybe I'll just take my chances then," he shot back, thoroughly annoyed as he strode for the door. "After all, I'm the one who has her heart."

"And I'm the one who has her faith, Doc," Chase called from the sofa, so may the best man win."

Sam froze with his hand on the knob, the preacher's words stabbing right through the heart.

May the best man win.

He hung his head because deep down Sam knew that wasn't him. And as much as he hated to admit it, Chase was right. Shannon *did* deserve a man of faith and not some player just going through the motions. He expelled a loud blast of air, fraught with frustration before he slowly returned to where Chase sat, face void of the smugness Sam had expected. Instead, all he saw was quiet concern that, knowing Chase Griffin's reputation as a standup guy, he suspected was as much for him as it was for Shannon.

Chest rising and falling in a show of surrender, Sam dropped into the hewn log chair and reached for the coffee, downing a long swallow before he clunked the mug back down. Slapping his palms on the arm of the chair, he met Chase's gaze with a steady one of his own. "Okay, Rev, you're right—Shannon *does* deserve a man of faith, and because I love her, I'm willing to do whatever it takes to get to that place. But I gotta tell you, man, I never expected bribery to be in your bag of tricks."

With a steady air of calm, Chase reached to pull two battered Bibles from the shelf beneath the coffee table, his faint smile somehow disarming the rest of Sam's resistance. "Well, I take my cue from St. Paul who said, 'I have become all things to all men, that I might by all means save some.'" He slid one of the Bibles across the table, his smile easing into a grin. "Which in my book, Doc, may occasionally include a little arm-twisting."

Sam snatched the book up and flipped through the pages, his mouth skewing to the right. "No kidding. But I'll agree with you on one thing—Shannon's definitely worth it." He unleashed a heavy sigh of resignation. "So I guess that means you win."

"Not me, Doc, *you*," Chase said with a faint smile, opening his own Bible on the table before nailing Sam with an understanding gaze that somehow promised adventure. "In every possible way."

CHAPTER THIRTY-SEVEN

T*ing-Ting-Ting.*

Tess held her breath when Ben stood up at the other end of her wrought-iron patio table, clinking a spoon to his iced tea glass while her family and his glanced up. Happy and full from a BBQ feast in celebration of Lacey and Jack's one-year anniversary, everyone stilled as Ben's eyes met hers with a smoky look that tumbled her stomach. "First of all, I'd like to propose a toast to Lacey and Jack on their one year of marital bliss."

Glancing at Lacey and Jack, Tess's eyes immediately flooded with tears, Ben's words reminding her of all the miracles God had wrought in the last year. Her eyes flicked back to Ben, and her heart swelled with a pulse-pounding love she'd never expected to feel again. But feel it she did, to the depth of her soul, for the man at the end of the table with whom she would soon share a name, a home, and a life. A tingle shivered her skin. *Not to mention a bed,* she realized with a flush that toasted both her body and her cheeks. The thought compelled her to upend her own iced tea with shaky hands before Ben could even finish his toast.

"So here's to a lifetime of joy to the best daughter and son-in-law a man could ever have—may your many years together be exceeded only by the happiness they bring."

"And the babies they bear," Cat piped up with a lift of her glass.

"Hear, hear," Shannon said with a wide smile.

"Wish I could second that," Jack said with a grin, "but then Lace and I'd be too tired to take care of them." Arm looped around Lacey's shoulders, he pressed a kiss to his wife's head before he raised a Red Bull in the air, a definite sparkle in his eyes. "But we *are* hoping to get a jumpstart on a houseful of kids soon, beginning with one precious little girl …"

"Oh my gosh—you're pregnant?!" Cat's eyes all but bugged out of her head while Tess caught her breath, hand to her heart.

"In a manner of speaking," Lacey said with a sheen of joy in her eyes, clutching Jack's hand. "We've applied to adopt Debbie."

Whoops and hollers circled the table as everyone congratulated Jack and Lacey, plying them with questions that elicited both laughter and tears.

Jack hoisted his Red Bull once again. "Miss Myra says everything is in order so barring any unforeseen glitches, which is highly unlikely, it's just a matter of time. So here's to the perfect adoption *along* with the perfect house since we haven't had much luck finding it yet." He shot Ben a sheepish grin. "And I'm pretty sure Ben would like his back."

"Well, you and Lace could always move in with us for a while …" Cat finger-shot a crumb at Jack. "But I'm not giving Jack's bathroom shelf back, just saying …"

"Don't worry, Cat," Ben said, pinning Tess with a possessive look, "you won't have to." He carried his iced tea to where Tess sat welded to her chair, hands sweating more than the glass in her hand. With a calm and steady smile, he gently hooked her elbow to lift her to her feet, shoring her up with a firm hand to her waist—completely necessary given the wobble of her legs. She and Ben had announced they planned to date at a family BBQ over a month and a half ago, but marriage was something else altogether. *Especially* since none of her family except for Lacey and Jack had even a clue how deeply Tess and Ben felt about the other.

Depositing a kiss to Tess's head, Ben tightened his hold with an awkward grin. "I've asked your mother to marry me."

"I knew it!" Cat shouted, jumping up with an I-told-you-so grin.

"You *knew?*" Tess gaped at her daughter, the flush in her cheeks burning more than the heat of Ben's hand on her waist.

"Knew what?" Davey wanted to know, glancing up from his Power Ranger action figures long enough to blink at his sister.

Ben left Tess's side to squat next to Davey's chair, squeezing Davey's shoulder like she'd seen him do a dozen times over the last month as he made an effort to bond with her son. An effort that had paid off with Davey's instant attachment to the former grump next door through games of catch and a lucrative job walking Ben's dog, Beau. "That your mom and I want to get married," Ben said gently, "that is, if it's okay with you and your sisters?"

Davey's eyes expanded, as wide as the moon pies Ben had introduced him to and supplied weekly. "You mean you're gonna be my dad?" he whispered, the hope in his eyes a testimony to the grace of God. Not only in changing a bitter recluse like Dr. Doom into a man now treasured by his family and hers, but in healing Davey's heart over the loss of a father he adored, forging the way for Ben to step into the role.

"Nobody can take the place of your dad, bud," Ben said quietly, his voice suddenly as unsteady as Tess's stomach, "but I would love to be your stepdad because I love your mom and I've always longed to raise a son. That is, if you'll have me."

Saltwater sabotaged Tess's eyes all over again at the crack of Ben's voice, the sight of Davey launching into Ben's arms almost more joy than she could bear. "You bet, Dr. Carmichael," he shouted with a tight squeeze, and Tess would have laid odds there wasn't a dry eye at the table.

"Oh, Mom, I couldn't be happier for you!" Shannon said with a soggy hug, a toss-up as to which of the females was weeping the most.

"Well *I* sure could be happier," Cat said, a tease in her voice despite its nasal tone from crying. "As long as you don't get married till *after* Thanksgiving, that is. Shan bet you'd tie the knot before the holidays, but I bet her fifty bucks you wouldn't till after."

"Wait …" Tess paused in the middle of wiping the wetness from her eyes, jaw sagging. "You not only *knew* we'd be getting married, but you bet as to *when* it would be?"

Cat gave a casual shrug. "Come on, Mom, we figured you and Ben had to be more than friends as early as last summer because, duh … you're like the Queen of Obvious."

"I'll second that," Ben said with a grin, cuffing Davey's shoulder before he rose, hand still firmly anchored to her son's shoulder.

Tess blinked, her brain on overload. "But … but how on earth did you guess?" she said, too shocked to acknowledge Ben's remark. Her eyes lighted on Lacey and Jack, the only ones who knew she and Ben were totally smitten. "Wait a second, you two didn't spill it, did you?"

Jack raised a palm, his grin as guilty as Lacey's. "And suffer the wrath of Dr. Doom and Tess O'Bryen?" He slanted back in his chair with a lazy smile. "I have a medical degree hanging on my office wall, Mom, so give me some credit, will you?"

"Us, too," Cat said with a bear hug of her own, pulling away to snatch a tissue from a box Lacey had retrieved from the kitchen. "I thought Shan was awful at being sneaky, but you take the prize, Mom." She blew her nose, then dabbed at her face with a grin. "I mean how many walks can one person take at night when she works at home and can work out during the day?"

Tess could only stare, dumbstruck.

Shannon kneaded Tess's shoulder. "And really, Mom, how many batches of monster cookies can one mother make before a daughter gets a tad suspicious?"

Tess stared at Ben. "Do you believe this?"

He slipped an arm around her waist again. "Unfortunately, yes, because you're an open book, Teresa O'Byren." He deposited a kiss to her head, scooping her close. "Deceit just isn't in your DNA, sweetheart, which is one of the reasons I fell in love with you."

"So …" Cat handed her mother the box of tissues and sat back down, idly licking the spoon from her empty dessert plate. "Let's start with the most important thing, shall we?" She pointed the spoon at her mother with a determined squint. "When are you getting married, because I have fifty badly needed bills riding on this wedding happening *after* Thanksgiving, people, and not a day before."

Ben gently nudged Tess to sit, claiming Lacey's chair beside her when Jack tugged his wife onto his lap. Shifting closer, Ben casually circled Tess's waist with one hand while he wove his fingers through hers with the other, jumbling her thought process when his thumb slowly skimmed back and forth on her palm.

"No offense, Cat," Ben said with a lazy smile, his smug tone indicating he was completely aware how his touch could muddle Tess's mind, "but if I win this debate, young lady, you're going to take a loss." His fingers nipped at Tess's waist. "But your loss is my gain."

"Ben's right, Mom—why wait?" Slipping back into her chair, Shannon offered an innocent smile, which now held a touch of mischief. "The way I figure it, you and Ben have had a close relationship since Lacey came back, at least based on the upsurge of monster cookies and bacon. And you've known each other forever, so it's not like *that's* an issue," Shannon reasoned, "so I say the sooner the better."

"The better for you, you mean," Cat said dryly, the twinkle in her eyes meeting the glaze in Tess's. "*And* Mom, apparently, given the loopy look on her face."

Ben leaned in to press a kiss to Tess's ear, his words husky. "And trust me, Teresa Catherine, there are more loopy looks from where that one came from," he whispered, fingers lightly skimming from her hip to the side of her thigh.

Tess blasted to her feet, suddenly in dire need of more tea.

Cold, *cold* tea …

"Who needs a refill?" she asked, painfully aware her smile was way too bright.

"Sit, Mom, I'll get it." Shannon rose with her usual sensitive efficiency, snatching Tess's glass up before Tess could grab it for herself. "Anybody else need anything?"

"I'll take more chocolate milk, sis," Davey said with a swoop of his favorite Power Ranger action figure while Cat stood to follow Shan.

"Thanks, Shan," Tess said with a tight-lipped smile aimed directly at Ben. "And bring Ben more ice water, will you? *Heavy* on the ice." She ignored the grin he gave her, along with the knowing look in his eyes.

By the time the girls were back with drinks, Tess had scooted her chair a safe distance from Ben, who now focused his attention on Lacey and Jack, grilling them on their house-hunting status. "What about that house you liked on Loon Lake?" he asked, "the one without a dock?"

Jack sighed, arm limp over Lacey's shoulder. "Mold." His lips skewed with disappointment. "Which is more hassle than we want to deal with right now, plus cleanup would cost a fortune."

Lacey sagged against Jack's chest, her tone as glum as his. "There's just not anything decent on the water within our price range, Daddy, which means we either give up our dream to own a home on the water or move into an apartment for a few years.

"Or maybe you could rent to own ..." Ben said slowly, idly reaching for Tess's hand on top of the table, giving it a light press to signal the subject they'd already agreed upon.

"Ha!" Lacey issued a grunt. "As if *those* kind of opportunities grow on trees."

"They do on family trees, sweetheart," Tess said with a misty smile, shock registering on both Jack and Lacey's faces when realization dawned in their eyes. She squeezed Ben's hand back. "After all, your dad and I only need one house to live in, and Davey, the girls and I are rather partial to ours."

Lacey sat straight up, saucer eyes trained on her dad. "B-But ... but ... when I was at your office last week, your colleague Dr. Morris said he made you an offer you couldn't refuse," she stuttered.

Ben grinned over the rim of his ice water, Adam's apple glugging as he watched his daughter. "That's what he thought, but turns out I could." A muscle suddenly flickered in his jaw, and Tess knew he was battling the onslaught of emotion when his voice wobbled into a near whisper. "That house didn't provide you with much joy in the past, sweetheart, but I'm determined it will in the future—if you and Jack want it."

"If we want it?" Jack gaped at Ben, struggling with a few emotions of his own as he blinked hard to dispel moisture from his eyes. "It's more than we ever dreamed possible, sir, but your house is worth a fortune, and this just wouldn't be fair."

Ben lost the battle when a sheen of tears glazed in his eyes. His jaw quivered as he reached to squeeze his daughter's hand. "It wasn't fair how I treated Lacey and you in the past either, Jack, but God's given me the chance to try and make it up to you, so don't deny an old man his one shot at making amends."

"Amends aren't necessary, Daddy," Lacey whispered, flinging herself into her father's arms. "Your love is all I ever need."

"You have it, sweetheart, always, but I'm afraid amends are necessary for me," he rasped, eyes closed as he held her tight. "That is, if you and Jack actually *want* the house, because I don't want to twist your arm."

"No arm-twisting needed, sir, I assure you," Jack said with a hardy pump of Ben's hand before coming over to swallow Tess up in a big hug. "Mom, we can't thank you enough." His voice cracked, and Tess clung with all of her might, throat too thick with emotion to do anything but cry.

Cat's chuckle helped to temper the tears. "Gosh, Lace, this means I can keep raiding your closet."

"Not after I change the locks," Jack said with a grin. "With a key for Mom and Shan because at least I can trust *them* not to erase my scores on the Xbox."

Cat delivered a mischievous smile with a toss of her hair. "No sense in keeping the lowest scores when a superior gamer is in the house, now is there, Jack?"

He grinned and pelted her with a balled-up napkin before facing Ben again, his smile fading into a determined clamp of his jaw. "Sir, Lacey and I can't thank you enough, but the only way we would even consider this is if we agree on a fair-market price with interest."

"Agreed," Ben said with a counter thrust of his chin, reminding

Tess that her future husband was no slouch in the stubborn department. "On the fair-market price, Jack, but not on the interest. The loan will be interest free or nothing."

"No, sir." Jack's jaw rose to meet Ben's. "I wouldn't feel right about that, so I insist on interest of some kind."

A faint smile shadowed Ben's lips. "Now I know one of the reasons I always gave you so much grief over the years, Jack—you remind me of me." He huffed out a sigh as he dragged Tess's chair closer to his, draping an arm over her shoulder. "Fine. One percent interest, take it or leave it."

Jack's temple twitched briefly before he extended his hand, the determined glint in his eyes not unlike that of the man Tess was about to marry. "I'll take it, sir—for now." They shook in agreement. "But as soon as Lacey and I are financially able, we renegotiate the interest in your favor, agreed?"

"And if I don't?"

Lacey joined the fray with a jut of her own chin. "Then we keep looking for a house."

Ben shook his head, his smile veering off-center. "You two deserve each other," he said with a chuckle, planting a kiss on Tess's head. "All right, deal."

"*Eeeeeek!*" Lacey squealed as she jumped up to hug her dad again and then Tess, finally plopping back onto Jack's lap. "We have a house, Brye, can you believe it?" She settled in with a giggle, grabbing her Diet DP. "So I guess that brings us back to the question of the hour, you two—exactly when *are* you tying the knot?"

Ben's satisfied smile told her he thought he had the edge for his choice of an immediate ceremony with a few family and friends rather than a more official December wedding for propriety's sake. "The sooner, the better, as far as I'm concerned," he said with a kiss to her cheek, deliberately brushing his mouth against her ear in a loud whisper. "You know, so the kids can finally be on their own with me out of their hair?"

Smile tipping, Tess shot him a narrow look out of the corner of her eye. "Why, how thoughtful, Dr. Doom."

"You have no idea, Teresa Catherine," he breathed softly, his low chuckle purling warm in her ear, "yet."

Giving up the ghost, she shook her head, her laughter as soft as his. "All right, Dr. Carmichael, you win—the Saturday after Thanksgiving."

"Yes!" Cat fist-punched the air.

"Nope," Ben countered, "two weeks. That's more than enough time to plan a small, catered affair for family in my backyard like we discussed, Tess, so there's no reason to wait. It'll be perfect."

"Two weeks?" Tess whirled to gape at him.

"It does make sense, Mom," Jack said, "getting married and settled in before the holidays hit, which are always crazy enough without a wedding in the mix."

Tess's smile took a left. "Et tu, Brute?"

Jack grinned. "Face it, Mom—we're all going to feel a whole lot better when you're happily married and life settles down."

"Especially me," Ben murmured against her hair, his gentle massage of her shoulders reminding her of all the benefits in store. "And I'll even pay Shan the fifty dollars."

"Well, that settles it, then!" Cat checked her phone calendar. "Saturday, October 1st sound okay?" A grin suddenly slid across her face. "And, hey, guess what? This is a calendar app that lists all the special days of the year, and you'll never believe what October 1st is!"

Tess glanced at Ben, mouth skewing to the left. "National Arm-twisting Day?"

"Nope." Cat glanced up, eyes twinkling. "National Homemade Cookies Day." She put a hand over her heart. "It's a sign!"

"No kidding?" Ben grinned ear-to-ear, bending to deposit a kiss to Tess's cheek. "I'd say it's a done deal, then, Tess, wouldn't you?"

Tess rolled her eyes, unable to suppress a chuckle. "Do I have a choice?"

"No!" the entire table shouted in unison, including Davey and his Power Rangers.

Tess shook her head, a smile breaking through when she

realized this was what she'd wanted all along, if not compelled to give her family time to adjust. Releasing a heady sigh of surrender, she patted Ben's sandpaper cheek with a tender smile. "I didn't think so."

CHAPTER THIRTY-EIGHT

It *shouldn't be this way.* Despite a joyous engagement, a heady sea breeze, and a melon moon hovering over a river shimmering with stars, Shannon couldn't fully enjoy the beauty of the night.

Because of Sam.

Carefully picking her way down the stone pathway to their dock where Ben and her mom had been shooed during dishes and cleanup, Shannon was grateful the newly engaged couple would be by themselves. Lacey and Jack had gone home, and Davey and Cat had long since gone to bed, so Shannon hoped an hour and a half of alone time was enough for the two people whose advice she desperately needed. She hadn't wanted to discuss Sam with Jack because the two men had become too close as friends, and Shannon wanted more objectivity to the counsel she sought. Right now, she needed wisdom forged through experience, and nobody had dealt with trust issues in a relationship more than her mother and Ben.

Squinting down the moonlit ramp, she was relieved to see two Adirondack chairs facing the water, linked by a single clasp of hands. With a final prayer for wisdom, she made a point of rattling the ramp as she walked, the whisper of swaying marsh grasses urging her on. "Mom?"

Two heads turned, silhouettes of surprise against a harvest moon. "Shan?" A hint of worry threaded her mother's tone as she pivoted all the way in her chair to watch Shannon's approach. "Everything all right?"

"Yes," Shannon whispered, apology lacing her words. "And then again, no."

Ben immediately rose. "Here, Shannon, take my chair. It's getting late, and I should head home."

"No, please, Ben, don't. I actually would like your opinion on something as well as my mom's—the male perspective, if you will." She started to drag another chair over, but he quickly picked it up and set it down next to her mother's before returning to his own seat.

"What's this about, sweetheart?" her mother said softly, rubbing Shannon's arm with a tenderness that never failed to soothe.

Feet tucked beneath her, Shannon slanted back in her chair, arms resting on its sides while she stared at the moon-ribboned river. "It's about Sam, Mom," she whispered, giving her mother's hand a gentle squeeze before facing her with a timid gaze. "I … haven't mentioned this before, because I didn't want to worry you, but I have" —a lump bobbed in her throat as she forced the words out on a rasp— "strong feelings for Sam."

Her mother stared for several seconds while her chest rose and fell in a silent sigh. "I wondered, sweetheart, because Jack warned me that Sam could charm a bird out of a tree."

A rusty chuckle slipped from Shannon's lips as she stared out over the water. "Yes, well, he certainly charmed this bird, no matter how hard she clung to that stupid tree."

"Oh, honey, I am so very sorry." Her mother leaned in to bundle Shannon in her arms, causing tears to prick at the back of Shannon's lids. "Does Sam know?"

Shannon nodded. "He does now. I told him last night." She nibbled the edge of her lip as she pulled away to peek up at her mom. "Right after he told me he broke it off with Jasmine because he has feelings for me."

Tess's lips parted in a surprised smile. "Seriously? Well, honey, that's wonderful news!" She paused, obviously noting the troubled look on Shannon's face. "Isn't it?"

"For most women, I suppose," she whispered, her mouth tipping off-center, "but you and I both know that when it comes to being in love, I'm no longer 'most women.'"

Tess gently brushed the hair from Shannon's eyes, ducking to offer a tender smile. "Honey, what happened with Eric is in the past, and God has redeemed both it and you."

Shannon blinked hard to clear the threat of tears. "I know," she whispered, "and I truly believe that, I do. But—"

"You're afraid." Tess stared her down, lips pursed in mother mode over the damage that had been done to her daughter.

Shannon nodded. "Petrified. What happened with Eric almost destroyed me, Mom." Her mother's face swam before her in a blur of tears, and she fought the rise of a sob. "I can't go there again, ever. It would kill me."

"No, it wouldn't, sweetheart." Tess gently laid her hand over Shannon's, the glow of love in her eyes a balm to Shannon's soul. "You're no longer that woman, Shannon. I've watched your faith grow to invincible heights as your dependence has grown on an invincible God."

Shannon sniffed, offering a nod of thanks to Ben when he produced a fresh handkerchief from his pocket. "Then why don't I feel like it?"

Tess smiled, briefly massaging Shannon's shoulder before settling back in her own chair. "Because you're focusing on *your* strength instead of God's, Shan, which we all know from painful experience, is no strength at all." She paused, head tilted in contemplation. "Which, in fact, is actually the perfect place to be for a person of faith."

Shannon slid her mother a sideways smile. "'For when I am weak, then I am strong'"?

"Exactly," Tess said with a heft of her chin. "God sure nailed St. Paul and each of us to the wall when He said, 'My grace is sufficient for you, for My power is made perfect in weakness,' because frankly, Shan, we human beings flat-out don't like being weak." Tess paused to graze a gentle hand to her daughter's cheek. "But the truth is, it's that very weakness—that futility and failure, that utter despair—that brings us to the bottom line." Her smile quirked. "Finally letting go and letting God carry us through."

She shifted in the chair to face Shannon. "And you know what, Shan? I saw that firsthand with you, after Eric. You were as low as a human being can go, honey, because everything you put your hope in was either gone or helpless to deliver you from the darkness in your soul. Except God." Tears sparked in her mother's eyes. "And it was His power that was made perfect in your weakness, sweetheart, when He opened your eyes to the reality that everything of value is in Him and only Him. You've always had a strong faith, Shannon, but never like now. Now your faith has been forged in fire to produce a gleaming treasure of truth."

Tess cradled Shannon's hand, the shimmer of saltwater in her mother's eyes matching her own. "And that is that no matter who, no matter what, no matter why—your peace, your joy, your hope rests only in Him, Shannon. Not in Eric. Not in Sam. And not in your own strength or anyone else's. *In Him and only Him.*" She nodded to the canopy of stars overhead where a brilliant moon underscored her statement with a slash of gold glittering across the water. "The Lover of your soul, darling, Whose unfailing love—unlike Eric's or any others'—will last forever."

I have loved you with an everlasting love …

Heaves rising, Shannon flung herself into her mother's arms. "I love you, Mom," she whispered, her words thick with congestion, "and I'm so grateful for the legacy of faith that you and Daddy instilled in our family."

"Oh, me too." Her mother's raspy whisper confirmed Shannon wasn't alone in her tears.

"Here." Shannon pushed Ben's handkerchief into her mother's hand. "I think you need this as much as I do."

"You ladies keep this up, and I'm gonna need it too." Ben's husky tone rescued the moment, prompting a mother/daughter grin punctuated by matching sighs.

"So," Tess said with a dab of her eyes, reverting to her transparent tone that said she would not let her daughter leave until every hint of fear was routed out. "Do you love Sam, sweetheart?"

Shannon expelled a weighty sigh of surrender. "Unfortunately."

"And he loves you?" Ben asked, brows in a scrunch.

She peeked over at Ben with a chew of her lip. "I think so—he said he's falling in love with me."

Tess tipped her head, eyes in a squint. "Then other than your fear of relationships, *which* we are going to pray about," she emphasized, "what's the problem, sweetheart?"

Shannon plopped her head against the back of her chair, venting with a long, wavering breath. "He's a player, Mom, or he used to be, and I guess I'm just not all that sure he can change to be a man who will love only me forever."

Ben grunted. "Trust me—he can change. Maybe dragging his feet all the way," he said with a tweak of Tess's neck, "but for the right woman and with God's help? He can do it."

"Agreed." Two tiny lines dug in at the bridge of Tess's brow. "But you said he's changed so much already, Shan, making great strides in the faith you've introduced him to, right?"

"Yes, he has, definitely," she said with a slow nod. "He's grown a lot in his faith since we've been friends, and he's even gone to church a few times, but …"

"But what?" her mother asked, her gaze probing Shannon's.

Shannon jumped up to walk off some of her restlessness, the same restlessness she saw in Sam at times when he got bored, his interest waning in things he thought would make him happy. Like all of his trappings. Scores of women. Jasmine.

Me?

"I guess I'm just not sure how capable Sam is of fully committing, whether to God or to a woman." She moved toward the edge of the dock overlooking the water, buffing her arms as if she could somehow warm the chill that blew through her every single time she thought of Eric.

"Ours is a forever love, Shan, I promise," he'd once told her. Only it hadn't been, and the scars were still buried deep in her heart, begging her not to go there again.

"He's a good man," she continued, "but his values have been

so shallow for so long that I wonder if he's even capable of the kind of deep commitment I crave in a marriage." She turned to face them again, shoulders and heart in a slump, both over the potential risk to her *and* telling Sam no. She gave a small shrug. "I guess I'm just not sure which way I should go."

"You don't trust him." Ben's soft comment reverberated loud in her ears.

She paused. *Don't I?* She closed her eyes, and Sam's handsome face suddenly appeared, his deep-down serious demeanor and tender smile telling her that she did trust him. With her life. He suddenly winked, and his face morphed into Eric's, taking her stomach for a tumble.

Just not with my heart.

"I guess not," she whispered, "at least not enough for a love that would last forever, so I suppose I have my answer."

"Not necessarily." Ben rose from his chair and paced the dock like Shannon had with hands in his pockets before he halted to peer at her mother. "Tess? Did you trust me when we first fell in love?"

"Ha! Are you kidding?" She sat back with a toss of her head like he'd just asked the world's stupidest question. "Not on your life, Dr. Doom."

His mouth slid sideways. "A simple yes or no would have sufficed."

Her face softened. "Come on, sweetheart—you were a widowed womanizer who shut people out with hedges and padlocks, including your only daughter. *And* you had about as much use for God as you did for your perky neighbor."

His smile crooked. "Yeah, but they both got me in the end."

Folding her hands on her stomach, Tess released a contented sigh. "Yes, we did, and it was a team effort."

"My point exactly," he said to Shannon, feet straddled and hands still in his pockets as he pinned her with a piercing look. "There was nobody more shallow than me, Shannon, and if it hadn't been for the prayer and persistence of a perky and pesky neighbor poking her nose into my life, I would have never known the depth of love I know today. Not only with God and your mother, but with her family and mine."

Hope flickered in Shannon's heart. "So you're saying I should give Sam a chance?"

"What I'm saying *is*," he said quietly, "I believe change is possible for any man who opens his heart up to God. Jack's told me a little about Sam's history, and like Sam, I never knew real love either—the kind that lasts forever—until the day your mother introduced me to the One Who loves forever. You better believe that kind of love changes a man, Shan." His gaze flicked to where her mother sat in the chair with tears in her eyes, the love flowing between them as strong as the current swirling down the Skidaway River. "And trust me, sweetheart—that kind of woman makes *him* want to love *her* forever." Expelling a sigh, he returned to his chair, taking her mother's hand in his own while his gaze connected with Shannon's. "And if He can do that for an old grouch like me, Shannon, He can do that for Sam too." He squeezed Tess's hand before sending Shannon a wink. "And for you."

CHAPTER THIRTY-NINE

The end.

Unleashing a contented sigh, Shannon sank back against her headboard, legs stiff from an afternoon of furious writing to meet her deadline. She stared at the last page of *Love Everlasting* on her computer screen, the novel her freelance editor had talked her into ghostwriting, and a heady smile curved on her lips. No, not the end—the beginning.

Just like for Sam and me.

She closed her laptop, the story between a princess and a playboy having taken a twist she hadn't expected, providing a fairytale ending that made her heart sing. Not unlike her relationship with Sam, she supposed, where she hoped and prayed for a fairytale ending too.

Glancing at her alarm clock, she jumped up to get ready, heart thudding that in two short hours, she and Sam would go out on their first date. She put a hand to her stomach to quell the excitement churning and headed for the shower, more than well aware that a bit of worry was in the mix too. Her feelings for Sam were stronger than she ever dreamed possible, and certainly more than she ever wanted, but her trust factor came in a poor second. As her best friend, she trusted Sam with her life. But as a man who held her heart—and her life—in his hands? She fought off a cold ripple of concern that rained down along with the cold water in the shower.

Not so much.

Putting on the finishing touches of makeup she seldom wore, Shannon heard the doorbell ring, and grabbed her purse. She compelled herself to descend the steps far more slowly than the adrenaline that surged through her veins. But when she saw Sam laughing with Cat and her mom in the foyer, her tendons went limp at the back of her knees. Flashing a dimpled grin, he could have walked right off the runway in a tightly tailored charcoal fitted suit with a mauve silk tie, hands leisurely in his pockets as he towered over Cat and her mom. And when those deep umber eyes glanced up to connect with hers, she thought she might swoon, never more grateful for the banister that helped her stay up.

"Wow." That's all he said as she met him at the door, but his look of stark approval said far more, dusting her cheeks with a warmth that did a slow spiral throughout her entire body.

She didn't even notice the flowers until Cat waved a long florist box in her face, dropping her jaw when her mother also held out a gold two-pound box of Godiva chocolates. "Oh, Sam, you didn't have to do this," she whispered, opening the floral box to reveal a dozen red roses.

He gave a shrug that came off more as an awkward schoolboy than a seasoned player. "Sure I did, Shan," he said, the husky tenor of his voice assuring her he meant every word. "First dates should be special." His eyes held an intensity that purled heat in her middle. "Especially when the girl is as special as you."

From that moment on, the evening had been a whirl of wonder. Sam spoiled her rotten with dinner at Savannah's finest restaurant followed by dancing at a trendy club, all culminating with a decadent dessert at Lulu's. They'd wined, they'd dined, they'd laughed, they'd cried, all the while Sam treating her like a goddess for six incredible hours. *Which* produced more tingles than any romance novel she ever read or could write. Smiling, she released a satisfied sigh as he regaled her with a darling story about the flu-shot debacle with the Brinker twins.

Thank you, Lord, for the best night of my life!

The Vette veered onto her street, and her pulse surged till she thought she might faint.

Uh … *and* the most nerve-wracking! Because laughing and talking with Sam Cunningham was one thing, the easiest thing in the world for her to do. But the kisses that were sure to follow her evening of bliss? Shannon fought a gulp as Sam eased his car into her driveway. She was more nervous than a sixteen-year-old on a first date—hands clammy and the skin beneath her silk halter dress just as bad. When he finally turned off the car and angled her way, she was hyperventilating so fast, she prayed she wouldn't pass out.

"I don't want this night to end, Shannon," he whispered, lacing his fingers through hers with a smoky look that stole all moisture from her throat. She held her breath, expecting him to kiss her, but he only grazed his fingers down the curve of her cheek. "Take a walk with me?"

A gust of relief rushed from her lungs as she nodded. He gave her hand a squeeze and got out to open her door. "I don't know about you, Angel Eyes," he said softly, securing her hand in his as they walked down Bluff Drive, "but this was one of the best nights I can remember."

"Me too," she whispered, the heat of Sam's hand against hers making her warm all over. She peeked up with a shy smile, hardly able to believe she and Sam Cunningham were dating.

"You know what's really freaky, Shan?" Pausing, he looped an arm around her waist to face her head-on. "One day we're the best of friends, and then the next?" He feathered her hair away from her face while moonlight highlighted his handsome features. "I'm so head over heels, all I can think about is holding you ..." His eyelids shuttered halfway as he traced her mouth with the pad of his thumb. "Kissing you ..." Her stomach quivered when he bent in to gently skim his mouth against hers, the taste of him almost buckling her at the knees. As if sensing the effect he had, he groaned and clutched her closer, devouring her with a kiss so urgent, it completely consumed her, taking possession with a fierce urgency as if to stake his claim.

He pulled away, and the separation was almost a physical ache, her lips following as if he were a magnet. Eyes closed, her body swayed forward in a dizzy lean, desperate to recapture the sensation of his mouth. His husky chuckle lured her eyes open as he cupped her face in his hands. "You know, Shan, I thought a walk might be nice and safe, but I'm not sure anyplace would be safe when I'm with you."

The heat pulsing through her converged in her cheeks as she nibbled on the edge of her lip. Her smile was shaky and shy, and she was quite sure the glow of love in her eyes was brighter than the harvest moon overhead. "I think I know now why they call you Dr. Love," she said softly, the sigh that sifted through her lips as wobbly as her limbs. "That kiss was …" A warm shiver skittered across her bare shoulders, and she wasn't sure whether it was the sea breeze or Sam. "Unlike anything I've ever experienced before."

"That's because it's not just a kiss," he whispered, bowing his head to touch his forehead to hers, "it's the gift of my heart, Shan, all wrapped up in the need to cherish both you and this fragile feeling inside that I never, ever expected." His quiet sigh feathered her face. "After a lifetime adrift, you anchor me unlike anyone I've ever known, Shannon, and just being with you completely calms my soul." He paused and she felt his smile rather than saw it. "Of course it would appear that you also stir my body with a passion that is anything *but* calm, Angel Eyes. Which," he said, putting distance between them with a gentle brace of her arms, "is why I'm going to employ some of that famous will power I've fine-tuned over the last few months to avoid serious temptation." He grazed her lips with a bare breeze of a kiss. "*And* Jack's fist."

Grinning at the reference to the teasing threat Jack had made when he discovered she and Sam planned to date, she stood on tiptoe to return a tender kiss of her own. "I can't tell you how much I appreciate that, Sam, because I'm not sure I could survive too many kisses from the notorious Dr. Love. At least, not unscathed."

He threaded his fingers into her hair to cradle her head with an intensity that stilled her, the unflinching sobriety in his eyes revealing the core of the man she'd come to love. "You have my word, Shannon, I will do everything in my power to try and never hurt you," he whispered.

Try. One word that reminded her there were no guarantees in love. But somehow she sensed Sam was different. He would never betray her like Eric, she just knew it. A shiver tiptoed down her spine.

Would he?

"You cold?" He took off his jacket before she could stop him and draped it over her shoulders, bundling her in a magical cocoon of his warmth and scent. "We should get you inside," he said softly, "even though I really don't want to go."

"Hey …" She glanced up, the dark stubble on his jaw making him look like a pirate in the moonlight. "Ever been in a dory?"

One corner of his mouth jagged up. "I've never been in a boat, period."

She blinked, mouth hanging open at the notion that Sam Cunningham, all-around sportsman and man about town, was a complete landlubber. "Never?"

His smile was sheepish. "Not even a canoe at Camp Hope," he admitted, nudging her hair over her shoulder. "Still love me?"

"Mmm, I don't know …" She wiggled free from his hold, a mock serious look on her face as she perched hands on her hips. "I'll have you know I'm Queen of the Dory, mister, a title hard-won against both my brother and sister in a race timed by my father."

A competitive spark lit in his eyes. "Ahhh … an overachiever. That's my girl." He trailed her lip with a glide of his thumb, his eyes following the motion before they connected with hers in a potent look that pooled heat in her belly. "Queen of the Dory, huh? So I'm in good hands if I ever go with you?"

She swallowed hard. "You won't be in *any* hands, Dr. Cunningham, I promise, because I'm as adamant as you about not rocking the boat. Besides," she said with a wiggle of brows, feeling as impish as Cat, "each person has to sit on his or her own bench seat several feet apart, so we don't upset the balance."

Stepping closer, he slid his hands into his coat and around her waist, a bob in his throat telling her he was feeling the intensity of attraction as much as she. "And we wouldn't want to do that, would we?" he whispered, enfolding her in a hug before he deposited a kiss to her hair, finally resting his head on top of hers. She felt his chest expand and deflate. "This is going to be harder than I thought, Shan," he said quietly, his shaky sigh feathering her hair.

Tell me about it. Shannon slipped out of his jacket, handing it back before she took his hand. "Come on, Doc, your moonlight sail awaits."

"Whoa, wait a minute ..." She practically bounced off his chest when he jerked her back, his body rooted to the street more firmly than the lampposts lining Bluff Drive. His brows lifted high as he put on his jacket. "You don't mean *tonight*? In my good clothes and shoes?"

She giggled, his obvious reluctance making her grin. "Yes, tonight, mister, and I promise neither you nor your beloved wardrobe will get wet."

"B-But … can't we just sit on the dock?" His voice hitched as she dragged him across the street.

"Nope. The chairs are too close and the moonlight too tempting. It's best in the dory, where we can enjoy the beauty of the night while we keep our distance." She halted halfway down the ramp, brows in a scrunch. "You *can* swim, can't you?"

"Oh, now there's a confidence builder!" He eyed the row of Adirondack chairs with a look of longing. "Yes, I can swim, Teach, but just barely."

"Don't be such a baby, Sam." She grinned while she retrieved two life jackets from the storage closet, kicking off her heels before leading him to the dory that was tied up to the side of the dock. "This will be an adventure you'll never forget, I promise."

"That's what I'm afraid of," he muttered, peering over the side with a suspicious squint.

She tossed the life jackets in the boat and hopped in, taking her position at the stern to lower the trolling motor into the water. "Come on, Sam, get in. We'll just putt upstream a bit and float down. Trust me, you'll love it."

"You, I trust," he said with a wary look, "but this sad excuse for a boat?" His smile went flat as he carefully removed his shoes, placing them beneath an Adirondack chair prior to methodically draping his jacket over the back. "Neither I nor my J. Crew loafers and favorite 'trappings' are feeling too cozy about this." With painstaking care, he slipped his "preowned" Rolex watch into his blazer pocket, then began unbuttoning his Armani slim-fit dress shirt, the one he'd told her he only wore for special occasions.

"For goodness sake, Sam," she said, watching as he took the shirt off, revealing a well-muscled T-shirt beneath. "We're *not* going to get wet."

He cocked a brow as he meticulously laid the shirt over his blazer. "Well, my prized wardrobe won't, that's for sure," he said with a ghost of a smile, shocking her when he began to unbuckle his belt.

"Sam!" She jolted straight up in the dory, slapping a hand to her eyes while her stomach whirled like an eddy in the river. "What on earth are you doing?" she rasped, peeking through two fingers in case he planned to remove his trousers as well.

He grinned as he whipped off his belt, neatly coiling it before placing it on the seat of the chair. "Versace alligator—stiff price, but worth every penny."

A knot ducked in her throat. "You *do* plan on leaving your trousers on, right?"

Hands perched low on his hips, he glanced down at perfectly pressed gray trousers, his little-boy grin sputtering her pulse. "Well, I don't want to, Teach, but it might look suspect if they fish me out in my boxer briefs after I drown, you know?"

"You are *not* going to drown, Sam Cunningham!" Smiling, she shook her head.

"I already have," he said with a weighty sigh, gingerly stepping into the bow of the boat. Easing down on the bench seat, he snatched one of the life jackets and put it on, his smile far drier than he obviously expected his clothes to be. "Into the sea of love, as evidenced by the fact that I'm willing to get into a boat not fit for a bathtub, on a body of water that's churning my dinner."

Shannon's gaze softened, suddenly remembering Jack mentioning something about Sam's aversion to large bodies of water. "Look, Sam, if you really don't want to go—"

He gave her a shuttered look that wobbled her tummy more than the rolling dory, making her grateful he was at the other end of the boat. "Too late. I've already stripped down to near humiliation, Miss O'Bryen, so let's get this moonlight sail underway. Besides," he said, looking downright adorable with his life jacket tightly tied at his neck and palms knuckle-white on the bench, "your virtue has never been safer. Because as much as I want to kiss you right now?" His smile tipped starboard. "You have my word—it sure won't be me rocking this boat."

CHAPTER FORTY

"By the power vested in me by the state of Georgia …"

Tess blinked hard to battle her tears, the sound of Pastor Chase Griffin's voice flooding her heart—and her eyes—with so much happiness, she felt ready to bust right out of her snug floor-length sheath gown. Who would have guessed she'd one day marry the crotchety neighbor next door in an intimate ceremony beneath a twinkle-light tent in Dr. Doom's own backyard? She breathed in the heady scent of her small gardenia bouquet while the pink shadows of dusk cast its ethereal glow, her pulse thrumming along with the music of tree frogs and crickets.

Dr. and Mrs. Ben and Tess Doom. Her lips quivered into a wobbly smile as she stared at Ben Carmichael in his crisp, classic tux, so utterly handsome and soon—so utterly hers!

"… I now pronounce you husband and wife."

The tiny gathering of family and friends erupted into applause at a smattering of candle-lit tables, spoons clinking against glass complemented by whoops from her daughters and whistles from Jack.

"You may now kiss the bride."

And, oh—Lord have mercy—did he! Tugging her flush, he dipped her back for a kiss straight out of the movies, the taste of Ben and monster cookies sweet in her mouth. "You've been into the cookies already," she whispered, and his lips curved against her smile.

"Couldn't wait," he said softly, pulling her back up to caress her with his eyes, the promise of untold joys warm in his gaze. "Still can't."

"I now present to you Dr. and Mrs. Ben and Tess Carmichael."

The guests lunged to their feet, clapping and cheering while Chase shook Ben's hand and their children doled out misty hugs and tears to both Ben and her.

"Oh, Mom—you two are going to be so happy, I just know it!" Shannon whispered. She hugged Tess tightly while Cat flirted with Chase. "And nobody deserves it more."

"Oh, I don't know …" Tess cradled Shannon's face in her hands, a secret smile tipping her mouth. She glanced at Sam while he laughed with Ben and Jack a few feet away. "I know *somebody* who does if my prayers have any say. And from that look I've seen in Sam's eyes lately whenever you're around, I wouldn't be all that surprised if it happens pretty fast." She tucked a wisp of hair behind Shannon's ear. "Jack says he's head over heels."

A pretty blush stole into Shannon's cheeks, her lovesick smile in Sam's direction confirming that her daughter felt the very same way. "Mom, it's only been two weeks."

"But you've been close friends for almost five months now, sweetheart, in an extremely honest friendship where you've shared and prayed about everything, yes?"

Shannon hesitated, her good mood dimming enough for Tess to notice. "Most things, yes ..." Her chin suddenly lifted with a bright smile, as if she were anxious to change the subject. "But now that we're dating, definitely *all* things." Her gaze flicked to Sam and back with a telltale shift of her throat. "And soon."

"Good girl." Tess gave her a hug.

Shannon kissed Tess's cheek just as the musicians struck up the dinner music. "Now, go," she said with a renewed twinkle in her eyes. "Ben's headed this way, and he looks *prettttty* hungry."

Tess turned, and her stomach did a dizzy whirl, but not from hunger. She pressed a shaky hand to her abdomen, hardly able to believe she was actually Ben's wife—poised on the threshold of sharing a future and a life with the man she adored.

Not to mention a bed … Battling a gulp, she gave him a shy smile as he approached, food suddenly the last thing on her mind.

"It's time to eat, Mrs. Carmichael." He took her in his arms, punctuating his statement with a slow and luxurious kiss. "Because I guarantee you, we're going to need our strength," he whispered, his husky tease fluttering her stomach when he ushered her to their table.

The evening was a beautiful blur—a hazy kaleidoscope of faces and memories in the making and some from the past. Tess released a wispy sigh against Ben's shoulders as he held her close in one of the last dances of the night. A hint of melancholy stole in when she glanced at his slate patio with its stone fire pit, where Adam and she and Ben and Karen spent many a summer night. Now Chase and Cat sat there in the same British green Adirondack chairs along with Lacey and Jack and Sam and Shannon, the latter two couples sharing two of the four chairs.

A bit of moisture sparked in Tess's eyes when Jack nuzzled Lacey's neck while the couples talked, so grown up and ready to start a family of their own. And, *oh*, how she prayed for a bounty of children to fill their house with the same love and joy that they'd given her.

She watched as Sam pressed a kiss to Shannon's cheek, bundling her close, and Tess smiled, hoping he was the answer to a mother's prayer. Getting to know him better over the last few months had deepened her affection for the man Shannon loved, even if Shannon's trust level still suffered the effects of a painful past.

Her gaze trailed to Cat, who was laughing at something Chase said, and Tess's heart cramped in her chest. If only her daughter's flirty smile meant that they were a couple too. But, unfortunately, Cat harbored other ideas about what she wanted in a man. Ideas that caused Tess no little worry over her daughter's future, which appeared as tenuous as her faith. Expelling a heavy sigh, never was Tess more grateful she could turn her children over to a God Who loved them far more than she.

"That was an awfully big sigh, Mrs. Carmichael," Ben whispered against her hair, the vibration of his husky tease skimming her skin with a delicious heat. "Either one of supreme contentment *or* wedding remorse."

She smiled up at him, falling in love all over again at the look of tenderness in his eyes. "Definitely the first, Dr. Carmichael, although there may be the tiniest tinge of the second." She stood on tiptoe to slowly fondle his lips with her own. "But *only* that we didn't do this sooner."

His groan melted into her mouth when he wrenched her close to finish the job with a kiss that weakened her at the back of her knees. Her body was limp when he finally pulled away to touch his forehead to hers. "We need to go," he rasped, his breathing as ragged as the air pumping in her own chest.

Tess blinked, realizing the evening had come to an end, but her life with Ben Carmichael was about to begin. And it would start at The Bohemian Hotel on Savannah's Riverfront.

In a corner riverview suite.

Tess gulped, suddenly shyer than she ever expected to be.

Followed by a week in Hawaii in a house on a very *lonely beach.*

She peeked up with a nervous chew of her lip. "Now? Before the reception is done?"

"*Now*," he repeated, emphasizing his intent with a heated gaze before he playfully tugged on her ear with his teeth. "Before my will power is *done*." As if he could sense her jitters, he gently tunneled his hands through her hair, bracing the back of her head with a quiet intensity she'd come to know and love. "I've waited all of my life for you, Teresa Carmichael. You're the woman God created for *me*—to love, honor, and protect—and I'm ready to start right now." He leaned in to nuzzle her mouth with an almost reverent kiss that totally disarmed her before his mouth curved into a slow smile against hers. "Preferably in that order." Cupping her face with gentle hands, he caressed her jaw with the pads of his thumbs, those hazel eyes potent with love. "You are the perfect woman for me, Tess, and far more than I ever dreamed I could have." His Adam's apple ducked several times as his gaze flitted to her mouth and back. "And God help me, woman—I want to be alone with my wife."

His wife. Saltwater immediately welled in her eyes.

And *her* husband, gifted by God.

"Okay," she whispered, her throat doing a little ducking of its own, "but I'm going to warn you right now, Dr. Carmichael—it's been almost ten years since this so-called 'perfect woman' has" —her cheeks flamed hot as she worried her lip, suddenly feeling like an awkward teenager all over again— "well, you know, so not only am I probably rusty, but I'm a *whole* lot older too."

He grinned and deposited a kiss to her nose. "When it comes to the woman for me, you're sheer perfection, Tess, just the way you are." He laced his fingers through hers with a firm confidence that helped to settle her nerves. "And when it comes to the other, Mrs. Carmichael?" Tugging her toward the house, he kindled her with a smoky look that whirled her stomach before slipping her a wink. "Just follow my lead."

CHAPTER FORTY-ONE

"Okay, boys—you sure I can't get you anything else?" The pretty halter-clad waitress at Rocks on the Roof smiled, her gaze sliding from Sam to Jack to Chase in a flirtatious manner while she waved the dinner check in the air.

Sam plucked it from her hand before Jack could, his smile subdued considerably given the spark of interest in the girl's eyes. "No thanks, Emily, and the bill is all mine."

"Oh, no you don't," Jack and Chase said in unison, both reaching into their pockets.

Sam tucked a credit card into the leather bill holder and handed it to Emily before Jack or Chase could even retrieve their wallets. "Go, Emily, please, before they make a scene."

"What are you doing, Ham?" Jack said, credit card finally in hand. He nodded toward the bill. "Between this and that fancy blazer you're wearing, dude, I'm starting to worry Augustine hiked your salary when you got back with Jazz."

A grin eased across Sam's face as he brushed a piece of lint from the new Ralph Lauren sport coat he bought for his next date with Shan. "Nope. This is just my way of saying thanks for saving my life." He nodded toward Jack. "First you in hounding me to death to go to church and *then* introducing me to Shannon." His gaze flicked to Chase with a sheepish smile. "Then *you* in putting the hammer down to help me see the light." His expression sobered as he thought about the gift these two men were, opening his eyes to a faith that not only saved his life, but his soul as well. He swallowed the lump of emotion clogging his throat. "I've never had friendships like this before," he said quietly, "and I can't thank you two enough for putting up with me."

Jack pocketed his credit card while Chase did the same. "Don't thank me, bro, thank my sister. As far as I'm concerned, Shannon saved your butt, not us. Although I suppose we *did* earn that dinner, eh, Rev?"

"I know I sure did," Chase said with a mock scowl, upending the rest of his water. "This is the second time I've had the girl of my dreams stolen away by some fast-talking joker. Truth be told, I'm glad both of you are off the market, although without Lacey or Shannon, there's not too much catching my eye at the moment."

Grinning, Jack slapped Chase on the back. "Cheer up, Chase, there's always Cat," he quipped, although Sam knew Jack would like nothing better than seeing his wayward sister corralled by the no-nonsense preacher.

"Yeah, sorry about that, Rev," Sam said with a rueful grin, "but Jack's right. Cat needs you way more than Shannon does, so the way I figure it, it all worked out the way it should." He drew in a deep breath as he scratched the back of his head. "Or at least I hope it does …"

"What's that supposed to mean?" Jack said, eyes in a squint.

"It means, O'Bryen, that like it or not …" Sam took his time answering while Emily delivered the ticket with a sultry smile, her close proximity making him uncomfortable with a woman for the first time in his life. He signed and handed it back with a polite smile, along with his usual healthy tip. When she left, he reached into his pocket to produce a velvet box, chuckling at Chase's low whistle and the wide span of Jack's eyes when Sam revealed a diamond ring. "I hope to become your brother-in-law in the not-too-distant future."

"No kidding?" Jack jumped up to pump Sam's hand, a contest as to whose grin was wider. "Does Shannon know?"

"Not a clue," Sam said with a smug smile. A mix of pride and love swelled in his chest over the way he'd kept his relationship with Shannon aboveboard *and* kept her off the scent of a proposal despite seeing her every day for a month.

"I want to take my time to really get to know you, Shan," he'd told her that night in the dory, even though he already suspected she was the one. And when they'd danced every single dance at Tess and Ben's intimate garden wedding almost two weeks ago, he'd known for a certainty he couldn't wait much longer to make her his wife.

"So, when are you going to pop the question?" Chase wanted to know.

"Saturday night when we celebrate our official one-month anniversary. I know how much she loves to cook, so I thought I'd pull the stops out and take her to the 700 Kitchen Cooking School at Mansion on Forsyth Park." He gave them a wink. "Already arranged with the chef for a surprise in her dinner roll, so I can't wait to see her face." He pocketed the ring and grinned like a fool. "And I can tell you right now, this will *not* be a long engagement if I have any say."

Chase cuffed Sam's shoulder. "I'm happy for you, man, and I sure hope I have the honor of officially ending your illustrious career as Dr. Love."

Sam chuckled as he put his credit card back in his wallet, shooting Chase a wicked grin. "Oh, I'll still be Dr. Love, Rev, but I'll only be making house calls for one woman."

"Good to know, Ham." Jack rose to his feet, one side of his mouth inching up in a wry smile. "Because I'd really hate to mess up the pretty face of one of my best buds and brother-in-law." He pushed in his chair. "And speaking of house calls," he said with a glance at his watch, "I'm late for mine right now."

Following suit, Chase stood as well. "I'm afraid I need to head out, too, Sam—early meeting with the board." He eased his chair in with a crooked smile. "I don't have the practice of burning the candles at both ends like you, Doc."

Sam laughed while he checked his phone. "Yeah, well the fires on both ends have been effectively doused, I assure you, by both you and Shan." His smile skewed as he returned a text. "And I'd be leaving, too, if I hadn't promised two college buddies I'd meet them for a drink, trust me."

"Don't forget Augustine's in early tomorrow, bro, so not too late if you value your job." Jack pinched Sam's shoulder on his way out. "Thanks for dinner, Sam, and I couldn't be happier with the news."

"Me too, Doc." Chase offered a quick handshake. "Appreciate the dinner—the best I've had in months. But then a pastor can't afford what you high-rollers can."

"Can I get you anything else, Dr. Cunningham?"

Sam glanced up in surprise, wondering how Emily knew he was a physician.

She gave a slight shrug, her megawatt smile putting him on-guard. "Your friends kept calling you 'Doc,' so I just assumed."

Sam quickly rose. "Actually, I'd love a cappuccino, Em, out on the terrace if that's okay. I'm meeting more friends in a few minutes."

"Absolutely, Doc." Her head tipped in question. "And … anything for your 'friends'?" The question seemed to beg an answer as to whether his friends were male or female.

Sam paused, wondering if Reece still put away the Wild Turkey like he used to. No doubt, Zach was still hooked on Bud Light. "Yeah, Em, thanks for asking—bring me a Wild Turkey on the rocks and a Bud Light too, if you will."

"Sure thing, Sam," she said softly, way too much familiarity in her tone. Her over-the-shoulder smile lingered as she headed for the bar, and he instantly made a beeline for the terrace, completely ruined for other women by the one girl he hoped to make his wife. Shannon was truly one of a kind, and gratitude instantly flooded his soul while moisture flooded his eyes. "Thank you, God," he whispered as he made his way to the far end of the terrace.

Sinking into the plush cushions of a rattan sofa seating, he fixed his gaze on the Savannah Bridge at night. The cable-stayed bridge was all lit up like a grand lady adorned in glittering diamonds, and he couldn't count the times he'd sat up here with various women. But not once had he truly appreciated the beauty of Savannah's historic riverfront. With a tangerine moon drizzling over an indigo river, the distant call of foghorns merged with the pungent smell of the salt marshes that so reminded him of the ocean mere miles away. But tonight, he saw and heard it all as if for the very first time, suddenly painfully aware how empty his life had been.

Before Shannon.

"Here you go, Sam, one cappuccino, a Wild Turkey on the rocks, and a Bud Light." Emily bent over to set the drinks down, providing an ample view of her V-neck halter and a killer smile. "How about something sweet to go with that coffee, Doc?" she asked, her voice suddenly husky and low.

Patting the washboard stomach he worked so hard to maintain, he tempered his smile to cordial. "No, thanks, Emily, couldn't eat another thing."

"I wasn't talking about food," she whispered, slipping a piece of paper with what looked like a phone number on it under the Wild Turkey. "I get off at eleven if you change your mind." Tossing him a secret smile that carried all the way to the door, she disappeared back inside, and Sam shook his head, amazed he'd ever been attracted to women who came on to him like that.

"The hot girls are still hitting on you, I see," a familiar voice said with a chuckle that harbored a trace of envy. "Bet you have to carry a stick now that you have your MD."

Sam glanced up to see two of his fraternity brothers approach with lurid grins, taking him back to college days when he took full advantage of women who hit on him back then. He hadn't been a player until Amber betrayed him, having an affair with her professor while she wore Sam's two-bit diamond ring. From that point on, he took whatever women were willing to give, and the lewd looks on Zach's and Reece's faces reminded him it had been plenty. The thought made him feel both nauseous and dirty at the same time, and never had he craved a hot shower more.

"Naw," Sam said as he stood to shake their hands, "she's just hoping to boost her tip."

Zach elbowed Reece with a snicker. "Yeah, I'll bet she is—delivered personally to her apartment."

"You guys haven't changed a bit, you know that?" Sam sat back down and lifted his cup in a toast. "But it's still good to see you. What are you two clowns doing in Savannah anyway?"

That's all it took to unleash ten years of crazy catch-up, nearly bringing Sam to tears with laughter, reminding him just why he'd been friends with two of the fraternity's funniest guys. They'd made him laugh and forget while he made them popular with the ladies, a trade-off that had served them all well.

He learned they were married to sisters and each had two kids, although it sure didn't show in their actions when Emily delivered more drinks and another cappuccino. They practically drooled, as if one out-of-town trip had dropkicked them right back into college.

"So, enough about us mortals," Reece finally said, giving Emily a wink when she delivered his third Wild Turkey, "I want to hear how the Greek gods live, Ham, so fill us in."

Taking a careful sip of his third cappuccino, Sam paused, well aware there was a time when he would have dazzled them with his conquests of women, but just the thought of that now left a bad taste in his mouth. So he told them how much he loved practicing medicine instead, and the satisfaction of giving back to society with the volunteer work that he did.

Reece guzzled half of his drink while he slid Sam a knowing look. "Sounds good, man, but that's not the kind of 'satisfaction' we want to hear about, Ham, and you know it. Have a heart, man—Zach and I have a ball and chain now, so we want to see how the other half lives."

"Yeah, dude," Zach said with a lift of his beer, "I'll bet your bedroom has a revolving door, so fill us in."

Rarely did Sam ever blush, but he could feel the heat crawling up his neck right now, singeing his skin with both shame and disgust. He set his cup down and sat back with a stiff fold of arms, as if he could ward off the regret that kept slamming his conscience. "Actually, I'm about to get engaged, I hope, so my days as a player have officially come to an end."

"Seriously?" Reece stared in disbelief, half-empty glass mid-air.

"Seriously." Sam draped an arm over the back of the rattan sofa, striving for a calm and casual air that didn't come easy with three cappuccinos jacking him up. "I met the woman of my dreams, so I'm done with the whole singles façade, and happily so."

"No kidding," Zach said with a grin. "Well, what do you know—life *is* fair! Congratulations, Sam. She must be some girl."

"Oh, she is, trust me." He could no more stop the goofy grin from his face than he could stop the flow of the river below. "She's one of a kind—sweet, smart—"

"And hot?" Reece upended his drink with a sly smile.

Sam laughed. "What do you think, Reece?"

"I'm guessing she's the hottest thing in Savannah, knowing you, Ham."

Jasmine's image suddenly popped in his mind, and Sam reached for his coffee, shocked that the notion of a well-stacked knockout no longer appealed. "She is," he said quietly, "a true beauty on the inside and out, and I'm a very lucky man." Thinking of Shannon, he smiled, rib cage expanding with pride that she belonged to him. "And you know the best part?" He glanced up with a sincerity he had never shared with the two men before. "She's the purest woman I have ever met, body and soul."

Reece almost spit out his drink. "Pure? Dating you? I don't believe it."

"Wait …" Zach stared, eyes gaping. "You mean you two don't—?"

"Nope," Sam said, quickly cutting him off. "She's a woman of faith, man, and she's opened my eyes to it too." He lifted his cup in a toast. "And to be honest? I've never been happier."

"Wow, man, that's great." Reece waved Emily down, wagging

his empty glass in the air. "So, what's this angel's name? Mother Teresa?"

Sam grinned along with Zach and Reece. "Close. Shannon Terese O'Bryen. And you're right, Reece—she is an angel." His smile faded when Reece exchanged a quick glance with Zach. "What?" he asked, the caffeine in his system morphing into overdrive.

"Hey, man, I don't know how to tell you this, but my wife's friend knew a Shannon O'Bryen at Georgia State and she was no angel, but it's probably not the same girl."

Sam blinked. Shannon went to Georgia State before she transferred to Armstrong State in her senior year. His heart slowed to a hard thud. "Probably not," he said calmly, forcing a casual demeanor despite the sweat glued to his collar. "What about her?"

Reece's gaze flicked to Zach and back before a knot ducked in his throat. "It was a big deal, Sam, made the papers and everything, according to my wife." He hesitated for several seconds before he continued, all humor gone from his eyes. "She was a home-wrecker, man. Had an affair with one of the top professors, busting up his marriage in a messy soap-opera story. The wife was so devastated, she tried to shoot them both when she found them together, right before she drove off a bridge. She survived, apparently, but the marriage sure didn't."

Sam couldn't breathe, the air in his lungs like toxin.

"Yeah, there was a big scene in the quadrangle caught on video, apparently," Zach said, his eyes as somber as Reece's, "where the wife was screaming and waving a gun, calling this Shannon a whore and saying she ruined the lives of her and her five children. It's all you saw on the news for days, especially after this Shannon tried to run, ending up driving off a bridge just like the wife. I'm telling you, man, it was freaky—a veritable reality show that rocked the campus."

Sam's voice was barely a whisper as he stared at Reece like he could see straight through him. "Was she from Atlanta?" he rasped, hoping against hope that she was.

Reece's gaze never budged from Sam's as he thumbed the side of his empty glass, not answering right away while he gave it a slow spin. "No, man … Isle of Hope," he said quietly, expelling a wavering sigh.

Clink. "Here you go, boys."

Sam almost jumped out of his skin when Emily set the drinks and steaming cappuccino on the table, her brows in a bunch when she noticed the zombie look on his face. "Can I … get you … anything else?" she said softly, as if aware something had just rocked Sam's world.

"Yeah." He gave Emily a glazed look while he slumped back in his seat. "A double Chivas," he muttered, desperate to numb the awful ache in his heart. His body felt sick as he took a heavy swig of his cappuccino, the strong brew burning as much as the angst in his gut. He stared straight ahead while fury surged through his bloodstream along with the caffeine. "And keep 'em coming."

CHAPTER FORTY-TWO

"Okay, Shan, something's fishy here," Lacey said with a pursed smile, fishing rod in hand and brow angled high, "and I don't think it's that bass you just caught, girlfriend."

Shannon glanced up from where she was hooking her nice-sized catch to the stringer, a smile tiptoeing around the edges of her mouth. A crisp sea breeze ruffled her hair while a pale white moon danced on the water, reminding her that these unseasonably warm October nights wouldn't last forever. "Why, whatever do you mean, Lace?"

Cat popped her hook from her Adirondack chair, casting a sideways smirk at her sister. "She *means*, Shan-*none,*" she said with a wicked grin, employing the nickname she'd coined for her sister after Shan told them about her strict moral policy with Sam. "Your lips have been squirming all night like they're just aching to laugh, and those stars in your eyes are so bright, I'm tempted to wear shades. So you may as well spill it, sis—what juicy facts are you keeping from us?"

"Nothing," she insisted, unable to thwart the smile that inched across her lips. "I promise."

"All righty, then ..." Lacey strolled over to where Shannon was rebaiting her rod, and lasered her with a look that said Shan was on the hook along with her fish. "Then what do you *think* you know, Miss Squirmy Lips, because something's up between you and Sam, and we want to know what it is."

"Yeah, you two getting serious or something?" Cat said, tongue rolling inside her cheek. The gleam in her eyes assured Shannon there was a tease on its way. "You know, like maybe you've graduated from holding hands to a kiss on the cheek?"

The cheeks in question immediately heated over the memory of countless goodnight kisses at the door that focused on far more than her cheeks …

"Well …" Shannon plopped back in her chair between Lacey's and Cat's to deliver a sideways peek with a chew of her lip. "Maybe …"

Lacey whirled in her Adirondack chair, pinning Shannon with a threatening smile. "So help me, Shannon O'Bryen, if you don't give us the scoop, I'll get it out of Sam myself."

"*No!*" The furnace in Shannon's face cranked all the way up to flashpoint, her mortification blazing that Sam might think she put Lacey up to it. She put a cool palm to her heated skin. "Please don't say a word to Sam, Lace, because I would just die if I was wrong, but I think …" She nibbled the tip of her pinky, the hint of a smile just barely sneaking through. "He may be pretty serious. Like … marriage serious."

"*Squeeeeeeee!*" Lacey dropped her rod and launched to her feet to squeeze Shannon in a noisy hug while Cat stared, open-mouthed, a smile slowly curling on her lips.

"Well, holy bucket of worms, sis, that has to be some kind of record for a guy like Sam Cunningham or *any* guy!"

Shannon put both hands to her burning face, shoulders in a scrunch. "Stop it, you guys! Just because I think it doesn't make it true. Sam and I are just dating, and for all I know, that's all it might ever be."

"Oh, *puh-leez!*" Lacey said with a roll of her eyes, retrieving her rod to make another cast. "Jack says the man is so far gone, he should be committed."

Committed. Shannon caught her breath, her dream of Sam committed to her sapping all oxygen from her throat. *Oh, Lord, if only …*

Cat put her rod down to focus on her sister, shimmying her chair around till she was facing her dead-on. "So, why do you think that, Shan?" she asked with a probing stare, knees bunched and bare feet curled over the edge.

Shannon shrugged, almost wishing she hadn't been born with this crazy sixth sense that could bode either good or bad. Good if she was right that Sam was serious enough to commit to her alone. But bad if this uneasy feeling she'd been having all night was more than indigestion. "It's a bunch of little things, really," she said carefully, hoping she wasn't reading too much into Sam's words or actions the last month.

"Such as?" Lacey laid her rod aside, now sideways in her chair with knees to her chest.

Shannon sighed. "I know this sounds silly, but he's had this look in his eyes ever since Mom and Ben's wedding. Kind of a heated intensity that defies his typically casual air." She pursed her lips, head in a tilt. "It's … almost like a horse at the gate, you know? Eyes searing the track while its body stills, every muscle twitching till the stall opens up."

A husky chuckle tripped from Cat's lips. "That sounds like Dr. Love, all right—a thoroughbred just waiting for that doggone gate to swing open."

More heat pulsed in Shannon's cheeks as her teeth tugged at the edge of her smile. "I hate to say it, but that's it exactly. And then he keeps saying over and over how he wants to take the time to really get to know me better."

"So?" Lips pinched to the right, Lacey peered at her through squinted eyes, as if trying to assess each word out of Shannon's mouth. "That's a good thing, right?"

Shannon tipped her head, mouth compressed in thought. "Yes, but it's almost like the man doth protest too much, you know? Like he's trying to throw me off track or something. Plus, I don't know the details because Sam doesn't like to talk about it, but he had a really bad experience with a girl he was engaged to in college, not to mention his rocky relationship with Jazz. So he's made it perfectly clear that when he *does* get engaged again, he plans to take lots of time to make sure it's the real thing." She huffed out a sigh as she stared out at the water. "And let's face it, one month does not a commitment make."

"Ahem … almost six months," Lacey corrected, "since you

two forged a close friendship the night of the fundraiser."

One side of Shannon's mouth nudged up. "Driving a soused Romeo home with puke on his tie hardly qualifies as a close friendship, Lace."

Cat grinned, eyebrows jiggling. "Apparently it does for Dr. Love."

"*Anyway,*" Shannon said with a patient smile, "he's taking me to 700 Kitchen Cooking School on Saturday night for our official one-month anniversary—"

"Wait a minute—a cooking-school date?" Cat's feet thudded to the wood planking when she sat up in the chair, posture stiff as two tiny lines puckered above her nose.

The indigestion that had been churning in Shannon's stomach all night kicked up a notch because she knew what Cat was asking. Why would Sam resurrect painful memories with a date that included a cooking class, when it was the very thing Eric had loved to do? "Sam already knows Eric and I loved cooking together *and* that since the breakup, I avoid it like the plague." A wispy sigh drifted from her lips. "But he told me he doesn't want anything to remind me of Eric, so he wants to erase those painful memories with good ones."

"*Or,*" Cat said with a sly cock of her head, "he wants to make good and sure he eats well if you two do tie the knot."

A shy giggle slipped from Shannon's mouth. "I thought of that."

"Well, I think it's sweet and very smart, but then we already know Sam is a genius because he's in love with you."

Ridges buckled Shannon's brow as she slumped back in her chair. "I sure hope so," she whispered, "because I sure am with him, and to be honest, I never thought I could feel this way again or ever trust another man."

"Oh, get real, sis." Cat settled back, palms flat on the wide arms of her chair. "Anybody with eyes in their head can see how gaga Sam Cunningham is over you, so as far as I'm concerned, you're home free."

"Maybe not," she whispered, the roiling in her stomach

starting to rival the roll of the river.

"What do you mean?" Lacey studied her with a sober gaze, as if she already knew what was coming.

"I mean, I never told Sam the whole truth about Eric," she said quietly, wishing a hundred times over that she had.

"What?" Cat sat straight up once again, mouth gaping.

Shannon shook her head, understanding her sister's shock perfectly. She and Sam were best friends, confiding in each other about almost everything. But fear had kept her from revealing her most debilitating secret, something that no one in her life knew but her family. Because the shame was still too deep, and Sam's faith had been too shallow, hinging so precariously on the very morality that Shannon espoused. And yet, here they were in a relationship that might be heading toward something more, and the guilt was eating her raw. Because if Sam and she were getting serious, this was something he needed to know.

She blinked hard to thwart a sudden sheen in her eyes. "When we were just friends, I couldn't tell him, Cat, not only because I was ashamed, but because he always made such a big deal about my so-called wisdom and morality, saying that was the biggest reason he trusted me like he did." Her gaze trailed out to the water, the river dark and ominous as the moon crept behind a threatening billow of clouds. "So when we started dating, I knew I needed to tell him, but every time I got up the nerve, it seemed like something derailed it. Then at Mom and Ben's wedding, I sensed things might be moving more quickly between us, so I tried to tell him that night, insisting I had something painful he needed to know about my past. But he just shook it off, saying that he did too, but it could wait because he didn't want to spoil the moment."

Her eyelids flickered closed, the weight of her guilt prompting a fresh wash of tears. "So I didn't push it, rationalizing that we'd just started dating and I would tell him if we got more serious." A muscle convulsed in her throat. "But now I'm worried we have and Sam still doesn't know. And to be honest, I'm worried sick that it will ruin everything."

"Oh, honey." Lacey squatted in front of Shannon's chair to hug her, the tenderness in her voice helping to ease Shannon's fear. "If Sam truly loves you—and I suspect he does—this may come as a shock, yes, but it won't change what you have." She paused several seconds, her silence heavy with conviction. "But you have to tell him soon, Shan," she said softly, "whether he wants to hear it or not."

"I know." Shannon's hand quivered as she brushed the moisture from her eyes. "So I guess I'll tell him Saturday night, then, although I don't know if he'll want to see me anymore after I do."

"Stop it!" Cat jumped up to grip Shannon's arms, bending to peer into her sister's eyes. "The guy loves you, Shan—anybody can see that—so I doubt he's going anywhere."

"And more importantly," Lacey said quietly, "God loves you and redeemed you, my friend, just like He redeemed me from all the horrible mistakes I made before I came back to Isle of Hope."

"And, man, were there some doozies!" Cat gave a sober nod, earning a thin smile from Lacey before her sister-in-law turned back to Shannon.

"Besides," Lacey continued, "it's not like Sam was a Boy Scout before you stirred his faith, so if anybody should understand, it should be Dr. Love." She gave Shannon's hand a pat. "So don't you worry, sweetie. We'll just pray about it right now, and everything will work out, you'll see."

Tears blurred in Shannon's eyes as she gripped Lacey's hand, craving her assurance. "You really think so, Lace?" she whispered, the barest trace of tremble in her tone.

"Nope." Lacey stood to her feet, her stance strong like a woman whose faith had been through the fire and back. "I know so, Shan, because we serve the very God Who created hope for moments like this." Her eyes brimmed with moisture, just like Shannon's. "And God's hope, my sweet friend, *never* disappoints." She reached to give Shannon a tight hug that coaxed even more tears from her eyes. "And neither does God."

CHAPTER FORTY-THREE

Shannon glanced at the clock, then stared at the ceiling of her bedroom, wondering if she would even fall asleep tonight. It was well past two in the morning, but the conversation with Cat and Lacey had heightened her awareness to the fact that she was desperately in love with Sam Cunningham—or Dr. Love to the Memorial nurses, she reminded herself—and needed to tell him the truth. *Which* meant she was also incredibly vulnerable to being crushed a second time.

Her eyelids lumbered closed like they were made of lead, but not before a pool of tears brimmed, alerting her to the fact that this gnawing indigestion in her gut had flared into full-blown nausea. Because frankly, she wasn't sure she was strong enough to go through it again …

When you are weak, I am strong …

The sweet whisper of God's Word opened her eyes once more, but this time it was to the hope that she was no longer alone in the battle.

The Lord will fight for you; you need only to be still.

"Thank you," she said softly, so very grateful for God. He had fought for her with Eric—for her very life as well as her soul—and she had no doubt that the strength seeping into her bones right now was His, not hers. More tears pricked, but these were tears of joy over a God Who had called her out of the darkness into His marvelous light. She had been on the brink of death in so many ways, but God had shown her through the pain that she—Shannon Terese O'Bryen, the shy and quiet twin that nobody noticed—was His "very own possession," no matter how far she had strayed from His hand.

And, oh, how she had! She'd been raised on a solid faith and yet, just like her father, she had fallen, exchanging the love of God for the love of man, a human frailty of epidemic proportion. But God had turned even that around for good when He'd brought her to the pinnacle of faith, revealing to her soul the only truth she could really cling to … and the only truth that really mattered.

I am God, and there is no other …

"My soul finds rest in God alone," she quoted softly, and knew to the core of her being that it was true. She'd already proven she couldn't rest in her own strength or goodness because it had failed her so miserably before. As much as she loved her family and friends, they could not provide the true rest she craved for her soul. And even if Sam did love her with the everlasting love for which she so longed, it would never still her, steady her, save her like the unfailing love of God.

"I have loved you with an everlasting love; therefore I have drawn you with loving-kindness. Again I will build you up, and you will be rebuilt."

Rebuilt.

Which meant that no matter what happened in her life now or in the future, in her relationship with Sam or anyone else, the Lover of her Soul would not forsake her like man was so prone to do.

At the thought, peace flooded, and her limbs slowly sank into the rest she needed. Eyelids edging toward sleep, she prayed a final Scripture, the words soft and warm on her lips. "Let the morning bring me word of Your unfailing love, Oh Lord, for I put my trust in You. Show me the way I should go, for unto You I lift up my soul."

Brrrrrrrrrrrrr.

Shannon startled in the bed, her silenced cell phone vibrating her stomach as much as her nightstand. Her heart turned over when she saw it was Sam, and lunging for the phone, she answered, barely able to hear her own breathy voice for the pounding of her pulse in her brain. "Sam?"

"Ain-chell Eyes ..."

Her stomach bottomed out as her heart stumbled in her chest, the slur in his words painful proof that he'd broken his promise to himself to never get drunk again. "Sam—what's wrong?"

"Come on, Teash, does somethin' hafta be wrong for me to see my bes' girl?"

Alarm prickled her skin. The thought of Sam driving drunk catapulted her from the bed. "Where are you?" she whispered, the sound harsh in a house where everyone else was sleeping.

"Right outside, babe, so come on out. And, Shan ..." The husky chuckle that usually fluttered her stomach now roiled it instead. "Don't bother to put on a robe."

Hands quivering, she ripped her pajama bottoms off and put on a fresh pair of shorts, barely able to latch the hook of her bra beneath the T-shirt she wore. Snatching her purse off the dresser, she slipped on her Sperrys and silently opened the door, holding her breath as she eased it closed before tiptoeing down the stairs. With the utmost stealth, she locked the front door behind her and hurried to where Sam's Vette was parked in the street.

"Give me the keys," she said in a terse tone she seldom used, Sam's recklessness unhinging a deeply buried temper few knew she had.

"Hey, babe." His eyes were mere slits as he stumbled out of the car, swaying conspicuously when she stepped back from his reach. The lazy smile on his face dissolved into hurt. "Come on, Shan, I need you ..."

"You need me all right," she said in a near hiss, "to drive your sorry butt home." With pickpocket speed, she plucked the keyless entry remote from his trousers and slipped it into the pocket of her shorts.

His suggestive chuckle reeked of alcohol. "I knew you'd come around eventually, Ain-chell Eyes. Most women do."

"Yeah?" She smacked his arm away, pushing and prodding him to the passenger side of the car none too gently. "Well, I'm not most women."

He skidded to a halt like he wanted to respond, but she just yanked on his shirt that much harder, dragging him all the way.

"Hey, you're gonna rip my favorite Armani," he groused.

"Better than your jugular, Doc." She jerked the passenger door open and shoved him in on top of his precious suit jacket that was folded neatly on the seat, not a bit sorry when he bumped his head on the roof.

Slamming the door, she almost smiled when she saw him grapple with pulling his jacket out from beneath his hard-muscled bulk. But, not quite. His mood was considerably testier when she got in on the driver's side. "For crying out loud, Shan, have a li'l respec' for my things, will ya?" he muttered, refolding the jacket just so before laying it over the console.

She fought the urge to roll her eyes as she started the car, figuring she'd have to give him one thing—he was the neatest drunk she ever saw. "I have respect for your things, Sam." She turned the stereo down, not missing the irony of Keith Urban's song, "Stupid Boy," blaring through the car as she eased it down the street. "It's their owner I'm not too sure about right now." She slid him a peeved look, her tone a clear reprimand. "Especially somebody stupid enough to drink and drive, so you'll excuse me if I'm not very happy with you right now."

"Yeah?" His voice rose in volume, making the slur all the more noticeable. "Well, I got news for ya, babe, that goes both ways—" His words strangled into a groan as he began to fumble with the handle of his door. With split-second precision, Shannon squealed to a stop on the side of the road and flung her door open, rushing to the other side to yank him out of the car. The moment his feet hit the pavement, it was his dinner that went "both ways"—from his precious Armani shirt right on down to his beloved Cole Haan brogues, baptizing them with the foulest vomit she'd ever seen or smelled.

"I don' feel so good," he mumbled, looking for all his strapping six-foot-one height like a sick little boy battling the flu.

"I imagine not," she said with a quiet sigh, her heart softening despite herself. "Not with a bottle of poison in your gut."

"Chivas," he corrected. "Some of the fines' scotch in the

world—aged twelve years."

"Yes, well your liver just aged twelve years, too, bucko, not to mention your shoes."

Swaying on his feet, he looked down and emitted a rusty groan, giving her pause when she thought he was going to spew some more. "Noooooo … not my Cole Haans …"

"Yeah, never mind the liver," she muttered, leaving him to bemoan the fate of his shoes while she rifled through both her purse and the glove compartment for tissues or towels. She came up empty, so she quickly scanned the yards on Bluff Drive, spotting a sprawling bed of giant hostas. Plucking several leaves off the bottom of a plant, she returned to where Sam sagged over the hood of his car, arms braced as if to hold himself up.

Without a word, she squatted to clean off first his shoes and then his slacks the best she could before rising to attend to his shirt.

"Thanks," he whispered. His voice was hoarse as he took the hosta leaves from her hand to finish the job, his shame evident in how he avoided her gaze.

Against her better judgment, she gave his arm a tender squeeze, then left to hunt for a tissue in her purse again, finding only a sad, crumpled one smeared with lipstick. "Here," she said in a gentle tone, carefully wiping any excess from his face and shirt before handing him a mint. "Hopefully the worst is over and we can get you home to bed."

He nodded and tumbled back into the car, deathly quiet while he settled back against the headrest with eyes closed. For all she knew he slept all the way to his townhouse, never uttering a word, and she was glad. He was in no condition for serious conversation right now, and there was a ton of that needed before she'd resume this relationship again. The nausea in her gut took over, exacerbated by the stench of vomit that permeated despite the open windows. She couldn't afford to marry a man who drank to excess, especially one who'd promised he'd given it up. He'd had dinner with Jack and Chase, so she knew little or no drinking was involved. But he'd mentioned meeting up with some old fraternity brothers after, so they must have twisted his arm. Even so, could she trust a man who could break a promise so easily?

"Ours is a forever love, Shan, I promise …"

The memory of Eric's words struck hard, echoing in her brain along with something Sam once said.

"Promises are nothing more than a puff of air. But my word is my unbreakable bond, as honest and pure as I can ever hope to be."

Putting her blinker on to turn into his complex, she chanced a peek at his profile, suddenly realizing he wasn't asleep at all. Yes, his eyes were closed and his head was back, but his stubbled jaw was far too steeled for a man in repose, clearly indicating he was pretending to be asleep when he wasn't. Goosebumps pebbled her arms as she pulled into his parking spot, wondering if there was anything else he was pretending about.

"I won't hurt you, I give you my word," he'd once told her. A cold chill iced her skin, matching the sleet suddenly slithering her veins.

Had that just been pretense too?

CHAPTER FORTY-FOUR

A towel wrapped around his waist, Sam stared through bleary eyes, his mind foggier than the mirror despite twenty minutes in a hot shower. Grabbing a washcloth, he wiped the steam away, wishing he could wipe away this night from his memory as effectively.

"She was a home-wrecker, man. Had an affair with one of the top professors, busting up his marriage."

Fresh fury surged through his veins along with fresh pain. How had he done it again? How had he fallen in love with another Amber?

His shoulders went slack as he leaned against the sink, his breathing as erratic as the thoughts ping-ponging in his brain. He sucked in a shaky breath. No, she wasn't another Amber, not even close. Amber never would have cleaned him up and driven him home. Nor would she be rattling around in his kitchen right now, making him breakfast, judging from the bacon smell that made him want to puke all over again. He glanced at the now half-empty cup of coffee she'd set on the bathroom counter while he'd been showering around the corner, and he had no doubt whatsoever that Shannon O'Bryen was one of the kindest, most gentle human beings he'd ever met.

But, she wasn't innocent and pure as he'd supposed. His mouth tamped in a thin line as he put toothpaste on his toothbrush, scouring till his gums were as raw as his heart.

Not by a long shot.

And for some reason that rankled more than anything else. Because he'd thought he found an angel. A pearl among women. When all along she was no better than anyone else. Her purity was nothing more than a façade, as surface as all those trappings she often accused him of. Which galled him all the more when he'd taken such great pains to treat her with respect and admiration, cherishing her for the priceless treasure she was.

Because you love her. Not because you thought she was pure.

Moisture burned at the back of his eyes as he sagged over the sink, biceps bulging while he braced stiff arms to the granite surface. He did love her, he knew it deep down in his soul, but his image of her was tarnished, which could very well tarnish their relationship as well. Because right now all he felt was white-hot anger that he'd been duped, sold a bill of goods as tainted as her so-called purity.

A swear word hissed through his teeth as he ripped the towel from his body. He balled it up and hurled it across the room, too inebriated—and too embittered—to even consider forgiving her for what she had done. Maybe tomorrow when the booze wasn't clouding his brain, but not tonight. His jaw hardened as he jerked a fresh T-shirt over his head, teetering precariously while he donned a clean pair of pajama bottoms. No, tonight, the alcohol told him she was no different than the dozens of women he'd brought to his bed, each and every one hoping for a piece of his heart. Well, only one woman possessed it, but she'd wounded it through her deceit, and with the Chivas in his bloodstream as toxic as his thoughts, he intended to make her pay.

Slapping the light switch off, he paused for several seconds with his hand to the wall, dizzier than he'd ever been in his life. But then he'd drank more tonight than he ever had in his life, making his drunk the night of the fundraiser look like a tea party. He waited for the dizziness to subside, then finally stumbled into his darkened bedroom. Hurling the covers and sheets aside, he tumbled into bed and closed his eyes, nausea threatening when the room began to spin. He quickly jerked his eyes open, rolling onto his back with a groan.

"Sam?"

He fought the softening of his heart at the gentle sound of

her voice and the accelerated thump of his pulse as she slowly approached. The calming scent of vanilla invaded his senses like a drug when she sat on the edge of the bed, fusing with the alcohol to heighten months and months of pent-up desire. "Are you hungry? I made you an omelet."

"Yeah, I'm starving," he whispered, hooking her waist to roll her over his body and pin her to the center of the bed, "but not for food, babe."

"Sam, stop it!" Shock edged her voice as she tried to squirm out of his arms, but he only held on tighter, silencing her with a kiss that unleashed a groan deep in his throat. "I need you, Shan," he whispered, voice hoarse as he tried to kiss her again.

"Sam, no!" She pummeled his chest, and his anger suddenly swelled, the thought of her and that professor pulling the pin in his grenade.

"What's the matter, Shan?" he said, eyes itching hot as acid coated his tone. "You only put out if a guy's married?"

Her limbs froze, her face as stricken as her body, and in that moment, the pool of pain in her eyes felt like he'd plunged a knife into his own heart instead of in hers.

His rib cage constricted, regret choking his air. "Shan, I'm sorry—"

Crack! She all but unhinged his jaw with the blur of a palm to his cheek, clocking him so hard, he had stars in his eyes.

Before he could even move, she scrambled off the bed to flee, the trail of her broken sobs shattering him like he'd just shattered her. "Shannon, wait, please!"

But she didn't. He heard the slam of the front door when he tried to follow, too dizzy to make his way down the stairs.

"Dear God, what have I done?" he whispered, crumpling over the banister at the top of the steps.

But he already knew.

He had single-handedly destroyed the truest love he'd ever known.

A groan scraped through his lips as he slowly slumped to the floor with his head in his hands, confirming once and for all what he'd been told all of his life.

He didn't deserve love at all.

CHAPTER FORTY-FIVE

Tess stirred from deep slumber, the still of the house not quite right. Mind hazy from sleep, she listened, but all she heard was Ben's soft snores beside her and the deep bong of the grandfather clock downstairs chiming the hour of five. Glancing out the window, she peered into the night, the predawn sky as dim and dark as her soul suddenly felt. Which made no sense at all because since she'd married Ben, she'd never been happier.

A loud snort escalated Ben's snores to chainsaw level, and she couldn't help but smile as she shook her head, giving him a gentle nudge to make him stop. Her smile grew to a grin when he emitted several growls before rolling onto his side, hooking her into the spooning position she so desperately loved. His soft moan in his sleep feathered her ear, and tears immediately pricked at the back of her eyes. "Thank you, God, for the love of this man in my life," she whispered, never believing her future could hold such joy. Ben shifted against her with another contented moan, and the press of his body reminded her of just one of the many ways that love was manifested, quickly spiking her pulse. Releasing a contented sigh, she closed her eyes to attempt more sleep, but something unknown still stood in the way.

Restless, she carefully tugged from Ben's hold and padded to the bathroom, hoping to slake her uneasiness with a quick glass of water. She headed toward bed again, sleep calling her back, but when her feet detoured to her bedroom door, she eased it open with the utmost care.

And then she heard it—muffled and barely there—but the sound of weeping all the same, and instantly she was awake, a mother in tune with a child's pain. Pulse pounding, she tiptoed to the end of the hall where grief seeped beneath Shannon's door and inching her hand forward, she felt her stomach twist along with the knob. Instantly her rib cage shrank, the sight of Shannon weeping while curled beneath the covers shivering Tess's soul as much as her daughter's heaves shivered her bed.

"Shannon?" Tess rushed to lay down beside her, cocooning her in comfort and love like when Shan was small, a tender twin too fragile for life's injustice. "Sweetheart, what's wrong?"

"Oh, M-Mom …" Voice breaking on a loud sob, Shannon turned and clung to her mother, her anguish wracking both of their bodies. "It … h-happened a-again …"

Tess's blood chilled in her veins. "What happened, darling?" she whispered, her head tucked to Shannon's while she clutched her with all of her might.

"S-Sam … h-he hurt me …"

"What?" Tess whirled, turning on the nightstand lamp to the dimmest level before holding Shannon at bay, searching her tear-stained face and swollen eyes. "How?"

Shannon sat up with a soggy tissue in hand, heaves quivering her body so hard, Tess was tempted to turn on the heat. "He f-found out the f-full story about Eric b-before I could tell him and he—"

Tess's body deflated with a silent groan just as Cat's groggy voice drifted from the open door. "Hey, what's going—" Her sleepy eyes widened when she saw Shannon's swollen face. "Shan?" She bolted to the bed and squatted before her, grazing a hand to Shannon's leg. "Why are you crying?"

"Sam," Tess said in a terse tone far too hoarse, quickly swallowing her shock that Shannon hadn't told him everything about her past. Sweeping Shannon's hair over her shoulder, she handed her the tissue box, noticing for the first time the profusion of crumpled tissues littering the floor and bed. "So, who told him, sweetheart?"

Shannon shook her head, sending more rivulets of tears down her mottled cheeks. "I don't know, Mom, maybe the fraternity brothers he m-met with last night, but he treated me terrible, m-making me feel so dirty again …"

"What a slime bucket." Cat's blue eyes snapped, all sleep apparently forgotten.

Tess laid a hand on Cat's arm, pretty sure the fire in her daughter's eyes matched hers to a sizzle. "Cat, would you mind fixing Shan some Sleepytime tea with lots of cream and just a touch of sugar like she prefers? It looks like she hasn't gotten much sleep, and she'll need her rest."

Cat rose. "Sure, Mom, but first I want to hear what that creep did to her."

Dabbing her eyes, Shannon sniffed, more tears welling. "He came by last night, drunk out of his mind, and I couldn't let him drive like that, so I drove him home."

Cat strolled to the window, mouth twisting in a dangerous smile. "Oh, good, his car is still here so I can initial it for him."

Tess fought the squirm of a smile. "Catherine Marie, as tempting as it may be to key that young man's car right now, that's not the response of a Christian woman."

"Wanna bet?" Shannon blew her nose, her snide remark coaxing a grateful smile to Tess's mouth.

Cat waltzed back over, hands on her hips. "Just give me the word, Shan, and I'll put a little sugar in his gas tank along with your tea."

For once, Tess was thankful for Cat's irreverent humor, relieved when she spied a ghost of a smile on Shannon's face. "Actually, Cat, I prefer honey," she said in a nasal tone, "both in my tea *and* on his prized pearlized paint job." She snatched several more tissues from the box, putting them to good use. "And if you have enough to fill the pockets of that expensive jacket he left in his car, that would definitely sweeten the deal."

A wicked grin slid across Cat's face. "Oh, you bet. Even if I have to drive all the way to Kroger to get it."

"So, what happened after you took him home?" Tess asked, anxious to get to the heart of the matter. "And I sure hope you railed on him for driving and drinking."

"I did." Shannon shifted to sit against the headboard with the box of Kleenex securely in her lap. Her mouth hitched on one side. "Right before he spewed his dinner and a bottle of scotch on the side of the road, so I cleaned him up with a bunch of leaves."

"Ooooo, poison ivy, I hope?" Cat arched a brow.

Another sliver of a smile shaded Shannon's lips. "Unfortunately, no." A tiny touch of tease glimmered in her eyes instead of tears, giving Tess hope that this situation would not bring her daughter to the brink of despair like before. "But on the bright side," she said with a tip of her head, "his new shoes, shirt, and car will smell like a sewer for a very long time."

"Good." Cat cocked a hip with a stern fold of arms. "That's a good smell for rats."

"So, what happened after you got him home?" Tess shimmied back against the headboard, too, thinking she might need a cup of tea as well.

A weary sigh drifted from Shannon's lips. "I helped him upstairs to take a shower while I fixed him coffee and breakfast."

Cat groaned, mouth dangling as she stared at her sister in disbelief. "Seriously? You are *way* too nice of a person, Shan. You sure wouldn't catch me cooking for any wasted womanizer." Her smile veered diabolical. "Unless I had ipecac on hand."

Shannon chewed on her lip, the hint of a guilty smile peeking through. "Don't think it didn't enter my mind, but his clothes and car already smelled like a tavern outhouse on a sewage swamp, so I didn't want his beautiful house to smell like that too."

"Bleeding heart," Cat mumbled.

The smile dissolved on Shannon's lips, eyes brimming with tears once again. "And that's exactly what happened, sis, because he made my heart bleed. When he didn't come down to eat, I found him upstairs on his bed in the dark, and he ..."

Tess's body went stiffer than the wood against her back. But when a sob broke from Shannon's lips, she folded her in her arms, soothing with a gentle hand to her hair. "It's okay, baby, no wound is too deep for God, so go on, sweetheart ..."

Shannon nodded against her shoulder, fingers gripping Tess with a ferocity that revealed the depth of her hurt. "He p-pulled me into his bed, wanting to make out, and when I wouldn't, he … he … said …"

"Said what?" Cat's tone was deadly.

Shannon's hand shook as she grabbed several tissues to blow her nose before slumping against Tess's shoulder. "He said, 'What's the matter, Shan? You only put out if a guy's married?'"

"I'm gonna kill him …" Cat paced back and forth several times before returning to the window with a perilous glint in her eyes.

Swallowing hard, Tess caressed a hand to Shannon's cheek. "He … didn't do anything else … did he, sweetheart?"

A grunt slipped from Shannon's mouth, so out of character, Tess had to bite back a smile. "Not after I left the imprint of my palm on that pretty-boy face of his." Her lip began to quiver as she rubbed her hand. "It still hurts, but not as much as his jaw, I hope."

"Yes!" Cat shot a fist in the air. "So, what happened next?"

Shannon's shoulders lifted in a pathetic shrug, the threat of more tears brewing in her eyes. "I left," she whispered, "and I've been crying ever since."

Cat slammed a hard-knuckled fist into her palm. "So help me, I'm gonna murder him …"

Lips twitching over Cat's dramatics, Tess gave her drama-queen daughter a patient smile. "Tea now, darling, homicide later."

"Oh, right." She hustled out, turning at the door with a salty smile. "Don't worry—I'll bring the tea *before* I go to Kroger."

"Mom, what am I going to do?" Shannon whispered after Cat left. "I love him even still."

Tess pulled her close, and Shannon rested her head on her shoulder. "Of course you do, darling. That's the beauty of love gifted by God—it never fails." She gave her daughter a squeeze. "But it's also vulnerable to hurt, as each of us knows all too well. What Sam did, sweetheart …" She expelled a wispy sigh. "Well, it was wrong in every way—spiritually, physically, mentally, and emotionally." She hesitated, grateful Cat had left the room because she'd never understand what Tess was about to say. "But … I have learned from a lifetime of doing wrong and being wronged, Shan, that the true path of love looks beyond *our* pain caused by others, to the hurt that caused *theirs*." She softly skimmed her palms up and down Shannon's arm. "And then," she whispered, tears pricking over a lesson she'd learned so many years ago, "we have to look beyond *their* hurt to God's. Because it's *His* pain that makes it possible to forgive and love others the way He has called us to do."

"I know you're right, Mom. I should have told him sooner and I meant to, I swear. But a part of me was so very afraid of this—his lack of respect, his disappointment, his rejection." Her shiver rattled them both as she held onto Tess more tightly, the gouge of her fingers a true measure of her angst. "So very afraid I would lose his love."

"Oh, darling, I don't think so." Tess pressed a kiss to her tousled hair. "If anything, this will serve to strengthen it."

Shannon issued another grunt, and this time Tess allowed a smile, her head bent to her daughter's while Shannon expelled a heavy sigh. "I don't see how."

"Exactly," Tess said with a soft chuckle. "Faith isn't something we see, darling; it's something we believe deep in our soul. And I promise you that when coupled with prayers of obedience, that beautiful blindness will open your eyes to all that God can do on your behalf. *And* Sam's."

Shannon lifted her head to peer at her with questioning eyes. "How?"

Tess's low laughter rumbled in her chest. "From the lovesick look in Sam's eyes over the last month, I imagine the truth of your relationship with Eric came as quite a blow."

"Ya think?" One edge of Shan's mouth inched up. "The man puked on his shoes for heaven's sake, Mom, and for Sam Cunningham, there's no greater sacrilege than that."

Tess chuckled, easing the tension at the back of her neck. "The shoes'll come clean, Shan, just like Sam's heart after he sees the truth in the light of day. And when that happens—aided heavily by your forgiveness and prayer, mind you—the man addicted to designer clothes and expensive shoes will suddenly realize nobody's perfect." She gave Shannon's waist a light pinch. "Not even the amazing young woman he's put on that lofty pedestal." She shifted to face her daughter. "Because you see, darling, it's the truth that will set both you and Sam free to be all that God has called you to be, not Sam's pie-in-the-sky idea that you're the perfect woman. Trust me, I know."

It was Tess's turn to grunt as she plopped back against the headboard. "When your father and I were first married, the poor, deluded man had me on a pedestal much as Sam did you." She scrunched her nose. "Until I charred both that pedestal and too many meals to count. Year after year, my humanity kept chipping away at it, and when I put my job before him?" Her smile sobered into regret as her gaze trailed into a distant stare. "It cracked that stupid pedestal all together, tumbling both me and our marriage into an awful abyss."

Shaking off the malaise that always arose when she thought of Adam, she huffed out a cleansing sigh. "So you see, sweetheart, as I have told you countless times, as people of faith, we have a built-in insurance policy to cover all of our disappointments and pain."

Saltwater brimmed in her daughter's eyes again, but Tess suspected these were tears of hope when Shan offered a wobbly smile. "All things work together for good for those who love God," Shannon whispered, "and have been called according to His purpose."

Tess beamed. "And what are two of His purposes in a situation like this?"

Shannon's lips twitched with another smile. "Pray for them which spitefully use you and praise God in all things."

"Yes!" Tess punched a fist to her palm. "Because—"

"It's not God Who needs our praise," Shannon interjected, "it's us, since praise, prayer, and obedience unleashes the power of heaven."

"You *were* listening!" Tess said with a wide grin.

Like the tide coming in, the saltwater dribbled down Shannon's cheek to pool in the curve of her trembling smile. "Always," she rasped, flinging herself into her mother's arms until both of them could do nothing but weep. "I love you Mom."

"I love you, too, Shan," Tess whispered, eyes squeezed tightly against the fresh flow of tears. "*So* very much!" She settled against the headboard again and patted Shannon's knee. "So … what are you going to do?"

Shannon's sigh could have ruffled the curtains. "Well, first I'm going to praise God in this situation and ask Him to turn it around for my good and Sam's. Then I'm going to pray that I can eventually forgive that sorry excuse of a boyfriend."

"Eventually?" Tess angled a brow.

Shannon huffed out a sigh. "I will forgive him, Mom, I promise, but right now it's just so raw, you know?"

Yes, she knew. All too well she knew.

"So I think I need some time to just pray and think about all of this, and especially get past the humiliation all over again." She peeked up, eyes moist. "Sam made me feel so ashamed, Mom, that I don't have the strength to even face him right now, even though he's called and texted a dozen times since I left his house." Her rib cage rose and fell. "And to be honest, I'm still so hurt and angry inside, I thought I'd give him a bit of the cold shoulder, just to let him stew for a while, you know?"

"Stewing's good …" Tess volunteered.

Shannon stared out the window where the first shimmer of dawn spilled across her sill in subtle shades of pearl and pink "At least till I figure out what I really want. Sam may not want me anymore, but if he does, then I need to decide if I can marry a man who resorts to a bottle whenever he hits an emotional blip in the road."

"You're a wise woman, Shannon O'Bryen."

Shannon peered up. "I have a wise mother," she said with a misty smile.

Squeezing Shannon's hand, Tess rose while her stomach emitted a noisy growl. "Hey—you feel like breakfast? Or do you want to sleep in?"

Shannon yawned, shimmying her toes under the covers. "I think I better get some decent sleep or forgiveness will be a lot further away," she said with a wry smile, "but thanks, Mom, for everything."

"You're welcome, sweetheart, and I'll just check on your tea. If you're asleep when Cat brings it up, I may just drink it myself because the calming effect will do me good. *Especially* if your sister is on her way to Kroger."

"Good plan." Shannon's grin was sleepy as she curled into a cozy ball. "G'night, Mom."

"Good night, Shan, and by the way, I like your plan too." She gave Shannon a wink at the door. "Cold shoulder … warm heart."

Expelling a weary sigh, Tess closed the door and sagged against it with eyes closed, thinking she was way too keyed up to sleep now. "May as well have some tea too," she muttered, startling when her eyes opened to see Ben standing at the end of the hall.

"What's going on, Tess?" he said in a gravelly tone, his morning voice always lower than normal.

Her shock seeped out on a wavering sigh as she put a hand to her chest. "Good night, Ben, you scared me half to death!" she whispered, praying Davey didn't wake up while she hurried down the hall.

"Why are you up?" he asked, hair tousled as much as his well-muscled T-shirt and pajama bottoms while morning bristle shadowed his face.

"Shan wasn't feeling well, so Cat's making her some tea." She cupped a hand to his jaw, eyes tender as she brushed a kiss to his lips. "Today's your day to sleep in, Ben, so go back to bed and I'll fill you in later, okay?"

Turning, she started for the stairs when he hooked her arm, all but bouncing her back. "Aren't you coming? It's not even light outside yet."

She stood on tiptoe to give him another quick kiss. “I don’t think so, babe. After talking to Shan, I’m wide awake, so I’m pretty sure I wouldn’t be able to sleep.”

Slipping his arms around her waist, he drew her in close, nuzzling her neck before he swooped her up to carry her back into their room. With a kiss that muffled her squeal, he kicked the door closed with his foot, his groggy voice way huskier than usual. “Who said anything about sleep?”

CHAPTER FORTY-SIX

"I'm gonna kill him."

"Probably not," Chase said to Jack with a wry smile, finger calmly pressed to Sam's fancy doorbell. "That's why you asked me along, remember? To ensure restraint?"

Ignoring Chase's remark, Jack pounded a fist on Sam's front door. "Open up, Cunningham, you have some groveling to do—"

"Settle down, O'Bryen," Chase said in the military monotone he'd always employed to diffuse volatile situations. "Losing your cool won't help anything."

"Wanna bet?" Jack delivered another bludgeoning blow, his lips clamped in a hard smile. "It'll help me feel a whole lot better when I mess up his pretty face." Cutting loose with a questionable hiss, Jack abandoned the front door to scrounge for the key Sam hid under one of his potted palms. "I don't have time for this garbage," he muttered, snatching up the key to rattle it in the lock.

"Sure you do." Chase strolled in behind Jack after he hurled the door open, quietly shutting it again while Jack stormed through the foyer. "Friendship is always worth the time."

Jack grunted, scouring Sam's great room before tearing down the hall to the kitchen. "That remains to be seen. Cunningham?" His shout echoed in the hallway as he rampaged back to the foyer, threats ricocheting off the vaulted ceiling. "You're going to pay for what you did to my sister, you blood-sucking lowlife."

He tore toward the staircase, and Chase halted him with a firm hand and a sober look on the second step. "We both agreed we'd handle this like rational human beings, Jack, who also happen to be close friends with that blood-sucking lowlife."

He shook Chase's hand off. "You agreed, not me." He started up the steps.

"*You* agreed by inviting me along, Doc," Chase said with a firm hook of Jack's arm, "asking me to keep you from doing something stupid, so I am."

Jack paused on the second step, his scowl going flat. "Yeah, I know—what was I thinking?"

Chase scratched the back of his neck. "Uh, that your temper might get the best of you, maybe, with a very good friend?" His smile veered toward dry. "No matter how incredibly stupid that friend has been."

Jack issued another grunt as he kneaded the bridge of his nose. "Yeah, well maybe his stupidity is catching because right now all I want to do is blacken his eye."

Chase nodded. "I hear you, man, but if you do that, I'll have to blacken yours per your request to keep you in line no matter what, which I told you I'd be happy to do." A slow smile curled on his lips as he slapped Jack on the back on his way up the stairs. "Biblically speaking, of course, as in an eye for an eye?"

Jack winced as he followed Chase up. "That can't be legal for a pastor," he muttered.

"Tough love," Chase said with a grim smile. "Better than incarceration for manslaughter."

Jack rubbed his neck. "Yeah, I guess. But you may have to remind me in a few seconds, 'cause just thinking about how Sam hurt Shan boils my blood, you know?"

"Yeah, I do," Chase said quietly, thinking Shannon had been through enough grief in her life from what Jack had told him; she sure didn't need more from Sam, the guy who *claimed* to love her. He tamped down his ire with a press of his jaw. "Somebody you trusted hurt somebody you love. And not just anybody, but one of the most kind-hearted, gentle, and gracious human beings alive," he bit out, suddenly wanting to take a swing at Sam himself. He slowed as he reached the landing, expelling a slow, arduous breath while he shot Jack a tight-lipped smile. "It's downright scary how quickly emotions can boil over, isn't it?"

"Tell me about it." Jack cuffed Chase's shoulder as they strode down the hall to Sam's bedroom. "Sam is my best friend along with you, Chase, so I gotta tell you, I'm more than a little shocked at how much I want to take a swing at the guy."

"I'm not." Chase stared straight ahead, anger licking at the edge of his restraint. "Shannon is one incredible woman."

Jack paused outside Sam's door to deliver a somber smile. "Thanks for caring about her like you do."

Chase never blinked. "I love her, man, as a friend. But I gotta tell you, Jack, if this bozo screws it up, I promise you right now, I have plans to love her as way more."

Jack smiled. "You're a good friend, Chase."

"You're darn right I am." His smile flat-lined. "Or I would have fought you tooth and nail on Lacey, and Sam on Shannon too."

"I know. Thanks."

"Don't mention it," he said, smile wry as he nodded to where Sam lay sprawled like a scarecrow corpse in the middle of his bed. "But *do* stop me from slapping Pretty Boy around if he gets on my nerves, okay?"

Jack put two palms in the air. "Hey, no promises, dude, especially since there won't be anyone holding me back."

Chase grinned. "Could get ugly, Doc."

Jack flashed some teeth of his own as he strolled into Sam's room, ripping the sheet off his friend's back. "No worries, Rev, I have a medical degree—I can patch him up after we dress him down." He kicked Sam's leg none too gently. "Hey, jerk—wake up!"

Nothing.

Chase ambled over to shake Sam hard. "Sam—wake up!"

Still nothing.

"I guess our boy had a little too much to drink," Jack said with a wicked smile. "He's probably dry, so I'd bet he'd like some water."

A slow grin inched across Chase's face. "Good idea," he said, heading for the door. "You scout out his bathroom, and I'll scrounge in the one down the hall." He strolled to the guest bathroom and found a tumbler that he filled to the brim with water. Striding back, he faced Jack on the other side of the bed with a crooked smile before leaning forward to sniff. "Smells like he needs a shower too."

"That's a given." Jack held a similar tumbler full of water over Sam's body. "Thought about using toilet water," he said with a dark smile, "since Ham has an unnatural aversion to dirty water from some childhood trauma, but figured I'd show him *some* mercy."

"Unlike he did for Shannon." Chase doused a sudden flare of anger just like he planned to douse his good friend. Smile hard, he leaned close to Sam's ear, which was the only part of his head visible beneath a feather pillow. "Sam," he whispered, "would you like some water?"

The pillow rose and fell in even rhythm, and Jack exchanged a grin with Chase before both unloaded their liquid stash like flood stage at Niagara Falls.

A low moan sounded beneath the pillow as Sam shuddered, finally stirring like a man rising from the dead. A very wet and groggy man.

Pelting the pillow off, Sam flopped on his back with a strangled sound between a gargle and a groan, black stubble peppering an open jaw. His rumpled T-shirt appeared to be stained with vomit, and his usually shiny black curls looked like they'd been combed with a Weed Eater.

Chase caught a sniff of bottle breath and wrinkled his nose. "I don't think I've ever seen the meticulous Dr. Love quite so disheveled before. Nor smelling worse."

"Yeah." A gleam lit Jack's eyes. "I say we take a picture for the bulletin board at Memorial."

"No way, Jack," Chase said with compassion in his tone, "not until the man's had a real good shower first."

A slow grin curled Jack's lips as he bobbled the glass. "Good idea. See you in a few."

The second round of H2O did the trick, resurrecting Dr. Love with a curse that defiled the air, along with his breath. "What the—?" Sam opened his eyes—if slits can be considered open—and immediately sank back on the bed with a rusty groan. "Tell me I'm dreaming, please," he said in a scratchy tone.

"Wish I could, slimeball, but the nightmare you put my sister through is real enough, Cunningham, so get up because I'm just itching to knock you back down."

"Jack …" Chase's warning tone did little to temper the fire in Jack's eyes.

"No, Rev, let him," Sam said, regret riddling his tone while he laid flat on his back. "I deserve it."

"You're darn right you do, Cunningham, so get up."

Sam started to rise, and Jack took a step forward with hands knuckled tight, looking for all his prior promise of restraint as if he were ready to pop Sam the moment he stood up.

"Put the guns away, Jack," Chase said quietly, blocking Jack's way while Sam rolled out of bed with a groan. "We're doing this the civilized way, remember?"

"He doesn't deserve 'civilized,' Chase, not after the way he wounded my sister."

"I don't," Sam said in a voice that sounded more like a croak, body swaying almost imperceptibly as he stood before them both with sorrow in red-rimmed eyes. "And I don't deserve Shannon either," he whispered, eyelids weighting closed as he ground the pads of his fingers to his temple. "I'm not good enough for her."

"You got that right, Cunningham." Jack cauterized Sam with a hard glare, his body all but twitching with the need for retaliation.

"So, do it, Jack," Sam said quietly, his somber gaze so spidered with red it looked like a roadmap. "Bloody me, flatten me, and beat me to a pulp, because it sure can't feel any worse than I do now."

Chase sighed as he braced both of Jack's shoulders. "Go make some strong coffee, will you? And I'll be right down while Sam cleans up."

"Ain't enough soap in the world," Jack hissed, scorching Sam with another look before he finally left the room.

"You should have let him deck me." Sam's voice was barely a whisper as he dropped to sit on the edge of the bed, shoulders slumped and head in his hands. "He needs the release … and so do I."

"Why'd you do it, Sam?" Chase slowly lowered to sit beside him, hands loosely clasped. "Over and above the bottle of scotch, what possessed you to reopen the wounds that almost destroyed Shannon's life?"

"How much do you know?" Sam whispered, the question hoarse with pain.

"Everything. From Shannon's painful past, to what went on here last night, till she cried herself to sleep early this morning."

Sam lifted his head, a sheen of moisture marring his gaze as he lagged into a lost stare. "Shannon is the world to me, Chase, everything I ever dreamed of … and everything I've never been. Clean. Pure. Untainted by my world, which in my mind has always been a cesspool, no matter how hard I try to dress it up. So when my buddies from college told me the truth about her …" His eyes met Chase's. "I lost it. All I could think of was her sleeping with that slimeball professor, not giving a whit that she was destroying a marriage."

"She didn't know," Chase said quietly. "Not that what she did wasn't wrong, because it was, but Jack told me the jerk lied to her. Told her he was divorced when he wasn't."

Looking away, Sam slashed shaky fingers through his hair, his tone gruff. "Come on, Rev, Shannon's one of the most brilliant women I know. She couldn't figure out that a professor on campus is married? Even if she wasn't smart enough to research it first, somebody had to tell her."

"Nobody knew."

"What?" Sam stared, brows in a bunch. "What do you mean nobody knew?"

Chase stretched out his legs. "I mean it wasn't a professor on campus; it was a visiting speaker from Stanford, highly regarded in his field." He slid Sam a sober look. "He met Shannon during his visit and arranged to take a six-month sabbatical at her university. To do research, Jack said, but it's pretty clear what that research involved."

Sam's jaw dropped. "What a lying sack of—"

"Yeah, he was," Chase interrupted. "It appears he proposed just to coerce Shannon into intimacies, keeping her in the dark along with his wife and children." His gaze drifted off like Sam's had before while a nerve twittered in his cheek. "Jack said even as a little girl, Shannon was always so innocent and vulnerable, the twin who always did what her mother asked and always gave in to her sister. While Cat climbed trees and beat up boys, Shannon was the gentle dreamer who always played dress-up as a bride, longing for a fairytale marriage and vowing to save herself for Mr. Right." Chase's mouth twisted. "Only Mr. Right turned out to be Mr. Dead Wrong, a creep who managed to disarm both Shannon and her faith.

"I didn't know," Sam whispered.

"Of course you didn't because gossip isn't interested in the truth."

Sam peered up, both fatigue and regret etched in his brow. "What happened with the wife? I heard she went ballistic when she found them"—a knot ducked in Sam's throat—"you know, together, and that she pulled a gun."

"That much is true, causing a huge splash in the papers when the wife trashed his apartment before taking a potshot at her husband and Shannon in the quadrangle." His mouth thinned into a hard line. "Right before she drove off a bridge, further exacerbating an already volatile and high-profile drama, which fortunately the wife survived." Chase expelled a harsh breath. "But Shannon almost didn't. She was so traumatized she fled and totaled her car on the way home, ending up in the hospital pretty banged up." He flexed his fingers, barely aware he'd been clenching them while his gut cramped over the awful guilt and anguish Shannon incurred. "Jack said the entire mess triggered a year-long breakdown for Shannon, robbing her of the will to live. The guilt was bad enough, but the papers raked her over the coals so much, Jack said she'd wished she had died in that crash. Apparently she dropped out of school and slept most days for a solid year, little more than a zombie the entire time." His jaw ached from clenching his teeth. "And all because of some sleazebag player who promised to love her forever."

Sam hung his head, arms limp over his legs, and when his shoulders began to shake, Chase realized he was weeping. "God forgive me," he whispered, the sound as broken as the man.

"He does, Sam," Chase said quietly, "and so does Shannon."

Sam shook his head vehemently, voice harsh. "No, I don't deserve it, and I definitely don't deserve her."

"None of us do, man, which is why the grace of God is so awesome. Unmerited favor, Doc. Can't earn it, can't steal it, can't buy it." He laid a hand on Sam's shoulder, a hint of jest in his tone. "Although God knows you've tried, more than any human being I've ever seen."

"Yeah, I have," Sam said numbly, eyes glazed with moisture as he stared straight ahead. "'Trappings,' Shannon calls them, all those things I do and buy to make myself feel worthy."

Chase exhaled softly, grateful Sam had filled him in on his abandonment by his mother at a very young age. He paused. "Worthy enough so someone will stay forever?"

Sam laughed, the sound bitter as he slapped at the wetness in his eyes. "Yeah, something like that."

Chase squeezed Sam's shoulder before letting go. "I will never leave you nor forsake you," he quoted from Scripture, just saying the words out loud bringing a calm to his soul. "And He won't, Sam, and I say that from hard experience. He never deserted me in the burnt-out hovels of Iraq when enemy fire was raining down, nor when snipers picked off my buddies like fleas on a dog. And you know what?" Tears stung the back of his lids as he thought of the irreplaceable friend who had tirelessly tried to teach him about faith. "Not even those buddies who knew Him," he whispered, "because the moment a bullet stole their last breath, *He* became their next, standing right alongside to usher them into a world without hate and pain. A world that makes this one look like a trash heap, man, where all the abandonment, all the betrayal, all the sin of any kind, is burned away by the blinding beauty of His unfailing love." Emotion grew thick in his throat. "A love that will never—just like our God—leave us nor forsake us."

"Love Everlasting …" Sam whispered, staring off into space once again. "Something Shannon talks about a lot."

"Because it's something she discovered when she was in the bowels of hell, just like I did in the crossfires of Iraq, and like Jack did with his father and Lacey with hers. 'I have loved you with an everlasting love,' God said, which is the only thing we can really bank on in this life, Sam, the only thing we can truly put our confidence in. Not in things. Not in people. And definitely not in ourselves."

Sam grunted.

"And you know the best part? Nothing you do or say can take it away. Nor anything anyone else does or says—*nothing*! 'Neither death nor life, nor angels nor rulers, nor things present nor things to come, nor powers, nor height nor depth, nor anything else in all creation, will be able to separate us from the love of God.'" He slapped him on the back and rose. "So. What are you going to do about Shannon?"

Sam gouged at the bridge of his nose, eyes closed and a pained expression on his face. "Apologize if she'll let me, although she hasn't answered my texts or calls between the time she left last night and when I finally fell asleep." He exhaled long and slow, as if letting everything go. "And then I'll leave her alone, which is what she obviously wants."

"Do you love her?"

Sam gave him a slitted stare. "No, Rev, I just sucked down a bottle of scotch and puked my guts out because I'm mildly attracted to her."

"You can be a real smart aleck, you know that, Cunningham?"

"Humph. Can't be too smart—I just blew it with the woman I love."

"So fix it. Spend some time on your knees—both with God and with her—then take it from there."

Sam shook his head. "I don't know, Chase, she deserves so much better than me."

Chase slacked a hip with a roll of his eyes. "Don't tell me we're back to that 'worthy' whine again. Well, you know what? She *does* deserve better than you," he said with a wry smile, "but I don't plan to make a move because she wants you, lughead." He took a sniff. "Although the way you reek right now, I sure don't know why."

Chase hesitated, wishing for the briefest of moments that he was in Sam's shoes despite the way that he smelled. "So treat her like the treasure she is, Sam, and be the man that she needs you to be. Which means no more turning to the bottle when things get too tough or lashing out at her when she falls from grace, because she will, man, like every single one of us. Just love her for who she is, not who you want her to be—just like God does with us."

He paused to draw in a deep breath, slowly releasing it again. "And above all else—never, *ever* take your hurt out on her, because hurt stabs blindly, Sam, but when it's done—they're not the only one bleeding." Giving Sam a jostle with his foot, Chase ambled from the room, turning only when he reached the door. "And get a realllly hot shower, will you? Because right now, you stink a whole lot more than your life."

CHAPTER FORTY-SEVEN

"Come on, Shan—you sure you don't want to go to Cold Stone?" Lacey wiggled her brows. "Jack's buying," she said in an obvious attempt to prod Shannon to go out. She rose from the Adirondack chair between Shannon's and Cat's with a jut of her lower lip, the mournful wail of a loon underscoring her sad face as the shadows of dusk stole away the light of day. "You've been cooped up here for two solid weeks except for work and church, sweetie, and Cat and I both think you need to get out."

"Hey, guys, I *am* out," Shannon said with a chuckle, arms wide to indicate the great outdoors where she'd been spending all of her evenings for the last few weeks. "I told you, Lace—I'm just taking some time to think and pray, kind of like a retreat." She rested her head on the back of her chair with palms flat on its wide arms. "Besides, I like to watch the lazy roll of the river."

Cat chuckled. "And I like to watch the grass grow, sis, but preferably at Cold Stone. Come on, Lace, leave her be. She's happy 'communing with God,'" Cat said with a droll smile, the tease in her tone indicating she'd been around this mountain with her sister before. "She's been assuring me all week that she wants for nothing right now."

"Uh …" Shannon shot her sister and sister-in-law a faint smile, waggling her brows like Lacey had. "Except maybe a cheesecake fantasy to go?"

"Yes!" Cat pumped a fist in the air. "She *finally* wants ice cream again, which is definite progress. Even *if* it's not the type of 'fantasy' I'd like her to indulge in." She pressed a kiss to Shannon's hair. "You want anything else, sis?"

Sam Cunningham with extra sprinkles?

"Nope, just the fantasy, please, and you'll find me right here."

Indulging in a little fantasy of my own.

"No doubt about that." Lacey bent to give her a quick hug before following Cat to the ramp, tossing a wink over her shoulder. "And we'll order yours right before we leave so it won't be mush by the time you get it, okay?"

"Perfect. Thanks, guys, I really appreciate it."

Sinking back into her chair, Shannon released a peaceful sigh, the sound of water lapping the shore working its magic, along with the shimmer of the river against a scarlet sky. An osprey glided over the fiery horizon, its graceful dance in natural rhythm with willowy grasses that swayed and shushed on the shore.

Chin lifted, she closed her eyes to feel the caress of a sea breeze mingling with the salty scent of the marsh, and her rib cage expanded with gratitude for the God Who had set her as free as the osprey overhead. "Thank you, Lord, for your unfailing love," she whispered, saltwater flooding her eyes like it flooded the grassy shores at high tide. Because she knew that although Sam had hurt her deeply, God had used it to bury the past. All of it.

The pain of Eric's betrayal.

Her deadly, deep-seated need for approval.

And the shame of losing that very approval from both God and her family.

A single tear slithered her cheek as she relived Sam's rejection that night, the loss of his approval the final blow to a stronghold that had held her in bondage far too long.

Am I now trying to win the approval of human beings, or of God? If I were still trying to please people, I would not be a servant of Christ.

So for one week she'd done exactly what her mother said—praise and prayer—and in the process she discovered a freedom she'd never known before. A freedom she wouldn't have known at all if God hadn't used the pain of Sam's rejection to reveal that her past was over and done. And in its place was a hope as bright and shiny as the dawn of a new day, where the God of Hope promised to give her a future and a hope.

A future .... She opened her eyes to scan the heavens, listening for that Still Small Voice she so trusted to guide her. *I need to know, Lord—will that be with Sam?*

She thought so. She hoped so. But she promised herself she'd give it time to think and pray, to make sure it was what God wanted her to do. Sam seemed to want it—he'd called and texted every day, begging to see her, sending her gifts, emailing his hopes for the future. But Shannon never responded directly, only through Jack, allowing vague assurances from her brother that his sister just needed more time.

She spied the osprey soaring overhead once again and a soft smile lighted on her lips. The bird's whistling call reminded her of a teakettle on the boil, and her thoughts suddenly leapfrogged to Sam. On the boil, indeed—her feelings for him steeped strong and too hot to handle. Her smile took a slide to the left. Which was exactly why she needed this time alone. She couldn't think clearly when Sam was around, because one word, one moment, one kiss had a way of bubbling her emotions, causing good intentions to float away in a fog as quickly as the steam whistling from the teapot.

And the truth was—this decision was too important to allow Sam to sway her in any way. She loved him with everything in her, and although the last month of dating had helped to assuage her fears about his prior "player" tendencies, she couldn't help but wonder if one month was enough to know for sure? To base a future on? True, he no longer flirted with other women in her presence or even glanced their way, focusing only on her in a manner that made her blossom and bloom into the woman she'd always hoped to be.

Cherished forever by the man that she loved.

But forever was a very long time. Especially if a man didn't accept you for who you were and belittled you for the things that you did.

Or loved his "trappings" far more than his wife?

Shannon absently nibbled her lip, worry lines crimping her brow.

Or resorted to alcohol whenever things didn't quite go his way?

Rising from the chair, Shannon sighed, the wispy sound more in tune with the mournful call of the loon than the cheerful chatter of the osprey that soared high in the dusk. Her eyes scanned the heavens as she sought her answer, seeking the guidance of the only One she could truly trust. "So, what do you say, God?" she said out loud. "Is Sam the one for me? Will You give me a sign?"

Silence reigned for several moments while Shannon closed her eyes, waiting for an answer. But the only thing she heard was the rising trill of tree frogs and the hoot of a faraway owl, obviously tuning up for the night. That and the husky clear of a throat.

"Uh, if He doesn't get back to you right away, can I take a shot?"

She spun around so fast, she almost tipped over. And might have, if not for Sam's firm hands, which steadied her waist, but did absolutely nothing for her heart. It shot straight to her throat while her pulse took off in a sprint. "Sam!" she rasped, barely able to catch her breath as she splayed a trembling hand to her chest, "I didn't hear you …"

"I know," he said quietly, his sheepish smile fading a lot more quickly than the prickles of heat searing her skin. "In fact, you haven't 'heard' me at all, Shan—not my calls, not my texts, not my tokens of apology for a solid two weeks." He offered a slight shrug, along with a repentant half-smile. "So I decided to plead my case in person."

She took a step back, arms crossed and cordoned to her waist like a barrier in an effort to maintain some calm and control. *Please, Lord, lots and lots of control …*

As if sensing her withdrawal, he backed up as well, hands buried in his pockets while he stared at his feet. He peered up with a half-lidded smile. "Jack said you're going to be published—is that the book you were ghostwriting?"

She nodded, still unable to believe her name would be on the novel she'd just written. She had poured her heart into it—just like she had in her friendship with Sam—baring her soul in a story that so mirrored her own. Her heart skipped a beat. Only Princess Olivia and her former playboy had a fairytale ending …

Shannon sighed, the joy of publication dimmed by her situation with Sam. "It seems both the author and her editor loved the book so much, they insisted my name be listed as co-author." Her lips lifted in a tremulous smile. "Along with a potential contract for a book of my own."

His face lit up as he stepped forward, arms raised like he wanted to give her a hug. "Wow, Shan, that's wonderful," he said, quickly dropping them back to his sides when she withdrew a few more inches. "Sounds like a happy ending for both Olivia and you." He slid his hands back into his pockets as if he didn't know what else to do with them before his gaze gentled with hope. "I'd like to give you a happy ending, too, Shan," he said quietly, "if you'll let me."

"I will, Sam, I promise," she whispered, gaze tender. "But right now I need more time."

"And right now I need *you*, Shannon," he said firmly, closing the distance with a pained look of regret. His eyes locked on hers while he gently skimmed his palms down her arms. "I 'need' you to forgive me for hurting you the way that I did because I can't live with myself if you don't."

"I've forgiven you, Sam …" She eased from his hold once again, his touch waging war with her resolve as she fought the seduction of those eyes. She'd always preferred to think of herself as more spiritual than physical, but Sam Cunningham had a way of blowing that assessment right out of the water, unleashing desire in her like no man ever had. Chewing on her lip, she tried to resist to no avail, peeking up at the man who possessed the power to disarm her, body and soul.

"But not forgotten," he said quietly.

"No." Her response was almost inaudible, barely wisping past her lips.

Exhaling loudly, he plunged his hands in the pockets of his

prized Armani trousers once again, the matching charcoal jacket perfectly tailored to showcase his broad shoulders and narrow hips. It was complemented, as always, by a crisply starched Armani dress shirt, complete with silver stud cufflinks, and his favorite "new" Ralph Lauren tie. Her lips twitched in a near smile. One that was vomit-free, apparently.

As always, he looked like a GQ ad with a hint of scruff on his hard-sculpted jaw and dark curls groomed to perfection, just begging to be mussed. Those potent eyes refused to let her go, disarming her as they penetrated into her very soul. "Why didn't you tell me, Shan?" he whispered, the hurt in his face damaging her far more than it did him.

Looking away, she swallowed hard, knowing full well he deserved an answer, deserved an apology as forthcoming as his, and one unhindered by fear. "I wanted to, Sam," she whispered, the heat of her shame creeping into her cheeks, "but after we became good friends, I … was afraid. Afraid it would ruin your opinion of me, and all those seeds of faith I was trying so hard to sow." She bit hard on her lip, scarcely aware of the taste of blood as tears burned beneath her lids. "And then when we began to" —a lump bobbed in her throat— "have stronger feelings for each other, I tried a number of times, but something always seemed to get in the way." Sorrow welled in her eyes as they connected with his once again. "Until I was in so deep, I was petrified you'd turn me away."

He hung his head. "Fears well-founded, apparently," he said quietly, his voice heavy with remorse. Expelling a weighty sigh, he looked up, a glint of promise in his gaze. "I'll never hurt you like that again, Shannon. I swear."

"I hope not." Her features turned tender. "But saying it doesn't make it so, Sam," she said softly. "It needs the test of time."

He nodded, head bowed once again. "Does that mean time together? Or time apart?"

Her sigh floated on the same breeze that ruffled the dark curls on his head. "Time apart for a little bit longer, I think, just to make sure it's what God wants me to do, then ample time together if He tells me you're the one."

He looked up beneath those nearly illegal lashes, mouth tipping up on one side. "So it's Him I need to be talking to, not you?"

Her lips curved in a shy smile. "That would definitely help."

"Good." Within two firm strides, he had her in his arms with hands locked at the small of her back, wise enough to leave several inches between them. "Because I've been talking His ear off nonstop since the moment you walked out of my door, Shannon O'Bryen, and He and I are on sound agreement on one very important thing." He cradled her face in his hands, the intensity in his eyes all but welding her to the spot. "We belong together, Shan, and I have never been surer of anything in my life. Give me the chance to prove it to you. To show you that I am exactly what you need because God knows you are everything I need and the only thing I really want."

"Oh, Sam …" She blinked away more wetness, a tug-of-war tearing her apart. "*Never* have I wanted anything more, but deep down inside I need to feel *His* peace, just to be sure." She cupped his bristled jaw, desperate to make him understand. "I've learned the hard way that I need to *see* love in action as well as hear it," she whispered, the truth of the Scripture she'd read that morning still emblazoned in her mind.

Let us not love with words or speech but with actions and in truth. This is how we know that we belong to the truth and how we set our hearts at rest …

Her heart bled through her tears as she gently tugged free of his embrace. "I need to know that our love is more important to you than your pride and your image and your fairytale idea of what pure love should be. And to know you'll seek your comfort from God and me and not from a bottle." Body quivering, she took another step back. "To know, Sam, that after God, I'm the most important thing in your life, your source of comfort and confidence like you are to me." A sad smile trembled on her lips. "And although I hope and pray we belong together, too, I need time to see your commitment in action rather than in words if we do get back together again."

His Adam's apple hitched hard in his throat. "If?" The question came out strangled and hoarse, and her heart cramped at the hurt that flickered across his face.

"*When*," she said quickly, anxious to reassure him that she wanted this relationship to work as much as he did. "Maybe another week or so, just to give us both a little space to really think it through." She caressed him with her eyes, hoping he could see the love she harbored inside. "And pray."

Head tipped, he squinted up at her. "Somehow I was afraid you'd say that." Expelling a cumbersome sigh, he fished his keyless remote out of his pocket, brows in a lift. "And there's nothing I can say to change your mind about starting our relationship over tonight?"

She shook her head with a timid chew of her lip. "I would like a little more time, Sam, just to make sure this is what God really wants us to do." She gave a faint shrug, smile shy as she hugged her arms to her waist. "It sounds silly, I know, but I've asked Him for a sign, something so out of the blue, that I'll know it's from Him."

"Okay." With a resigned nod, he traced a finger down the curve of her face. "Well, before I go, you need to know, Shannon, that I love you more than anything in this world, and I will wait as long as it takes. But, as you so wisely pointed out, actions speak louder than words, so you not only have my word, Shannon O'Bryen, you will have my actions to prove that nothing is more important to me in my life than you." He leaned in to slowly graze his mouth against hers, so excruciatingly tender, it brimmed more tears in her eyes. "Good night, Angel Eyes." With a final skim of his thumb to the curve of her jaw, he turned and strode away with purpose.

Right into the lake.

Ker-splash!

Air seized in her lungs as she froze, feet fused to the wooden planks for several horrifying seconds. And then with a cold rush of adrenalin, she dropped to the edge of the dock to peer into the swirling foam of the river, eyes gaping wide. "Sam?"

Nothing but bubbles rose to the surface, and with a horrendous squeeze of her stomach, she screamed all the louder, her heart hammering out the seconds. "Sam—where are you?!"

Her hands and feet started to tingle and she felt lightheaded, her breathing coming out in short, shallow gasps. "Sam!" she shouted again, her voice hoarse and heaving. *God, please—where is he?*

"Over here," a rasp sounded, the frantic splash of water tearing her gaze to the ladder at the far end, where Sam was hacking as he climbed onto the dock. She stared in disbelief while he stood there, dirty water sluicing down from every inch of his Armani. Head cocked, he flashed some teeth as he tapped water from his ear. "Sorry—guess I took a wrong turn."

She stormed over to where he stood shivering, seaweed on his shirt and Cole Haans in a puddle. "What on earth are you doing? Are you *crazy?*"

"As a matter of fact, I am," he said with a proud grin, casually dumping water from one shoe and tossing it to the side before he emptied the other. His dress shoe leaked as he pointed it at her. "About *you*." Flipping it over his shoulder, he paid no attention when it plunked right back into the river.

"Oh my goodness, Sam—*stop!*" she squealed, hand to her mouth to stifle a giggle.

"Because it's not the shoes," he continued, peeling off his socks and then his jacket before methodically sailing each over his head. "And it's not the Armani or the Rolex that I care about, Angel Eyes—it's you." He put the watch to his ear and grinned. "Ah … but still ticking, just like my heart." His brows beetled low with a scrunch of his nose. "Unless, of course, you say no to ever marrying me at all."

Hands cupped to her mouth, she burst out laughing, the sight of Sam Cunningham soaked to the skin somehow making her happy.

"Oh, you think this is funny, do you?" He sloshed over to where she stood, a veritable T-shirt contest with his stained Armani shirt molding to every sculpted muscle. "Well, this is every favorite thing in my wardrobe, kiddo, but none of it means squat if I can't have you." Teeth chattering, he stared her down. "I'll g-give you all the time you need, Shannon, to prove you're the m-most important thing in my life after God—but let's start over right now, *t-tonight*. Because frankly, Angel Eyes, b-being without you for even one m-more day is far more terrifying than freezing my b-butt off from dirty water in the d-dead of October, trappings and all."

"Oh, Sam—you're freezing!" Rushing to the storage closet, she returned with a tattered blanket and draped it over his shoulder before tugging him toward the ramp of the dock. "You're going to catch your death if we don't get you changed out of those wet clothes right now."

"Oh, I'm going to change all right." Lips turning blue, he stopped cold to pierce her with that do-or-die look beneath water-spiked lashes, the hope in his eyes igniting that in her heart. "Into the man you deserve if it means giving up everything from Armani to Chivas because you, Shannon Terese O'Bryen, are the only thing I want and everything I need."

She plunked her hands on her hips, chin in a jut that would make her sister proud. "If you think I'm going to give in, Sam Cunningham, just because you pull a crazy stunt like this, then you're all wet."

He blinked, water sopping onto the deck in a puddle around his bare feet.

A giggle bubbled up as she circled her arms to his waist. Standing on tiptoe, she lightly brushed her mouth against his with a misty grin before hugging him with all of her might. "And given the state of your soggy Armani, Dr. Love," she said with a definite peace in her heart, "you most certainly are."

NOTE FROM THE AUTHOR

Although this is largely a work of fiction, two things are very real. First, Isle of Hope, Georgia is not only a real place, it's one of the most beautiful and historical locales in the U.S. Located fifteen minutes from Savannah on a peninsula that becomes an island at high tide, Isle of Hope possesses a unique low-country charm and a rich and vibrant history.

Almost a world apart from the continental U.S., Isle of Hope is a sleepy tidal island with a strong sense of community where picture-perfect cottages reside next to lush waterside manors and the historic Wormsloe Plantation. Dating back to the early 1700s, Wormsloe Plantation is the oldest of Georgia's tidewater estates and has served as a military stronghold, plantation, residence, farm, tourist attraction, and historic site.

With a unique Southern charm all its own, Isle of Hope's seaside beauty and low-country allure has drawn moviemakers and photographers to its shores for years, boasting such films as the Oscar-winning *Glory*, the original *Cape Fear, The Last of the Belles*, *Forrest Gump*, and *The Last Song*. And, with a name like "Isle of Hope," it was—for me—the perfect setting for a story of hope restored.

The second "real" thing about this series is the estranged relationship between heroine Lacey Carmichael and her father in book one, *Isle of Hope: Unfailing Love*, which purposely mirrors my own relationship with my dad. Although Lacey's circumstances and mine are totally different, the bitterness and unforgiveness is much the same, as is the road to restoration for both Lacey and me, miraculously wrought through the unfailing love of Jesus Christ, truly a God of hope and healing.

And now, I have a favor to ask. If you enjoyed this novel, would you consider posting a brief review on *Amazon* and *Goodreads*? It can be as short as one or two lines, merely stating why you liked the book. Most people don't realize how critical good reviews are to a novel, but so many readers base their book-buying decisions on the number of good reviews posted, that that's the best way to bless your favorite authors. And if you *do* post a review, *please* let me know through the Contact Julie tab on my website so I can thank you personally.

I hope and pray you were blessed by Sam and Shannon's story and that of the Carmichaels and O'Bryens, two families who had to learn—as I did—that the true "Isle of Hope" resides in the heart of a Savior Whose love never fails.

Hugs,

Julie Lessman

AUTHOR BIO

Julie Lessman is an award-winning author whose tagline of "Passion With a Purpose" underscores her intense passion for both God and romance. A lover of all things Irish, she enjoys writing close-knit Irish family sagas that evolve into 3-D love stories: the hero, the heroine, and the God that brings them together.

Author of The Daughters of Boston, Winds of Change, and Heart of San Francisco series, Julie Lessman was named American Christian Fiction Writers 2009 Debut Author of the Year and has garnered 18 Romance Writers of America and other awards. Voted #1 Romance Author of the year in Family Fiction magazine's 2012 and 2011 Readers Choice Awards, Julie was also named on Booklist's 2010 Top 10 Inspirational Fiction and Borders Best Fiction list.

Julie's most recent novel, Isle of Hope was voted on Family Fiction magazine's Best of 2015, and Surprised by Love appeared on Family Fiction magazine's list of Top Ten Novels of 2014. Her independent novel A Light in the Window is an International Digital Awards winner, a 2013 Readers' Crown Award winner, and a 2013 Book Buyers Best Award winner. Julie has also written a self-help workbook for writers entitled Romance-ology 101: Writing Romantic Tension for the Sweet and Inspirational Markets. You can contact Julie through her website and read excerpts from each of her books at **www.julielessman.com**.

OTHER BOOKS BY JULIE LESSMAN

The Daughters of Boston Series

Book 1: *A Passion Most Pure*

Book 2: *A Passion Redeemed*

Book 3: *A Passion Denied*

The Winds of Change Series

Book 1: *A Hope Undaunted*

Book 2: *A Heart Revealed*

Book 3: *A Love Surrendered*

Prequel to The Daughters of Boston and Winds of Change Series

A Light in the Window: An Irish Love Story

The Heart of San Francisco Series

Book 1: *Love at Any Cost*

Book 2: *Dare to Love Again*

Book 3: *Surprised by Love*

The Isle of Hope Series

Book 1: *Isle of Hope: Unfailing Love*

Book 2: *Love Everlasting*

Book 3: *Love Unchanging* (coming 2017)

Novellas

Hope for the Holidays Historical Collection

With This Kiss Historical Collection

Home for Christmas Historical Christian Romance Collection

A Glimmer of Hope: Novella Prequel to Isle of Hope
Cowboy Christmas Homecoming

Writer's Workbook

Romance-ology 101: Writing Romantic Tension for the Inspirational and Sweet Markets

Made in the USA
Lexington, KY
27 March 2019